SHEILA'S MEN

Jenna Ashlyn

Cover design by Vila Design

Published by Van Rye Publishing, LLC
Ann Arbor, MI
www.vanryepublishing.com

ISBN: 979-8-9851099-0-0 (paperback)
ISBN: 979-8-9851099-1-7 (ebook)
Library of Congress Control Number: 2021949580

Warning

SHEILA'S MEN is a fictionalized account of one woman's real-life struggle to escape abusive relationships and is intended, in part, to help others recognize and escape such relationships. As such, this book necessarily contains language and scenarios related to self-harm, suicide, and abuse (emotional, physical, sexual, and financial) that might be triggering for some audiences. Reader discretion is advised.

Dedication

Dedicated to the women traveling their own journey.

And to the men that inspired it all, may God have mercy upon your souls.

Contents

PART I

Chapter 1

NOBODY NOTICED ME ... unless I was naked. Men's faces flooded my mind as I approached the bridge for the last time. Looking up, I shivered in the snow as the sidewalk rose into the night and lights cast their glittering reflection on the untouched path ahead. My nightgown was icy against my flesh as I carefully placed my journal in a plastic bag, knowing they would find it long before they found me. I couldn't be rescued, but maybe others could be.

My toes shivered as I gripped the steel railing and began to climb. It was only a few steps and a moment of bravery, then . . . it would be over. I was only visible when men wanted me for something I didn't want to offer. They were oblivious to the love I longed to give. I was a notch on the bedpost, a trophy on the shelf, earned and forgotten. I was familiar with icy bitterness because that's all men had given me. That's why I had chosen that night. The stars were out, the moon full, and the snow gave me a runway to freedom.

Peering over the edge, I watched silver ribbons reflect off the Kanawha River, and soon, they would be the last thing I saw as I dove into the river's treacherous depths. This is where it connected to the Ohio, and together, their undertow would pull me to the bottom where many had fallen during the bridge collapse years before.

Around me, cars sped by in falling snow. Nobody noticed me. They were busy. Their laughter echoed against concrete and steel as they traveled. In the back of pickup trucks, I watched packages of red and green slide as the trucks turned to cross the bridge. Smiling girls in pigtails anticipated their destinations, with only thin glass separating them from the bitterness of the world. They were oblivious to me. Like always, I was invisible—a shadow of who I should have become.

Gripping the railing, I looked into the light and remembered. Like everyone else, my story began . . . in the beginning. The children rushing by in warm cars reminded me of my childhood. And as my life began playing out before me, I tried not to think of him, the one who could have been but wasn't.

My childhood seemed perfect. I went to church every Sunday, was active in the community, and always smiled. My parents were the picture of a perfect marriage. They went out with friends on Saturday nights and left their children together in one house while they had their adventures. Of course, nobody knew I was being touched by my brother's friends.

When we were all home together, it was worse. My father was always angry with my brother. I hid from the turmoil by locking myself in the bathroom and plugging my ears against their screams. When things got quiet, I would venture out to see new holes in the walls where my father's fist had missed my brother's face.

Then, one day, my mother caught my father cheating. He had stashed a notebook full of love letters from his mistress that I unfortunately found. Of course, it wasn't the first time he cheated, and my mother made sure I read the letters, even though at ten years old, I didn't understand. It seemed my mother was constantly finding evidence of a new affair. After a while, I became friends with some of the women. It was nice to have a friend to talk to, but eventually, that, too, would end because the truth would come to light.

My parents separated a few times and talked of divorce but always got back together. My mother would say they needed to raise their children together. It was a vicious cycle. On Sunday, we were the perfect family, but by Monday, we were destroying kitchen walls.

As I developed into a woman, boys noticed—at least, a few did. They would catch me playing video games and sneak up behind me. Their hands explored my body as I sat frozen, afraid to move. Then, the next day, they were kissing their girlfriends, and it only made me lonelier. After all, I was the youngest and wasn't ready to be kissed.

2

That's what my parents and their friends seemed to think. They never asked questions or wondered what happened during late-night games of hide and seek or sleepovers supervised by teens.

Of course, I never said much of anything because there was nothing wrong with being touched, right? At least, that's how it felt at first. During the school year, I was a nerdy little girl who nobody noticed, but every summer, starting at only four years old, I was sexually assaulted. I tried to speak up a few times, but nothing ever happened. I was simply told that boys will be boys and was dismissed. My parents didn't believe me when I told them an older boy held my head underwater until I agreed to put his penis in my mouth. They just wondered why it took me forever to learn how to swim with so many of the older boys teaching me.

After Church, the men I knew gathered at our kitchen table to complain about their wives withholding sex. They hated that they couldn't touch their wives. I remember them saying that it's a wife's duty to submit to her husband, especially in the bedroom. I knew what that meant from a very early age. They didn't realize that I could hear everything they said through the thin wall that separated me from them. That made it easy for them, and soon enough, they would touch me instead because I was "a good girl."

Now, as I stared at the midnight river, my mind raced with memories of late-night dinners and promises of love. Hadn't I fulfilled every expectation of a good wife, a willing partner, and a mother? Why hadn't I found love?

In the distance, the stars peered through the clouds as snow fell around me. The hills cradled the river like a blanket as I looked at the town I called home. Looking through the windshields of those who drove by me on the bridge, I watched a man take his wife's hand and kiss it gently as they drove. She looked at him the same way I had looked at my ex-husband, but my marriage was a lie—hopefully, hers wasn't. Love was a joke. It was fun to imagine, but it didn't exist, not for me. The slush was frozen in splatters up to my knees, but no one noticed. Music drifted through windshields as merriment and joy were surrounded by darkened silence. I smiled, knowing the pain would soon

3

be gone.

After I had discovered my own husband's infidelity, I was broken, but I remained strong for my daughter. I hoped to survive on child support. After all, there was no one to watch Terra, and her father had vanished, so I found a small, subsidized apartment. Remembering my childhood, I knew I had done nothing wrong. I felt the greatest revenge for my childhood and my husband's infidelity was to find happiness and a man who appreciated me, but that's what I had been trying to do my entire life, unsuccessfully.

Chapter 2

S ITTING AT MY neighbor's computer, I typed hesitantly. *Seeking companionship, short-term relationship, long-term relationship,* I wrote, and I clicked all the extra boxes. Finding my best photo, I typed a little about myself, and suddenly, I was on the market, ready to be wooed. Of course, I spent a few minutes searching for someone interesting. *You never know who you're going to meet online; you might as well give it a try.* The life of a single mother isn't glamorous, but online, you can be whoever you really are. Guys can get to know you before worrying about your children. Of course, you should always be honest. But in the real world, people only see children, nothing else, and I was more than that.

As I scanned through pictures, no one caught my attention. Then, I saw a pictureless ad. I read his words eagerly. It talked about how he always felt like women never gave him a chance because he was a bigger guy. He wanted someone to hold at night, who would see him for who he was. He talked about getting a fresh start in life. It sounded like something I could have written about myself, so I sent him a message and my phone number.

As I stepped outside my tiny apartment, the air was crisp and the breeze blew gently through the dancing leaves. The streetlights lit the sidewalks in golden trails that weaved through the apartment buildings. I enjoyed my evening walks. With Terra's window open, I was able to hear any noises as she slept. I kept her window in view, almost walking in circles. Then, as the evening grew darker, my phone rang.

"Hi . . . I got a message online, and I think you gave me your number," a man said when I answered.

"I must have. My name is Sheila," I replied, trying to sound confident. "What's your name?"

"I'm Trenton. I'm glad you messaged me."

"Why?"

"You seem sweet. There's not a lot of ladies like that these days."

"I'm more interested in getting to know a person, not a picture."

"That's brave," Trenton answered.

"Maybe . . . but looks don't count for much. I would like to get to know you first. I don't want to see a picture right away."

"If that's what you want, that's what you'll get. A lady deserves to get what she wants."

"If you say so."

"Well, I'm tall, dark, and handsome. I'm a bit of a lady-killer, I guess." Trenton laughed. "I'm actually sad you don't want to see my picture."

"Sounds a bit arrogant."

"Maybe a little, but not really. Do you ever go to church?"

"I used to. I haven't been in a long time. It's something that I've been thinking about. I just don't like going alone. Watching all the happy couples together makes me kinda miserable, and I'm not easily accepted, or at least my ministry isn't."

"I know what you mean. What's your thing? I work a lot with the youth, trying to help them make good decisions so they don't make the same mistakes I have."

"That's awesome. I work with the youth sometimes, but I'm a dancer. It's very misunderstood around here. I like to sing, but they always ask me to dance. I don't think they like my voice."

"That's sad. I wouldn't let them do that to you if I was around. I would remind them of God's mercy, his faithfulness."

"I just think they like it when I dance. I really get into it. What's your favorite song?"

"That's an easy question. Let me sing you a couple lines . . ."

After Trenton sang the first verse, I listened to his breath catch as he cleared his throat. *Wow, he really means it. He really wants to be a better man than he was. He's humble, knows his flaws, and wants to really serve God. The words he sang say it all.* I had always loved church, and I wanted to be like the couples I saw sitting on the pews holding hands and sneaking kisses as they worshipped.

Every night, Trenton and I talked, and he told me about his business. I loved offering suggestions. I had always been good with advertising. Unfortunately, I hadn't been able to do much since I became a mother. It was refreshing to have someone respect my opinions. When Trenton spoke, my pulse quickened. I longed for his phone calls and our conversations. I had always wanted to connect with someone.

Then, one day, the calls stopped. And eventually, I was forced back to online dating sites. I missed Trenton but knew to cut my losses. He was only a man I had the privilege of talking to, who had occupied my time and made me smile. That was enough.

When I checked the messages I had been neglecting, my inbox was full of men asking random questions. I answered several, but only a few could hold a conversation. I quickly tired of one-word responses and nude picture requests. There was only one man interesting enough to have a good conversation with, and I agreed to meet him.

I'll never forget meeting Matt. Pulling up beside his silver dodge, I glanced over at him and was immediately captured by his blond curls— just not in the way you would assume. *He looks young*, I thought. *This feels weird.* My thoughts were racing as a cold chill ran up my spine. Matt's T-shirt hung loosely against his body as he stared ahead, his tanned skin glowing in the sun as he waited for me.

Many of my initial phone conversations with Matt had been awkward. At first, it was a simple hello. Then, as I slowly opened up, we talked about our exes and how things didn't work out. Matt seemed kind and worth meeting. After all, what did I have to lose? With a sigh, I closed my eyes and rolled down my window. Matt's face lit up as his eyes met mine, and for an instant, I forgot his youthfulness.

"I'm excited to finally meet you," Matt said. "I love talking to you on the phone. I'm glad you answered my message."

"Yeah, me too." Trying to smile, I watched Matt shut off his car and fumble around as he climbed out. *He must love his car; he's care-*

ful. Abruptly, he reached for my door handle and opened it, reaching for my hand. Staring at his hand for a moment, I noticed his fingers were short and wide compared to mine. His skin was cold. Looking at his large build, it felt like ice running down my back as his breath caressed my cheek.

"Do you wanna go for a drive?" Matt asked.

"Um . . . sure, sounds good," I answered. "Where do you want to take me?"

"I don't know. We could go down to the park and talk for a little bit."

"That makes sense."

As I climbed into the car, I clutched my phone tightly and took a deep breath. *Meeting someone online is always a little scary at first. It's going to be okay, though. Give him a chance.* Looking across the dash of Matt's car, I didn't notice even a speck of dust. It had that new car smell, and even the carpet was immaculate. Glancing over at him, I watched him wiggle in the driver's seat before leaning up to start the car. *This feels weird.*

When we finally parked by the river, I was ready to climb out. *Hopefully, he wants to talk and get to know me. That would be nice.* Thankfully, Matt rolled down the windows, pulled back his seat, and sat sideways. Brushing my hair away from my eyes, I looked down at my phone as Matt's hands wiggled the shifter. He touched it with a gentle firmness that directly contrasted with the jerking motion he enlisted to pull up the emergency brake. Shifting in his seat, he leaned back and started thumbing through channels on the radio.

"What do you like to listen to?" Matt asked.

"I listen to about everything, I guess, just not country," I answered.

"I thought everyone listens to country."

"Not me. It reminds me too much of childhood."

"Ahh . . . I get that."

"I like a lot of music, including some country, just don't listen to it much."

"I listen to a lot of different stuff, too. I like the 80s channel and Octane."

"What's that?"

"It's rock. Here, I'll show you."

As Matt pushed the button on the radio, loud guitar music started screaming through the speakers as though it were yelling at me. My face drew up at the noise, and he quickly turned it down. "Too much?" he asked.

"Probably just that song. I don't like it when they scream." I laughed.

"You have a point. So, what do you want to talk about?"

"I don't know. Tell me about you?"

"I don't know. I'm just me. I like music, I like you, and I want to know more about you. Tell me about your divorce. How's it going with you and your little girl?"

"It's going okay, I guess. It's slow. We never hear from my ex. It's hard sometimes. My mom doesn't help. She always said she would be there if I needed her, but she's not. We're making it day by day. I can't complain," I answered.

"I get that. Well, *I'm* here for you. Who's watching her now?" Matt asked.

"My sister. But she's busy a lot."

"Isn't everyone always busy?"

"Of course, they are. Why wouldn't they be?"

"How are you handling the divorce? You said he cheated, right?"

"Yeah, he did. I was heartbroken. I think I still am. I'm honestly not sure I'm ready for this. I keep thinking about everything we went through, and I . . . I don't get it."

"I can't see why he would cheat on you. You're beautiful."

"There's something beautiful in everyone. You have to look for it."

"Well, you don't exactly have to look for it when we're talking about you."

"*He* didn't think so, obviously. I haven't had time to deal with it like I should. I want to be strong for Terra. I watched my mom stay with my dad when he cheated, and I was miserable. All they ever did was fight, and I don't want that for Terra."

"Of course not."

9

Looking at my phone again, I caught my reflection mirrored in it. *He's full of shit; I'm not beautiful.* My eyes were swelling as I thought about my ex and about me being alone with Terra, not knowing where our next meal was coming from. Bitterness started to rise in my cheeks as I thought about how Terra discovered his letters.

"I don't think I'm ready to be dating, Matt. You seem sweet, but I don't want to be thinking about him while I'm with you. I don't think that's fair."

"There's no harm in being friends. We can see what happens from there," Matt mumbled. His eyes narrowed as he looked at me, his lips pursed as he swallowed against his words, and his gaze raked across my body. I felt merciless and tried to keep my eyes closed, but I heard his sighs and felt the rough jerking motion as he shifted gears and music blared through his speakers.

"Matt, I'm . . . sorry. I would like to get to know you first. We can always use more friends, right?" I asked.

"I want to be your friend, and if you're not ready, I'll wait," Matt answered. "I'm not easy to get rid of."

"Are you sure? I'm not rejecting you. I just need more time."

"Yes, I'm sure. I really like you, and I want to help in any way I can."

"I appreciate that. I'm going to get back to Terra. Thank you for taking me down to the park. I enjoyed it."

"You're welcome. Can I call you tonight?"

"I would like that."

"Can I at least get a hug?"

"Um, yeah. I guess so."

Lunging forward, Matt wrapped his arms around me. They felt gentle against my body as he pulled me close. *Maybe he isn't so bad after all.* Matt made me question what I wanted. He was the first guy from online dating I had met in person, and it was miserable. I needed time and wished I could talk to Trenton.

When Trenton called again, he apologized. Hearing his voice again sent shivers down my spine. His voice was barely a whisper, but I knew it instantly. My knees buckling, I collapsed to the moonlit grass. A rush of spoken words invaded my mind as I knelt under my favorite tree. I wasn't ready for a relationship . . . unless it was with Trenton. All thoughts of meeting Matt faded as though he never existed. When Trenton asked me to meet him, I agreed.

Finally, I was pulling into a restaurant and waiting for Trenton. It had been a long time since anyone had bought me dinner. Stepping out of my little car, I greeted Trenton with a hug. When his arms wrapped around my waist, I felt his strength grasp me, pulling me closer. There was no hesitation, no awkwardness, and no voice telling me to run.

"It's great to see you, Sheila. You know, you said on a first date, it was a good idea to get that first kiss out of the way so it isn't awkward," Trenton reminded me. "Can I kiss you?"

"I did say that, didn't I?" I blushed. "Why—"

Stepping toward me, Trenton's lips captured mine before I could finish speaking. His hands gripped me tightly, pushing the air from my lungs. "It's nice to meet you. Thanks for the kiss," Trenton said as he winked.

"You seem a little smug about that."

"Nah, I know a good thing when I see it. I shouldn't have waited to meet you. You are more beautiful than I could have imagined."

"You *can't* be serious. I bet you say that to all the girls."

"What other girls? Nobody ever gives me the time of day. What do you think?" he asked, stepping back as he gestured toward his body. "Am I too big for you?"

"No! Of course not! I couldn't imagine being that shallow. I'm as curvaceous as they come. So, why would I judge you?"

"You might be surprised. You are stunning and way too good-looking for me."

"You need to stop feeding me lines, Trenton."

"Don't be silly. I'm not feeding you lines. I didn't expect you to look nice. But if you think I'm feeding you lines, I'll stop."

"Thank you. So, what do you have planned for us?"

"Let's go in and have dinner. Then maybe we can drive around. How does that sound?"

"That could work. I'm not picky. Hey, we have to start somewhere, right?"

I loved going to Fred's. It was one of those hole-in-the-wall restaurants only locals knew about. Sliding into a booth, Trenton handed me a menu. The words blurred like the fine print in an eye exam as I tried to remember the menu items. But the only thing I saw was his eyes . . . watching me. Trenton had a surprisingly rough sophistication and carried himself like a celebrity. "Maybe I should order the special," I said as I sighed.

"But you don't even know what it is."

"I know, but I'm too distracted to look at the menu."

"What has you distracted?" Trenton laughed. "I'm not distracted at all."

"Right . . . that's why you haven't even picked yours up? I know I'm gorgeous, but we have to eat."

"You are, that's for sure, but I'm interested in more. I've loved talking to you. Your mind is better than your body."

"How do you know *that*?" I asked.

"We've been talking for a while. I feel like I know you. We are connected—like we were meant to find each other. I wish our server would hurry up." Trenton winked. "I don't want to be in here all night."

"Yeah, but I promise the food is worth it."

"I'm becoming less and less interested in food. I would love to get you alone so I can taste your lips again."

"We don't have to be alone for you to kiss me, Trenton. You can do that anywhere."

"There's nothing like privacy."

"I thought you wanted more than to get me alone."

"I do, I'm sorry. It's easier to talk to you on the phone. There's something about you. You are making me crave you."

Trenton had been the listening ear when I needed to talk. Our conversations had been hypnotic, and I couldn't stop thinking about him. I craved his attention. Watching him, I knew there were other women. There was no other explanation for his inconsistent phone calls and waiting a month to meet in person. Unfortunately, it had been a while since a man had given me attention.

Looking across the table at Trenton, I knew I could keep his attention by giving him what he wanted. If I made an impression, maybe this man would think I was good enough to keep around. *Maybe I could finally have something I want. I want him to touch me. Will his touch be as sweet as his words? Maybe if I let him have me, he will forget the other women. If I'm good in bed, he won't have any need for anyone else. I hope he keeps telling me I'm beautiful.*

"Actually, I have a job to do tomorrow, close to where you live," Trenton stated dryly. "I don't have much money. Do you know of any cheap hotels?" he asked.

"No, but you're welcome to my couch," I answered. "I mean, I guess you can stay with me." *This is my chance to show him how special I am.*

"I'd like that."

I felt Trenton's eyes roam across my body as I sat quietly across from him, and I knew my fate was sealed. Obviously, Trenton didn't have a lady close by to take care of his needs, and I was more than happy to oblige. Tonight, I would invite him into my bed and hope he would enjoy me enough to come back. His eyes were savagely lustful as he watched me nibble. My legs quivered imagining his touch. I remembered how he had shared his favorite song with me. It was a song about moving away from past mistakes and becoming a better man. *Make me a better woman, make me feel loved, and I will make you the happiest man alive. Just try me.*

It wasn't long before our food was ordered and consumed. Stepping outside, we leaned against our vehicles. *Make your move. I'm ready to be captured. Be gentle with me, and I will give you the world.*

"I love that shirt," Trenton stated, staring down at my breasts. "Did you do that on purpose?" he asked, playing with the string at the top of my modest blouse.

"I don't . . . know. What do you mean?" I questioned, glancing down at the little string that hid the small keyhole above my cleavage. "I didn't think it showed anything."

"You're being silly. You look so sexy. I must have you. Can I have you, Sheila?"

My heart shivered as I pulled away and looked down at my baggy clothes and unshaved legs. Suddenly, it didn't matter that he wanted to meet me at night or that he had vanished for a month. I wanted to prove to him that he was an idiot for making me wait. All I knew was that my little girl and I were alone. Many men had visited my apartment—strangers that heard about a new single mom in the apartment complex—and all of them made me uncomfortable. Trenton might have been questionable, but when I was around him, nobody else existed. With him, there was a possibility of a future. My ex-husband had left me with nothing—no skills, no money . . . only the impossible task of raising a little girl on my own.

"It's getting a little chilly. Climb in the truck with me, and we'll drive over to where it's . . . quiet," Trenton whispered.

"If that's what you want."

As we climbed into his vehicle, Trenton quickly pulled to a dark part of the parking lot and unbuckled his seat belt. Sliding against me, his hand reached behind me and pulled me against him as his lips captured mine. Taking a deep breath, I pulled away and stared into his eyes. They were open, and his chest was moving quickly as he parted his lips and pulled me tighter against him. His kiss grew deeper and harder as he grabbed my arms and pushed them against him, burying me in his strength.

"You don't need to get away. I'm not going to hurt you," Trenton gasped between kisses. "Please touch me. I bet you know how to touch a man."

Oh, God! I know this is what I wanted, but do I really? Is this what I should do to keep him around? Within moments, I distanced myself from my thoughts enough to surrender to Trenton's will. I had trained most of my life to please a man. I was used to it. For me, it was easy to think that by pleasuring him, he would take care of me in return. That's what I saw growing up. So, it didn't take much for me to not only touch him but bury my head in his lap and make him explode. I had a knack for going on autopilot. Those were moments I didn't need to be present for. Distancing myself via autopilot protected my mind. No man had ever had the privilege of having my mind and body at the same time,

14

and I was certain they never would. Everything I knew made me believe that *this* was love.

"So, can I come home with you? Or did you want me to find a motel?" Trenton asked.

"Um, yeah . . . you . . . can stay on the couch," I stuttered. "Take me back to my car, and you can follow me."

On the way home, I calculated my next move. *I can do this. He thinks I'm beautiful, he keeps saying it. Of course, he means it. He was moaning a lot. I wish he would have said something, though. Oh, God! I'm halfway home. I can convince him. I loved the way he kissed me. Don't hesitate, do it.* My thoughts were racing again.

Walking into my apartment, I grabbed Trenton's hand and led him upstairs. *Don't change your mind. It's just sex, nothing more. This is how you will get him to come back.* Sitting on the edge of my bed, I closed my eyes, knowing he would come for me. *It's going to happen, and then, if you do a good job, he will give you his heart.* Trenton had told me endlessly about his hopes and his dreams, including finding true love. He had talked about going to church and singing for the choir. He wanted to follow God and start a new life, and he needed a strong woman by his side. He wanted to take me away from the harshness of poverty and food stamps—a world I longed to escape.

That night, Trenton ravaged me. His body pinned me against the bed, and his hands put me in a million positions as I dutifully moaned. Allowing Trenton to take what he desired, I waited for morning to rise through the darkness. Awakening the next morning, I smiled as I felt his body next to mine.

"You were amazing last night, Sheila. I've never seen anyone like you." Trenton smiled. "I can't believe you let me have you so fully, so completely."

"I enjoyed it, too," I whispered, sliding my hand to this thigh. "Do you want more?"

"Twice?!"

"Of course, why not? Don't you want me?"

"Only an idiot wouldn't want you, especially if they've already had you." Trenton moaned as he once again climbed on top of me. "You are

15

mine. Promise me that no matter what, you will belong to me. I don't want anyone else to touch you ever again. YOU. ARE. *MINE*."

Closing my eyes, I smiled and moaned in agreement. Relaxing against Trenton's thrusts, I nestled against his arm and waited for his satisfaction. Arching to meet his thrusts, I moaned, clawing his back to heighten his pleasure. I dutifully served him.

As Trenton headed for the shower, I listened to the rustling sounds of Terra's movements approaching from the other room, and soon, she was staring up at me. Her blue eyes sparkled as her red pigtails bounced into my bed. I loved those moments with her. Every morning, she would climb in beside me, and we would sleep for a little longer. I had left her with a neighbor girl the night before, and I was glad to have her beside me again. I hated leaving her.

Life was tough as I struggled to pay bills, even in a subsidized apartment. I knew I would have to do something soon to provide for Terra. I just didn't know how to work and take care of Terra without a babysitter. Pulling back the comforter, I tucked Terra in beside me and sniffed the top of her hair. I was thankful to be dressed. She always came in as soon as she awoke, and Trenton had unlocked the bedroom door just in time. Coming in after his shower, Trenton admired Terra with a smile.

"I have to work. I'm sorry, I wish I could stay. I will call you tonight, though," Trenton whispered as he kissed me passionately. "Thank you for everything. You were amazing. You might be everything I've ever wanted. And you have a beautiful little angel."

After a while, I scooped Terra into my arms and headed downstairs to scavenge for food. Finding a loaf of bread, I made toast and sprinkled it with cinnamon and sugar to make it different than the day before. I had another week before I'd have food benefits again, and as always, I was already planning my midnight trip to the twenty-four-hour grocery store.

It happened like clockwork, every month. I would grab Terra and go to the store, fill my cart, and wait for midnight when our food benefits returned. It was hard not to buy snacks and unhealthy foods because by then, I was starving. The last few days of the month, I often lived on very little, sometimes not eating for days, to make sure Terra had food. I would crave a treat that first night having benefits again, and I often splurged on cookies and pizza rolls. Then, toward the end of the month, I would run into ice cream and soda and all the things I missed.

Walking through the store, everything looked amazing. Sometimes, a couple of steaks seemed like a good idea. At other times, it was a frozen chicken pot pie. We had little money to spend on food, so that first shopping trip was always intimidating. Regardless of how hungry I was, I knew the first purchases of the month would set the course until I had food again. I often felt like a failure because I would always splurge a little, and those splurges would equal less food later.

I hated our apartment. Every night, flashing lights of cop cars were there for a new drug bust or domestic violence case. When the sun went down, their lights came out. It was like having Christmas year-round but without the benefits. It had become so routine that I couldn't sleep without the commotion.

Watching Terra devour her morning delicacy, I thought of Trenton and allowed myself to dream of a modest brick house on a hill surrounded by evergreen trees. I wanted to watch Terra wait for the bus from my window instead of having to stand there guarding her from other kids. I imagined having dinner ready for Trenton after his hard days at work. The thought of meatloaf, mashed potatoes, and fresh rolls with real butter made my belly growl as I watched Terra with her Cinnamon toast. *He will call, don't worry.*

As Terra finished, I thought of the perfect distraction. Turning on the TV, I found our favorite music playlist and cranked the volume loud enough to disturb the neighbors. As the bass began to echo against the walls and shake the carpet beneath our feet, Terra came running, and before long, the coffee table had moved and pillows were flying across the room.

Dodging each of Terra's throws, I grabbed a pillow and bopped her on the head. As I ran to grab another pillow, Terra chased after me. Her messy hair was flying as her little arms hurled pillows my way. I managed to sidestep each one until Terra decided to throw *herself* at me instead. Catching her in my arms, I lifted her toward the ceiling and

began to spin until we were both dizzy and collapsed on the couch.
"Mommy, dance with me!" Terra pleaded.
"No, you can't make me!" I laughed.
"Oh, whatever. You know you want to."
"Nope, not gonna happen."
"Fine, I'll just dance without you!"
"You wouldn't dare."
"Oh, yeah? You think I won't? Just shows how much you know."
"I'm your mom; I know *everything*."
"Not a chance that you know everything."
"I don't see you dancing."
"Oh, you will," Terra teased. Whipping her red hair around, she started to walk to the center of the room. "You'll see. I don't need *you* for *me* to be able to dance. I can do it all by myself."
"You can't." I giggled.

With a knowing look, Terra quickly turned to face me. Her arms twirled as her head bopped side to side. She had so much attitude as she bent her knees and began hopping in a circle, shaking her head. She ran in place, tossing her hair like the singer of an 80s hair band. Then, just as quickly, she dropped to the floor, moving in a circle as she crawled on her hands, her belly poking out of her pajama top.

"What is that supposed to be, break dancing?" I teased.
"It's whatever I want it to be! There are no rules in dancing."
"Oh, well . . . forgive me for asking!"

Jumping up from my position on the couch, I grabbed Terra's hands and pulled her from the floor. Twirling her in a circle, I dipped her almost to the floor. Walking on my knees, I grabbed a rose from the table and, placing it between my teeth, I grabbed her. Together, we stiffly shuffled from side to side until I lifted her above my head. Terra's laughter echoed through the room as I tossed her to the sofa. Running to her, I buried my hands in her stomach, tickling her until she cried for me to stop. Collapsing beside her on the floor, she quickly rolled on top of me. Her little arms wrapped around my neck as tears of happiness ran down our faces.

"What do you want to do today, baby girl?"

"Don't call me a baby, Mom. I'm getting older, ya know. I'm not a ba . . . by," Terra mocked.

"Okay, fine, princess. What will it be? How can I serve you today?" I laughed.

"You're crazy, Mom."

"Maybe a little."

"I want to ride my bike, I think. Then, maybe we can get dirty with finger paints or write on the sidewalks with my special chalk. What do you think?"

"Sounds like a plan, my dear."

"Then what are you waiting for? You better get dressed! We have a lot to do today! Come on, I will help pick out your clothes," Terra directed, running upstairs to my closet.

Terra kept me busy throughout the day. Still, I caught myself thinking of the night before and how Trenton had taken me through the night and how well I had served him. I cleaned, I cooked homemade vegetable soup from the cans that remained in the pantry, and I danced to some of the songs he had mentioned to me. As the streetlights came on, a knock came at the door. Quickly running my fingers through my hair, I smiled and headed for the door. My heart raced, excited to feel Trenton pull me into his arms. *He didn't call! He stopped by instead!*

"*Matt?!* What are you doing here?!" I exclaimed, opening the door to the wrong man. "How did you find me?"

"I'm sorry, I didn't mean to catch you off guard. I had to see you. I thought you might need a friend." Matt smiled. "You haven't been answering my calls. I was worried about you. You said we could be friends and that you weren't ready, and I respect that. I stopped by the gas station and didn't want to eat alone. Do you want a cheeseburger?" he asked, holding up a brown paper bag.

"Ummm . . . yeah, come in," I answered as the overwhelming scent of greasy cheese filled my nose. "I'm starving! It was hard to keep up with Terra today, and I didn't have time to eat. You have perfect timing; I just put her in bed," I lied, trying to control the sound of my stomach growling. "It's always good to see a friend."

"I'm glad," Matt said, pushing his way through the door. "I had to

19

do a little work to find your apartment, but it wasn't too hard."

"Oh, I thought I told you which apartment I was in." I lied again.

"No, you said you would text me. You must have forgotten."

"I'm sorry, how forgetful of me."

As Matt handed me a sandwich, I felt his eyes roam, resting on my breasts. Matt's eyes pierced my skin like daggers. *Why is he looking at me like that? I thought he understood we were just friends. I'm not ready to be in a relationship with him. I'm not sure I like him. I like Trenton—I felt connected to him—not Matt. I don't know why, but Matt is intimidating. He makes me feel small—antlike. What am I supposed to do? I'm hungry. I want to be a friend, but he's staring at my breasts.*

"Can you hang out here for a minute, Matt? I don't mean to be rude, but I need to run to the restroom. I'll be right back." Closing the door behind me, I quickly dialed Trenton's number.

"Hey, I didn't hear from you after you left this morning," I stuttered.

"I can't talk right now, Sheila. I like you, but I want you to know . . . I enjoyed last night. You are so intimidating, so beautiful," Trenton said, trying to hide the sound of another woman giggling in the background.

"Oh . . . really? I wasn't sure how it went."

"Oh . . . yes . . . I want more of you. I want you to make good on those promises. I don't think I'm ready for something as special as what we could be, though. Can you give me a little time?"

Why do I hear another woman's voice? I need an answer. What am I supposed to do? Placing my phone on the counter beside me, I stared at my reflection. I had failed, and now, this man who I had wanted to be a friend was waiting for me. *I need to get to know Matt better. Maybe it's his age that made me feel weird. I've never been with a younger guy. He brought me food, and I'm hungry. He's always trying to call and spend time with me. How bad could it be? Everyone deserves a chance.* Looking down at my phone, I remembered Trenton's kiss, knowing I would be weak if he called again. I knew I wouldn't easily forget him even if I wanted to.

Pinching my cheeks, I headed back to Matt. I needed to make the best of the situation and forget about Trenton, at least for the time being. With my head swimming with thoughts of the night before, I returned to the man I'd rejected.

"So, what made you think of me?" I asked Matt.

"What do you mean? I haven't been able to *stop* thinking about you." Matt laughed. Grabbing my hand, he ran his thumb across mine and smiled. My body tensed at his touch. "You know you're beautiful, right?"

"No, why would you say that? I'm just me. I didn't know you thought of me like that." *Why do these guys keep saying that? It's like they can't think of anything else to say. I mean, come on, how gullible do they think I am?*

"Of course, I do. Why wouldn't I?" Getting up from his chair, Matt's shadow moved behind me, and his hands gripped my shoulders. "Is this okay?"

"I . . . guess."

"What about this?" Matt asked as his hands traveled down the front of my wrinkled blouse to the top of my breasts. "Can I touch you here?"

So much for being friends and respecting boundaries . . .

Matt's strong hands cupped my breasts as I fought against my instincts and leaned against the back of my chair. Looking across the table, I felt like I owed him for bringing me food. Did it matter if this man touched me so closely, in my home, at my table? It was like most of my childhood. How many times had I paid for someone's kindness with a little touching or a kiss? There had been *many* times, and I found myself distant as Matt began to loosen the buttons on my blouse. I was frozen, unable to move as he explored. This was how I normally reacted. I had always let things happen, never feeling like I had much of a choice.

"I want to fuck you," he whispered. "Can I have you?"

My mouth fell open as Matt stared down at me, his once kind eyes now intensely dark. While I found his confession and asking for what he wanted sexy and commanding, as he hovered above me, he felt like a threatening thunderstorm. His body was ready to strike me with bolts of electricity if I didn't obey. *I don't want this.*

21

Leaning down, Matt captured my lips in his as he pinned me in the chair and began kissing me like a barbarian. I couldn't breathe. Pushing away from him, I stood up and looked over at him. *Am I brave enough to say no? Do I have the courage to stand up for myself?* But I knew it was too late. Matt's animal instincts had taken over. I saw it in his forceful gaze. *What would he do if I resisted? What if I screamed? What if he hurt me with Terra upstairs, asleep in her bed? Do I have a choice?*

Closing my eyes, I took another breath, and with shaking hands, I began to unbutton my blouse. Taking Matt's hand, I placed it against my flesh and let him take control. Keeping my eyes closed, I imagined myself as a child, swinging on my mother's porch swing. I thought of the sunlight that danced through the maple leaves as I swung back and forth. It was where I went when I needed peace.

Thank God for autopilot.

Chapter 3

A S THE BRIDGE ROSE away from the ground below, I glanced back at my journal. My journey had taken me farther than I'd ever been from its gilded pages. My heart pounded like native war drums, echoing against the green steel that rose like a labyrinth above me. The traffic slowed, and the lights grew dim as I glanced at the apartments below. Their warmth taunted me. Life danced forward and wouldn't notice my exit. It had a lot of feigned smiles and innocent dreams to steal from women like me—those who were raised to believe you "reap what you sow," "Karma is real," or my favorite saying, "do unto others as you would have done unto you." They were fairy tales. The world was fake, and laughter was only the melodic undertow of fools.

On this bridge was my final truth. I felt betrayed as I stared below at warm porch lights. Life was a lie. Love wasn't real. I had only known hate and manipulation. That's why I wouldn't be missed. And I certainly wouldn't miss the world. Soon, my body would be as frozen as my heart.

As I looked ahead again to the steel beams that beckoned me, I thought of Trenton and Matt. How was I so foolish to believe either of them had ever loved me? All I wanted was to be loved and wanted.

* * *

A week after being with Matt, my mind was swamped with thoughts of both him and Trenton. But eventually, I forgot Trenton and his promises of a better life. Thankfully, Matt had left a few minutes before Terra had awakened. As nice as Matt seemed, I couldn't picture myself with

23

him. Guilt had washed over me like a bad batch of soup for allowing him to have me after being with Trenton. I despised myself for what happened that night. I didn't want to be touched, and I cried each time I thought of being with Matt. I couldn't stop questioning my instincts. I hated to disappoint him but was glad he agreed to take a step back and wait. I only hoped that night wasn't the first of many like it. I was afraid to hurt Matt but terrified of what he was capable of.

Together, Terra and I sat cuddled up, watching her favorite movie. A beautiful girl who lost her father would soon meet her prince and be rescued from her evil stepmother. Terra smiled as the fairy godmother made the girl's perfect dress appear, and I was overwhelmed with the urge of wanting to give Terra everything she wanted. Her red hair was tousled and matted against her head from a sleepless night, and there were stains on the bottom of her nightgown from spending too much time in it. We didn't have a lot of furniture, so we spent a lot of time on the floor. I wanted a good life for us—one where we didn't have to worry about where our next meal would come from. That's why I started thinking about Trenton again and couldn't stop. It would be so much easier to have someone take care of us.

Reaching down for my phone, I pulled away from Terra and headed toward the kitchen. Dialing Trenton's number, I resolved to try one more time to make something of him. He was the only one I saw a future with. I missed his voice, his smile, and his laughter. I longed for him.

"Trenton," I spoke into the phone, "I haven't heard from you, are you ok?"

"I'm sorry, babe. I've been busy with work, but I've been thinking about our night together a lot."

"*Really?* What . . . about it?"

"I think I'm stupid for being afraid. You are *such* an amazing woman, and I saw how you live and I . . . I want to take care of you."

"What do you mean 'how I live?'"

"I mean, you don't have much. And that's okay. But you were fun to be with. I don't want you to worry anymore."

"I'm not worried about anything. Terra and I, we're fine," I lied.

"I'm sure you are. That's not what I mean. I want to give you more. If you stayed with me, you would never have to worry about going out in the middle of the night for groceries or eating cinnamon toast for dinner. You deserve better, and I want to be the one to give you a new life."

"Thank you," I answered.

"So, I've been wanting to ask you: will you be my girlfriend?"

"*Really?!* You want *me* to be your girlfriend?"

"Absolutely. I would ask you to marry me, but it seems a little soon," Trenton joked. "What do you think? Do you think we could make this work?"

"I'm sure we could figure it out. The way I see it, we are meant to be together. It's up to us whether we screw it up or not."

"Ok, well, I need to go. Can I come see you tonight?"

"Of course, you can."

"Until then . . ."

I spent the day cleaning and scrubbing the apartment and myself. I wanted to be perfect for Trenton. Somehow, he had managed to squeeze every ounce of love from my heart. He was a one-way trip into the unknown, and I was ready to board the train. Visions of the magical train ride that lay ahead filled my head.

Buttoning the last button on my goodwill dress, I waited for Trenton. I knew it wouldn't take long for a proposal, and then we'd be together. I was tired of worrying about money and where Terra and I were going to get food. But most of all, I imagined Trenton's constant passion. I imagined us singing together in church and praying together. I loved the idea of church services and Sunday dinners—the way it was meant to be. On many occasions, Trenton had talked about going back to services. He had loved working with the youth, and I had a knack for relating to teenagers. I imagined myself working as his secretary and using my skills to help his business grow. Together, we could conquer the world.

"So, what are you thinking?" my sister, Tasha, asked from across the table as I approached.

"I'm hoping this works out. Trenton seems to have it together, you know?" I answered, grabbing a cup of coffee.

"You always say that, Sheila. Maybe it shouldn't matter if he has it together or not."

"Yeah, I feel bad that I keep thinking of it that way, but there is so much to him. I think I got lucky this time. He's smart, funny, car—"

"Make sure you like him for the right reasons," Tasha interrupted. "I've never known you to act like a gold digger. That's not your style."

"I want Terra and me to be safe."

"What about that other guy who keeps calling?"

"You mean Matt? I don't know. He's just a friend."

"Maybe you should focus on taking care of yourself before getting involved with either of these guys."

Startled, I quickly stood as the phone interrupted our conversation. Walking to its place on the counter, I snatched it up when I saw Trenton's number.

"Hey, I'm exhausted, and my leg hurts. I don't think I can make it there tonight," Trenton stated before I even said hello. "Would you meet me at the hotel in Jackson?"

"Um . . . long day?"

"Oh, God, yes. It was awful. Why don't you call me when you get here, and I will sneak you inside?"

"Yeah, if that's what you want. I already have my sister here to watch Terra. I was hoping you could meet her."

"I'd rather us be alone tonight if you know what I mean."

"Yes, of course. I'll be right there."

"Trenton isn't feeling well, Tasha. He asked me to meet him. I hate leaving you guys, but it shouldn't be more than a couple hours, okay?"

"Fine . . . if that's what you want to do."

Watching Trenton step into the moonlight when I arrived felt magical. Quickly, I ran into his arms, smelling the fresh hotel soap on his skin. The breeze caressed me as my body was crushed against his, and he swiftly pulled me inside the hotel.

"I'm so happy to see you. It felt like it took forever for you to get here." Trenton smiled.

"You said your leg was hurting. What's wrong?"

"I get blood clots sometimes. I needed to get off it."

"That sounds scary."

"I'm used to it. Come here, sit down with me. You know, you're wearing an awful lot of clothes. I don't think that's necessary."

Grabbing my dress, Trenton started carefully unbuttoning me, and soon, I was beneath him, eagerly accepting his presence in my body. My best dress laid crumpled on the floor as Trenton plunged savagely inside me. My body ached as I tried to wrap myself around his large frame as he groaned above me. Closing my eyes, I allowed myself to drift away, letting him fulfill his needs. As with any man, it didn't take long before he collapsed beside me. It never lasted long.

"You know something I told the guys at work today?" Trenton asked.

"What's that?" I inquired, hoping he would cuddle up with me.

"I said, 'If you feel like the girl you are with is too good for you, then you've found the right one.' And . . . you're too good for me, Sheila."

"Why would you say that?"

"You just are. It's hard to explain. You know what else is interesting? The best way to attract a woman is by sleeping with another woman. They are more likely to try to compete. It's like they sense it. Women are easily manipulated."

"I have a guy like that. I told him I wanted to be friends, but he hasn't gotten the hint yet." I laughed while, at the same time, my phone buzzed from the table.

"Answer it."

"But I'm with you right now, Trenton. Why would I?"

"Don't be rude; answer it." Trenton laughed.

With a sigh, I picked up the phone and greeted Matt.

"Hey, I haven't heard from you in a few days and wanted to see how you are doing." Matt said through the phone.

"I'm fine, just been busy with my little girl. Listen, I can't talk right now. Can I call you another time?"

"Of course, sorry to bother you."

"Ok, talk to you later," I stuttered. *Why do I feel so guilty?*

27

"Well, that seemed awkward." Trenton laughed from the bed.

"He honestly scares me. Matt acts respectful, then tries to be flirtatious. I'm not sure how to handle it."

"I'm sure you'll figure it out. But remember, these tits are mine. Nobody is *ever* allowed to touch you again, not ever. Even if we break up, your body belongs to me. You promised that only I could have you, remember?"

"Of course, I do. I'm all yours, Trenton."

"That's right. Even if we break up and you're with some other guy, if I call you, I want you to run to me so I can have this body of yours." He laughed. "No matter what, YOU . . . ARE . . . *MINE.* I love how you put yourself on display, completely at my mercy. It lets me know I can do whatever I want to you, and you won't complain."

Lying beside Trenton on the bed, I opened my body for him to enjoy. Cupping my breasts in his hands, he teased my nipples, squeezing them between his fingers. Sliding his hands down my body, he threw my legs open around him as his eyes raked over my flesh. Taking his hands, he gripped my thighs and pulled me toward him. Leaning over me, he nibbled at my breasts as he groped my thighs, manipulating my body to his will.

"Listen, as much as I would love to enjoy you again, I have an early day tomorrow." Trenton groaned. "You make sure to come when I call, ok?"

"Of course. I guess I will go then. Will I see you again soon?"

"Yes, absolutely. That's why you're my girlfriend, isn't it?"

Why does he want me to leave so soon? Did he just want to see if I would come running to his side so he could play with me? So he could screw me?

Rushing home to Terra, I remember thinking about how much I enjoyed being with Trenton. But I hated that Trenton and I talked more on the phone than in person. It was only about sex when we were together, but he had chosen me to be his girlfriend. Trenton loved when I surrendered to him. Of course, attraction didn't matter when his touch felt like ice against my flesh. It was frightening to submit to his power, to hear his words as he took me. I felt like property—a toy in his hands. As offensive as it was, it was just as sexy.

I wanted to be on display for Trenton, walking around his house all day, ready to be enjoyed whenever he beckoned. I wanted him to brag to his friends that his girl was always happy to serve. With anyone else at any other time, I would have been offended by the things I wanted to do to and for him. My mind swarmed with conflict at his ideas even as I embraced them.

* * *

Sitting across from Tasha the next morning, I quietly sipped my coffee, unsure if I wanted to talk. Glaring at me from above her cup, I knew she had something to say, and so I waited.

"You know . . ." Tasha began.

"There it is. I knew it was coming."

"What?!" Tasha sighed. "You don't want to hear how Terra woke up wondering where you were? You used to never leave her alone, not for anything."

"I know. I don't know what it is about Trenton. I can't stay away."

"I don't think everything is right with him, Sheila."

"Well, I know it's not perfect right now, but Trenton works a lot. It will get better. Are you sure you're not just upset because you don't want to watch Terra?"

"Nooo . . . it's because you hate leaving her alone. I know this has to be eating away at you."

"Of course, it is. I miss her like crazy. I don't know what else to do. I like him. Pretty soon, I will get it together. It's the beginning. It's not going to hurt anything to make a few sacrifices right now."

"You should figure out how to take care of Terra on your own. It's better to be single than to mess around with a guy who doesn't respect you."

"What makes you think Trenton doesn't respect me?" I asked.

"Maybe because you only see him in the middle of the night, you never know when he's going to call, and he's supposed to be success-ful. Shouldn't he be taking you *and* Terra out if he actually cares about you?"

"It's because he works late, and that's all the time he has. I'm sure he will when he has a day off. I don't know. Maybe I should give Matt a chance. I just don't like him. It's awkward."

"No, I think you're afraid of being alone."

"I don't know what else to do, Tasha. My ex left us with nothing. He won't even come babysit so I can get a job at night. Even that wouldn't be enough to take care of her properly anyway, though."

"It doesn't matter, Sheila. You have to start somewhere. I know you are attached to this guy but probably for the wrong reasons."

"I don't know . . . maybe. I'm hoping. I feel like I'm not ready for a relationship until I'm with Trenton or hear his voice, and then it's like magic. He's the only thing I can think about."

"It's weird. You're suddenly obsessed with this guy, and I don't think he's treating you right." Tasha sighed. "Remember that old camera I got you. You were so good with it. You should try taking pictures for people."

"I don't know how I would get started."

"I'm sure you'll think of something. You are a lot smarter than you give yourself credit for."

Sitting down across from Tasha, I knew she was right. Trenton seemed like a kindred soul. I remembered all the conversations we'd had—the late nights, the laughter. I couldn't think of a night without him. Every day I didn't see him felt like an eternity. I was lucky to have him in my life. Glancing over at my phone, I shuttered when it rang. I knew it was Trenton before I even saw the number.

"I can't make it tonight," Trenton whispered. "I'm in the hospital. I have a blood clot in my leg. They think I might need to have another filter put in."

"*Oh, my God! Trenton!* Let me see if I can get a sitter, and I will be right there. Are you okay?"

"I'm in a lot of pain, and Sheila, I want you to know that Marsha is here too. She lives close by, and she's just a friend. I hope you don't mind."

Wait . . . what? Who the hell is Marsha? Be cool, Sheila, be cool.

"I'm just glad you're not alone. I will be there as soon as I can."

Rushing to gather my things, I quickly ran out the door and darted off to cling to the man who was supposed to change our lives, with barely enough gas to make it there. *He understands how difficult things are for me. Surely, he will give me gas money. There's no way he would leave me stranded, right?*

After a few wrong turns, I searched the halls for Trenton's room. I had expected there to be a couple of machines hooked up to him, but there were none. Wrapped up in a thin hospital blanket, Trenton seemed fragile, so I headed for the chair under the window and laid down, waiting for morning.

* * *

Listening to the mumbled sound of nurses, I slowly opened my eyes to the blinding light of Trenton's hospital room. The closest nurse was laughing at something Trenton said as she pumped up the blood pressure cuff around his arm. He simply smiled up at her. Glancing over at me, his gaze locked with mine for only an instant, and again he looked away. I felt like an intruder, hoping he would greet me with appreciation. But instead, his eyes ignored me. My heart grew cold watching him smile up at the nurse. I was only a few feet away, but it felt like a million miles as I waited for her to leave.

"Come here, Sheila," Trenton suggested dryly.

"I'm here. Good morning," I replied.

"I need to ask you something."

"Of course, anything."

"Were you with another man? Recently? After you were with me?"

"What do you mean?" I answered, reaching for his hand. "I was *before* we were a couple. Why do you ask?"

"I heard you were with him the day after you were with me."

"Like I said, it was before we were a couple. It was after we first met, not—"

"Why are you acting like this isn't a big deal, Sheila? I know things. I have spies everywhere!"

"I . . . I didn't have a choice. He just showed up at my apartment."

"How did he know where you live unless you invited him there? Did you take him there like you did me?"

"No! Not at all, he just showed up, and he brought me something to eat. That's all it was."

"I know you let him have you! You know how I feel. You belong to *ME*!"

"I know, of course, I do. I'm all yours whenever you want."

"I don't believe you."

"What does it matter? We weren't a couple. I called you that night while he was there, and you were with someone else. I heard her in the background. You dismissed me. What was I supposed to do?"

"You were supposed to wait for me." Trenton shrugged, reaching for his wallet. "And another thing . . . when you left the hotel, I was missing $100. Why did you steal from me?"

"What are you talking about? I wouldn't steal from you!"

"Then why is the money missing?"

"I don't know. I was with you every second I was there. I didn't even go to the restroom. How could I have taken anything from you?"

"I don't know how, but I do know the money is gone. I can't do this, Sheila. I can't be with a thief."

"I'm not a thief! You can't ask me to come here and then decide you don't want to be with me. I don't understand."

"What don't you understand?"

Sitting down by the window, I dropped my head in my hands. I felt the tears welling up in my eyes as my hands began to shake. Looking into Trenton's stern eyes, I felt lost, confused. Still in yesterday's clothes, I ran to the restroom. Splashing water on my face, my breath escaped in sobs as I hoped the running water would hide it. My feet felt like ice against the hospital tile. The mirror's light was blinding through my tears. After a few moments, I brushed the tears away, knowing I had to ask Trenton for gas money.

"I think you need to understand something," Trenton stated as I opened the bathroom door. "I have been with a lot of women, and I messed up my marriage. I regret almost everything I've ever done. I even told Marsha this, and she didn't like it at all. I even regret being with her, but you . . . I'll never regret you. You were . . . wow. And that's a compliment—a big one."

"I'm glad you don't regret me, but I wouldn't steal from you, and why do you think I would? That hurts."

"I don't know, maybe you didn't, but Marsha seems to think you did," Trenton answered. "Why don't you blow me as a hello, and we can start this day over again."

"I'm all for starting the day over, but I can't go down on you in the hospital. What if someone comes in. Besides, you're not well right now. What if I accidentally hurt you? You have to be careful."

"That's a shame. I would love to cum in your mouth right about now."

"It's not a good idea. What if your blood clot moves?"

"I'm not worried. In a bit, they're going to take me to put the filter in, and everything will be fine. I've had one before. It's not a big deal."

"Trenton, I hate to ask, but I barely had enough gas to get here. Can you spare anything to help me get back home?"

"What?! You won't give me a blowjob, and now you're asking me for money after you took $100 from me? I will give it to you this time, but I won't anymore."

"I didn't take any money from you."

"It doesn't matter, here take this. You don't think it was a big deal you cheated on me, do you?"

"I didn't cheat. You were with someone else, and I didn't think I would ever hear from you again. I don't understand! You just asked me to go down on you?"

"No, it's not okay. You know what? Marsha wouldn't steal, and she wants to be with me. You should leave. I can't stand the thought of you being with another man."

"But you and I weren't even together yet. It was before you asked me to be your girlfriend. I didn't cheat on you. You know, I would have gone to the ends of the earth for you. I wanted to marry you, sing with you, and spend my life taking care of you. And now, you want to toss me to the side because you *think* I cheated on you? I swear if we had been together, I wouldn't have let another man touch me."

"But you did. Sheila, why don't you leave? Marsha will be here soon. *Go.*"

With a face full of tears, I ran out the door, thankful Trenton had given me a little money to make it home. Pain shot through my body as my heart dropped. Ice snaked through my spine as I shivered from a moment of regret. I knew I hadn't stolen from him, and being with Matt had only been to protect my daughter. Yet, one moment had destroyed me—a moment that should have never been in question. I had been honest, and my honesty had only shattered my hopes and dreams in an instant.

Approaching my car, I watched a chubby short-haired blonde approaching the hospital entrance with a balloon and a smile. I knew it was Marsha. She thought she had won a prize, but he wasn't a prize worth having.

I wasn't going to be alone, and I wasn't going to be tossed away so easily. I had misjudged Trenton. He wasn't appreciative of my gifts. And as the ice of my heartbreak turned to anger, I dialed Matt's number. If I could be ready for Trenton, then I could be ready for Matt. I refused to be alone when I had someone who was always checking on me, always close by, and smart enough to want me. So, as I watched Marsha proudly find her way to Trenton, I committed myself to Matt.

I heard Matt smile when I asked if he wanted to give us a try. My body shook as guilt washed over me with its cold despair. I believed I deserved it. Maybe I wasn't good enough for Trenton, but Matt was willing to give me—with all my flaws—a chance.

Chapter 4

NOW, AS THE BRIDGE'S arches loomed above, I stared down at the waters turned black by darkness. I had made it to the top. It wouldn't be long. I felt naked standing there, hollow from the memories that ravaged my mind. My heart felt the guilt of those nights and the regret of sudden decisions. My life had never given me a choice to be anything more than what I was: a woman lost, drowning in her addiction to the passionate fire of men. My journey to the bridge had been inevitable. This was where I was destined to rest. My childhood had been the first step, my divorce the second. Trenton and Matt were merely stepping-stones leading me to the path I was destined to travel.

Even though men had touched my body, seen it, and embraced it, my heart had always remained frozen within a robotic frame. I had never allowed men to touch my soul. It was reserved, but for what I didn't know. If I tried to release my soul, my mind would escape the men's embrace, and I would stand alone.

My palms shivered against the railing as I clung to it, leaning over to see the thin waves lick the rocks below. The edge of the river taunted me as it had for years, beckoning me to join the lost and weary that had gone before. I had a long leap ahead of me. I only needed to find the strength to climb over the edge.

As I watched the water kiss the shore, I began imagining things. I imagined the water's cold fingers caressing my body, pulling me deeper into its depths. Closing my eyes, I felt the heat of the coming embrace and the air brush across my skin with smoking cold. The scent of burning flesh burnt my nose as silence engulfed me. At that moment, I knew

I had been removed, taken from the bridge.

Instead of the icy bridge, I was surrounded by the heat of desolation. In a moment of emotion, my mind had taken me away, and now I stood surrounded by fire. Everything had turned gray. The crisp air had shifted to smoke, and my feet stood in the shattered glass of memories. I saw all of my memories, in thousands of tiny mirrors that covered the ground like sand. Each mirror taunted me with a memory regretted. Around me, all color had vanished. The world once cold was now hot with suffocating smoke that rose from flames that licked the ground. I was surrounded by The Gray. In an unending loop of despair, fire scorched the earth, and black waves reached for me with oily fingers from an ocean cresting gray.

My body burnt against the escaping embers from the flames surrounding me. I felt each of them strike me as fire licked my hair. The smoke pushed me forward like a wave until the pressure buckled my knees. The shattered sands dug at my hands, cutting into my tenderness as I watched the oil crawl to me. I searched for relief from the trap ahead of me, only to discover a burning tree, beckoning. Pushing away from the black ocean, I clawed at the rocks, tugging to escape as I watched my life play out in mirrored sand. I pushed, trying to scream, but only silence escaped my lips. My body ached as the satin gown that once protected me melted in the heat. I was naked, unprotected against the heat and crashing oil that called me.

I felt my body slide against the shattered sands as I pulled back from the forceful smoke that tugged at me until, at last, I stood. I watched silently as men rushed past my vulnerability. Blinded by smoke and flame, they ran with torches to the shore, igniting the waves. They struggled against the smoke as it lunged at their bodies. It twisted around them, wrapping them in fire like an invisible enemy. Their mouths opened, their eyes widened, and they screamed in silent agony as they fought against the waves. But the smoke tossed them into the ocean that reached up for them with claw-like waves, and they were pulled within. One by one, they sank as The Gray overtook them.

I once again stood alone as flames licked my flesh. Quickly, I ran toward the tree. My gaze forgot the smoke that burned my eyes and took my breath as I darted through the rocks, trying to reach the lowest branch. I needed to climb, to find what was beyond, but the flames pressed against me, hindering my ascension. Looking up at the flaming tree, I felt its cold ripping through my body. I felt its impending death echo as another wave of men appeared, racing against the smoke. But as they topped the rocky hill, their eyes narrowed, and their torches fell to the ground. One by one, they circled me. Their crimson eyes discovered me. They noticed my pale breasts against the blackened sky.

The men's faces curled in silent growls like lions ready to devour, reaching for my naked flesh. Yet, I stood locked—frozen—only steps from the flaming tree. I felt it. Even as it burned, its branches waved. The men moved, reaching around my body. They stretched their wooden fingers around me. My feet stumbled back against the rocks as the tree drew me closer until, beneath it, I lay in the heart of the fire.

* * *

The night sky radiated with light as I reclined in Matt's car. In front of us, the water of the Ohio River looked beautiful. As the barges crept by, the water rippled against the darkness like a satin sheet flung on a bed. Around us, the geese waited for the bread we kept to ourselves. With each breath, I felt the tension in my shoulders release as Matt took my hand in his. A smile crept across his face as he noticed me watching him.

"I'm glad you're here with me," Matt said.

"Me too. It's peaceful."

"When I was getting my divorce, I used to sit down here all the time. I wouldn't have made it through it any other way. People don't know me. My ex's family . . . they said I was mean to her."

"Why would they say that?"

"They said I left her screaming when she needed help out of bed. My ex-wife was in a wheelchair. Her family left me with her, and I never had a chance to get out or do anything. I was tired and frustrated sometimes, but I never hurt her. They sent me to a crisis center. I don't why, but at least I had a moment's peace. I made a big mistake while I

37

was there. It had been a long time since my wife and I had been intimate, and there was this girl . . . When I got out, things were never the same again. Everyone in town knew where I'd been. They made fun of me, and I couldn't even go to the gas station without someone calling me a freak. I was afraid to go anywhere."

"Oh my God, people are cruel," I reassured him, squeezing his hand. "I would never judge you."

"You're the first person I've talked to in a long time. It was hard for me to say hello. You looked so pretty in your profile picture. You're too good for me."

"Why would you think that?"

"You're beautiful, sweet . . . and I have nothing to offer you."

"I don't need anything."

"Everyone needs something."

"I wouldn't worry about it. It's enough to enjoy someone's company."

It made my heart ache listening to Matt's story. In my mind, his story played out like a movie. I imagined him being stuck at the crisis center against his will. I saw him being taken from home and thrown into the sterile rooms of the crisis center. It was probably the best place for him, and I couldn't imagine people making fun of him for being there. In my mind, I saw those people in front of me. I watched them see their own guilt in his eyes, reflecting their pain onto him.

"Bullies, Matt. No doubt they've been there too and wanted to make you feel small so they could feel better about themselves," I continued reassuring him.

"Maybe, but . . . it doesn't make me feel better. When I'm with you, all that goes away."

As Matt leaned toward me, his strong arms wrapped around my shoulders and pulled me closer. I felt small in his arms as he lowered his lips to mine, and I knew my resistance was over. *Maybe, like everyone else, I have misjudged Matt.* Closing my eyes, I answered his lips with mine in a conversation only flesh can understand. I felt his pain melt into mine as I tried to take his pain away. *Nobody deserves to feel like a monster.* In that moment, I wanted to rescue him from the past. *Everyone deserves a second chance.*

"There's something I've always wanted to do," Matt whispered, pulling away. "I wanted to have someone to do it with me, though—someone who gave me hope. I never thought that was possible . . . until now."

"Oh, what's that?"

"I've been carrying around my old wedding band for a long time. I think it's time to throw it into the river."

"Then let's do it. Maybe it will help you move on. Hell, maybe I should do that too."

Shuffling through my purse, I pulled out my ring. If he could do it, so could I. It was only a small gold band. I had tried to sell it, but it hadn't been enough gold. They had taken my diamond, and that had supplied Terra and me with a month's worth of groceries, but the band hadn't left my bag.

"Come on, let's do it!" Matt laughed.

Rushing from the car, both of us ran to the edge of the dock. The wood beneath us shook, echoing our excitement as we approached the edge. Taking my hand in his, Matt smiled, and, without a question, both of us took our rings and threw them in. "AHHHH!!!!!" we both screamed into the night.

Finally, our rings were gone. I felt a weight lift from my shoulders as I watched them sink into the murky depths of the Ohio River. *The past was over. It was time for a new beginning.* Looking into Matt's brown eyes, I smiled. *It's funny how things work out sometimes.*

"Come home with me tonight," I suggested while giggling.

"Are you serious?"

"Yeah, why not?"

"I don't know. I'll have to check with my mom."

"Wait . . . what?"

"She gets angry if I don't tell her where I am."

"But you're a grown man, have been married and divorced. She knows that, right?"

"She knows. But I don't want to piss her off. She's a little crazy sometimes."

Walking away from me, Matt grabbed his phone and began to dial her number. I watched him pace in front of his car, staring at the ground. The joy was sucked out of the moment as his free hand balled up into a fist when his mom answered. I only heard his voice raise a few times, but it was enough. I tried to give him my sweetest smile when he looked up. *He's way too old to need his mother's approval. I appreciate respect, but this is a whole other level of crazy.*

Finally, Matt hung up the phone and returned to me with a smile. "Are you ready for me to take you home?" he asked.

"Of course!"

Taking Matt's hand, I followed him to the car and climbed in beside him, thankful Tasha had taken Terra for the night. Looking over at him, I knew I needed to get his mind off his mother and whatever trouble he had at home. When we entered my apartment, I led Matt to my bedroom, inviting the inevitable. *It's time to show him what I'm capable of. He's only had a taste.*

As I often did, I turned off my emotions and let a man partake of my gifts. I spoiled Matt with my body, knowing he had plenty of built-up frustration needing to be released. I was good at that. My body was strong and could take the aggressive lusts of an angry man. I invited him to use me. I loved the look of pleasured men and their expressions as they plunged within my flesh. It gave me a satisfaction I couldn't find elsewhere. It was a drug and I an addict, forever craving the look of a man enjoying my body.

In those moments, the pain didn't matter. A man could be as rough as he needed to be, and I would only encourage him. I could handle it. Matt must have been frustrated because he lasted the entire night until he could no longer cum. Eventually, my river of moisture dried out, and I was left with nothing but the pain of his continual thrusts.

Thank God for autopilot.

As my eyes opened the next afternoon, I rolled over to check my bed, fully expecting Matt to have fled, but he hadn't. Instead, I was engulfed by his chocolate eyes staring down at me. *Oh great, a morning person.*

"I need coffee," I mumbled.

"You drink coffee?" Matt laughed.

"Of course, I do, don't you?"

"No, never could stand the stuff."

"What?! Are you crazy? I can't live without coffee!"

As I willed myself from the bed, I felt my legs shake as my feet hit the floor. Pain shot through my back as I stood, reminding me of how frustrated Matt had been. My body felt torn as I stumbled my way downstairs to the coffee pot with him following close behind me.

"Have you actually *met* Terra yet?" I asked as I sat at the table, awaiting the nectar that would enliven me.

"No, I haven't. I think she was asleep last time I was here."

"Well, she should be home soon. You can meet her, unless you're uncomfortable with that?"

"Sounds great. I love kids."

Smiling to myself, I thought of Terra's absent father. It would be nice to have a man around the house. *Maybe he could find a job or other ways to contribute. Or I could get a job.* As I settled down with my first cup of coffee, Matt watched quietly.

Before long, the door creaked open, and Terra rushed into my arms, oblivious to the man sitting across from me. Holding her in my arms, I smelled strawberries as her hair brushed against my cheek. As I took a deep breath, I scooped her up into my arms and rested my cheek on top of her head. Her arms wrapped around my neck like a necklace as I squeezed her tightly. Terra's blue eyes gazed into mine as I quickly kissed her forehead while my fingers tickled her until she collapsed like a rag in my arms.

"I love you, baby girl. I missed you sooo much."

"I missed you too, Mommy!" she squealed. "I love you." Turning in my lap, Terra glanced across the table and looked back at me, her eyes wide. "Who is this person? Why is he visiting us?" she asked, grasping the side of the table. "I don't remember asking for visitors."

"I'm sorry, I will make sure to ask you next time," I teased her.

Matt giggled. "My name is Matt. You must be Terra. I'm happy to meet you," he said, reaching for her hand. Slowly, Terra reached her hand out to him while she looked back at me. Gently, Matt took her little hand in his and kissed the top of it. "I hear you're quite the princess." He smiled.

"Well, that's what Mommy says, and her opinion is the only one that matters," Terra answered, snatching her hand back.

"Is that how it works?" Matt asked.

"Of course, how else would it be?" I confirmed.

"Well, I guess I don't know."

"It's nice to meet you, Matt," Terra said, sliding off my lap. "Mom, I'm going to go watch TV."

"Do you mind if I join you?" Matt asked.

"That's up to Mommy. I don't make the rules around here. But I'll warn you now, I'm going to watch princesses, so you might as well get used to the idea."

Slowly, Matt followed her to the sofa and sat beside her while she turned her favorite movie on. Looking back at me, he shook his head in amusement before turning his focus back to Terra. Watching him carefully, she scooted to the edge of the sofa and began swinging her legs off the side.

It seemed awkward at first, and then, as the movie progressed, I watched Terra warm up to him. Matt was quick to bring her snacks and adjust her pillows so I could take a break. The entire time, he barely took his eyes off me, knowing I was watching. Terra was never a child to trust easily. She knew her father had hurt me, even if she didn't understand how or why. She knew, and it made her capable of going from sweet and innocent to sassy and mature in an instant.

"Hey, Mommy, can I play with your hair?"

"I guess so, go get the stuff," I answered.

Running to the bathroom, Terra quickly returned with a basket full of her favorite hair jewels, tiny rubber bands, and hairbrushes. Grabbing my hair, I felt pain just from looking at the tiny basket. Terra playing with my hair hurt on a normal day, but this time, my hair was even more in disarray, from my night with Matt.

"Terra, why don't you do *my* hair instead?" Matt suggested.

"You want me to do *your* hair?" Terra laughed.

"Of course, I want to look pretty, too. And that will give your mom a few minutes to finish her coffee."

"She's almost finished the pot already!"

Good man. I dodged a bullet on that one.

Slowly, I made my way to the restroom to ease the tangles from my hair. It took a little longer than normal, even after using Terra's detangling spray. Heading to the living room, I gasped. Matt did not have just one tiny rubber band in his hair but several. His blond hair stuck out in tiny tufts all over his head. The room was full of laughter as Terra added ribbons and bows over each ponytail.

"I think you need eye shadow," Terra suggested as she giggled.

"Oooh, sounds wonderful. I've always wanted to try blue eye shadow. It might make my brown eyes POP!" Matt giggled.

Never turning down an opportunity, Terra quickly ran back to the bathroom, returning with another basket full of makeup. Closing his eyes, Matt sat perfectly still while she pulled at his eyes with the slimy eye shadow I had gotten her years before. It wasn't long before his hair was done and his face was covered in glitter makeup. And finally, Terra placed a small crown on his head.

"There, now you can be a princess, too. It's perfect. Now you have to stay like this until you leave."

"Can I see?" Matt asked.

"Of course, but if you take it off, you have to leave."

"Your wish is my command," Matt answered, reaching for the mirror. His eyes wide, he gasped. "You're right; it's perfect. I've never felt so beautiful."

"Told you."

Knowing the movie was almost over, I went and sat beside them. Giggling to myself, I was amazed that such a big man had allowed a little girl to dress him up. *Maybe I can love this man.*

The rest of the evening was full of laughter, feather boas, and pillow fights. It was weird to watch Terra slowly open up to a man. It seemed the more Matt endured her torture, the more she welcomed him. As the day progressed to night, I began to forget the aches and pains that shot through my body. It seemed normal, natural. What was a little pain in comparison to having an apartment full of laughter? For a moment, life seemed almost perfect, and then it was time for the man who had ravaged me the night before to return to . . . his mother.

As I tucked Terra into bed, I made my way to the bathroom. Armed with music and a glass of wine, I settled into a tub full of bubbles and closed my eyes. As the notes of my favorite songs danced through my head and the bubbles caressed my skin, I let my mind wander. *Perhaps this isn't so bad. I could love Matt. He seems to adore Terra.*

My mind quickly wandered to the camera I kept locked in the closet. When I was younger, I loved taking pictures, and some even said I had a gift. I knew I could run a small business, especially with a little help from Matt. I only wished it was enough to make me forget Trenton. My time with him had ended abruptly, and even though I had swiftly moved on, he hadn't escaped my mind. No matter how hard I tried to push thoughts of him away, somehow, he remained.

As the bubbles vanished down the drain and my glass ran empty, I wrapped myself in the scent of my favorite lilac lotion and let my hair rest against my curves. I never felt more beautiful than after a bubble bath. Every bubble took a worry or a fear and tossed it away. I was reborn a little each time the water drained and I stood naturally before the mirror, covered in the softness of my skin. That night, I hoped the bubbles would take away my memories of Trenton and give me peace about Matt, but they didn't.

Hearing a knock at the door, I quickly grabbed my robe and headed to answer it. I rarely had visitors, but at that hour, it could have easily been a police officer asking if I knew anything about a neighbor— something I hated. I always kept a robe close by—one that covered me enough to avoid gossip.

As I opened the door, my heart caught in my throat as I stared into Trenton's eyes. My breath stopped as I watched him caress me with his eyes. My legs shook as I stepped to the side, allowing him to enter my home. I knew I couldn't leave him outside with everyone watching. *Trenton and Matt at my apartment on the same day . . . again. Why does this keep happening?*

"You're out of the hospital?" I asked, noting the obvious.

"Yeah, I had to see you again. You left so abruptly that I didn't get to say goodbye," Trenton answered, resting his hands against my arms. "I'm sorry."

"But . . . I thought you were with Marsha."

"I was . . . until I realized I had lost you. Sheila, I don't know what I'm doing. I'm so confused."

"What do you mean? You said you wanted to be with *her*."

"I did, but I don't. I don't know. I can't let you go."

"But you *did* let me go."

"I didn't mean to. I don't know what happened. I don't remember most of what happened at the hospital. I remember you leaving and me waking up seeing Marsha beside me instead of you."

Tears gathered in the corner of Trenton's eyes as he took my hand and held it to his heart. Staring at the floor, he caressed my hand. His eyes fluttered as he gulped down the air that came in shaky gasps.

"Trenton, you dumped me. You told me you wanted to be with her. I can't guess what you want."

"I want *you*, Sheila. I'm sorry if I hurt you. I don't know what I want anymore. I want you, but I want her."

"That's not fair."

"No, it's not. I'm sorry. Please let me make it up to you. Let me show you how much you mean to me, how much I want you."

"I'm not going to let you have whatever you want."

My heart quaked at the idea of betraying Matt so early in our relationship. He was trying to do the right thing, trying to be a man. He was honest, and while he was a little rough with me, he was kind. My heart ached, longing to touch Trenton as we sat together on the sofa. I wrapped my robe tighter against my body, trying to hide my flesh. I had never betrayed anyone, and I knew how it felt to discover the person you trusted had given their body to another. I didn't want that for Matt.

Still, I wanted Trenton, and I wanted to believe that everything at the hospital was a drug-induced mistake. I wanted to unwrap my robe and welcome him. Looking at his sad face, I knew I couldn't resist him. He fed my addiction. He understood it and was happy to oblige, to let me see his satisfaction, and to allow me to fulfill him with my body. It gave me a rush like a strange drug that spoke for me. While bubble baths made me feel reborn, sex gave me purpose. With Trenton, it was potent—a high I couldn't turn from. I felt alive because he wasn't shy to tell me his desires. The knowledge that I was competing for Trenton's affections only made me want to please him more.

Trenton's eyes beckoned me as his lips stayed silent. My breath echoed in my chest. My heart rattled like a drum as his hand touched the belt around my robe. Reaching his hand to my face, he pulled my lips to his as he ripped the robe from my body, revealing my flesh to his. I was lost, detached from the reality I had created.

Trenton's body made me feel alive, desired, and sensual that night. As he kneeled above me, I forgot everything. I came to my senses only long enough to feel his hands tug me into another position as I surrendered to him.

Why do I desire this man? How does he feed my passions so easily? I don't understand. I wish he would just STAY! I don't know if I will ever be able to forget him. Why can't I feel this way with Matt? Why can't I resist Trenton? I suck at this. I'm a horrible person. If only he hadn't visited me. I wish I'd never met him. But then . . . I would have never felt this. Trenton, you are my fantasy. I crave the competition, the passion, to be chosen by such a strong man. DAMN! Why? Trenton doesn't deserve me, but I know nobody will ever capture me the way he has. I'm so screwed. Why does this have to be so hard?

As I laid before Trenton that night, he told me more of his confusion between Marsha and me. I hated him, and yet . . . I loved him. I longed for the conversation to be different, but I still allowed him to enjoy my body, to feast his eyes on my breasts. I remained on display, his hands caressing each curve of my body as he continued to apologize for being with Marsha. I loved watching him take my body with his eyes. It made me hungry for him. But my mind was only there long enough to feed my desire, and I was gone again, on autopilot, allowing him to take control of my body as my mind escaped.

Thank God for autopilot.

Chapter 5

S TANDING IN THE KITCHEN, I watched through the dusty window as children played outside. Summer was raging, and water fights were everywhere. I was thankful Terra didn't notice. She was inside, busy watching princesses' dreams come true. As I sipped my coffee quietly, Tasha's words echoed through my mind: *Remember your old camera? You used to be good with it.* Then it hit me like a hammer to my chest. *Maybe I could do something.*

Slamming my coffee down on the counter, I headed to the closet and pulled out a bunch of old sheets and, of course, my camera. With the sheets, I could make backdrops and take pictures of the neighborhood kids. Glancing around the apartment, I found places where I could easily set up small sets for photography. With a few lamps, sheets, and a little creativity, I knew I could make something happen.

That night, I rushed to make flyers, and by the next day, everyone knew about my one-day photography event. For next to nothing, my neighbors could come and get their pictures taken before school started, and it would give me enough money to buy Terra school clothes and a few groceries. I resolved to run my little business with every bit of knowledge I could dig from my exhausted brain.

On the day of the event, people filled my apartment, awaiting their chance to get in front of the camera. I remember smiling more than I had in a long time. Every kid in the complex was there, and the money came, too, but I didn't notice. I was busy helping kids pose. One after the other, I took each of their pictures, and not just one picture. No, I gave them a full thirty minutes each. Our home was filled with laughter and smiles as excitement filled the air. It filled my heart knowing I did something to not only help myself but them as well.

I remember Terra running around, working hard to keep up as my assistant. Between sessions, she would gather the stuffed animals and flowers I used and put them back in the corner. When I needed her, she would find the perfect item to help the process along while Tasha counted the money and kept us all organized. That day, I felt a new era dawning. As pictures were edited and sent to customers, I was filled with pride. Before long, my photography business was enough to keep us in bologna sandwiches for the entire month, and cinnamon toast became a snack instead of a delicacy.

As business progressed, Matt always made sure to visit. It was the perfect way to celebrate. We would all three dance in the living room. Pillow fights were our favorite thing. I loved when Matt spent the night. He always woke up early and tended to Terra. Together, they would eat cereal and watch movies. It was the only time I ever slept.

Of course, Matt made sure I was up for most of the night. He had a way of making sure I was exhausted, and I loved every minute of it. It seemed that unless I was working with my latest photography client, Matt and I were always together. Those days flew by quickly. Matt was considerate, and when I ran out of money, he would take his mother's credit card to the gas station and load me up on snack cakes and pizza. He was a relief when things got hard.

One of my favorite memories of those early days was going up to Mound Hill for a picnic. Matt and I would sit in his car, overlooking our small town for hours. We didn't talk much, but again, we didn't need to. I remember how the breeze felt as it drifted through the car windows as we leaned back, enjoying the silence. Matt's hands always seemed to find my flesh, even when it was covered. His touch was always gentle in the beginning and grew more passionate and aggressive as evening descended upon us.

I remember the feeling of the rough wooden picnic tables as Matt laid me on top of them, his hands ripping my panties away from my body. Matt was always eager to enjoy me, and that made me proud to know I satisfied him easily and often. I took comfort in knowing he would never stray from me.

It wasn't long before Matt slipped a tiny engagement ring on my finger. Although it should've been a good day, I was disappointed. It wasn't the size of the ring but that I was an afterthought. Matt had come into some money, and after he spent most of his cash on a new game system, games, and rims for his car, he bought me a little ring. He said it seemed like a good idea at the time, but it seemed to me like an afterthought. I always felt guilty for feeling that way. Still, I accepted it and began planning our future.

My new photography business grew quickly, and I was soon able to move away from the apartments and the aggressive children that lived there and into a small house. I had grown tired of the constant battles with sirens and nightly arrests. Of course, Matt moved with us because his mother had become stricter. They were constantly fighting, and the stress was unbearable, and I was excited to see how much fun the three of us would have without the worry of gossiping neighbors living close by.

The next year went by in a blur of laughter, but something didn't feel right. I wanted time—needed time—to make sure Matt and I were ready. I wanted us to have a beautiful future, but I had trouble picturing it. I couldn't stop thinking about my ex-husband and how he had betrayed us.

Chapter 6

A ROUND ME, THE SMOKE swirled against the gray sky. Peeks of flames danced across the ground as I lay beneath the burning tree. Around me, a vine emerged. It crawled from the ground like a spider, creeping up my spine. Soon, another tendril followed, twisting its way around me. The vines arose, slowly wrapping their arms across my breasts and my waist. Their strength felt like hands carrying me as they pulled me back against the tree. Frozen, I clung to their embrace as their tendrils pulled me closer to the heart of the tree. I felt its rhythm. It echoed through the vines like the pulse of a million drummers, covering me in its enchantment.

Vine after vine twisted around my body, wrapping me against the tree, creating a sanctuary. They hid me from the shadowed figures of beastly men that lunged for me. Trembling, my hand clutched at the soot surrounding me. The vines grew closer together, and The Gray was slowly hidden from my vision as they covered me. I was left with a room of twisted vine walls. Along the walls, blue threads began to rise, glowing with light as they climbed, twisting through the vines as tiny flowers emerged.

In the tree's embrace, I arose and stood against its heart. Its radiance echoed through my flesh, pulsing within the tree's essence as I stood, protected by mossy veins of blue. In a crack, I watched as men arose from their hunt for me, rushing toward the devouring black that beckoned them. They ran into the smoke blindly as the black ocean reached out with its oily fingers, rising from its depths to capture their souls. Their mouths opened in voiceless screams as they were thrown within the depths of the oily waves.

The fire raged electric with each soul cast within the depths. The waves darkened as water turned to blood with each soul defeated. Yet, they came rushing. In groups, they ran toward the shore. Their white flames plunged into the darkness, striking at the heart of the smoke that swirled to carry them to the depths.

There was no hope for them—no defeating the darkness that raged within The Gray. My arms ached against the vines that embraced me. Pulling against them, I climbed to the branches above, searching for a vantage point, my escape, and freedom. Resting, I laid within the curve of the tree's bottom limb as vines followed me, covering my flesh in a blanket of moss. Around me, I watched the tree turning black as its energy surrounded me. Its essence grew weaker as it fought to shield me from suffocating flames surrounding us.

Around me, the tree's branches glowed with silvery light echoing from within, but the vines were fading as I clung to them. I clung to the only life that had tried to save me. I clung to the vines and to the tree that stood dying as tears escaped me. I felt its anguish as it struggled against the flames, against the heat. Its farthest branches turned black as its life was taken. Slowly, the light was fading inch by inch from its father limb, rising closer to me with every moment that passed. Life . . . was fading.

Watching the sky fade into gray as blue faded from the depths of the ocean black, I remembered the first moment I felt my life draining. Watching the essence of the tree fade, I remembered the pain and the overwhelming rush of ice that took my body over time. At first, it felt as it must when a limb is frozen, sleeping as its strength is slowly drained and your veins begin to tingle as razor blades scrape your skin from within. I remembered fighting against it, reaching for my own escape, knowing I needed time.

* * *

"I think you should move out for a while," I suggested to Matt quietly from behind a kitchen chair.

51

"But why? You don't want to break up with me, do you?" he asked.

"No, I need space. I need time to heal. And I'm not sure you should be living here before we are married. I feel guilty."

"I can't leave you! I don't have anywhere to go," Matt pleaded, grabbing my arms firmly with both of his hands.

"You don't get it, Matt! Everyone keeps saying this is wrong! I have talked to our pastors and explained the situation, that I'm trying to help you and that you have nowhere to go. They keep saying we're living in sin. We're going to go to hell. What if something happens to one of us or to Terra. I don't want to die and end up burning for all eternity. I can't do this. I'm desperate. I've tried to see if there is somewhere else for you to go, but nobody is listening to me! They don't care. All I ever hear is that you shouldn't be here. Nobody talks to me anymore unless they are saying that. I don't know what else to do!"

Looking into the living room, I saw princess dolls and play tiaras lying on the sofa. I watched Terra play with the couch pillows. She was tossing them to the floor as she tried to hit the dog. I watched her smile as the pillows missed our cocker spaniel, who played along, getting closer and closer to Terra. *I have to do something. I have to protect Terra. No matter what, Matt has to leave. At least for a little while, and then we can hurry up and get married. I can't live like this. I want to do what's right, what they expect. I can't lose my friends.* Darting off from the corner, Terra ran past me to the screen door, searching for a ball.

"Terra!" Matt snarled. "Your mommy wants me to leave. *You* don't want that, do you?!"

"No, of course not," her innocent voice stuttered. "I like you."

Escaping Matt's grip, I watched her. Taking a deep breath, I leaned over the hot water in the sink and closed my eyes. My stomach turned into a giant knot, and sweat beaded on my forehead. My heart raced, and I felt my skin turn red as I tried to catch my breath. Then, I felt Matt's hands snatch my shoulders. My body spun, and he was looking down into my eyes as I shrank against the counter. The wood pushed into my lower back like a sword as he pressed against me.

"I don't care what anyone says, I don't think you want me to leave. And Terra doesn't want me to leave." Matt growled, getting closer and closer to my face as he slid his hands down to my arms. I felt blood rising to my skin, burning bruises into my back as his body pushed me farther into the countertop. I struggled to breathe as I arched backward, gasping for air. "I'm never going to leave you, never. I love you. You're mine. There's nothing you can say or do that will make me leave. Even if I do go to my mom's, you won't find a way to get rid of me. I AM NEVER GOING TO LEAVE!"

"I wouldn't try to get rid of you," I whimpered. "I think Terra and I just need some time alone. We need time to figure out how to *be* alone. I want to do what's right. I don't want to lose my family, my friends, my faith."

"They're wrong. I don't care what you have to lose for us to be together. You don't have to be alone. I'm going to stay and help you through this. I told you, I'm not leaving." Slamming his fists against the counter, Matt spun and stomped away.

I fell to the floor like a crumpled piece of paper. My heart pounded in my ears as tears streamed down my face. I barely caught my breath as the pain in my back echoed. *I need time alone. Why can't he go and give us a little space to figure this out? I WANT to marry him, not because I have to and not because it's convenient. But I want to love him, and I'm not sure I do or can. I can't find out the answer if he's always here. The people at church say we're living in sin. I keep asking for the pastors to help me, but they won't do anything! They say I have to do this. I have to find a way. I'm trying, but he's not listening. I just want to be happy, to feel loved. And I don't feel that with Matt. I don't know if it's him or me or if I just need time, but something needs to change. Why can't he understand that? Why did he freak out? He thinks I hate him. He doesn't have anywhere to go. What's wrong with me? What do I do now?*

"Oh, stop crying. I'm here to help you," Matt continued, returning to the kitchen. "*See*, you don't want me to leave." Taking my crumpled body in his arms, his hands rubbed my shoulders while he said all the right words—words that only made my tears grow colder as my body shook at his touch. Thankfully, Terra was occupied with our dog as my tears grew harder and Matt tried to hold me in his arms.

Later that evening, I laid on the couch staring at the ceiling as Terra and Matt played on the floor. My mind wouldn't settle, my heart continued to race, and I knew I needed something. Glancing down at my phone, it instantly lit up as though it were responding to the thoughts in my heart. And like clockwork, there it was, my favorite text message.

Can you call me?

Are you okay, Trenton?

Yes, I just need to talk. I need a friend that gets me.

Give me a minute.

Casually, I set my phone down and headed to the kitchen, being careful not to draw attention to myself. Quickly, I opened up one cabinet door after the other. I searched randomly, investigating cabinets I had already memorized.

"Matt, I want to make an apple pie. I don't have the stuff I need, though. Do you mind if I run to the store really quick?" I asked.

"I hate apple pie," Matt answered.

"I don't think you've had mine. I have my own recipe. I'm really proud of it."

"It doesn't matter, but I guess I can try it."

After leaving, I stopped a few feet from home and grabbed my phone, anxious to know if Trenton was okay. It seemed like that's how Trenton and I handled things now. We were friends, and sometimes, we needed to talk. Glancing back toward the house, I felt guilty. *Matt would be angry. He wouldn't understand.* I wanted honesty, and even as I feared Matt's anger, I knew it would be better if I told him about my old friend. My heart skipped a beat as I dialed Trenton's number.

"What's wrong?" I asked.

"We got into it again."

"What about this time?"

"Marsha wants to get married. But I'm not sure that's what *I* want. Actually, I *know* that's not what I want."

54

"What do you mean? Why wouldn't you want to marry her?"

"Well, I don't know. It doesn't feel right. And she's not . . . *you.* What would you do if I left her? What if I came to you?"

"You're never going to do that. We've never had a real conversation while we were together. That only happens on the phone."

"Maybe, but that's because you're so . . . never mind."

"Well, I don't know. I'm with Matt now. He asked me to marry him a while back."

"Why didn't you tell me?"

"How could I? What do you even remember about me?"

"I remember everything: your sweet voice, the way your lips taste, and the tenderness in your touch."

"Trenton, you can't say that to me anymore."

"I know, but I do. How did you get away tonight?"

"I'm driving to the grocery store."

"I wish I was there. I wish I had never been in that hospital. It would be me in your house, me holding you through the night. It would be me making love to you, playing with your daughter. He's a lucky man."

"I don't feel lucky."

"What happened?"

"Everything . . . and nothing," I whispered into the phone.

Gripping the steering wheel, I pulled into Foodland and headed inside. I didn't have time to stay on the phone. Matt always watched me closely, and I hadn't told him about Trenton. I was afraid he wouldn't understand, and right then, Trenton wasn't making it any easier. Taking a deep breath, I ignored my heart.

"I asked Matt to leave, and he refused. He pushed me up against the counter. I think I have bruises."

"*What?! Why?!*"

"He said he would never leave me, that I was confused. I'm not sure he's wrong."

"He shouldn't do that. Are you okay?"

"No, not really. But I don't have a choice, do I?"

Quickly grabbing everything I needed, I headed for the checkout. It was a record-setting shopping trip. I needed to be alone, to hear Trenton's voice without interruption. Just for a few minutes, I wanted to be heard. My back ached as I carried the bags and threw them into the trunk. I walked as fast as I could just to shut the door of my car to the outside world, returning to my solitude with Trenton.

"I'm going to come after you. I have to find a way to get away from Marsha," Trenton whispered. "And I can't let Matt do that to you. You're mine. You remember that, don't you? You promised me."

"I know I did, but you belong to Marsha now."

"A part of me will always belong to you. Don't *ever* forget that."

"I couldn't, even if I tried. Are you going to marry her?"

"What did I just say? I'm coming for you. I will call you when I get my truck fixed."

"I thought we were supposed to be friends, Trenton. How can you say that to me?"

"You know how I feel about you, Sheila. I promise I will come for you as soon as I can. Is there any way you can get him out of the house? Can you find your way to me? That would make it easier. I don't want to wait, Sheila. I don't want to marry her."

"I don't think I can. I wish, but I tried to get him out of the house, and he refused to leave—*refused*. I can't do this on my own. I need help. I would rather be alone to figure out what I want."

"Don't worry; I'll find a way. Wait for my call. It won't be long. I'm going to come for you, and we will be together."

Quickly, I rushed home and waited . . . for weeks. Then, when it had been long enough, I told Matt about Trenton. I spoke the truth of who he was and how we became friends. I told him about Trenton's health problems, his business, his problems with Marsha, and how I normally tried to give him advice. For once, Matt was understanding. He trusted me. I didn't mention the last phone call since it wasn't my typical conversation with Trenton. A moment of panic had overcome Trenton, and while I knew he missed me and wanted me, I knew he wouldn't come for me. Marsha seemed to have imprisoned him because now, he never came, not even for lunch. My heart hoped, but my mind knew better.

I tried several more times to convince Matt to leave my home, asking him for private time. I visited the pastors of our church and begged them for help again. I felt guilty for breaking the rules and living in sin, but Matt wouldn't leave.

I talked to Trenton every day for a while. He always complained about Marsha and talked about not wanting to be tied down. He was like me in that he didn't feel he had a choice. It hurt me to watch his pain, but it was a nice distraction from my own. Eventually, his calls stopped again, and I was left with my own personal torture. So, I pretended Matt hadn't pushed me up against the counter and that he hadn't growled at me. After all, he had only acted out of fear. His mother treated him badly, and I felt guilty knowing he didn't have anywhere to go. I couldn't abandon him.

That call, that moment in the grocery store, was in November, just before Thanksgiving. Trenton and Marsha were married in December. And I, with tears in my eyes, gave in and finally married Matt in January.

Chapter 7

OUR WEDDING wasn't special. Hardly anyone was there to wish Matt and me well—only a few obligated relatives. And while I had wished for snow to cover the landscape outside the church windows, it didn't show up either. My dream of a glistening white wedding was canceled by a muddy January.

I remember crying as I took Matt's hand on our wedding day. After many attempts at trying to get him to leave, I had failed. I had asked for advice from the pastors, my family, and my friends, but Matt prevailed. I decided the best way to move forward with my life was to marry him. It was an act of surrender. Sure, I had my moments of love, where I missed Matt, needed him. But the moments of regret had already overtaken me. I wish I could say I was happy on our wedding day, but I wasn't.

Matt had his bad moments, but overall, he was a good guy, and I believed he was misunderstood. I dedicated myself to him and kept my occasional calls with Trenton friendly, nothing more. I had made the choice to be with Matt and to make a family with him, and I honored my vows.

The years flew by for a while, and there were smiles, laughter, and occasionally moments of peace. Sometimes, when I missed Trenton, I would sing a song out toward the moon. Then, we didn't seem so far apart. But mostly, I had forgotten Trenton. I only thought of him occasionally, as a friend.

With Matt's mother's help, we were able to make a down payment on a house—one to call our own. And as the years passed, Terra's needs began to change, and my photography business wasn't enough. I had chosen to keep my rates low to help others, offering a service most couldn't afford. That left me with limited funds. It was enough to pay our bills in our new home but nothing more. I held many events and raised my rates but kept them affordable. But as Terra needed more clothes and school supplies, it grew harder.

Unfortunately, Matt refused to work. He had never held a real job, only the occasional odd jobs for his mother. While that helped sometimes, he made sure he always got something of his own out of it. That wouldn't have been a bad thing if I would have been able to pay the bills on my own. But we were living month to month, session to session, and I wanted a better future for us. Terra needed more. It was time for me to go to work. So, after months of trying, I finally found a job.

It was my first day at The Outlet, which had hired me to help run its service desk but only for a few hours a day, a couple days a week. I had my eyes set on the future, and I wanted the kind of experience that looked good on a resume. More than anything, I wanted to learn. Thankfully, The Outlet's flexible schedule allowed me to continue my photography business on the side. There was no way I was going to return to subsidized apartments and living on cinnamon toast for dinner.

As I pulled in front of the store, I thought about Terra being home with Matt and shuddered. Looking up at the aged Outlet sign, I knew I had made the right decision. I needed a little more money to help keep us away from the apartment we had escaped. And yet, with each step I took, it felt like there was concrete in my legs as I knew I would be away from Terra more than I ever had been. But I had to provide for her. Terra deserved the best I could give her. This was only a small start, but it was a start.

I spent the first few hours sitting behind a computer, learning the basics and The Outlet's policies. Everyone seemed happy to meet me, or happy to gossip. I wasn't sure which they preferred, but I welcomed the company. I wasn't used to sitting alone in a tiny closet-like space working on tedious videos and quizzes, and I kept my phone close by in case Terra needed me.

Then, finally, it was time to start the actual work, and my new manager, Teddy, led me to the service desk. I watched two little bru-nettes already working there, scurrying around like squirrels as people approached them. One of them, who wore her hair in a ponytail, was helping a customer return a shirt. The little brunette smiled broadly as her foot stomped against the padded mat at her feet. Her fist clenched behind the counter as the customer shook her head, her tongue wagging as she pointed at the brunette. I felt the frustration from twenty feet away and pitied her, but I knew that soon I would be dealing with angry customers too.

"Meg, Rylie . . . this is Sheila. I need you to train her on what she's supposed to be doing here and how to keep the customers happy," Teddy instructed, pushing me inside the little cubicle.

"Uh . . . hi," I said, trying to sound polite. "What can I do to help?"

"Are you kidding me, Teddy? Right *now*? We're not getting enough hours as it is. How are we going to fit someone else into our schedule?" The brunette with the ponytail scoffed.

"Meg, we discussed this," Teddy replied. "You need someone to cover your days off. We *need* her, and she's way too smart to be a cashier."

"Fine." Meg scoffed again.

"I want you to be personally responsible for her training, Meg. You are the trainer, after all."

I immediately admired Meg's feistiness. She had stood up to a man twice her size. With his dark hair and large hands, Teddy was a bit intimidating at first, but his smile . . . well, it would make anyone smile. Approaching the angry customer, he had Meg calm within moments.

"I gotta go. Take care of her. This one is special." Teddy winked at the duo of brunettes. And with that, he quickly walked away, into the store. His large frame dominated the aisles as he went on to his next task. I couldn't help but stare and wonder at having such an unusual creature as a boss. He was a mix of common and culture you didn't see in Gallipolis. Yet, here he was, the assistant manager of a rundown Outlet that was threatening to close.

"Okay, what did he say your name is again?" Meg asked.

"I'm . . . I'm Sheila."

"Well, there's a lot to learn, so you might want to get a notebook. Write down everything I say. You're going to need it."

The next few weeks were a blur of numbers, passcodes, and rules. Meg wasn't kidding when she said there was a lot to learn, and she tried to help me, but it was difficult for me to keep up. Even as she taught me, I felt her resentment. Every chance she had, she would escape to the jewelry counter to help other customers or visit the cashiers. Every time I needed help, she rolled her eyes and went over procedures again. I never managed to write everything down; it was impossible, but I tried. Every day, there was a new rule I hadn't discovered, or a new passcode, or a new situation I hadn't encountered. But I persisted and was soon working alone.

It was easier for my new "friends" to escape then. Now, they were able to leave me alone for entire shifts as they collected online orders and ran the registers when someone called in sick. My little service cubicle got lonely, and Teddy quickly became my only friend. At night, when we closed the store, he would talk to me about my day and ask about my daughter. If I needed a specific day off, he made sure I got it. The other girls hated me even more for that, so I made a point to volunteer for holidays so they could be with their families.

Each night when I returned home, I went straight to Terra, even if she was asleep. She had grown much older, but I needed her as much as she needed me, if not more. Tucking her in bed, I would hold her in my arms and ask about her day and what she had done with her dad. (She called Matt her dad because my ex had completely disappeared.) After that, Matt was sure to occupy my time as I fixed dinner, cleaned, and fulfilled whatever else he had deemed my wifely duties.

On my days off, which weren't many between The Outlet and my photography, Matt always wanted me to himself. There were many days that Terra was sent to her room to play while he had alone time with me. I missed her terribly but felt I had no choice but to keep going. Each time I suggested that he get a job, Matt refused, saying it was impossible to find a job.

I remember one awful day in particular—well, it was many days. I felt like my words didn't matter to Matt anymore. I was growing and changing, and I knew it. I needed more, wanted more. That day, I laid naked in our bed with my vagina sore from Matt's thrusts and stared up at the ceiling, too dazed to even consider counting the tiles as I had often done after he had taken me.

"Matt?"

"Sheila?" he responded in a teasing way as he giggled.

"I would like it if you touched me more."

"What do you mean, we just fucked? I always touch you."

"I mean, you know . . . a little foreplay."

"I sucked on your nipples. What more do you want?"

"You only do that for a couple seconds, and honestly, you don't seem into it. I would love it if you played with me sometimes. You know, took your time, helped me get wet before—"

"You're *always* wet! Why would I need to do that?"

"I'm *not* always wet. It would be nice if you tried to seduce me a little."

"Again, I don't understand. I thought you like it this way. You never seemed to mind before, and I touch you a lot."

"I don't feel like you do. I would like to take our time a little bit."

Watching Matt stomp around the bedroom gathering his clothes, I remembered all the times he said it didn't matter how I felt. I remembered him brushing my hand away when I tried to touch myself. He would tell me I wasn't allowed to have an orgasm. Even as he told me how much he touched me, I remembered being pushed down face-first on the bed as he pulled my dress up and plunged his cock inside of me. Then, I remembered the times he would stand in front of me after Terra had boarded the school bus. He loved catching me with a cup of coffee and pulling his pants down in front of me while I sat there. He wouldn't move; he wouldn't ask. He expected it. If I didn't respond immediately, he would wiggle his cock in front of me until I put it in my mouth and started sucking.

Then, I remembered how he would push my face down on the kitchen island and pull down my pants while I was talking to Tasha on the phone. That's when it hurt the most. I was completely unprepared, but I wouldn't miss a beat. I never reacted. Matt liked it when I struggled to keep my breathing normal while I talked on the phone. I wasn't allowed to hang up either. If I was tense and it hurt, then it was even better for him.

"I thought since I suck your dick all the time, maybe you could go down on me, or you could touch me . . . down there . . . a little," I pleaded.

"Nah, you know I can't do that. Every time I look at your pussy, I remember how sick my ex-wife was. She kept getting these awful yeast infections, and it stunk. Remember I tried to go down on you once a long time ago, and I almost threw up. Besides, you keep asking for this, and I keep telling you that I already touch you. I don't know what you want."

"I'm *telling* you what I want. I want you to take your time."

"Fine, I will suck on your nipples more," Matt responded, slamming the door behind him.

Looking back at the ceiling, I covered myself and held Matt's pillow. I pushed it tightly against my body, trying to fill the void between my breasts. It ached, especially after sex. My legs curled up as I rolled to my side. The alarm clock glowed a fiery orange as the minutes slowly changed, and my body quivered against the cold that invaded my mind. This time, I had managed to remove my shirt. I had often pushed it up myself, hoping Matt would touch my breasts for a moment before he threw me down or unbuttoned his pants and pushed my mouth down on him.

Soon, I heard the lawnmower start, and I pushed my aching legs over the side of the bed. Pain shot through my back as gravity took its toll, and I quietly embraced the pain. Thankfully, my robe was close. Its softness caressed my skin like an embrace from a teddy bear as I pulled it around me. Glancing down at my phone, I sat on the side of the bed and texted Trenton, hoping he would be there. I needed a friend—anyone I could talk to, even if only for a moment.

Trenton?

I'm here. Are you okay?

I don't know. Can you talk? I texted.

For a moment, I stared at the phone, wondering what I would say if we talked. I hated texting Trenton. He had his own life to live, after all. But sometimes, it was nice to hear his voice. Before I could think a second longer, the phone rang.

"It's me, baby. What's wrong?"

"Trenton . . . I . . . I . . . don't know what to say," I answered, heading to the window to check Matt's progress on the lawn.

"Say whatever you want. *You* contacted *me*, remember?"

"I . . . I think Matt's gay. I feel like he doesn't want me."

"Didn't you say he has sex with you all the time?" Trenton asked in disbelief.

"Yeah, but . . . I'm always face down, or he has his eyes closed. He barely touches me. I asked for him to give me a little bit of foreplay, and he reminded me that when he tried to go down on me, he gagged. I remember it. I was so humiliated. He doesn't even undress me sometimes. He keeps my shirt on. I don't understand."

"Yeah, there's something wrong with him. I can't understand why he would be like that."

"You never went down on me either, though."

"No, but I wish I would have tasted you. I will never forget what you felt like and the way you looked." Trenton snickered. "Still, no regrets."

"Do you think he's gay? Maybe I'm just a cover so his mom doesn't know or something."

"I don't know. That would make sense, I guess. Sheila," Trenton whispered, "do you regret me?"

"No. I wish we would have talked more when we were together. Maybe we would have had a chance to build something."

"I'm glad you don't regret me. I have been thinking about you a lot."

"It's a little late, Trenton. We're both married now. We have been for years."

"But I'm here."

"Not really. What if Marsha knew you were talking to me?"

"I don't care what she thinks or that we're both married. Sometimes, I miss you. I shouldn't have taken you for granted."

"It's a little late for that now. I care about you, but I'm not trying to bring up the past. I honestly just needed a friend for a minute."

"Wait, did this stuff with Matt just happen?"

"Yeah, I'm watching him mow the lawn from the bedroom window."

"What the hell?! He fucked you and went outside to mow?!"

"Um, yeah."

"He's gay. Damn, here I wish I had one more night with you, and he's out there acting like none of it matters."

"You won't come see me, Trenton. We tried. I thought it would be nice to have lunch, but you never showed up."

"I couldn't. Marsha has a pretty tight hold on me. I wish she was half as warm and loving as you are."

"You married her, though. If you hadn't, I probably wouldn't have married Matt. I would have found a way out. We could have disappeared."

"I'm thinking about leaving her."

"You always say that."

"I mean it this time."

"I better go."

Placing my phone on the nightstand, I wrapped my robe tightly around me and headed for the bathroom. As the warm water flowed and bubbles arose, I listened closely to the lawnmower echoing against the house. As I immersed myself within the water, I let it take me. The soft bubbles wrapped themselves around my aching muscles as I laid back against the tub and closed my eyes, letting their warmth embrace me.

I can't remember the first time I put bubbles to water. I'm not even sure what gave me the idea. I'm sure it was something I saw on TV. Maybe it was rich women on the soap operas my grandmother watched. Of course, it could have been advertisements for barbie dolls and all their implied elegance. The idea of bathtubs filled with water and bubbles up to your neck seemed like something only rich, elegant women could do. Watching them engulf themselves with bubbles seemed too much for a little girl with no luxuries.

No luxuries is an understatement. I remember our tiny bathroom and our "little house," as my mom referred to it. Looking back, it was barely more than a shack. Our home was nestled quietly among the trees on a gravel road with only two windows on the side as you approached it. It was often overlooked by the few passersby that dared to approach the old road. That was . . . *if* anyone found the road. Nestled among the trees, you would easily mistake our road for a driveway as it closely resembled two small paths with grass growing up the middle. Small as it was, our home seemed like a hospitable place along the old road with its two maple trees and half-laid sidewalk.

My favorite place was the bathroom. There was only a small window and a dirty screen to remind me there was more outside. Occasionally, a soft breeze would enter the muggy space and overwhelm my nose with the scent of honeysuckle, which engulfed the outside. I was always drawn to the bathroom's ivory paneling with gold veins that tried desperately to look elegant. If I looked long enough, I saw screaming faces overlapping each other, especially on the longest wall, which was barely five feet long. Sometimes, I looked for hours, getting lost in the faces. Somehow, their screams made me smile.

At times, I would rest my back against the bathroom door and allow myself to slide to the old linoleum. Clutching my knees to my chin, I would often hide from my parents' screams and the sound of fists hitting wood-paneled walls. When I was truly desperate, I'd imagine I was deep within the jungle with screaming baboons and thuds of falling timber. Of course, even in the lush jungle, I would imagine pools of hot bubbling water. As I turned the water on, I tried to muffle the sound of my family fighting. The water always reminded me of TV advertisements that simply said, "Calgon, take me away."

When my brother and I were young, we always had to take turns using the bathwater. There was a rush to try to keep the water warm. Drawing fresh water wasn't an option because we used a shallow well that was always running out of water. My parents were constantly conserving water or "priming the pump."

The idea of a bubble bath seemed like something from a fairy tale.

It was as elusive as finding my own personal prince charming and being whisked away to a far-off castle. It was a beautiful fantasy. Unfortunately, that was all it could be at that time. After all, bubbles—or fancy soaps of any kind, no matter how inexpensive they were—were considered wasteful and frivolous by my parents' standards. It was just the basics for us, even if my parents didn't always follow their own rules.

But that was then, when I was a child. Unfortunately, it didn't seem my circumstances had changed much. Now, as an adult, I still feared violence and being yelled at for wastefulness. *Maybe one day, that will change.* As I drifted away within the bubbles, I considered my circumstances. *Why does Trenton always seem to want to be with me? It doesn't seem right. If he meant the things he says, he would be here with me. Maybe I've misjudged Matt. He's mowing the lawn, something that needs doing. Maybe I'm overreacting. This is how Matt shows me he loves me.*

Determined to stay positive, I thought of the bubble baths that had come and gone, and I relished each bubble—how they gently kissed my skin and eased the pain. Leaning my head back, my body rested.

"What do you think you're doing?!" Matt yelled from the bathroom door. "You know you're not supposed to be in here. I'm dripping with sweat, and I have to take a shower. You're supposed to meet me at the back door and help me undress."

"Matt, I'm so sorry! I must have fallen asleep," I answered, jumping out of the tub.

"You know to make sure the bathroom is open when I get done mowing. Hurry up and take my clothes. And get me a fresh glass of water. It's hot out there."

Dripping with bubbles, I emptied the tub and grabbed Matt's dirty clothes. The grass stuck to me as I headed to the washer, the stench of his sweat covering my arms. Within moments, I returned to him with a glass of water, knowing that if I didn't hurry, he would put his fist through the door again. As I struggled not to slip on the tile floor, I remembered him throwing me against the wall, his hands digging into my shoulders, leaving bruises.

"Bring me fresh clothes and socks!" Matt demanded.

Running to grab his clothes, I searched his drawer for socks and placed them on the counter where he liked them. Catching my breath, I gazed at Matt's shadow against the shower curtain and cringed. *No, don't act like that. He's tired from mowing the lawn. Matt has never hit you. He only pushes you around a little. When he gets angry, he hits the wall or the door.*

"Do you need anything else?" I asked sweetly.

"No. But what are you going to fix for dinner?"

"I don't know. What do you want?"

"I want McDonald's."

"It will take me a little bit to get ready, but I can do that."

"Try to hurry. Nobody cares what you look like; just go."

As the weather grew colder, Matt was inside the house more. I tried to be a better wife, and even when I was tired, I didn't complain. It was nice when Matt started making me coffee in the mornings when I got up, and sometimes, I got to sleep in while he played video games. Things seemed better. I loved that he had started doing little things for me. Matt would let me know my cup of coffee was waiting as he screwed me every morning, and he even made sure he was quick so the coffee would still be warm when he was done with me.

Chapter 8

L IFE WAS FADING within The Gray. Around me, blue had vanished from the sky, and the pulse of the tree that echoed around me slowed, steadily fading. Each beat, each strike of its rhythm, grew weaker as the tree was overtaken by the smoke that raged around us. Turning black, the vines relaxed, breaking against my skin, falling to the fires below. The fire, once blue, slowly changed to the smoke of embers engulfed, rising into the night. Below me, smoke rose into The Gray as men continued to fade.

Lightning strobed against the oily waves. My heart stopped within the blinding light that ripped across the sky, striking the beastly men that ran for the black waves. The weakened vines draped across me as life gave its final gasp. It beat like a gong, echoing through my spine as my teeth clenched against the flash that covered me in the icy heat of death. But it wasn't *my* death. As the tree glowed blue one last time, it faded, its light vanishing in an instant like a switch gone dark. And I stood alone, grasping at the branch above me as its life drained from my fingers, knowing its hope had faded long before I came.

In the distance, red smoke arose from a place beyond my sight, and I saw rocks breaking against the heat as life became gray. The ground shook beneath me as I clung to bark turned to steel. Looking down upon my once snowy curves, ash painted my flesh, hiding me against the sky. My fingers clamped against the branch above me as tremors echoed against its skin and vines fell to the sharp rocks below. Slowly, I eased myself down, watching for the next tribe of men, not knowing if I had seen the last. Still, my heart felt them, and it heard a battle rising in the land through deafening silence.

Frozen and hidden against the tree, I watched men arise again, chasing the smoke that entangled them. It came faster now, their deaths a ballet of lifted limbs and spinning heads dropping suddenly behind the curtain of smoke grown thicker. My lungs burned like swallowed flames as the men's voiceless screams rippled against my flesh. I felt their anguish as their light was ripped from within.

Stepping away from the tree, I reached for the sharp rocks that rose beneath me. Hiding behind them, I awaited the men. From a distance, I watched them standing guard like soldiers marching against living smoke. Their faces were soft with moments and memories, but with every step they took away from their camp, I saw their essence fading. As they approached me, blue eyes turned black, their cheeks sank, and their lips shriveled as their minds were stripped. What once was human turned beastly as the heat rose like a veil around them.

As the men approached, I remembered that men once trusted would change. I remembered the loneliness of standing alone in the snow wishing my husband would have arrived. I remembered how our love had once burned through the night but had become a whimper as my mind drifted. I thought about how many times I had felt lonely and vulnerable to the advances of men as I grew weak and starved for gentle hands that caressed and lips that kissed.

Quietly, I hid within the branches of the flaming tree, hoping the men couldn't see me, knowing I wasn't safe. From my spot in the branches, I remembered the pain Matt had often caused and how I believed that *I* was the problem. I believed that his aggressiveness was *my* fault. I blamed myself for every time he hit the wall, the door, or the refrigerator. I remembered how desperately I tried to cater to his needs, and I remembered the bridge. *I must have jumped. I must be dead. I wish I would have gone to a good place, free of men that act like animals. This must be my Hell. Now, the men around me don't even try to hide their beastly nature.*

* * *

Heading to work, I listened closely to the weather forecast. It was calling for snow and lots of it. I was only fifteen minutes away from work, but it felt like forever as I watched snowflakes fall. The temperature was plummeting, and I felt my heart drop as I entered the store.

Meg was the first to call for Teddy. The weather was the perfect excuse for her to abandon me, and soon, she was gone for the day. Customers were leaving the store as quickly as they entered it as the snow continued to fall. Outside, I saw the gray parking lot quickly turning white as glossy patches rose from the slush. One by one, the cashiers left and the stock boys vanished, and before long, only five of us remained. I watched women get calls from their husbands, volunteering to take their wives home.

"I wouldn't let my wife drive in this," Teddy stated. "It's not right."

"Don't worry. You're stuck with me unless we close," I answered. "My husband isn't coming for me."

"Why not?"

"He's just not. Matt wouldn't think of it."

"I've never heard of that. 'Wouldn't think of it?'"

"Uh, no."

"Well, you're a tough girl." Teddy winked. "I'm gonna call the district manager again and see if he will let us close. There's no reason to be here."

That night, Teddy and I were the last ones to leave the store. As he locked the doors, we walked to the back together to secure the money in the safe, just like any other day. I saw him differently that day. I saw him as a person, a man—more than just a manager. I felt his frustration, and I dared to believe he didn't want to return home to his wife. As we walked past the lighted Christmas trees, I thought I saw tears in Teddy's eyes. Regardless, I refused to acknowledge seeing any weakness in him. I was paid to respect him. He was my boss.

I had grown to appreciate Teddy, even when others feared him. He was rough when he got angry, and he had a habit of slamming his fist on the counter when the other girls would call for help, but he never did for me—not once. As we finally set the alarm and headed out to the icy parking lot, I dreaded the drive home. There were several inches of snow on my windshield, my wipers only worked occasionally, and I hadn't heard a word from Matt. I hated being right. He hadn't thought of it.

"Do you have a scraper?" Teddy asked as I started my vehicle and stepped back outside.

"No, I keep meaning to buy one, just haven't."

Without looking up, Teddy headed to my side and began cleaning off my vehicle. I watched his height come in handy as he easily cleared the car of ice and snow.

"Do you live far?"

"I'm in Centenary. It's not too far."

"Out 141?"

"Yeah, basically."

"I will follow you as long as I can."

"Thanks, Teddy."

That night, I was thankful to be a good driver. I didn't slip—not once. When I got home, I was shaking from the drive home. I wasn't as brave as I pretended to be, and even the short walk from the driveway to our front door had been treacherous. Inches of snow and ice had fallen on the front porch, but the snow shovel and rock salt sat untouched in the corner.

Grabbing the doorknob, I pushed the snow away with my foot to get inside. Matt sat quietly in his chair, staring at the flickering television screen as I entered. He didn't look up, didn't ask if I was okay. Quickly, I shed my snow-covered shoes and went to Terra's room.

Crawling in beside Terra, I wrapped my arms around her and pulled the blanket over me as I continued to shiver, more from my nerves than the cold. Slowly, Terra turned to face me with tears in her eyes. "Mom, I miss you," she said.

"I miss you too, baby. What's wrong?"

"I want a new dad."

Me too, kiddo, me too. "What? Why would you want that? I thought you love Matt?"

"I did, but he's different since you started work. He just sits in front

72

of the TV all the time. I've been microwaving Hot Pockets and heating leftovers."

"He doesn't cook anything for you?"

"*No*. And he's always yelling at me when I didn't do anything wrong. He said he doesn't want to take me to dance anymore."

"Well, honey, getting a new dad isn't easy. I'm married to Matt. So, I have to make it work."

"Get a divorce."

"I can't just get a divorce. He wouldn't leave anyway. Where would he go? You know how much he hates his mother and grand-mother. They are mean to him."

"Can you get rid of him? I'll be fine on my own."

"I'm sorry, it's not that simple."

"Yes, it is."

"How about I try to make things better somehow?"

"I want a new dad."

"I don't know how, Terra. I'm not sure I can give you that, but maybe I can try to make him *like* a new dad?"

"I don't know, Mom, but I am starting to hate him."

"Okay, let me see what I can do."

She wants a new dad?! This is my baby girl! What can I do? My mind filled with dread as I thought about trying to get Matt to leave. Things hadn't been too bad, had they? Gently, I caressed Terra's back until she fell asleep again, and then I returned to the living room.

With a snort, Matt quickly turned off his game. Walking to my place on the sofa, next to his chosen perch, I sat down and watched him turn his phone over. "When did you get home?" Matt asked.

"A few minutes ago," I answered. "You seemed occupied with your game, so I went to tuck Terra in really quick to give you a few minutes. I walked right in front of the TV. You didn't notice?"

"No, I had no idea you were home. It's early for you to be home, isn't it?" he asked as his phone quietly dinged with a message notification.

"Yeah, it is. It was a rough night. We're in the middle of a snow-storm. We had to close the store."

"Seriously?! I had no idea. I wish you would have told me you were coming home early. I would have gotten off the couch and turned on the porch light for you."

"Well, I'm home safely. That's what matters."

"Yes . . . uh, yes, of course. Are you sure you were at work? You didn't go visit your boyfriend and forget what time you were supposed to be home?"

"Like I have time for a boyfriend! I'm basically working two jobs, plus doing stuff here at the house. Just look outside." *Did he seriously ask that?*

Standing up, Matt headed toward the front door and pushed it open. Looking back at me, his eyes crossed, and he quietly shook his head before finding his perch again. As I looked him over, I watched his phone light up again, and he quickly snatched it up.

"Who are you texting?"

"I don't know. Let me check." Matt hesitated, quickly thumbing through his messages. After typing for a moment, he held his finger down on the screen, and with a sigh, he placed the phone face down on his other side and smiled. "That was weird. It must have been a wrong number." He laughed nervously.

"Oh, of course, 'cause that happens all the time," I responded. *Why is he lying to me?*

"It's actually happened a couple of times. So, anyway . . . what are you fixing for dinner? I'm hungry."

Of course, you're hungry. You could have volunteered to fix ME something. I did just drive home in a snowstorm. You didn't even notice I was home. And then, you lied to me. And since when did you get a lock on your phone?

Without a word, I headed toward the refrigerator and grabbed a bag of frozen Chinese food and threw it on the stove. I pretended not to notice as Matt smiled and texted. I just stared straight ahead, focusing on dinner. I welcomed the warmth of the stove after the ice from outside seemed to have crept inside my body. I was shivering, but I wasn't sure if it was from the storm or from Matt.

If Matt didn't notice when I came home and walked directly in front of him, what else did he not notice? What had happened to take Terra from enjoying her time with him to wanting a new dad? I had so many questions, but my heart was locked on the tears in my daughter's eyes and the sadness of her words as she asked for a new dad. *What am I supposed to do? I only work about twenty hours a week and do photography on my days off. How could things have fallen apart so quickly?*

If Terra wanted a new dad, how was I supposed to do that? Of course, Matt was texting someone and was obviously lying about it. And yet, he accused *me* of being at a boyfriend's house? I had never even considered being anything but faithful to Matt. As I turned the vegetables in my largest skillet, I watched him smile at his phone, somehow oblivious to my presence. *Would he even notice? I'm lonely. Maybe I need a friend to talk to and not just on the phone. Someone other than Trenton. Yes, a friend.*

* * *

The next morning, I spent extra time getting ready. Work was hard, and sometimes, feeling a little better about myself gave me the confidence to stay there. Every day, we received phone calls from people asking if we would be closing our store permanently, especially when we had clearance sales. Looking around the poorly maintained building made me feel like I was lying when I told them we weren't. As far as I knew, we wouldn't be.

That day, I pretended to be confident. Spending extra time getting ready almost convinced me I was. When Meg arrived early for her shift, I was more than happy to exit the building. I'd had enough rumors and insane customer returns for the day. It never stopped. My feet ached as though I had been walking on hot coals for hours. Knowing Matt wouldn't notice I was missing, I decided to go for a little drive, and I eventually landed at a gas station on the opposite side of town. An old friend had worked there the last time I dropped by. Seth was dedicated to his lovers even though he had often been the sidepiece of married women.

Pulling under the gas station's sign, I hoped Seth would be there. He had always been kind, and we could talk about anything. Of course, college together had mostly been making fun of professors and talking about his girlfriend. Seth's dedication to Mary had always made me feel safe from his advances.

As I opened the glass door, I looked up and smiled. There he was, with his signature black hair and bright blue eyes, smiling back at me. Coming from behind the counter, Seth swiftly wrapped his arms around me. "Sheila! Why haven't you been around?" he asked.

"Well, I have this overprotective husband. You know how those can be," I teased him.

"You know I do! So, how's that going?"

"I don't know. It's going, I guess. Not too much to report."

"Hmmm . . . why don't I believe you?"

"Oh, well . . . you know you've always wanted to get me in your clutches."

"Nah, not me, never!"

"Right, sooo, how's Mary?"

"She's fine. Went back to her husband and can't decide between us. That woman is constantly breaking my heart. I don't understand her at all. She says she loves me, but . . ."

"Oh, crap. I'm sorry."

"Here, let me show you a letter I wrote to her last night."

Together, we leaned over the counter as Seth thumbed through his phone. *It's nice to be around someone who isn't trying to hide anything from me*, I thought. Reading through Seth's letter, I felt the pain in his words, and when I reached the bottom of his long message about his devotion to Mary, I frowned. Mary had read it and never replied. Looking into Seth's eyes, I saw his sorrow and his love for her. It was a combination that should never exist in a single moment.

"That sucks. She hasn't replied?" I asked.

"No, and she does this to me all the time. It will be next week, or maybe the week after, and she'll try to come around acting like nothing ever happened—like she never left."

"I hate the way she treats you. I always have. You deserve better, Seth."

"I can't get away from her. I love her."

76

"I know how that is."

"Uh-oh! I hear a story. What's up, babe?"

Quickly, I gave him a brief overview of Matt and Trenton and the hot mess I was. I thought it would have been a more comical conversation as Seth and I compared our misfortunes, but after a few minutes, I had tears in my eyes. It was then that I realized how much I needed to talk, to express what I was going through. I felt my heart drop as I heard my own story out loud. It's funny how that makes you see things in a new light, and I stopped caring. I stopped caring that Matt was lying to me and constantly throwing me down face-first on the bed. And I stopped caring that Matt never touched me. Looking into Seth's eyes, I knew we were both in pain—a pain that we couldn't describe. It was something that only happened when the heart betrayed the mind, and we both knew it well.

"You know, there's nothing wrong with friends with benefits," Seth whispered.

"But I'm married, and I go to church."

"Yeah, that may be true. But you are a breath away from doing something stupid, and if you're going to do it, I would rather it be with me. You can trust me. I can protect you. Sheila, you need attention. You are starved for it. I can see it in the way you move, the look in your eyes. We're both lonely, and we know neither of us will ever say a word to anyone . . . *ever*."

I felt a familiar chill run up my spine as I listened to Seth's words. I felt his gaze as if it were hands exploring my flesh. My mind was gripped with the talons of his words, and I remembered the pain I felt from my conversations with Matt and Terra the night before. The conversations echoed through my mind: *That's weird, it must have been a wrong number . . . I didn't know you were home . . . Are you sure you were at work . . . Mom, I want a new dad.*

Reaching up, Seth cupped my chin in his hand, and I didn't pull away. I let his lips touch mine. His arms grasped me tightly as I let myself go, and as he kissed me, he gently pushed me toward the back of the empty store. Seth's hand rested against my back as he softly whispered, "It's okay, I've got you. I won't hurt you. Let yourself go."

77

As I tasted Seth's bitter kisses, Matt's voice echoed in my head. I barely heard Seth's words as he undressed me, spreading a sheet on the cold floor. My thoughts were screaming through the whispers of his passion. Matt's words taunted me: *I didn't know you were home . . . Are you sure you were at work . . . It must have been a wrong number.* I was lost and tired of feeling numb, but my flesh slept, and I didn't even notice when Seth climbed on top of me and freed my breasts from their lacy cage.

I gasped as Seth's cold lips captured my nipple and sucked it into his mouth. I shivered against the concrete as the chill crept through the thin sheet. My breath caught in my throat like a block of ice as Seth's body captured mine. I gripped his shoulders and held him tightly, not wanting him to see the tears trailing down my cheeks as I remembered the things Matt loved to say when he pillaged my body night after night: *You're here to make me feel good . . . You don't deserve an orgasm . . . It's not about you; it's about me.*

I remembered Matt throwing me on the bed face down night after night. Even as Seth gently slid inside me, I remembered the pain, the bruises, and the tears Matt so often inflicted on my delicate flesh. Seth was better than being hurt, better than being told I didn't matter. I wanted to feel something other than pain, to forget the tears, and to matter to someone. And for the briefest of moments, I rested in his lust, enjoyed his gentleness, and felt like I mattered. But even in the arms of a man—a friend I trusted who promised to keep me safe—I found myself drifting away, drowning in the words that echoed, crying for change.

Thank God for autopilot.

"**Y**ou know, she never lets me touch her anymore," Seth confessed as we put our clothes back on. "It's been months since I've held a woman in my arms."

"Well, now it hasn't been," I answered.

"No, it hasn't. Thank you for that."

My heart fell, shattering against the concrete floor. *What have I done? Seth doesn't love me. Maybe Matt does, and that's why he's so protective. But . . . he hurts me. He's always hurting me.* Watching Seth buckle his pants, I knew I would never be happy with him. Our friendship didn't contain those deep sparks of beautiful moments and flirtatious embraces. No, Seth would forever be a friend, nothing more. *He loves Mary. And I . . . I'm not sure I know how to love—I've forgotten. Have I EVER truly loved? What is love anyway? Why can't I be like a man and just do what I want? What's stopping me? Obviously, I can get what I need.*

Chapter 9

WORKING AT THE OUTLET quickly became a burden. For every mistake I made, Meg despised me more. I admired her tenacity as she tried to make me as uncomfortable as possible. I couldn't blame her. She needed the extra hours they were giving me, especially when her boyfriend lost his job for doing something stupid.

The breaking point for me was when I discovered there was no way to move up in the company. I didn't want to stay at the service desk forever. I felt like an animal in a zoo every day that I got stuck alone there. I knew I didn't belong, and it was time to leave. When the opportunity to work at a new jewelry store came, I took it. At first, it seemed scary to leave a secure job and take a risk on something I had never tried before, but as I stepped inside the jewelry store, I knew I belonged there.

I'll never forget witnessing the birth of the new store. As I approached the new business, I saw men in dirty jeans. Everything was white as drywall dust flew through the air. The walls were bare as they were sanded smooth, wallpaper laid in rolls in the corner, and barren glass cabinets waited to be installed. Dirty ladders were scattered across the floor as remnants of new lights hung from the ceiling like streamers. I saw what it would become. Everything was there: the registers, the lights, the cabinets, the wallpaper, and the carpet. But all of it was covered, hidden in the process of construction.

Being there felt like watching a baby emerge from the womb, covered in white, waiting to be wiped clean and wrapped in love. Life was breathing within those walls as the baby store was slowly born. Soon, I would be there to care for it, laying out its diamonds and gold. I would be there to show her off to the world as she was discovered by our small town. I knew that like any newborn, caring for her would be hard, but every day would be rewarding. I may have only been an hourly employee, but I was the first hired for that store, and I felt like an expectant mother filled with fear and anticipation for what the future held.

I was ready for this new opportunity and for the hour-long daily drives for training. I had been warned that at the end of my training, I would be responsible for the new hires that would follow. I was ready to learn how to make this baby store not just another business but a blessing to our small town. My interviewer had told me stories of women being promoted to manager in a couple of years. Things moved quickly in their company, and I dared to believe anything was possible.

Looking out at the white-dusted floors and hanging fixtures, I felt a determination grow within. *This baby is meant to be mine.* My body tingled with pride and hope as I looked at the store, ready to begin its life—a life full of memories yet to be. And I carried that hope with me, safely locked away.

I had a few minutes to spare, and my heart was racing as I approached Seth's gas station. I didn't know what to do. I needed a moment of clarity. *Yes, he's a friend, but we're not close, not anymore. He's not the one I call when I'm stuck. Who do I call when it's about Seth?* And then, I knew . . . there was no one but Trenton. Pulling over at a park, I grabbed my phone as I had so often done.

Trenton? I quickly texted.

I'm here, he replied.

I need to talk. I think I've really gotten myself in trouble this time.

Give me a few minutes. Marsha is home.

Okay, try to hurry. I don't have long.

Leaning my head against the seat, I watched the river flow and let my mind drift. As I allowed myself to dream, I remembered the words of a poem I had written, which was so much more than a poem. The words were always so clear when I needed Trenton most. *My darling, please come to me.*

Looking at the steps leading to the riverfront, I imagined it decorated with tulle and flowers. I saw myself dressed in white, walking to Trenton, carrying flowers. His eyes smiled as we were united. I knew no matter how connected we were, we would never be married. I wasn't even sure I loved him anymore. Trenton was just Trenton. He was a part of me, almost as though we were one person. He was my voice of reason at times, my voice of rebellion at others. He had become more than he had ever been before. The years that passed between us had made it something else. I just didn't know what.

"Hello, Trenton?" I said, answering my phone.

"Hello, my darling Sheila. What's wrong?"

"I messed up. I did something I shouldn't have."

"What did you do? I hope you didn't do what I would do."

"Yeah, I probably did. Have you been with anyone other than Marsha?"

"Yeah . . . it's a long story. The woman who lives next door. She came over the other day. She said she had something wrong with her tub, and she was wearing only a towel. I couldn't stop myself. It's been forever since I felt anything toward Marsha. It just kind of happened."

"I cheated, too. An old friend from college. We talk now and then."

"Sheila, you're better than that. That's such a bad idea. What will Matt do if he finds out?"

"I don't know. Maybe he'll leave."

"I doubt it. He's living in a perfect world. He has you whenever he wants, doesn't have to work, and stays home doing God knows what while you're out there working your ass off. He's not leaving, Sheila. It won't be easy. Do you really want him to leave?"

"Yeah, I think I do. I just don't know what I would do, though."

"You would call me, come get me, and then you would be mine instead of his."

"I wish that were true."

"It *is* true."

Glancing back at the steps, I wished it were. My heart yearned for Trenton, to feel him in my arms, to feel his kiss on my neck. "I wish I believed you," I replied.

"I wish you did, too, but I know you don't," Trenton whispered. "I'm sorry for the way I've treated you. I have so many regrets. You deserve so much better than me. I have taken your friendship for granted. I've always felt like you would be there for me. You've always accepted me, and I never come. I never visit. I should have appreciated you more."

"Trenton," I sobbed, "I miss you. I miss what could have been."

"Sheila, break it off with the other guy, the friend. You don't need that in your life. It's only going to cause you trouble. It's not a good idea. You don't need him when you have me."

"I *don't* have you. You're not here. I am tired of feeling alone. Alone in my bed. Alone in the arms of my husband, not knowing what he will do to hurt me next and not knowing if he will ever love me the way he should. I feel like I'm a cover-up. Matt has to be gay to treat me the way he does."

"He's an idiot."

"Maybe, but at least he's here. The other guy is also here. But you're not Trenton; you never were. What am I supposed to do? It doesn't matter how much I love you if you're not mine."

"A part of me will always be yours."

"You're not here, though. I'm tired of being alone. I figured out how to survive and dig my way out of that shitty apartment. I did that alone, you know . . . without you. If you would have come to me, it would have been easier, but you never did. You never came back. You chose Marsha."

"I didn't have a choice. That day when I said I was coming for you, before we were both married, my truck broke down, and nobody could come get me but her. There was nothing I could do. I got evicted, and she had a place for me to live and took me in. I owed her."

"Why didn't you call *me*?"

"You were going through enough. I couldn't do that to you. How could I? I had to save myself first."

"You always had a choice."

"Sheila, I don't want you with another man. I'm telling you, you're better than that. This is not who you are."

"I don't know who I am anymore."

"You're not *that*, though."

As our conversation ended, I watched the river dance along the banks as the geese gathered amongst the cars, waiting for bread. I could relate as I watched them move from car to car, hoping for something to nourish their bodies until finally, they headed to the river to find it on their own. Looking at my reflection in the mirror, I noticed how my eyes had swollen. They were red from the weariness I felt inside. My lips quivered as I saw how far I had fallen, how weak and exhausted my face looked.

That night, I must have driven for hours. My excuse to Matt was that I was working late, but I really just needed a minute—a minute to think, to breathe, and to consider where I was, who I was, and where I was going. Sorrow had clutched my heart like an alligator ripping into its prey. I was tired of being the prey. What must it feel like to be the predator?

I didn't feel at home anywhere but when I was driving. That was my quiet time, my refuge. I missed Terra and how we used to cuddle up together in the morning and have dance parties in the living room. I missed the pillow fights, the cinnamon toast, and even the bologna sandwiches. Now, all we had was fast food and complaints about Matt. She was growing up, and it felt like I didn't know her anymore.

* * *

Climbing into my vehicle the next morning, I gripped the steering wheel and looked through the foggy windshield. My cold breath quickly spread against the glass as it came in the quick gasps of sleeplessness. Slowly, my hand rose to place the key in the ignition. My eyes drooped as I looked for the switch for the windshield wipers, and my fingers scanned the radio stations, hoping for something to help wake me up. Caffeine was too weak to keep me going, it seemed, and I had to push forward.

Terra's face was sad that morning as she clung to me. Our hugs goodbye were always rough, but that day, I felt it a little more. As I settled in, ready for the hour-long drive ahead of me, my eyes swelled, threatening the mascara I had carefully applied.

"Hey, can you bring home something from Parkersburg for dinner tonight?" Matt asked as he quickly ran to my vehicle.

"Yeah, I guess. You can't make anything for *me* tonight? I'm tired, and I honestly want to get home so I can rest and spend time with you guys."

"It will just take you a few minutes. I don't see what the big deal is."

"It's a lot more than a few minutes. Sometimes it takes forever to get through the drive-throughs, and all the fast food lately is starting to make me feel bad. I thought it would be nice if you cooked something. I got a few of those frozen dinners you can heat up. That would probably be better."

"No, I don't want to cook. It won't take you long, and it will be late, so there won't be any traffic."

"I know, but that late, we are stuck with the same fast-food places we always get food from. They are the only things open that late."

"Well, you'll be out of town. Maybe you can get us something good."

"I don't know, maybe. What are your plans for today, other than taking Terra to dance?"

"I don't want to take her. I hate that studio. Terra isn't making progress. Besides, why does she have to go at all? I'm going to be sitting in the parking lot for nothing."

"What? It's not that bad. I wish I could take her to dance. I miss it, seeing her with her friends, hearing the music, and watching them put the dances together. If I could take her, I would. You know how important this is to Terra."

There was no holding back my tears as Matt complained about the one thing I wish I could do with my little girl. It had always been our favorite thing to do together. Sometimes, I even had the opportunity to help with the class. Hearing Matt talk so negatively about something so important to Terra enraged me. My hands became fists on the steering wheel and my eyes narrowed as I thought of the good memories Terra and I had at dance class.

"Sheila, it's crap. That studio sucks, and I hate going. It doesn't matter what Terra thinks. You're not here to take her, and I'm not getting saddled with it twice a week."

"But MATT! Things are hard right now. I don't have time to take her. I have to work to keep food on the table and clothes on our backs. It takes money to keep our home."

"I know, but you got this! Oh, by the way, thanks for giving me the money to get the new NASCAR game. I can't wait to start playing it today."

"Ummm . . . you're welcome?" *I don't remember giving him money for another NASCAR game. He already has two.* "I have to go. Can you step back so I can leave? I don't want to accidentally run over your feet."

"Why be in a hurry? They will understand if you're a few minutes late. It's over an hour drive. It's not a big deal."

"I can't be late, Matt. I just started this job, and I want to do well. I have to learn to help the other new hires when they start."

"Yeah, but you're never home. What about our time together?"

"It's not going to be like this for long. Just a few more days, and then I will be here in town. I'm doing this for us. I promise it will get better. Can you please take Terra to dance class? I wish I could be with her, but I can't. We need you to do this."

"No, I'm sorry, I'm going to be too busy with the game to do that. You know I can't leave once I get started." Tapping the side of the vehicle, Matt finally stepped back. "Speaking of . . . maybe you should go so I can get started. Don't forget dinner tonight."

Quickly, I put my vehicle in gear and pulled away. Matt had already talked long enough that I would have to skip breakfast. My stomach was growling, and I knew those extra few minutes meant I would have to break the speed limit to get to the store on time. It would be another six hours before I had a chance to eat. That always made it harder to concentrate. The last thing anyone wanted to hear while they were looking at diamonds was the salesperson's stomach growling.

Then, I thought of Terra having to miss dance class. Matt had refused to take her the week before, too. She had cried on my shoulder that night and had begged me not to leave for work. I hated hearing her sob. Both of us wanted things to be the way they'd been between us before Matt. I felt helpless. Matt was there and claimed to love Terra as his own but refused to simply stop his games long enough to take her to do something that was important to her. I had only asked for him to take her to class and fix me something to eat. I was going to be gone for the entire day, another twelve-hour shift, while he stayed home playing video games.

I thought of the dance classes, the hugs, and Terra's smiles as she spun and turned to the beat of the music. I remembered all the times she was pulled to the front of the class to demonstrate. I felt the pride as her face lit up when her friends asked for help, and yet, he wouldn't take her. In that moment, if I had one wish, it would have been to be able to stay by her side. But I also remembered her bike getting stolen and how the other kids pushed her around and shoved her into mud puddles at the bus stop when we lived at the apartments. I had no choice. This was what was best for us.

* * *

After a few weeks, it was finally time to open our new store. My co-workers and I worked endless hours that first week—much more than I had expected. Together, we made an empty store beautiful. Those first few days, boxes were scattered across the floor as we opened displays and placed each piece of jewelry in cases.

When those first pieces of jewelry arrived, there was no room to walk, and we had to push boxes out of the way so we could sort them. Carefully, we sat in a circle on the newly laid carpet as we opened bags of diamonds and gold. I think there were twenty different categories and types that we sorted them into. Each night, we worked until we fulfilled that day's corporate task list. Some days, we kicked boxes out of the way to clock in, and others, we spent hours breaking them down until finally, we made new displays and locked away each sparkling piece behind glass.

Opening day came quickly, and the first weeks were gone in a whirlwind of sparkle. I remember falling in love with my first ring, one of the most meaningful in my collection. With a hefty employee discount, I ordered a two-tone silver and rose gold ring with a rope design. The marketing behind it reminded me that one day, I would be happy—I would find my future, and love was possible. Each time I looked at the tiny ring, I smiled, knowing it was a promise to myself. I never took it off.

As they had warned, I was soon training new team members about birthstones, diamonds, and how to talk to customers. I was doing well, and they needed a third manager to open and close the store in case of emergencies. I knew they were considering me, and that made me work even harder. I was always taking extra shifts and trying to learn from the managers.

It wasn't long before my paychecks finally allowed shopping trips and nice clothing for Terra and me. Our apartment was now nothing but a memory. I walked a little taller, spoke more confidently, and finally dressed in clothes I loved. I soon discovered I had left The Outlet just in time, as news of its impending closure spread across the community. I was thankful to have moved on. Working in jewelry felt like the beginning of a new life, and I knew something amazing was on its way.

Chapter 10

A S BEASTLY MEN VANISHED within living smoke, I crawled away from the dying tree and wilted vines that once protected me. The soot covered my skin as my hair slowly turned black from the ash and smoke that pushed against my flesh. The rocks scraped against my breasts as I clung to them, hiding, searching for life between their cracks. Hope tasted like salt upon my tongue as I traced the footsteps of faded men. *If only I can find where they come from, if I can find them before they change and their minds are stripped away by the smoke, maybe I can find shelter, a way out.*

Slowly, I crawled, moment by moment, step by step, and rock by rock. Each rock scraped me, and each of them painted me until my skin was as black as the land that surrounded me. I watched the men closely, their suits of gray assembling against a block building. They gathered commanding, gesturing against the smoke that arose. It pushed against them until they ran toward the darkness.

As I stepped from behind the rocks, I watched the men's faces change. Like animals, they emerged as their eyes turned crimson and drool came from their shrunken lips. With one step and then another, their minds were stripped, and they came for me. Their eyes locked upon my flesh, and they hunted me. My flesh trembled, and my throat collapsed as they approached. I ran for the tree as smoke swirled around me, stripping me of ashes, my pale skin reflecting the fire that erupted at my feet.

The salt upon my tongue changed to bitterness as my throat screamed, dry from air that ravaged me with its smoky caress. I remembered that touch—the touch of icy heat. It gripped me like a thousand hands as I threw myself beneath the tree. The fire grew hotter as flames turned red and licked my flesh. The tree above me burst into flames as I clung to it, like the men that had ignited, surrendering to lust. There was no safety, no peace . . . only fire.

* * *

Walking inside the dirty glass doors beneath the Outlet sign, I scanned the service desk for a familiar face. They no longer had to acknowledge me, so I wasn't sure what to expect. The only thing I knew was that The Outlet had the best towels in the area, and with my new, much higher paycheck, I wanted a few. That meant I probably couldn't avoid the staff, as the towels were directly in front of my old zoo enclosure—I mean, service desk.

Glancing over at Meg, our eyes met for an instant, and I almost saw warmth in her eyes. But I quickly dodged her gaze as a customer approached her with yet another return. Quickly, I grabbed my favorite hotel-quality towels and held them close to me like I was holding a shield. I headed for the registers.

"Hey!" Meg called out. "Come here; I'll check you out."

"Are you sure? I know how you hate that," I mumbled.

"Yes! Girl, we got this new guy in, and he makes you look like a genius. He makes me realize how hard this job is. Rylie left, too, and now, we're working our asses off. And if I hear one more phone call asking if we're closing, I'm going to scream." She laughed.

"Wow, that's a switch," I said sarcastically.

"Yeah, well, I get that. Say, how's the new job going?"

"It's great, actually. I love it there. I don't have to stand all day, and people are actually happy to see me."

"That would be a welcome change of pace."

"Definitely."

"You just didn't belong here. You're not like us."

"I know, but that's in the past."

"Yes, it is." Meg scowled as she handed me my towels.

"Sheila!" a familiar voice called from behind me.

Turning, I almost dropped my bag of towels as Teddy crossed the store to greet me. Before I could object, his arms wrapped around me and pressed me against him. Closing my eyes, I smelled his freshly-sprayed cologne against my nose as my face was buried in his chest. I felt Meg's eyes glaring into the back of my head as I pulled away.

"Are they looking for managers over there?" Teddy asked.

"No, they only promote from within, but the starting pay is good—a lot better than here. They're talking about promoting me soon. I don't know, though. It seems a little too good to be true. But I do hear you can move up fast."

"Shoot! Go for it, girl!" Teddy smiled.

"I will, don't worry about that." I winked.

"I bet you will do what you need to do."

"I have to. I have a little girl to think about."

"You got this."

"Thanks, Teddy. I miss you guys, but I have to get out of here. I'm on lunch, and I don't want to be away too long. You can stop by the store, though, ya know. We could hang out for a bit, talk about old times. You could talk to my manager if you're ready to get out of here."

"I don't know. I need something else, but I will let you go so you don't get in trouble."

"Okay, so I'll see you soon?"

"I'm sure you will." Teddy winked.

With that, I walked away from The Outlet for the last time.

* * *

Curled up on the couch, I cradled my phone in my hands, waiting for Seth's reply. We had been texting most of the day. We weren't talking about much, really. But being around Seth and having a friend to consistently talk to made me see things from a different perspective. I now saw Matt for what he was.

Matt didn't do much to help me during the day. When I would return from work, the house was always exactly how I left it, and dinner was never made. Seth made sure to tell me I wasn't being treated fairly and that if it had been *him* waiting for me to get home from work, dinner would be ready along with a hot bubble bath and a back massage. It was a good fantasy, but it didn't seem realistic.

If I'm being honest, I don't remember what Seth and I were texting each other that night, but he always enjoyed being flirtatious and telling me about all the things he wanted to do to me—after talking about Mary, of course. That night, the conversation had mostly turned to Matt and how sad the situation felt. Unfortunately, I had left my phone sitting on the couch at the wrong time.

Sitting on the edge of the toilet, I realized I didn't have my phone, and I shuddered. As badly as I wanted Matt to leave, I wasn't ready. I was afraid I would never be ready. I knew I didn't want to be a cheater. I had never been one before—not ever. Cheating made me feel like I had been rolling around in the mud of a coal mine. Still, I enjoyed conversations with Seth. He was great to talk to, and sometimes, I needed that more than I cared to admit.

"Sheila!" Matt screamed from the other room.

Oh . . . fuck. Closing my eyes, I waited. *Did he read my messages? What will he do? Is he going to hurt me?* Thoughts of Matt's fist crushing into my skull clenched my heart as I rushed to leave the bathroom. *I can't do this here. I need to be away from anything that could hurt me. The walls are too close. I won't be able to get away.* Throwing open the door, I stepped into the hallway, knowing he would be there.

Matt's eyes were red as he backed me up against the wall. His breath was hot as he leaned over me. My shoulders ached as he gripped them, pushing me farther into the wall.

"How could you cheat on me?!" Matt screamed. "I love you! I would never do anything to hurt you."

Watching Matt's jaws clench, my mind screamed with laughter. *Are you serious right now? What did you expect me to do? You spend all day playing video games. You won't touch me or kiss me. You refuse to tell me I'm beautiful. You won't talk to me, and when you do, you don't understand anything I'm talking about. You ask too many questions. It's like I'm talking in a foreign language. And . . . you would never hurt me? What do you think you're doing RIGHT NOW, slamming me up against the damn wall?*

"I can't believe you would do this," Matt continued. "Aren't you going to at least apologize? What did I do to deserve this?"

Is that a real question?

"Answer me!" he screamed.

Imagining Terra coming home to broken glass and an angry father, I stepped to the side, trying to escape Matt's grip. I hadn't answered him, but I needed to get away. I needed to feel safer before I spoke. Struggling against his hands, I gasped as he clenched harder against me, his face getting closer.

"I . . . I'm . . . sorry," I managed to sputter.

Throwing his hands down, Matt crossed the living room and plopped down on the sofa, staring up at me with his lower lip quivering. He waited for words I didn't have. I wasn't sorry, and I wasn't going to stop talking to Seth. It felt like Seth was all I had.

"I thought Seth was an old friend from school," Matt prodded.

"He is and nothing more."

"Sure seems like a lot more to me. Do you love him?"

"No, it's not like that."

"Then why did you cheat on me?"

"I . . . I . . . don't know. I've been struggling for a while. I've been asking for you to pay attention to me, to talk to me, to touch me, to do something *I* want to do . . . for a long time—years. I only wanted someone to talk to. I needed a friend."

"You're not supposed to have sex with friends."

Heading to the couch, I grabbed my favorite pillow and cradled it against my chest. My heart felt like a broken television lying on the floor for Matt to kick and step on. I felt the bruises rising through my skin as I rocked myself. Cold tears flooded my eyes as I stared at the phone I could no longer touch. *I want to feel important, needed. I want to know the man I'm with loves me, and you DON'T. I want to feel SOMETHING! Please appreciate me. What happened to the man who loved me, who tried to look out for and protect me? Why won't you TOUCH me or kiss me? I hate that I did this. I hate myself for allowing this to happen, but . . . I've asked you for YEARS to at least consider my feelings, but you NEVER have for more than a week!*

* * *

In the following days, with each moment that passed, I grew colder. I only thought of what led me there, and I hated both Matt and myself. I didn't speak for days. What I wanted seemed simple to me, and yet, what I felt didn't matter. I was overwhelmed with guilt.

Somehow, Matt didn't leave. And he didn't change. I felt like I owed him, so instead, a few days or maybe weeks later, we decided to experiment with couple swapping. Although I hated the idea, my sorrow wouldn't allow me to be touched by Matt, and even though he didn't hate me, I hated *him* more every day. I hated him for not leaving me. I respected him even less as he grew more aggressive. I had to check in with him wherever I went, even if it was the grocery store. I wanted him to leave, but I refused to admit it. I was afraid of what he would do to me, to our home, and to Terra. I wanted the opportunity to feel loved, but . . . Matt stayed.

I continued talking to Seth, but I never slept with him again. After a while, things returned to normal, and Matt promised to love me. I tried to focus on him and show him I loved him, even though I wasn't sure I did. I wasn't sure I ever had. Yet, our marriage continued.

Our first experiment with couple swapping haunted me for years. I didn't mind the phone flirtations, but meeting someone face to face was something else. Matt bore the scars of scraped knees for weeks while I laid in a vat of tears caused by what felt like the complete devastation of my mind. I ached from the inside out as I thought about the things I had done but felt powerless to stop. Each time we spoke to a new couple, I grew quieter and hated Matt more. I felt like a piece of raw steak behind glass, ready to be picked over by whoever may have wanted me.

In the shadows of my heart, I wanted to feel something. I wanted a man to recognize me for who I was and see past the sex my husband was offering them. Each time another man came and went, I was disappointed. I felt like a trophy sitting on the shelf, like I was shared by many but forgotten by all, like a woman to conquer, and like a stray kitten—admired for a moment but left by the side of the road to die.

We even had a threesome, but it left me feeling robbed. That's the only explanation. You see, many people think of a threesome as being a good thing—a fulfillment of a fantasy—especially when it's the idea of a woman with two guys, at least, from a woman's point of view. After all, how often does just one man manage to satisfy a woman sexually? For me, it had always been one of those things where I let him command me and do as he pleased, whatever that may be, without regard to my satisfaction. It's a rough gig, but I was used to it. When Matt approached me with the idea of a threesome, saying he wanted to try something different, I was intrigued—scared as hell but intrigued.

I will never forget that day. As was our usual, we looked online for someone to fulfill Matt's needs. After a few minutes, we found an older man who had experience with first-time three-way situations. I remember his picture. It seemed okay enough—nothing special, not particularly attractive, unfortunately. I had hoped Matt would back out, but he didn't, especially when the other guy showed interest in the same video games. They immediately wanted to develop a long-term friendship centered around sharing me.

When Terra left for school, I immediately hopped in the shower to prepare myself. Matt sat and watched. He made a point to pick out my lingerie and outfit for the day, making sure his property was ready to be presented to another man.

Sitting on the couch, I clung to my phone as the guys talked about video games. I felt their eyes on me as though I were already naked. I felt like a rabbit must feel while staring down a lion. My body shook, and my skin was as cold as ice as I picked up the phone and texted Seth. It was risky, but I needed help, and he was the only one who would answer quickly. With tears in my eyes, I watched Matt and the other man talk, hoping they would forget about me. I wanted to vanish into the couch, but their eyes felt like claws raking down my skin.

Seth, are you there?

Of course, I'm here.

I'm scared. Matt invited this strange guy over for a threesome. I'm scared. I can't believe Matt is going to do this after he was so angry about you and me.

Are you serious?

Yes, of course, I'm serious. I don't know what to do. I don't think I can get out of this.

Why would he do that? If he's going to share you, why didn't he call me? At least you know who I am.

Yeah, exactly. I don't understand. It's like Matt doesn't care that I'm afraid.

I'm sorry. I wish there was something I could do. Just try to stop it.

I can't. I don't know what he'll do. I better go; they got quiet.

Sitting the phone face down on the arm of the couch, I found myself staring into the eyes of an animal. Matt didn't look like my husband anymore. He was a monster, a beast. It felt like a bucket of ice crashing across my flesh as my eyes met his and he reached for my hand. Dutifully, I stood and waited for instructions.

"So, how do you want to start this?" Matt asked me.

"I . . . I . . . um . . . Aren't you in charge?"

"Do you *want* me to be in charge?" Matt asked.

"Yes, you always are, right?"

"Of course, I am."

Looking into Matt's beastly eyes, my soul pleaded with his. But I dared not speak up. I only hoped he would love me enough to recognize my terror, my hopelessness. Instead, he led me to our bedroom and told me to sit on the bed. Matt and the other man both stood in front of me as I stared at the floor, watching my toes squish into the carpet. My hands gripped the side of the mattress as I waited. Chill bumps raised on my arms as the men's gaze ripped across my flesh. I didn't move, didn't speak.

"Take off your dress," Matt demanded.

I stood in front of them and quickly pulled it over my head. As my bra and panties were exposed, I shivered, and my stomach jumped into my throat. As I closed my eyes, the two men stripped me of my bra and panties. I felt their hands on my breasts as they threw me on the bed. Pain shot through my skull as the impact jarred me into the moment. I wanted to escape, but I was there. I felt my legs being pulled back as Matt's cock drilled into me. The other man climbed on the bed, kneeled beside me, and tried to shove his cock in my mouth. Quickly, I turned my face away, trying to act natural to avoid tasting him. Closing my eyes, I focused on the familiar pain of Matt.

"She has some nice tits," the other guy stated, gripping my breast in his hand.

"You should try her pussy," Matt answered.

Holding my legs open, Matt gestured for the other man to take his place, and he entered me. *I better act like I'm enjoying it, or I will pay for it later.* Thankfully, I didn't have to make a lot of noise before Matt was kneeling beside me. Grabbing a fistful of hair, he forced my head over to him as he slapped my cheek with his cock. The head of it pressed against my lips, passed my teeth, and jammed the back of my throat like a dagger as I gagged from the impact. My hair felt like it was being ripped out by the roots as he forced his cock down my throat. Pain shot through my neck as Matt pulled at me. With my hands, I tried to hold him back, but he only pushed them away, pinning them under his knees. He was rough—harder than normal—as his hips thrust against my mouth.

"You should taste her. I never eat her pussy. If you do, I will suck your cock," Matt suggested to the stranger.

"Hell yeah, she looks good," he replied.

Pulling away, the man knelt on his knees between my legs. His hands forced me open, pulling and tugging at my delicate flesh. Finally, I was able to breathe again as Matt went between the stranger's legs. The other man groaned against me and paused as his penis was sucked into Matt's eager mouth. I heard the sounds, the groans. I felt Matt's body clinging to the other man's as he worked to please him. *No wonder Matt won't go down on me; I don't have the right equipment. Wouldn't he be happier if he admitted he was gay, or bisexual, or whichever way he wants to go? Then, he wouldn't have to pretend he's something he's not. He could let me go, and he could do what makes him happy. Maybe I'm a cover so his mother doesn't find out?* And slowly, I drifted away to the safe space in my mind.

Thank God for autopilot.

I don't remember what happened to my body after that. I remember how I felt and what I thought. Watching Matt enjoy sucking a man's penis made me sad for him—about him having to hide who he really was, that is. He was eager. He enjoyed it. More than that, he loved it. I felt bad for him and wished he would allow himself to be free.

Afterward, I told Matt I didn't want to be with other people anymore. I wanted to feel safe, respected. Watching my tears as I crumbled, he finally agreed. Matt was happy to have me all to himself again as long as he could sleep with other men.

* * *

The day after the threesome, I went to work like nothing had happened. I pretended my life was normal. Unfortunately, my store manager had an emergency, and with no assistant manager, the backup duty fell to me. I was charged with the task of managing several employees and two special events in the same week. Sitting behind the diamond counter, I scanned the store, knowing what was ahead of me. None of the other employees listened to me even though they knew I was in charge.

From across the store, I looked at the empty manager's chair, the quiet computer screen, and the empty desk calendar. Steadying my gaze, my eyes narrowed, I took a slow breath in, and I headed for the chair. *I can DO this. This is my chance to prove this store is meant to be mine.*

The events of the previous day echoed through my vision as I began to step slowly to the black office chair, and before I knew it, I was there and ready. A surge of power and fear shot through my body as I sat in the manager's chair for the first time. I waited only a moment, relishing the feeling. Thoughts of my first photoshoot in my apartment and the joy I felt at being able to help my neighbors rushed through me. I remembered where I had begun and how things had changed. No longer was I starving, waiting for my food stamp card to load. Now, shopping trips and scented lotions were the standard, bubble baths were common, and dinner out was a constant and not an impossibility. Sitting in that chair for the first time, I wanted to be more.

I had no control over life at home, but there at the store, I could be respected. I made people feel at home. I could give someone the opportunity to grow a job into a career. I could help people like me climb out of poverty. Our town had few opportunities. What if I was one of the people making a difference? Grabbing paper from the printer and the only red ink pen, I began writing a to-do list. It was a strong list that I knew I could implement—a step-by-step guide to our survival through two special events. I searched online, looking for clues, learning what to expect. I had never seen either of the events in my store, so I knew we had to start strong. And we also needed to hire someone or at least conduct some interviews.

Thumbing through the applicants, I felt empowered. I needed to find someone who needed a break, a chance. I had previously conducted a few interviews under Annette's—my store manager's—supervision, but now, I had the power to choose which people to interview. I looked for work history, longevity on the job, and their location. We needed people that could come to work quickly in case of call-offs. Then, as I looked through the list of names, I paused. *Meg? But she hates me. Isn't The Outlet shutting down, though? She was a hard worker. Maybe I should give her a chance. Maybe she's one of the people who needs a break.*

Staring at Meg's name on the applicant list, I remembered each sarcastic comment, each time she abandoned me at the service desk, and each time she rolled her eyes at me. *How ironic that the power is in MY hands now. I guess you should watch how you treat people.* Putting her name on the list, I asked another associate to make the calls and schedule the three people I had chosen to interview. *Remember, time management, delegate tasks.*

Pulling out the appointment schedule for the diamond event, I spread out the sheet on the manager's desk and shuddered. *I'm the only one with an appointment? How can that be?* Grabbing a tablet, I quickly wrote a marketing email to our current customers about the event and copied it down for the rest of the associates to copy. We had to move quickly to make sure we had more appointments, more of a chance to meet our goal. *I need balloons.*

Stepping outside the store, I watched cars in the parking lot drive by, each of them oblivious to my existence. I watched the trees on the hill sway in the breeze as I thought about the week ahead. Leaning against a concrete pillar, I felt its rough texture against my arms and the soft breeze that brushed the hair from my face. *We cannot fail, no matter what they think of me. They have to listen, and they know it. There's nobody for them to call. I have to do this and show them how wrong they are about me.*

I remembered all the times the store manager and I had discussed the other employees and the ideas we had for promoting our business, and I knew what must be done. I had her ideas and plenty of my own. But then, my phone vibrated in my pocket.

Sheila?

Yes, Trenton?

Call me NOW!

That's weird, I thought. *He's never that demanding.* Glancing back at the other associates in the store, I picked up the phone and dialed, hoping for a quick conversation. *At least I'm on break. I have fifteen minutes. I better follow the rules if I expect them to.*

"Sheila?!"

"What's wrong, Trenton?"

"I'm leaving her, right now. I'm in my truck. Where are you?"

Hearing his words made my heart sore. It pounded, it ached, and the all too familiar chill ran down my spine. *Finally, it's time.*

"I'm at work in Gallipolis. What happened?"

"Marsha cheated on me. I'm heading your way now. I hope my truck can make it."

"Are you serious? You're leaving her?"

"Yes, I will be there in about an hour. Send me your address. Is Matt still living with you?"

"Um, yeah. He's my husband. You know he won't leave."

"I don't blame him. I wouldn't leave either."

"Well, what are you going to do?"

"I don't know. I'll figure it out. I will help you get rid of him. Matt will leave, don't worry about it."

My hands began to shiver as I contemplated my future. I couldn't wait to see Trenton's face again, to feel his arms wrap around me. It had been years, but Trenton was Trenton. Thoughts of how far we had both come and how we always seemed to find each other floated through my heart. *It's been so long. I can't wait for this to finally be over so we can be together as we were always meant to be.*

Rushing into the store, I sat in the manager's chair and waited. I thumbed through emails, made checklists, and found the interview sheets for the next day. I had to distract myself as much as possible. My eyes watched through the wall of glass. *Trenton will be here any minute. Is this happening? Wait, it can't happen like this. He has to earn his way back into my life. I love him, but he can't come in and disrupt my entire life. I can't leave the store. How can I trust him? You're being ridiculous. You told Matt last night that you didn't want to mess around with other people anymore. You know how it makes you feel.*

As my mind raced, I couldn't stop staring out the window, hoping to see Trenton's dark hair coming across the parking lot. But he never came. Instead, Trenton texted me the next morning. He let me know his truck had broken down and that as soon as it was fixed, he would come home to me once and for all. I didn't believe him. I pretended the phone call never happened and went about my day, starting my interviews, going through my to-do list with a broken heart.

When Meg entered the store, I watched quietly from the back as she smiled. She sat at my favorite spot for interviews and waited. As I stepped out from the back with a clipboard, I watched her smile fall to her knees. A part of me wanted to laugh, but I felt bad for her. The job she had counted on at The Outlet had been taken from her. She was afraid for her future, and I knew it. *She needs a chance. Meg was only rude to me because I was taking away her hours. How would she act here? How would she work in a place that appreciates her?*

I asked the standard questions, but I remembered how much Meg cared about her job. By the end of her interview, it felt like talking to an old friend. When I talked to her about it months later, she said she had gone to her boyfriend's after the interview and told him I would never hire her and that she needed to keep looking for a job. But at the end of the interview, I knew without a doubt that she would be able to do amazing things. I quickly reported her interview to the higher-ups and made the appropriate phone calls to make sure she would be chosen. It felt good to help her, to do the right thing. I still smile about it years later, knowing she was the first of many hires. Even though we had started badly at another place, I grew to like Meg—if not love her—as a person.

As I wrapped up what I now lovingly refer to as hell week, I felt accomplished. Annette would be returning to a successful store. We had met our goal, and during our first diamond event, we had doubled it. I worked diligently that week, and the entire district noticed. I was proud.

Chapter 11

AS I WATCHED my district manager giggle with my store manager, Annette, I waited, wondering what would happen next. I had secretly applied for a position in Charleston as an assistant manager. They had passed me up for the promotion in my own store, and more than anything, I wanted to have the power to make a difference.

I knew they had made a mistake not promoting me, but that wasn't something I could tell them. I had worked harder, been smarter, and dedicated myself to our baby store. But the girl they chose instead of me had been just flirtatious enough to get the promotion. It was time to move on, and *nobody* wanted to work in Charleston. It was a dying store that everyone knew would close. They just hadn't announced it yet. That's why I had applied. I needed to prove them wrong.

Looking down Annette's shirt, my district manager leaned against a glass case as she leaned over, touching his arm. Annette talked about him constantly. It was maddening. If she didn't hear from him for a few days, she would panic, asking me if he "loved" her, was she still his favorite? It was obvious there was more going on than what either of them dared to admit.

"Sheila, can you talk with me outside?" my district manager asked abruptly, heading for the door. Outside was the only place anyone talked privately. Our small store and the ladies who worked there were accustomed to eavesdropping and gossip, which could ruin your life in a small town.

"Of course, I'm right behind you."

"So, why did you apply for the assistant manager position in

Charleston?"

"Honestly, I want a challenge and to learn from someone else. There are two stores in the mall down there, and it's a completely different environment."

"That's true. It would be difficult, though. It's over an hour away. Do you think you can do that every day for fifty hours a week, sometimes more?"

"Yes, I'm ready to prove myself."

"Listen, I know you love this store and that you were the original hire. Nobody can talk to people like you can. Why would you want to leave?"

"I heard you might be moving Annette to a different store next year. I would like to continue to grow and be ready to have a chance at being the manager here. But I need more training to do that." Looking directly into his eyes, I didn't waver from his gaze, and I didn't soften my approach. He knew I wouldn't flirt with him, but I *would* be honest, and I *would* earn my chance at running my store because, in my heart, it had always been mine—my baby.

"That is a possibility. If you're sure you can handle it, then you can start there on Sunday. Do you think you can wrap things up here in a couple days?"

"Of course, I can. I look forward to it."

"Well, you've done a lot here, and I appreciate you working when Annette was out with her daughter. You ran this store and kept things moving in the right direction. You hit our goal on your first diamond show with nobody to lead you. You stepped up and became the leader. All of your shifts were covered. I'm proud of you. I look forward to seeing what you can do. Don't disappoint me."

Walking back inside, I saw the store as it had been when we were opening. I remembered the drywall being finished and the wallpaper being hung. Annette and I had built that store from nothing. We had placed each piece of jewelry into the cases together. We were the ones who had fought to get the word out, to bring in business. I knew that one day, I would walk in, and it would be *my* store as it always should have been. I would find a way, no matter what it took.

* * *

The next couple of months went by in a blur of emotions. Within a few days of my conversation with the district manager, I learned how far gossip had spread in the company. One of my co-workers at my new store, Clark, quickly informed me about the rumors surrounding my name. Annette had told my new store manager that I was selfish and had a habit of stealing sales from everyone. So, Clark was surprised when I came in and taught them this magical thing called teamwork.

My new store manager, Kara, and I tended to butt heads about everything. One thing rang true, though, and that was my passion for my new team. Soon enough, the rumors of me being selfish changed to me being the one who helped develop the strongest team in the district.

Like clockwork, Diane, our sassy senior citizen, would greet potential guests that passed our store with charity teddy bears and a smile. Then, Clark and Kendall would welcome them into our store, often cleaning their jewelry. When the time came, they would invite me into the conversation, and together, we made people's dreams come true. We listened to our guests, and we got to know them. When things were quiet, we spent time listening to music and taking breaks in the parking garage. While we were successful, it sometimes felt more like a college dorm than a jewelry store.

Together, we were a band of misfits that nobody else wanted in their store, united into a team that others envied. It almost sounded like the beginning of a bad joke when someone described us. We had the curvy mom, the sassy old lady, the gay guy who just got out of jail, the conservative man who knew every word to "Dancing Queen," and the girl who didn't have a filter. Of course, the store was closing, so none of it mattered. And when Kara left, I became the "acting" store manager. That meant I had all the responsibilities but none of the pay. As time went on, gossip of our store closing and its lack of maintenance took its toll.

I was enlisted in a training program that required a lot of my time. I had to wait for Kara to leave so I could study because she was convinced I didn't need it. She had been promoted to store manager without the additional training. Of course, she, like my previous store manager, was highly flirtatious with our arrogant district manager. The same district manager who shook my hand when I stayed professional and politely refused his hugs, bragged on my accomplishments, but still required me to undergo intense training. I was the only one in the district to go through this training process—a process I was proud to complete, knowing I had earned any future promotions the right way.

One of my first full days being in Charleston, I was happy to see a familiar text message. I had been waiting for it. It had been a longer wait than usual, but I was eager to share the news of my new promotion with Trenton. He always seemed happy for me and was a voice of encouragement where Matt often failed.

Sheila?

Call me, Trenton, I quickly texted.

I can't call today. I'm at work.

Well, so am I. But I get it. What's up?

I wanted to check on you. It's been a while, Trenton texted back.

I'm good. I got promoted to assistant manager. I'm in Charleston for a while.

That's great. I'm proud of you.

Thank you. I needed that. God! I am so tired. I don't know how long I can do this.

You're strong. You can do it.

Sometimes, I doubt that.

I miss your voice, Sheila.

Are you sure I can't call?

I'm sorry, not right now. I got promoted, too. I'm the store manager at a furniture rental place now.

OMG! Really?!

It surprised me. I moved up fast. It makes me think . . . I miss running my own company, but Marsha doesn't want that anymore. She doesn't like how inconsistent it can be. She took the money from a job I had to do and spent it without me knowing, so I couldn't finish the job. It completely messed me up. I got in a lot of trouble.

I'm sorry, Trenton. Why did you keep the money in the same place? Was there anything you could have done?

No, I didn't think about it.

Not good.

No, it was bad. And I got arrested over it. So, I couldn't call you. That's why it's been so long. I'm sorry.

Why are you sorry, Trenton? It's not like you did it on purpose. Did she get you out?

Yeah, she eventually got everything taken care of. She couldn't live without my money, I guess.

I don't know why you have put up with her for so long.

I don't have a choice. I miss you, though. It should have been you. I regret leaving you. And if you're in Charleston, I don't know how I can get to you.

You wouldn't come anyway.

You don't know that. Do you regret marrying Matt?

Yeah, I do. You know that. Listen, I have to go. I have a customer. I will text you back soon.

Okay.

Putting the phone down, I closed my eyes and leaned back in the manager's chair that I now called home. I was tired of Trenton's empty promise not to be just a friend. He always claimed he wanted more. When the phone rang, I didn't check to see who it was calling. I was ready to tell Trenton how much I loved him, but I couldn't keep going on like this. After all, I could always call Seth if I wanted a friend. Of course, listening to him talk about Mary was always irritating. Why did so many women treat their men like crap? I was ready to talk to Trenton, to tell him how I felt, so I answered the phone.

"What are you doing?" Matt asked abruptly.

"Nothing . . . I . . . I . . . was talking to Kara and Clark about our next sales promotion. Why? Is everything okay?"

"I don't know, you tell me."

"What is *that* supposed to mean?"

"You know what I mean."

"No, I don't."

"You forgot to log off messenger. I was on it when you started texting Trenton."

Matt's words felt like I was being drowned in a bucket of ice. His tone was deep and angry—so angry that I was frozen, unable to speak. I knew he had a right to be angry since I texted that I regretted marrying him. That was something that he didn't need to know, not like that. I would have broken the news to him gently and not so abruptly. What if he hurt Terra? I heard her crying in the background but barely.

"What's wrong with Terra?" I asked.

"There's nothing wrong with her. You're hearing things. Stop trying to change the subject."

"Trenton is just a friend, Matt—a harmless flirtation. We both know it's never going to happen. It's not what it seems like."

"Then why did you say you regretted marrying me?"

"That's . . . something Trenton and I say to each other. It's part of the game, I guess."

"This isn't a game, Sheila. You know better. Who would be here to watch Terra? You better find someone to cover for you and get home *now*!"

"I can't come home. How am I supposed to do that?"

"I don't care. You need to find a way, or else . . ."

Hanging up the phone, I looked over at Clark with panic in my eyes. Unable to speak, I started to grab my things. What would Matt do if I didn't hurry and come home? Was he going to hurt Terra? It was an hour and a half drive home. What was I supposed to do? The thought of Matt hitting her flashed before my eyes, and I hit the floor, gasping for air. I remembered the times he left a hole in the bathroom door and each time he had locked Terra in her bedroom so he could be alone with me.

My heart was filled with a panicked hate, and I knew I shouldn't have been talking to Trenton. I missed Trenton, but I knew it was only because I needed the encouragement, the conversation, and the compliments. I knew that's all I was to him—a self-esteem boost and nothing more. That's why he would never come for me. Matt was the one at home taking care of my little girl. As I lay against the dirty carpet of our little jewelry store, my mistakes came for me like an avalanche of regret. This wasn't who I wanted to be. I had to fix this.

"Clark, I'm sorry, but I have an emergency. My daughter might be hurt. Matt is acting crazy. Can you cover for me?"

"*Go!* Sheila, it's ok! Just *go!* Be careful and don't worry about us. We have you covered. Nobody will even know you were gone."

"Are you sure?!"

"Yes, go. We got you."

Picking myself up off the floor, I ran for the parking garage. My baby was alone with Matt. He was angry, and she was crying. I was an hour and a half away. Panic covered my body with ice. My hands shook in the ignition. My heart raced. Violent visions filled my head. My teeth chattered as my foot pushed my vehicle as hard as it would go. I passed cars and ran red lights to make it come within an hour.

Running up to the porch, I threw the door open and ran inside. There Matt sat in his spot on the couch. With a stiff sniffle, he looked up at me with a narrow smile and a glint in his eyes as I threw my bags down and headed for Terra's room. Finally, I saw her placing her new doll in its bed, and without even noticing me, she grabbed the book that went with her doll and curled up on her bed to read. Her phone played her favorite song as she sang along in her pajamas.

"What's wrong, Sheila?" Matt asked, laughing from the other room. "Were you worried about something? Aren't you home a little early?"

"What do you mean was I 'worried about something?'" I answered, stomping back into the living room. "You told me to get home, or else."

"No, I didn't. Why would I say that? You should be at work. You're not needed here."

"That's not . . . What?"

"You seem confused. Do you know where you are?"

"I'm not confused. You called me."

"No, I didn't. I thought about messaging you because I saw that you were talking to Trenton on messenger, but I didn't. My phone hasn't worked all day."

"You called me about that."

"No, I didn't. You must be crazy. Why were you messaging him like that anyway?" Matt giggled.

"I . . . I . . . I don't know. It . . . makes us feel good for a little bit. It doesn't mean anything."

"That's kind of a sick game, don't you think?"

"I know. I have been trying to stop it. I have. I never expect him to contact me again, and then . . . he always does. But it's only messages and phone calls. That's why I stopped texting him so quickly."

"Then why do you keep doing it?"

"Well, we've gotten close over the years. I feel like I can talk to him about things, and he flirts, and he is never going to come here. So, he's not a threat. There's nothing to worry about."

"It doesn't matter. I'm not going to let you leave me. And I already told you once that *I* will never leave. You can't get rid of me."

Sitting beside Matt, I glanced down to the floor. Of course, I remembered that conversation. I remembered each time he told me to shut up, each time he made Terra cry, and the broken bathroom door. I couldn't forgive that. Looking at Matt's big feet without a single callous, not a rough spot, nothing but perfectly soft baby feet from a life of ease, I knew why I had let things go on for so long with Trenton. Maybe I was justifying my actions. I don't know, but I felt regret. *How could I love Matt if I'd never let Trenton go? Was Matt so bad of a man that I couldn't love him the way I should?*

I could only rationalize and guess at why I had done the things I had. Trenton was a fantasy—at least, my idea of him was. It wasn't real. Our connection, our magnetic energy, my attraction to him, none of it was real. He was the closest I would ever get to a man who loved music, respected my opinions, cared for me, and enjoyed intelligent conversations. That's why I had thought I needed him. But it was time to let go of the fantasy and live in the reality my regrets had created.

What I loved wasn't the real Trenton but the man I had dreamed of my entire life. The man who didn't exist. I knew I had to fix this, and even though Matt had tried to make me panic, hurt me, broke into my phone account, and made me miss work, I had to forget Trenton. Once. And. For. All.

"I'm sorry you had to read that, Matt. I didn't mean any of it. I want this to work. I want things to change."

"I do, too."

"Then let's focus on our marriage. Let's fix this. We need to make our family a priority."

"Yes, we do. Here, why don't you play this game with me?"

So, together, we played a game—one that I couldn't play, which only frustrated Matt more. Later, he told me he had messaged Trenton and solved the problem himself but that he had deleted their messages. Matt said that Trenton accused him of being gay, of not being able to satisfy me. They both called each other fat, and Marsha had even been involved. I guess it was a mess, but Matt conveniently made sure I would never see those last words. That day, I lost a friend and . . . my hope, even if that hope was never real. Talking to Trenton was something I enjoyed. It was a little mystery, a little flirtation, and the closest I would ever get to the man I dreamed of.

Even though I tried to play it off as nothing—even to myself—a part of me crumbled. No matter how many times Trenton didn't show up, I counted on him for one thing: to give me the illusion that someone cared. The last light that hung in my heart, the last sprinkle of fairy dust, and the last ember that kept my heart warm went out. My heart wilted, drying to a crumble.

Through the years, Trenton's random messages and calls had been the bread that kept me from hating myself because his words were often my thoughts. That night, as Matt fell asleep, silent tears soaked the blanket clutched to my heart while cries tremored violently within. I was unable to even allow myself the luxury of showing emotions.

* * *

Finally, after a couple of months of being the acting store manager, I had a day off. I was exhausted trying to balance work and our little family. Sitting at our kitchen table, I felt my head bobbing as my eyes started to close. Dinner was done, and Terra was satisfied in bed. Thoughts of work darted through my head around streaks of moments with her. I missed dance class again that week. I loved when they would call me out on the floor to help.

Then, I remembered Clark and Kendall laughing while listening to their favorite songs as we hoped a customer would dare to enter our shadowy store. How was I ever going to be closer to home? I kept telling Terra it would get better when I got moved back to my original store, but I didn't know if I would ever get the promotion. Glancing around the room, I noticed the dusty corners, the haphazardly placed bookbag in the middle of the floor, and the jacket thrown over the back of the chair.

Looking at Matt, I sighed in exhaustion. He refused to cook when I was on my way home. Going through a drive-through took forever and made me feel awful. It was always the same fast-food restaurants, nothing else was open, and I got sick of eating the same things every night. I wanted to savor every minute with Terra at home and drive there the short way, but every night I was always stuck waiting in line for dinner.

I tried to text Matt whenever possible so he could complain about Terra arguing with him about cleaning her room, doing her homework, or finishing her dinner. I wanted peace, but when I was home, they fought, and I listened to their screams. On a good day, he would send her away so we could have privacy. I wanted to spend time with my daughter, who was growing up without me, but those opportunities rarely came.

My responsibilities had changed. Now, I had to keep the store on track, attract customers, and keep my employees on task—or at least keep them from plotting the demise of upper management. Lunch breaks were a thing of the past. The idea of a phone call seemed like a luxury, but it wasn't exactly tempting to call and listen to Matt's complaints about Terra. I knew life would be better if I were home. But we needed to survive. We needed the money. We had come far, and this was about sacrifice. This was how we would make it. Terra wasn't being bullied anymore, and we had gas in the vehicle, food on the table, and decent clothes to wear.

Looking at Matt again, I saw him scoot his chair beside me and put his elbows against his knee. I knew he had something to say. I braced myself for another lecture about how bad Terra was or how he never got to see me. I found it ironic because he would push her away so we could be alone, but she saw me less than he did to begin with.

"I'm lonely, Sheila," Matt started. "All you do is work. You're never home anymore. I need someone to talk to. I want to try an open marriage so I can have someone to keep me company."

"Why would you want that? You want to date other people while I'm at work? That's a lot different than what we were doing before, and you saw how hurt I was."

"Well, I want to make some . . . friends . . . and see where it goes. You're always at work and barely pay attention to me. I never hear from you." Matt sniffled as a tear welled up in the corner of his eye. "I don't want to be alone anymore."

"Are you going to sleep with them?"

"I don't know, maybe. I'm not against it. But that would mean that you could do the same."

"I don't want to do that. We have sex *all the time*, no matter how tired I am. I always—"

"I'm lonely, Sheila. I want someone to spend time with."

"Matt, I don't know. I guess I need to think about it. I don't want you to feel lonely. Yes, I'm working all the time. It's not that I want to. I have to." *Don't I mean anything to you? Am I not good enough anymore?*

I made plenty of mistakes in our marriage, including cheating on Matt—an act that I had sincerely hoped would drive him away. But again, he refused to leave. Instead, we engaged in the fine art of swinging. I listened to him make another woman moan while I lay beneath her husband, and later, I closed my eyes when he invited another man into our bedroom. It, of course, had been a fantasy of mine, but when faced with it in reality, I had been filled with disgust. I wasn't attracted to the stranger who Matt invited to partake in my body. Perhaps it would have been a little more fun if the extra guy hadn't been nearly thirty years older than me and if I hadn't been nauseous at the sight of him. My fantasy became a nightmare as I watched Matt take the guy's penis in his mouth and then spread me open like a rag doll as he shared me.

I had felt that, maybe, I deserved it. After all, I was the one who had been seduced by a friend—a friend who was there when I needed him, there when I needed to talk. I felt obligated to share myself with my friend. He had given me more than I needed, and for that, I was grateful. But I *had* cheated.

After that, I fell into a deep depression. I pulled away when Matt tried to touch me. It took months for his knees to heal from where he had slept with another man's wife on our area rug—a woman who couldn't finish the job. I remember tasting her on him when I went down on him so he could cum. I had asked to *never* partake in sharing, swinging, or threesomes again. The cost was too much. I hated myself for everything I'd done. I knew other people seemed happy in those situations, but it had crushed me.

* * *

Over the next week, Matt asked me every day for an open marriage, and I kept asking questions. I should have seen his request coming, but I didn't. During sex, we always talked about our fantasies, and now, I asked him if he wanted to be with someone else. Of course, he agreed. He would change his story often, from wanting to make friends—by being on dating websites—to waiting to see what happened or keeping his options open as to whether he would have sex with them or not.

By the end of the week, I wanted the questions, the constant pleading, and the sobs of desperation to stop. I wanted Matt to leave. I wanted Terra to be independent. I wanted to be free from the constant turmoil that was my home. So, in the hopes that maybe Matt would fall in love and leave of his own free will, I agreed to the open marriage. Obedient, as always, I helped him make the perfect dating profile to attract women because he said he couldn't do it on his own, and he demanded that I make some for myself as well.

The morning after I had finally agreed to Matt's idea was one of the hardest. That was the day the guardrail between the road and the cliff started to look tempting. As my hands clutched the steering wheel, it was difficult to stay on the road. I needed to talk, but Matt had taken away the only people I talked to. I knew I had to be strong, be a leader, and face my team. Of course, they knew something was wrong the moment I arrived, fifteen minutes late.

"Why are the eyes of our fearless leader swollen and red this morning?" Jimmy asked, leaning against the counter.

"Oh, you don't want to know. You realize that part of my training is that I'm not allowed to let my personal life follow me to work, don't you? When I'm here, I have to be professional."

"But you don't follow their rules, Sheila," Clark piped in. "You never have, and that's what makes you such a good manager. That's why we love you; you're real. You haven't been corrupted by the corporate mumbo jumbo crap yet. So, tell us what's wrong."

"I don't know," I answered.

Leaning back in the manager's chair, I propped my feet up against the desk and closed my eyes. That wasn't my usual style, but this wasn't the usual day. Still, as I tried to rest my eyes from the long drive, I felt my co-workers' gaze on me. They weren't going to stop, and I loved them for that. They cared and not in an "I want to get in your pants" kind of way.

"You're not going to let me say no, are you?" I asked with my eyes closed.

"Um, no, not a chance," Jimmy answered.

"Okay, give me a minute. I'm going to get coffee. I don't think I'm ready to talk about it yet."

"I already got your coffee," Clark notified me, handing me a cup.

"Of course, you did."

Taking the cup from his hand, I stared at the white lid and felt the warmth burning through the cardboard slip meant to protect hands. I wanted to hold its heat to my body and bathe in its comfort, but all I could do was hold it with both hands as my breath came in shaky gasps. Looking into my co-workers' concerned eyes, I closed mine. I didn't want to see their reaction. I didn't want them to hate me.

"I'm scared," I finally said. *I can't believe that's the first thing I said.* "He . . . I mean, Matt . . . he . . . wants an open marriage."

"Why?" Clark and Jimmy asked simultaneously.

"He said he's lonely, that I work too much, that I'm never home, and that he wants a 'friend.' I asked if he would sleep with them. He said he was open to it. I don't know . . . he's been asking for a week, and I agreed to it last night. He immediately started making dating profiles. It made me sick to write them for him. The only thing I could think was, am I not good enough? Doesn't any of this matter? It doesn't seem fair. I don't understand. I want him to leave, but I'm working here, so far from home and from Terra. I don't know what to do."

I couldn't stop the tears from pouring. The little bit of makeup that remained was gone in a matter of moments. I couldn't see my co-workers' faces as they came toward me. I couldn't breathe. The thought of my husband with another woman was too much. The thought of what he was doing while I was at work, with the money I earned . . .

My body shook as Clark and Jimmy approached me and wrapped their arms around me. I felt the pain of icy screams clenching my lungs as I struggled to catch my breath.

"I can't breathe," I whispered.

"It's okay, we've got you," Jimmy reassured me.

"You're too good for him, Sheila," Clark jumped in. "He's not going to find anyone anyway. I wouldn't worry too much. He's an idiot for asking for something like that."

"Well, he did. You don't know Gallipolis. It's hard to tell what he'll find."

"It doesn't matter," Clark continued. "Just stop sleeping with him."

"I don't think that's what she needs to hear, man," Jimmy opined. "I'll take it from here."

Looking into Jimmy's eyes, I listened. I waited for his advice. Stepping away, Clark headed toward the edge of the store to play lookout as he often did. After all, when salespeople were around, customers didn't dare to enter. Instead, they made sure to go to the opposite side of the halls to avoid being spoken to. It was funny how corporate never figured that out.

"Jimmy, I can't stop sleeping with him. He won't let me."

"That's called rape if he takes you when you don't want it, if he tries to convince you to do things you don't want to do. All of that is rape," Jimmy asserted.

"But—"

"It is, Sheila."

"It doesn't matter. I'm sorry. I should be stronger than this."

"You're stronger than most. You don't give yourself enough credit."

"Thank you."

"I need you to listen to me now, okay?"

"Okay, Jimmy."

"Let him have his way with the open marriage. It will work out okay in the end. He's a fool, and he will screw it up. Maybe this is the beginning of the end. You never know. What I do know is that if he had to talk to you and try to convince you for a week and if he doesn't care how you feel, then you deserve better. Maybe you'll find better."

"I don't want to date. I've seen enough from the stupid crap I did in the past. I feel like I'm still paying for it. I feel like this is Matt's revenge. I don't know how to say it, but I think you understand what I'm trying to say. Maybe this is my karma."

"I doubt it. I think he wants more. He knows he can control you. You are far too beautiful of a person for that, Sheila. And I don't mean physical beauty. I'm talking about your heart."

"I don't know about that. I do mess up a lot."

"Think about it, Sheila. What have you been doing here while you're an hour and a half away?"

"I've been enjoying the freedom, knowing that Matt is not sitting outside spying on me. He used to sit outside of my old store for hours while Terra was at school, just so he could watch me. I feel more at ease. I can work better. I can breathe."

"But you haven't been cheating is my point. You're not a bad person."

"So, what do I do?"

"Just ride it out. Enjoy it a little. Do what you want. According to him, it doesn't matter anymore. But *be careful*."

"I don't want an open marriage, and we have to tell each other if we do anything with anyone."

"Then, if you don't want to do this, don't. Let him do his thing. You have to do what's right for you. Nobody else. *You*."

"Thanks, Jimmy."

"You know what *I* think you should do, don't you?" Clark asked as he came back into the store. "Get your flirt on. Do your thang." He laughed.

"You always think that." I giggled.

"Well, that's because it's true. Matt is giving you permission to have fun."

"I don't want to have fun like that. I want to *not* feel like a piece of meat."

"Well, good luck with that."

"Gee, thanks."

Unfortunately, Clark was right. Over the next few days, things got bad. My phone was going off constantly with guys that liked my picture. None of them held a conversation for more than a few minutes without asking for sex. I was tired of meaningless sex. If I was going to do this, then I wanted someone around who could be supportive, be polite, and be my escape from work and home—a friend who kissed me occasionally.

Kissing: that was another thing I missed. Matt never kissed me. I spent most mornings and evenings bent over the edge of the bed, thrown down and open, at Matt's mercy. I considered all the times he hurt me as he pushed me down on the bed, how many times he wouldn't take no for an answer, and how many times I silently cried in pain as he ripped into me before I was ready. I knew better than to say no. I had given up on that long ago. After all, he would whine until I gave in, or he would try to talk me into it. I had once loved sex, but now, it was painful.

I initiated sex a lot, too, though, because it was routine and because it caused Matt to act better and treat me nicer, and it seemed to keep Terra safe. That was the only thing that mattered. For years, I had been asking Matt to kiss me more, touch me more, and give me a little bit of foreplay. Of course, he listened for a few days, and then it would be back to his normal.

I dreamed of gentle kisses in the kitchen, sweet moments when Matt and I would say goodnight at the end of the day, and passion when those moments came. Instead, I got forceful kisses that felt like I was being swallowed alive and foreplay that lasted three to five minutes and felt like an obligation. None of it had true passion. When I would tell Matt what I wanted, he complained that he would never make me happy and suggested that I would never be happy with anyone. Matt would tell me that he was doing exactly what I had asked him to do.

I felt less for Matt each day. I'm sure part of it was my fault—how could I expect to receive tenderness, passion, and affection when I was never home? I always needed to sleep for work the next day, so of course, sex needed to be fast, and his needs had to be taken care of. So, frequently, the sex was hard and blindingly painful. I was thankful for autopilot.

Chapter 12

I N THE HEART of the fire, beneath the flaming tree, I hid. The heat danced in waves like a veil around me as fire erupted. I watched the men circling the tree as I lay beneath, unable to hide my flesh from their crimson eyes. I felt their thoughts as their eyes ravaged me. I felt their hands rake across my flesh, pulling me into theirs as they hunted me. I heard their laughter in my mind as they came closer and as my lungs gasped in tremors. Like an animal nearly dead, I watched the tree stretch its arms to me as it burned. The men twisted and reached, trying to escape the fire engulfing us as wood became steel within the flames.

Beastly ghosts of men dropped to their knees. Their eyes locked on my flesh as they crawled toward me. In my mind, I heard their growls like starving animals, focused and intending to rip into my body. I felt them coming closer. I saw their minds darkening as they gave into their primal urges. I was flesh for them to enjoy and nothing more. I had never felt more vulnerable as they lunged for me.

My eyes filled with tears as I watched the men slowly come for me. There was no hiding their intent or their desire, nothing to hide my nakedness from their hunger, and nothing to guard me from the inevitable. I knew that if they reached me, they would destroy my flesh with their instincts. Reaching for the branches of the flaming tree, I hoped for a spot not burning, not hot to the touch. I looked for something to grab and a way to climb away from the beasts that hunted me.

Then, I felt it: the edge of a vine, barely clinging to life. Grabbing it, I stood and looked up through the branches of the tree as parts of it slowly smoldered, the fire quieting itself among its branches. With a swift tug, I pulled myself up, away from the beastly men, just in time to feel a hand rake across my skin. Below me, they scrambled as I climbed blindly up the vine until I found a branch that was not burning. In the heart of the tree, I rested. Covering myself with the few remaining leaves, I looked out across the flames.

Flowers melted, vanishing within the smoke. Bushes disintegrated in the heat, and in the distance, I saw touches of blue within the black waves that oozed upon the shore. The shores sparkled with broken glass as the light from nearby flames danced across their mirrored surface. With each oozing wave, more glass appeared on the shore, shattering into smaller and sharper pieces. The shoreline grew.

Below me, the beastly men gathered, each of them breaking off a piece of the tree that protected me. Together, they lit their fires and ran into the smoke that surrounded us. Every few moments, another tribe of men would approach, unaware of my presence, and each of them disappeared within the smoke. The men were easily beaten as the living smoke wrapped around their bodies and carried them to the sea. With each soul it took, the ocean grew darker, and I knew that it wasn't oil that was making the water black. It was the blood of souls lost. Each one that was drug into the depths only made the fire stronger and the smoke thicker. Still, the men came systematically as though they had been released from a hidden dungeon. Each of them ran from the smoke behind me to the flames below until there were no men left.

From the top of the tree, I watched the land turn gray, and beastly men who once fought were chained and taken within the block building in the distance. My eyes strained, searching to see what lay within the building.

* * *

Every day, I drove back and forth between Gallipolis and Charleston on what was rumored to be one of the most dangerous roads in the state. Death was tempting. It would look like an accident. If I drove the vehicle as fast as possible, I would die instantly when I hit the guardrail or plummeted nose-first over the cliff. Or I'm sure the person driving the semi would be fine if I drove as fast as I could into them. Trucks were tough, and accidents happened on that road all the time. All it would take was one moment of bravery—just long enough to press the gas pedal to the floor and turn the wheel sharply.

After that, it would be done. There would be no turning back. It would be over—the pain, the suffering, and the trying to figure out how to move on. And Terra would be taken from Matt and placed somewhere safe. I couldn't think of anything else. I wanted to end it. I wanted freedom, and it didn't matter how I got it. I wanted to cry but couldn't.

At work, the pressure was on. I wanted to be reunited with my baby store. I was convinced that being there would fix everything. I wanted to be the store manager. I wanted to make Terra proud and to have the power to make a difference in other people's lives. Maybe then Matt would be more attentive. Then, I realized that it didn't matter how he felt. Quietly, I told Terra it was time she learned a few things around the house. She needed to be able to do laundry, cook basic meals, and get up for school. I was going to find a way out. It was time to fight back.

I knew there was a bonus program for store managers. Each year they would receive a bonus on the profits of their store, and it was substantial. I had to get there. The first bonus wouldn't be much at that store, but I knew that the second year, it would be more than enough to buy Matt out of the house. I made a plan that when that second bonus hit, I could get him to leave peacefully. It would take the one thing that he loved the most: money. That would be the perfect amount of time to help Terra be a little more independent—at least, enough to survive a few days a week without me.

I had it all figured out. Tasha could check on Terra a couple days a week, I would have a couple days off, and Terra would be able to heat leftovers or cook simple meals a few days a week. Together, we could do this. It was just going to take time and a little teamwork. And I had to get Terra ready. After all, she wanted Matt gone as badly as I did.

When I was in Charleston, I had everything I needed. There were plenty of guys to flirt with, supportive friends, and coffee. So, I made a game of it. My favorite game was to walk into the mall and find a couple. I loved the guys who stared into the distance while their women yammered about random stores and clothing. They seemed completely lost and oblivious to their surroundings until they spotted me. I made sure to make eye contact and look longingly into their eyes for a second or two longer than was normal. Within seconds, they would run into a wall, trip over their own feet, or completely miss their obligatory nod to the woman beside them. It was fun to watch them fumble and trip over themselves.

I hated men like that, so this was the perfect game for me. I had become *that* girl. After all, gone were the days of secondhand dresses and ill-fitting clothes. Now, I dressed to impress. My hair was always curled, and heels were my new sneakers. Then, just as quickly as I had appeared, I would duck into my shadowy store and hide at my desk. Still, I hoped that one day, in the midst of the convention tourists, I would find a compassionate intellectual who spoke to my soul—my personal prince charming.

I stayed with my co-workers most of the time, and we compared our soon-to-be closing store to the titanic. Everything was falling apart. We waited patiently for corporate to decide what to do with us. When corporate was looking, I was the best acting manager possible. I was dutiful, obedient, and inspiring to my team. But when corporate *wasn't* looking, the team and I engaged in karaoke, gossip sessions, and complaining about the evils of giant corporations.

Our store was closing, so we didn't matter to anyone. That gave us plenty of time for fun, games, and impromptu therapy sessions. I went from complaining about being in an open marriage to all of us agreeing that men are evil, manipulative bastards to toy with. I needed to learn how to play and use men to get a little boost of self-confidence. So, that's what I did. I talked to a lot of men. But those conversations were always cut short because I wasn't interested.

Until one man *did* interest me. He was tempting in a different way. A cheating pastor was a safe way to dive into a crazy story and have a little fun. I would never be able to truly be with him, and he could satisfy my need for attention.

I became the pastor's mistress—at least, in *his* mind. I was completely wrapped up in him—devastatingly so. Suddenly, everything made sense. I had always been religious, and here he was, a pastor, a man of God. It was almost magical, even if he was married. Slowly, through many phone conversations on my way to work, he convinced me that his wife was pure evil. She didn't listen to anything he had to say, never made love to him, and didn't support his ministry. I felt devastated for him. She didn't even trust him to visit the sick in the hospital. I wanted to believe there were good men in the world, so I dove headfirst into his words and into his story.

Chapter 13

"THERE'S SOMEONE HERE to see you, Sheila," Clark announced from across the store. "I thought you said you were going to keep guys out of here?" he teased, laughing.

"What do you mean? I didn't tell anyone where to find me," I answered, pushing away from the computer to peek through the small gap between the wall and the register where I was safely hidden.

Catching a glimpse of the man who stood a few feet away, I knew I was wrong. It was Pastor Ramsey. His elegant bald head reflected the small amount of light that remained in our little store, probably because his height put him so close to the ceiling. He was a big man, but only in the best of ways. And then, I remembered that I had told him *exactly* where to find me. I just hadn't expected him to show up.

"Clark, I'm going straight to hell," I mumbled as I carefully stood.

"Perhaps, but you might as well have fun on your way." Clark laughed, patting me on the back. "Now, get out there."

Looking back at Clark, I tried to smile. Everything with Matt had led me to this. A tall, handsome stranger had come to visit me. It was odd that out of all the men that had been sniffing me out, I had led this one straight to me. Perhaps it was a moment of weakness or shared childhood ideas; I'm not sure. But this was the first time I had allowed anyone who saw the dating profiles Matt made me create to meet me in person.

"I told you I'd find you." The pastor beamed. "I had a doctor's appointment, and I managed to slip away without my wife knowing where I am. I left my phone in the truck so she can't track me, and I left the truck at the hospital."

"It's been weeks since I've heard from you. I wasn't expecting you to actually show up." I laughed.

"Of course, I did. Most people don't understand me like you do."

"Well, we have the same type of background. I'm sure there are a lot of people like me out there. That seems like quite a lot of work to come see me."

"Well, you know . . . I'm getting a little frustrated in my marriage. I'm hoping that you might be different. I wish I could leave my wife. I seriously considered killing her off a couple times," he joked.

"Well, I don't want anything to do with that, Pastor Ramsey," I stuttered, looking at his crooked smile.

"Please, call me Ram. That's what my friends call me. I definitely don't want to be formal with you." He cooed and took my hand. "I love my wife, but I hate that she won't make love to me. She used to be up for anything and took care of herself. She was beautiful and kind. Now, she stalks me, puts trackers on my phone, and won't let me out of her sight."

"She won't make love to you? Does she do any of the things that a pastor's wife is supposed to do?" I sighed in disgust. "I hate women like that. All men have needs. What do women expect to happen?"

"Exactly, I need a real woman of God—one who will stand beside me, support me, and be encouraging to my ministry. It's more important than anything else in the world to me."

"Ram . . . you said you would never leave her?"

"I don't know anymore. I wish I could be free, but I have a lot of people that depend on me—an entire congregation. They look to me for answers, Sheila. What am I supposed to do? I'm a man."

"A wife is supposed to help. She's supposed to help you achieve your goals and be your strength when you're down. Your wife is supposed to be a safe place where you can run."

"She's none of those things." Taking my hand in his, Ram didn't try to hide his wedding ring. He didn't try to hide anything. He was honest, and his honesty was sexy. "Can you take a break? Maybe go where nobody can hear us talk? I don't want to cause any problems, but

I can't be seen."

"Sure, follow me. I know a place. It's where we go on break."

Walking out of the store, I turned to see Ram watching me, following me with his eyes. I felt my cheeks flush red as his eyes met mine. It was only a few steps to the employee hallway—an empty space we all had to travel that led us to the roped-off areas of the parking garage. Only a few people dared enter the space, making it one of my favorite places to hide. Grabbing the door, I entered and waited for Ram to follow me into the shadows. Leaning up against the wall, I watched him approach, waiting as the door closed firmly behind him.

I blinked as Ram leaned over me, his lips hunting mine. My breath caught in my throat as he lowered his face to mine and his hands grabbed mine. I felt his wedding band cut into my flesh as he pulled me to him. It had been forever since I had been kissed, and it felt like a winter rain spreading from my lips to my toes. Looking into Ram's eyes, I waited for him to release me, but he didn't. He continued kissing me, his lips biting at mine as I tried to catch my breath. Arching my back, I pressed my body against his, knowing that this might be the only moment we would ever share. This was the kind of kiss I craved—powerful and passionate. It was nothing like the bitter kisses that Seth had given.

"I ummm . . . I have . . . to get . . . a hotel . . . next week . . . so I can be here for an early morning meeting." I tried to speak through Ram's kisses.

"Mmm, count me in, baby girl. I am *definitely* up for that. You know what would be better, though?" Ram growled in my ear. "If you joined me at my church sometime. I want to take you right there on the alter. Maybe I could take you to the Sunday school room and bend you over the table. Mmm, that would be amazing."

"Ram . . . that sounds . . . delicious. I will have to do that if I ever get out of here early enough."

Pulling away, I headed to the door. I didn't want this man to know that I was hanging on his words. He didn't need to know it had been years since I had enjoyed a kiss, an eternity since I had felt desired. I wasn't sure about the idea of being the other woman, but it was exciting—the risk of getting caught.

I knew old thoughts and ways of thinking were overwhelming me, but Ram thought the same way I did. Leaving him behind, I took a deep breath and pretended to be confident. I walked with my head high as I made my way back to the store. I didn't want to admit to myself that I had been captured easily. It reminded me of Trenton and how quickly I had fallen for him, but at least Ram was honest. *I never knew if Trenton was lying. He had married someone else, after all. Maybe this would be my new future. Maybe I could stand next to this man as his wife one day. Maybe. Probably not.*

Collapsing in the manager's chair, I looked up to see Clark's smile. I knew my cheeks were flushed and had hoped he wouldn't notice. The last thing I wanted was to appear weak. I was done with being weak for men.

"Have fun?" Clark asked, taking the seat beside me. "It looks like you did."

"Yeah, it was just a kiss, though."

"One hell of a kiss, I'd say."

"Is it that obvious?"

"Definitely. You know, there's nothing wrong with having a little fun. Isn't that what Matt keeps pushing you to do? Who knows what *he's* been doing?"

"I don't want to be like that. I don't want to be weak."

"Then don't be weak; enjoy it. You have all the control you need. If Matt is going to make dating profiles for you and try to get you with other guys, then you are only doing what he told you to do."

"It's not that simple, is it?" I asked, staring at Clark's hands.

"Yeah, I'm afraid it is."

"I'm in control. I can do this," I asserted. "Ugh, no, I *can't* do this."

"Yes, you can," Clark assured me. "Maybe this guy is different. You never know. Don't give up."

"I don't want to get my hopes up. Did I tell you that Trenton texted me last week?"

"No! *Are you serious?* How long has *that* been going on now?"

"Seven years, Clark. Seven . . . years. And every time he texts or I hear his voice, I'm putty in his hands," I said, throwing my phone down on the desk. "I *hate* that I do that."

"Sounds to me like the pastor might be what you need. Seven years is waaay too long to be hung up on a guy."

"I'm not hung up on him. He's just a friend. I can talk to him about anything, always have been able to."

"But he uses it against you, doesn't he?"

"Well, yeah, he does. But at least I have someone to call. He might not answer or give advice or pretty much anything else, but that's all I have."

"Exactly."

"Yeah."

The rest of the evening, Clark and I watched people come and go from the food court. There was always something happening there. It was the home of tables, the strongest wi-fi, and the coffee shop. On any given night, we had the opportunity to watch catfights between teen girls, the homeless catch a nap, or mall security flirt with girls in other stores. That was where everyone gathered, and it was close to the convention center, so there was never a shortage of interesting people, deep conversations, and culture.

It was October, and the mall was already playing Christmas music over the loudspeakers. It echoed into our store, making it pointless to listen to our own music. With twelve-hour shifts, it got annoying fast. So, that night, as the mall closed and the music continued, I took a walk and started thinking. I walked with my head held high, and I was proud of how far I'd come.

Matt said he hadn't had any luck with dating sites and hadn't found a friend, which made it odd when he would show me pictures of nude women who texted him. Then, he would get upset when I received messages and accuse me of lying to him about what I was doing in Charleston. You know, while I was . . . *working*. I had no doubt that Matt was using his time and any money I left behind on other women. Ram was the only guy I had met, and all the other men I had managed to avoid.

* * *

The next week came quickly, and I told Matt that I had to work late and be at the store two hours early the next day, all of which was true. But I also had plans to meet up with Ram that evening. I was excited, and I couldn't stop thinking about his kiss. When I got to work that day, I was asked to work at our nearby sister store, and when I was given the opportunity to leave early, I headed back to my store to clock out.

"Are you staying at a hotel tonight?" Clark asked as I stepped into the store.

"Yes! Ram is supposed to show up. I can't wait! If that kiss was any indication, I have a wild night ahead of me." I giggled.

"Well, be sure to enjoy it. I can point you in the direction of a couple of bars if you want. You are bound to find a little fun that way." Clark laughed. "That's where I find most of *my* guys."

"I'm pretty sure we don't have the same type."

"I'm not sure about that; just look at you."

"Yeah, fat and sassy," I answered, looking to the ground. "I better check into the hotel. I'll probably be back. He might be meeting me here. I'm not sure."

Grabbing my red and black leopard suitcase, I rolled it out of the mall to the hotel across the street. It was a nice place, with clean rooms and its own restaurant. I had always enjoyed hotels. As I looked over the white comforter and fluffy pillows, I caught a glimpse of myself in the mirror. My eyes were a little swollen, and my makeup had worn off. I was wearing my favorite lace dress and a pair of heels. I needed rest.

Wanting to explore my surroundings, I headed toward the elevator, looking for signs of different amenities. Stepping out onto the second floor, I followed the signs to head outside to the courtyard. After stepping through the hidden doors and making my way through a mass of chairs, I stepped onto the balcony. It wasn't much of a view, but I saw the mall across the street and the lights of the other businesses in the distance. The streets were buzzing below me, and my head filled with emotions. The mall was nearly empty. From my perch, I watched the cars go by. They had no idea I was watching them. The people on the sidewalk strolled to their cars, shouting at one another, assuming they were alone.

As I headed inside, I checked my reflection and prepared myself to meet Ram even though he hadn't confirmed he could get away from his wife. I wasn't sure that I cared. Hell, I just wanted to be kissed again. Glancing at my conservative lace dress, I knew. *I will be kissed tonight. I can take control. This is MY life.* Ripping my favorite dress over my head, I removed the camisole top that blocked my cleavage and adjusted my breasts, then slid the dress back on. After removing my panties and applying fresh lipstick, I returned to my store to await Pastor Ram.

"Shit, girl, you look *hot!*" Clark squealed when he saw me.

"I thought you were supposed to be gay?"

"I am."

"Yeah, not convinced." I laughed.

"Hey, Ram called. He left a number for you to call." Clark handed me a slip of paper. "You know I don't mean anything by my comments, don't you?"

"Yes, I know. Of course, you don't. You're just trying to make a fat girl feel a little better about herself."

"I wish you'd stop that, Sheila. You're beautiful and probably one of the sweetest," Clark reassured me as he rubbed my shoulders. "Go call him."

Grabbing my phone, I headed to my desk and dialed the number. As Ram quickly answered, I heard a giggle in the background, and I knew without asking. I had traveled this path before.

"Sheila, I can't make it tonight. I can't get away from my wife," Ram whispered into the phone. "She has me busy with the youth tonight. I tried."

"Okay, that's fine," I answered dryly.

"I want you to meet me tomorrow at the church, though. I have to see you. I want to see you naked before God," Pastor Ram cooed into the phone.

"Okay, that's fine," I answered dryly.

"I want to make love to you in the holiest of places. I might bring an extra guy. You wouldn't mind that, would you? He could have his way with both of us."

"Okay, that's fine," I answered dryly.

"Okay, I can't wait to get you naked. I will call you and let you know when I can get away from my wife."

"Okay, that's fine," I answered dryly.

Hanging up the phone, I pushed my shoulders back and glanced over at Clark. Without saying a word, I headed back across the street and found my room. Staring at my reflection in the mirror, I looked at myself with new eyes. I wanted to be kissed—possibly more—and I was hungry. It took me about five seconds to make up my mind. I had never been in a bar alone, but at least it would be a somewhat classy hotel bar, and it had food, which I needed. It wouldn't hurt to see what kind of trouble I could get into.

PART II

Chapter 14

"OUR FEARLESS LEADER is *late*?" Jimmy laughed. "What did *you* do?" Clark chimed in.

"I don't know what you mean," I answered with a wink as I unlocked the gate to the store.

"You know exactly what I mean," Clark replied.

"No, I'm afraid I don't."

"You're not going to tell us, are you?"

"I don't know, maybe, maybe not. I've never been one to kiss and tell."

"Oh, now I knooow you did something. Come on; you have to tell us. Did you do what I would do?"

"Maybe. But with a little twist of my own." Twirling my skirt, I laughed at Clark and Jimmy as we clocked in and headed down the hall. My heels clicked against the tile as we cascaded to our sister store for our mandatory meeting. "I'm not sure how we're going to get through this meeting." I laughed. "I think I got even less sleep than usual."

"Of course, and you're not saying anything. You're a tease; you know that?" Clark replied.

"But I'm sweet and innocent, remember?"

"Uh-huh, and I'm the pope."

"Oh, really? You are? Why didn't you tell me before?" I teased Clark.

"Smart-ass."

"Come on, let's go outside for a minute before we get there. What are they going to do, start without us?"

"*Then* will you tell us something?" Clark pleaded.

"Maybe."

Taking a sharp left, I flew out to the parking garage and leaned against the railing. Running forward, my co-workers gathered like children waiting for a bedtime story. My smile broadened as they stood silently, waiting.

"So, I went to the hotel bar last night."

"*And?!*" Clark prodded impatiently.

"Well, there was this old guy flirting with this brunette, bragging that he took his little blue pill. She, of course, kept flirting with him, trying to get free drinks. I swear that guy was just like our district manager."

"That is *not* why you are smiling, though!" Kendall interrupted.

"Is that all you got?" Clark asked.

"No, of course not. It was funny watching them, and as the night went on, more guys flocked to that girl, and they kept buying her drinks. A few of them stared at me, sat next to me, and tried to buy *me* drinks, but I refused. I completely brushed them off. I just sat there waiting, kind of laughing at the little games they were playing."

"Continue. Come on; we need more than that." Jimmy laughed.

"Well, as I finished my drink, another guy entered the bar and sat a couple stools down from mine. He was kinda cute but nothing fancy—dressed nice, but not in a business snob kind of way. I refused his drink, too, but he was smart enough to ask why. I told him that I didn't need alcohol to have fun. If I was going to do something crazy, I preferred to remember it."

"That's great. Can I steal that line?" Clark asked.

"I don't think it will work for you, man. You *like* the free drinks."

"This is true," Clark agreed.

"So, anyway . . . I let him flirt with me all night. I made him work for it. He fed me so many lines, and the whole time, I dismissed him, until he started being honest. Hell, I already knew what I wanted to do, just wanted it on *my* terms. This was probably the craziest thing I have ever willingly done, but he left my room this morning. We exchanged first names, locations, and careers but nothing more. I think one of the cool things about it was that *I* was the one who asked *him* to leave the bar with me, not the other way around."

"Sooo, what happened?" Clark prodded me.

"I took him out to the balcony. What else could happen?"

"You did *not* ask a guy to leave a bar just to hang out on a balcony."

"Actually, I did. But eventually, I might have agreed to take Lance to my room."

"Lance, huh? That's a different name."

"I didn't bother to check if it was his real name. I liked the mystery of not knowing who he was, never seeing him again."

"So, you took him to your room? Then what? You're leaving out the juicy details!" Clark exclaimed.

"Oh, you want more?"

"Of course!"

"Well, I might have allowed Lance to go down on me for a while. I let him stumble around and tell me I was hot, unique, beautiful—you know, all the stuff I enjoy hearing. Poor guy enjoyed being between my legs. He didn't have much more to offer, but I had sex with him anyway, to see what it was like to be in charge. Now quick, we better hurry to our MANdatory meeting." I laughed.

Quickly, my co-workers followed as I led them to our sister store, where the other manager was waiting with coffee and donuts. The five of us barely got through the meeting as we laughed at everything he said. I almost pitied him. After all, that was the most fun any of us had ever had in a mandatory meeting. Don't get me wrong, we followed the rules and covered the material. But there were many times we erupted into laughter as Clark put a spin on every scenario we read aloud.

Heading back to our store, I collapsed in the manager's chair. Our joyful attitudes were squashed by the dreariness of the dying store. Christmas was coming, and I had applied for the store manager position in Gallipolis. As predicted, Annette, the district manager's favorite, was heading to another store. The entire team was anxious as each of them accepted either a transfer or severance package. Everyone knew where they were going . . . except me.

"It's bullshit that they haven't told you if you got the position yet,"

Clark asserted.

"That's the way they do things. They like to make you wait till the last minute, make you worry, torture you."

"They are good at torture," Clark agreed. "Wish it was the fun kind."

"No doubt! If they move me back to my store, I won't have time to prepare for Christmas, and you *know* they are expecting miracles."

"Of course, they are! But in their defense, you are a miracle worker."

"If you say so, Clark."

The day slowly drifted into darkness as we complained about evil corporations and Clark interrogated me about my mysterious encounter with Lance. Clark couldn't understand why I enjoyed the mystery of never hearing from the man again.

Even though my future hung in the balance, I smiled for the rest of the day. For once, things had been on my terms. I had drifted into autopilot, yes. But I always had, so it didn't matter. That night, I drove home, trying to hide my elation. I didn't want Matt to know anything. He had a knack for finding people. He would track down the guy, and I didn't want that to happen. I liked the way things ended—without obligation.

Before heading home, I pulled into the parking lot of my baby store. The staff had placed teddy bears in the window with a handwritten sign about charity. In the window, I saw a card table they had used to sit outside, and I smiled, knowing that without a manager, they were trying. I dreamed of the store being mine as it always should have been.

I imagined walking through the door again, but this time, the manager's chair would be mine. I wouldn't be borrowing it anymore. *I* would be the authority. I wanted to make donations to local charities, decorate for Christmas, and show my employees how they should be treated. I wanted that store to be a place of refuge and second chances. The people of Gallipolis deserved it, and nobody would be as passionate as I was about helping them.

* * *

138

The next week went by slowly. They were starting to clean out our back room, and the customers were gone. The customers thought we were already closed because of the darkness of the store. The tension was becoming too much as the days crept by.

Clustered together at the bridal counter, my co-workers and I propped our phones up, listening to our favorite songs. It was one of the few places still lit, so we gathered like moths. Our store filled with laughter as we sang along to the craziest music we could find.

"You know we're going to miss you, Sheila," Clark interrupted.

"If I ever leave." I laughed. "I wish I could take you guys with me. It's not going to be the same without you."

"Of course not, 'cause we're awesome!"

"I think they're going to screw me over. Annette is already at her new store. Gallipolis is sitting there without a manager."

"He needs to get off his ass. This isn't right. They moved Kara out immediately after they announced the store was closing. It's been months."

"I feel bad for wanting to leave you guys."

"Why? We know that's why you came here. We love you and want what's best for you," Clark encouraged me. "I don't know how you have managed to do it this long. That is a hell of a drive every day."

"I never thought it could be like this. I love you guys so much that it feels wrong to leave you behind."

"You have to, though."

"Look at us. I haven't heard anything, and still, we sit here acting like I'm going to leave. What if I don't? What if they fire me? What if they don't know what to do with me after this? I feel lost. You guys all know where you're going. I talked to the other managers and made sure you have jobs after this. But I'm hanging in limbo, waiting."

"If you don't get to go home after everything you've done for us, we'll raise some serious hell. I've never seen them make someone do as much training as they have you."

"I know. Nobody else has done everything I have, and sadly, I can prove it."

"That's because you're not flirting with him. You're not the typical skinny girl."

"Maybe. He always looks at me weird when he gives all the other managers hugs but I shake his hand. Sometimes, I think he uses his looks and flirts with them to keep them obedient. You should have seen the way Annette hung on his every word. I thought it was just her until I met Kara."

"I never thought he was good-looking," Clark opined. "That shit doesn't work on me, sorry. I don't see it."

"I kinda can, but I never cared about any of that. He's my boss, and I want to earn my promotion because I'm good at my job, not because I was willing to sleep with him. You know, people have reported plenty of affairs and sexual harassment, but they can never prove it."

"That doesn't surprise me at all."

"That's what makes me think this is the end for me. It's been too long, and he's silent. I wish it wasn't up to him. I hope someone notices that I'm running things well down here and that we're making our goals. I think I've done enough to prove myself."

"I got it," Clark said as the phone rang. "Sheila, it's for you. It's the district manager. I hope they can't hear us through the cameras."

"I'm sure they can't. Even if that was possible, I'm sure it's broken like everything else." My hand trembled as I reached for the phone. Looking back at my team, they stared wide-eyed, waiting and hoping. The store was silent as the lights flickered above and the mall bustled around us.

"Hey, Sheila, we need to talk," the district manager greeted me. "I have a few questions. As you know, you applied for the store manager position in Gallipolis."

"Yes." My voice shook as I answered him. With panicked eyes, I looked back at my team. They were leaning over the edge of the counter—not sitting, not standing—waiting for an indication as to why the district manager called. Shaking my head, I looked away again, waiting for his next words.

"I'm concerned that you might not be ready."

"Why would you think that?"

140

"You've only been with the company for a year, and nobody is promoted that quickly. But you have done the training. And you've worked hard in Charleston, and we appreciate that. Can you think of any reason that I shouldn't give you the position?"

"No, sir. I've done everything I can to prepare myself. I'm acting store manager now, and when they need something in Gallipolis, they call me."

"I realize that, but what will you do if you have a question or get stuck on something?"

"I'll call Annette or the other store manager down here. I have a good relationship with them, and I know they'll help."

"Ok, so you're sure you can handle this?"

"Absolutely. I think I've grown as much as I can down here, and I would like to come home before winter hits."

"I understand. So, if you think you're ready, then I would like to offer you the position. I would like you to start back in Gallipolis as the store manager on Sunday."

"Okay, I'll be there."

"Don't disappoint me."

Looking back at my team, I smiled. Rushing toward me, they gathered around, swarming me with hugs. I was speechless. *I finally made it!* Still, I knew I wouldn't be with them long, and the idea of a new team was frightening.

That night, I stopped in front of the Gallipolis store, stared in the window, and cried. I was excited for it to be mine as it always should've been and happy to see Meg in her new role. My district manager had called again, asking whether Meg should be promoted to assistant manager. She'd been calling me since Annette left, so I pushed for her promotion. Everything had changed in Gallipolis, but my heart hadn't left. Still, I knew I hated leaving my Charleston family behind.

I remember my first day as store manager. As was customary, I waited outside for another employee to arrive. We were never allowed to enter the store alone, for our own safety. Sunday was our shortest day, so I made a slim schedule—just Meg and me. We needed to discuss our ideas, and she could update me on the other employees. I decided to watch the store in action for a week before having our first meeting. A week wasn't much time to prepare and strategize for the holiday season.

Walking through the double glass door, my eyes rested on the manager's chair. Holding my head high, I pulled my shoulders back and walked toward it. Each step echoed in my mind like the seconds of a clock ticking. Setting my purse on the floor beside the chair, I ran my hand across the back of the chair and glanced down at the computer as I slowly lowered myself into position. Closing my eyes, I leaned my head against the back of the chair and sighed. *Finally!*

Chapter 15

"DID YOU MAKE a new Craigslist ad since you're back in Gallipolis?" Matt asked.

"No, I hadn't thought about it. I've been busy trying to get the store ready for Christmas. That takes a lot of planning."

"Are all your men going to follow you up here then?"

"What do you mean 'all my men?' I told you I only met that pastor. I don't want to date a bunch of guys."

"Maybe you should. You obviously can. I hardly get any messages. I met up with one girl in town, but she didn't want to hang out again because I didn't take my wedding ring off."

"You *are* telling them you're married, aren't you?"

"No, nobody talks to me if I do. I keep telling them I just want to be friends."

"That doesn't make sense to me. I'd think girls would be excited for a guy friend."

"Well, I asked if she wanted a kiss and if I could go back to her house. That's not a big deal, right? I figured out where she lives from her social media pictures. I drove by a few times, hoping to catch her there alone, but there was always an extra car in the driveway."

That's the opposite of being a friend. No wonder she didn't want to meet up again. Watching chips fall from the corner of Matt's mouth, my heart sank as he stared at the TV. He snacked mindlessly with his leg propped up, bouncing his foot. *He doesn't care how I feel, does he?*

"Matt, is this what you want? I'm home more now. I thought maybe we should focus on us for a while."

143

"Why? Are you afraid you might like it too much?"

"No, I thought you'd want to spend more time with me. You kept saying the open marriage was because you're lonely."

"I *am* lonely. You don't call, and I don't see you. It doesn't matter where you're working."

"What do you mean? I have a store to run. I have huge goals for Christmas. I have to get to know the team and hire a couple of new employees for the holidays. I have a lot on my plate."

"That's why we're in this situation. You have a better chance at finding someone to hang out with than I do."

"But how am I supposed to do that? If I spend our money on men, how would you take girls out without any money?"

"We are a team, aren't we? I watch Terra so you can work. So, the way I see it, part of that money is mine."

So, your plan is to take the money I earn working fifty hours a week and spend it on other women? I'm going to be paying for your dates? How is that fair?

Matt hadn't looked at me, and I knew he was lying about not getting dates because his phone was continuously lighting up with notifications. As always, it was on silent, and if I questioned him, his voice would raise and tell me how unfair it was that I got more messages than him. Yet my phone sat quietly with the ringer on in case an employee called. I didn't have the luxury of a silent phone.

"I guess I can do another ad if that's what you think I should do," I reluctantly offered.

"Yes, definitely. I'm curious to see who talks to you."

Pulling the laptop toward me, I found the section of Craigslist where I placed all my ads. After staring at it for a moment, I glanced up at Matt and knew exactly what to write. I talked about being busy, successful, and how I didn't need a man's money. I was looking for a friend to enjoy my free time with. I wanted a relationship where cuddling was common, and I mentioned how much I missed being kissed. Handing the phone to Matt for approval, he skimmed over my words and submitted it.

"You don't want to include any pictures? Maybe some nudes or

144

something? I'm sure you have a few."

"That's not what I'm looking for," I replied.

"Are you sure? Most girls have nudes on Craigslist. You probably won't get many responses without them."

I hope you're right.

The more he spoke and the more he did, the farther I drifted. I missed Charleston—the people, the atmosphere, and the unpredictability. It was impossible to guess the depth of conversations that could be had so far from home. While our town had its charms, we didn't have conventions full of different people every day. Our little town was predictable in a comfortable but boring way. Most importantly, the odds of me finding a man to enjoy life with—one who was caring, musical, respected my opinions, and loved intellectual conversations—was impossible. And I wasn't sure I was interested in a relationship—*any* relationship—anyway.

I missed my friends. I was only existing. I barely knew my team at the store, and Terra was in bed when I got home. I was out of my element, and as I sat watching my husband flirt with other women, I wished I was at work. Watching chips fall to his sweatpants, I wanted a divorce more than ever. As much as I wanted to cry, to cleanse myself of the pain that was building within, I couldn't.

"Did you get any replies yet?" That was the first thing Matt asked the next morning as I stumbled to my coffee. I just rolled my eyes as I noticed his clean clothes and brushed hair. Grabbing my cup, I curled up on the sofa, avoiding my phone.

"I haven't looked, Matt. I just woke up."

"You better check! You never know. Prince charming could have messaged you." He laughed.

"Pretty sure prince charming doesn't exist. Don't worry, I'll check it later. I'm not exactly in a hurry."

"Hey, can I get twenty bucks?"

I wonder who's going to be enjoying my husband and my hard-earned money today. "Get it out of my purse."

Hanging my head, I quietly sipped my coffee as Matt pranced like a dog in heat. *At least I didn't wake up with his penis in my face again.*

Sipping my coffee, I distracted myself with my mental to-do list. I didn't have much planned, but I needed a distraction. I was used to leaving early for the long drive to Charleston, and now, all I had was time. With cup in hand, I headed for the bedroom, trying to decide what to wear for another twelve-hour shift.

"Are you leaving early, Sheila?"

"Yeah, I think I'll get breakfast and take it to the girls." *Anything is better than being here.*

I must have arrived at the store an hour early that day. It didn't take long to get dressed and run out the door with my makeup and hairbrush in hand. So, there I sat, staring at the glass windows of my store, wondering what the day would bring. At that hour, there weren't many cars driving by, only those belonging to managers in neighboring stores. With the windows rolled up, I laid my head back and closed my eyes, dreaming of the center court in the Charleston mall and all of its interesting people. When my phone blinked, I quickly checked my email, only to see one with two words in the subject: *Craigslist, Teddy.*

Teddy?! No! It can't be. Dropping my phone on the floor, I bent forward to grab it, knocking my head on the steering wheel. My hands shaking, I opened the message. Scanning over the picture of my former boss, I froze.

You sound perfect for me. I live in Gallipolis, so we are close, and I work all the time too. I would love to find a friend who I could kiss. Don't worry; I'm not your typical guy from around here. I'm not from here at all, in fact. And I'm recently divorced. I would love to meet you. I hope to hear from you soon.

—Teddy

That's right; he doesn't know who I am. It's anonymous, and I didn't include any pictures. OH MY GOD! TEDDY?! DIVORCED?! I thought they were happy?!

I messaged Teddy back, teasing that I knew him and that once he saw my picture, he would want to have lunch. The store buzzed with speculation as my employees tried to guess the identity of my date, but

I kept it hidden. Remembering my anonymous night in Charleston, I felt empowered. *I don't have to do anything I don't want to do. I'm better than that. Teddy is just an old friend, and I don't have to lie about that.*

My lunch date with Teddy went well. It was simple. Together, we sat watching the river in the front seat of his car. We talked about The Outlet, Meg, and how I had given her and several others from The Outlet a second chance. Teddy took several old co-workers with him to his new workplace, where he, too, was a store manager. We discussed business, employee gossip, and other old co-workers. This was the one time being from a small town came in handy. Together, we had inside information about most of our applicants, so we knew who would be a good employee and who wouldn't.

My visit with Teddy ended with only a friendly hug. When I pulled into my parking spot at work, a familiar car loomed at the edge of the lot. Entering the store, I checked work phone messages, and I got updates on what had occurred during my absence before I sat in the manager's chair and waited for my phone to alert me.

Where have you been? I thought you never leave the store? Matt texted.

I went to lunch with a friend.

I thought you didn't have any friends here.

I have a couple. Besides, things are different now.

Things are never different, Sheila. People don't change. Who was it?

It was Teddy, my old boss. We talked about my promotion and The Outlet mostly. It gave us a chance to discuss some of our job applicants. It was nice.

You said you weren't talking to anyone. Why did you lie to me?

I'm not lying. Teddy messaged me this morning. It was a spontaneous thing.

You're not spontaneous.

That's not true, Matt.

I don't appreciate you lying to me. Come outside. I'm going to pull up.

But Matt, I'm busy.

As I sent the last message, Matt pulled in front of the store. My stomach churned as his eyes searched me through the glass. Revving his engine, he tapped the side of the car and beeped the horn from the edge of the sidewalk. Running to the doors of the store, I stepped outside.

"What is wrong with you?! I'm at work! You can't act like that. This is my job—the job that keeps you fed and a roof over your head. What is your problem?"

"What do you mean 'what's my problem?' I'm not the one who lied last night."

"Really? Then why are you out? Did you have a date?"

"Yeah, I did. And I look over and see you in some guy's car. I told you about my date last night."

"No, you didn't because I didn't ask. But I could tell by how you were acting. I thought you wanted me to go out?"

"Yeah, but I have to know who and when. You don't lie to me anymore, ok?"

"I didn't lie to you! And why do I have to tell you everything? That's not how you wanted this to work, remember?"

Turning around, I pulled my head up, swung the store's door open, and headed back inside. I didn't look back as I walked. I stared straight ahead. I knew he was there, but if I ignored him long enough, I knew he would eventually leave.

"Meg, ask me something and act like it's important," I directed her.

"Sure thing." Meg laughed. "What's his problem?"

"I don't know. I just had lunch with a friend. He does stuff like this all the time."

"Matt wants the open relationship for himself, not for you. He wants to keep control."

"That's not going to happen. I'm done with being controlled."

"I'm telling you, Sheila, he wants to be able to do whatever he wants. If he was okay with you doing it, he wouldn't spy on you all the time."

"I know, but he keeps pushing me to write ads and meet guys, then he gets mad about it. He makes no sense."

Together, Meg and I kept busy. She brought me paperwork to look at and talked with me until Matt was gone. After a while, Matt messaged again, and I pretended not to see it, knowing that no matter what I said, I'd have to face him. That was the slowest I ever closed the store.

As I left work, I stopped at McDonald's, making sure to buy Matt more food than usual. The longer he ate, the less he accused me of lying. As I laid on my pillow that night, letting the softness ease my tired muscles, my eyes closed. Hearing a metal zipper, my eyes shot open. Matt's fist snatched my hair, and as pain shot through my body, he jabbed the back of my throat with his cock. Gasping for air, I tried to scream, but Matt's grip only intensified with the force of his jabs. Spreading my body apart with his, I felt my delicate flesh tear against his hard cock as he ripped up my nightgown and thrust into my flesh.

Thank God for autopilot.

As the sun rose on the concrete sidewalk the next morning, I ran my fingers through my hair, combing out the remaining tangles from the night before. Watching my reflection in the mirror, I noticed that red rims had become my permanent makeup. My cheeks were swollen, and pain shot through my legs as I sucked on a new batch of cough drops. My stomach gurgled as I stared at the breakfast sandwich in the bag beside me.

I watched the world spinning by as people started their days with smiles and confidence. With a slow sip of coffee that I didn't taste, I imagined what life was like for them. They had a home, a safe place to go, peace, and love.

Love doesn't exist. Isn't Matt supposed to love me? If this is what he calls love, it's not for me. I want out. I want to feel safe. I keep hearing stories on the news of what happens to the wives of angry men. It doesn't end well. One of these days, his fist is going to miss the wall and hit my head. He brought home a gun from his mom's. Why did he have to do that when I asked him not to? I grew up around guns, but I don't know what he's capable of.

I keep giving Matt what he wants, and I never get anything in return. He thinks it's a huge thing for him to make me a cup of coffee in the morning. I wish he would at least bring me lunch occasionally. Is that so much to ask? A trip through the drive-through? To bring me a bottle of water INSIDE the store rather than making me stop in the middle of a sale to come out when he shows up after I beg him, and it's convenient because he was already there spying on me?

When Meg arrived to help me open, my sadness had turned to anger. I was quiet that first hour as diamonds were placed, ready to be discovered by new brides. I spent my day arranging them, magnifying them, and creating unique mixes of bands and engagement rings. I mixed gemstones and diamonds, white gold with rose gold, and tried enhancers with vintage-style rings. It was my favorite part of the job. When I was lonely, I spent hours designing, creating, and . . . dreaming.

Every day, I heard a new love story. There was the unexpected reuniting of old friends, the work buddies, and the ex-lovers. I loved when a man would come in to buy a gift for his wife. They were always looking for something special. After a while, it was sad because when their moment was over, and they left with their newest treasure, I knew I wouldn't get the same treatment from Matt.

I didn't want my marriage to fail, but it was impossible to think of things we could do together. We had no common interests, and I was always the one compromising, learning about things Matt loved. I had abandoned many of my passions, and that day, I remembered them. I missed photography, writing, and music. *Maybe I should buy a key-*

board. I would love to play one again. Or maybe I should pick up the novel I started writing.

As the day drew on, my thoughts drifted through the corridors of my mind—ideas of leaving Matt, and then hopes for renewing our marriage. I knew the man I had known was buried somewhere in his body. I only needed to find him again. Staring at diamonds sparkling in the case, I dreamed of feeling loved, cherished, and appreciated.

I was left with a lot of time to myself that evening. It was quiet, and my newest trainee was busy studying the assignments I had given. It was my third day as the new store manager, and I was already tired of quiet days.

As darkness fell in the mid-November sky, I watched cars fade into the night. It was the part of the evening where you watch the clock, ready to start packing away cases and cleaning glass. Still, I waited, not wanting to move because closing the store only meant I had to go home.

As the glass door opened, I launched to my feet, ready to greet the unexpected late-night guest. My head spun as I tried to focus my eyes on him. He was unlike any man I had encountered in Gallipolis. His thick gray and blond hair and unique way of walking were intriguing. His clothes were neat, and his button-up shirt was open enough for me to see the chain that hung around his neck. *He's handsome, and . . . What is he doing HERE? Probably from out of town, looking for a last-minute engagement ring. That's what always happens.*

"Good evening. How can I help you?" I asked in the customary way.

"Oh, I'm just looking. How are you?"

"I'm okay. It's been a long day, quiet. Are you looking for anything in particular? Shopping for your wife? Girlfriend? Both?" I laughed.

"No, I don't have time for that kind of drama."

"Oh? Okay, who are you shopping for?"

"I wanted to see if there's anything my daughter would like. I'm trying to teach her how a girl should be treated. I'm hoping that if I show her, then she won't accept anything less. A girl should feel important and cherished, and I want that for her."

"Okay, I can help you with that. Do you know her birthstone?"

"Yes, it's a blue topaz—December."

You have GOT to be kidding me? Is this guy real? Someone PINCH me! Leaning over the case of aqua blue stones, I placed my key in the lock and looked into his eyes. As he stared out from a sea of blue, I felt his warmth and saw what lay beneath his smile. I quickly looked back to the necklaces that lay between us. "That's not something I normally hear," I informed him.

"People don't buy stuff for their daughters?"

"No, not really. Only around holidays, birthdays . . . stuff like that. Are you looking for something for Christmas, maybe?"

"No, like I said, I want to see if there's something she'd like now. I bought tickets to the symphony, and I'm going to get her hair and nails done. I got her a new dress, and I thought maybe a necklace would be a nice finishing touch. I want her to feel like a princess."

I must have fallen asleep at the counter. I'm dreaming—that's the only explanation. This guy can't be real. "I've never heard of anyone doing that."

"You see, that's the problem. People don't appreciate each other. I want to show my daughter that relationships are supposed to be equal, even though they never are. There needs to be respect. That's why I don't have a girlfriend, too much drama. Too many people lying and not being themselves, and then years later, you discover that you don't even know the person you're with. Sometimes, *they* don't even know who they are. I will never get into another relationship. Every woman I've been with has screwed me over. That's why so many people are damaged. That's why I decided to go back to school. I'm studying psychology. I want to be a doctor so I can help people."

Staring into his eyes, I listened to more than his words. I watched how his lips moved, how his eyes grew softer as he spoke about wanting to help people, and how he watched his feet when he talked about how people lied about who they were. He talked about depression and trauma and how people hid their true selves. And I remembered my own pain—how unworthy I felt and how desperate I was for change. I longed for the idea of someone respecting and loving me enough to buy me jewelry just once. But I knew it wasn't worth it. When Matt and I had first started dating, he bought me food, drinks—little things that I needed. I missed that. Now, he was a different man.

"Sooo, what do you do if you give everything you can in a relationship, and they don't give anything in return?" I asked the man. "I work long hours and try to cook and clean on my days off. I get tired, and it doesn't feel like he notices. He just stays home."

"Honestly, you need to get out of the relationship. He's going to keep draining you until you reach a breaking point. Nobody can take that. Eventually, you'll snap."

"I don't think it's as easy as that."

"Well, everyone is different, but my advice is to get out."

After that, we looked at necklaces for a while until he found the perfect one to match his daughter's dress. He showed me pictures and told me about the date he planned for her. I was jealous, wishing someone would do something like that for me, even once. He had no idea that he was educating me as much as I was educating him. Yet, he denied women, stating how they all lied to him, caused drama, and weren't worth it. Honestly, he sounded the way I felt, and his sincere compassion captured my attention.

For a moment, as I talked with this man, my thoughts wandered, forgetting his denial and hatred for women. My heart saw his, and as I looked up at this man—who entered my store at closing, on my third day as manager, in Gallipolis where intellectual conversations never happen—I felt something.

"So, what's your name? I'm Sheila, by the way."

"I'm Michael."

"I'm glad you came in. I enjoy talking to you. Maybe you can stop by sometimes, and we can talk. You can never have too many friends, right?"

"I'd like that." He smiled.

Chapter 16

"WHO IS THIS GUY that keeps texting you?" Matt asked. "I'm not sure," I replied from the kitchen. "I haven't been paying attention to it. I was trying to make sure we have everything for Terra and me to bake something tonight."

"Well, maybe that's why you don't have anyone. It's because you ignore them."

"Maybe. You can check it if you want."

"Let me see . . ." Matt mumbled, scanning through my messages. "Are you sure you don't have anything to hide?"

"Yeah, why?"

Slamming down my phone, Matt stomped into the kitchen, his face stopping an inch from mine. I closed my eyes, waiting for the blow that was coming. I felt his breath against my forehead as his hands gripped my shoulders and forced me back against the counter. The wood dug into my back. As pain shot through my spine, I whimpered, clinging to the edge, trying to push myself away from the wood stabbing my back.

"The message didn't have a name, and it said he couldn't wait to fuck you again. That's literally what it said. Why are you lying to me? I thought you said you didn't have anyone following you and that you only had lunch with a friend. It doesn't sound like a friend to me. If you have time to fuck other people, maybe I should come to work and fuck you there. Maybe I should shove my cock down your lying throat," Matt screamed as his hand snatched my throat, tossing me toward the island.

"I don't know who it is. I don't know what you're talking about. I

154

didn't lie to you, I swear!"

"You're a liar. You need to stop lying to me."

Matt's face twisted into a growl, and he reached his hands to the bottom of my dress and lifted it up to my waist. Ripping my panties down, he shoved my face into the hard tile. His hand pushed against my neck as I heard his pants hit the ground and felt pain as he tore his way inside me. Closing my eyes, I froze, waiting.

"You need to tell me who that is. If you lie to me, you'll pay. Do you understand?"

"Yes, yes . . . I understand," I whimpered.

"Good! Now tell me who it was."

"I don't know, I'm sorry. I haven't talked to anyone other than Teddy, and it's not like that. We didn't even hold hands or kiss or anything. He wouldn't message me like that."

"You better find out, or I will make sure you can't go to work tomorrow."

"Okay, then let me go so I can."

"*NO!* Here, why don't you call him while I'm fucking you? Let him know what he's missing."

"You're hurting me! Why do you keep doing this to me?!"

"Shut up, Sheila! You're mine. I can do whatever I want with you. Do you want me to go harder?"

Matt's thrusts grew fiercer, and my arms burned as I held myself away from the counter, bracing against his thrusts. *I'm so tired of this. I can't take it anymore! He vowed to protect and cherish.*

Thank God for autopilot.

As soon as Matt was done, I grabbed my panties and headed toward my phone, texting the number. It didn't take me long to receive a reply. It was Pastor Ram, begging to see me. He wanted me to visit him if I could get away from my new job. He heard about it from Clark when he'd stopped by. It didn't say he wanted to do anything to me, just that he wanted to see me. Matt read it too quickly or read it wrong; I'm not sure which. But I replied and let Ram know that I didn't have time. He would have to come to me. Then, I read the messages to Matt, who grabbed my phone, not trusting me to tell him the truth.

"Well, you got what you deserved, and I feel better now," Matt replied smugly.

"What? Did some girl lead you on and not let you screw her?"

"No, I'm not trying to screw anyone."

"Oh, really? Is that why you used my money to buy condoms?"

"Whatever."

Heading to the restroom, I wiped myself clean as I waited for Terra to return from school. *I don't say anything when someone texts him, or sees him, or calls him. Why does he keep treating me this way and then getting mad when I do exactly what he tells me to do? What's wrong with him?*

When Terra came through the door, my spirits lifted. I only saw her a couple days a week, and I missed her. As she got older, she loved to bake. I found the perfect cookie recipe for us to try. We were going to make homemade chocolate chip cookie sandwiches with icing in the middle. From the pictures in Terra's recipe book, they looked delicious, and I had everything waiting on the counter.

"Mom, you're home!" Terra laughed, tossing her bookbag to the floor.

"Yes, *thank God*!" I laughed as Matt turned on the TV, ignoring us. "I found us the perfect recipe. It's been a while since we baked, and I know Daddy will love them. Do you want to see what we're going to bake, Matt?"

"No, not really. I don't care. I was going to get on my game," Matt replied, staring at his phone.

"Are you sure you don't want to help, honey?" I answered, trying to forget the pain. "I'm sure Terra would love for you to help."

"Yes, Dad, I would love that. We don't do anything together anymore," Terra agreed.

"No, I'm fine. Thank you."

Flour flew in the air as the mixer revved its tiny motor, and ingredients were added one by one. Hugging Terra, I took a spot of cookie dough and placed it on her nose as she prepared the five cookie sheets that I had waiting. The years had flown by, and she wasn't a little girl anymore. But when we were baking, she was still my little princess, dancing in the kitchen to the silliest songs we could find.

"Do you want to make the icing now or wait until they're out?" I asked.

"Hmmm . . . let's wait, so it's fresher."

"Okay, if that's what you want. Do you want to try to make it on your own this time?"

"Yes, Mom!"

"Awesome. Sooo, how's school? Any new friends, boyfriends, gossip?"

"Not really. Everyone is getting boyfriends, and I don't like anyone. They're all immature."

"Well, honey, they are boys! What do you expect?"

"I want someone smart who can make me laugh. Apparently, that's a lot to ask."

"I don't know. Maybe it is."

"Anyway, I don't want to talk about that. Let's just bake."

As we finished the cookies, Terra headed to her room and wouldn't come out for dinner. Every time I checked on her, she was buried in her laptop, saying she had schoolwork. As she often did, she looked at me with a grimace, and instead of asking for a "new daddy," she simply asked, "When are you getting a divorce?" I was truthful. I told her I didn't know how to get away from Matt. Terra never understood how afraid I was, especially since he brought a gun into our home. I didn't want to make him angry, and I was afraid to touch the gun or even know where it was because what if *I* got too angry?

As we prepared for bed, Matt grabbed my phone and started going through it as I laid down, counting ceiling tiles. He sighed a few times and then handed it back to me.

"When are you and Teddy going out again?"

"I don't know. Maybe next week. I think we have the same day off."

"Make sure you do. You need to go out on dates, and you said you didn't want to see the pastor again. Maybe you should tell him."

"I'm trying to ignore him. When I get random weird messages, I don't answer them. Normally, people go away. It's like an unspoken rule. Besides, he's married and won't come after me."

"Do you want me to contact him?"

"No, not really. I don't want it to be like Trenton. That wasn't fair. He was a friend. He wasn't a threat to you, and yes, I flirted with him and said things I didn't mean, but I could talk to him. He understood me, and you had to take away the one person who listened to me. I'm not going to forgive you for that. I was heartbroken, and you didn't even notice. We've been together long enough for you to be able to see when I'm hurting. It's not rocket science."

"Those are harsh words coming from you."

"Well, it's the truth. I always tell the truth, and all you think I do is lie."

"I didn't mean to hurt you when I got rid of him. I was trying to help our marriage."

"Yeah, right."

"What?! I'm sorry."

"Is that all you're sorry for?"

"Yeah, what else would I be sorry for? I wake you up for work in the mornings, I make you coffee, and I stay home and watch Terra. I treat you good, Sheila. What else would I have to apologize for?" Matt answered.

He doesn't think he's doing anything wrong. How can he rape me and push me against walls and not think he did anything wrong? Did I teach him that I like to be treated that way? What did I do to make him do this to me?

* * *

The clock pounded in my head. Its ticking grew louder as I stared blankly at the manager's computer. I had moments before the day would begin—moments to figure out what I wanted to check off my to-do list and prioritize for the day. My mind wandered through the last few days—well, years if I'm being honest.

"Meg?" I asked, staring at the screen.

"Yeah," she answered.

"Why aren't you a diamontologist yet?"

"Annette never brought it up. Why?"

"You're technically not supposed to be behind the diamond counter without it. It helps you learn more about diamonds. I want you to get that as soon as possible. Actually, I'm going to enroll a few of you. I want you to be able to answer questions without me. I can't be everywhere at once, and I don't want you to get in trouble with the district manager. If there's an engagement ring sold, there has to be a diamontologist on the sale. That might be why Annette's numbers were so high."

"That makes sense. She didn't allow anyone to have a bridal sale by themselves."

"Yeah, that's why," I agreed. "She should've offered you the training."

"I understand why she didn't." Meg laughed.

"Yeah, I don't want to be like that. So, I'm going to get you enrolled. And let's have a Christmas party for the team. We can hang stockings and do a gift exchange. What do you think?"

"*Yes!* That's a great idea!" Meg agreed.

"I want to decorate, too. I want this place to be warm and welcoming, like coming home," I said, even though coming home was not like that for me.

Smiling, Meg unlocked the doors and joined me at my desk as we planned how to decorate the store. I had seen a black tree and was desperate to have it. It was different and would make a great accent against the jewelry in the store. Within moments, we decided on a black and silver theme, and we both donated to our first group fund.

As my next employee arrived, I gathered the money and headed out for supplies. I felt like I was dancing on clouds as I stepped into Christmas decorations with thoughts of employee parties and stockings stuffed throughout the store. The team would be together at the store constantly over the next few weeks—sometimes, more than we were with our families—and I wanted it to be as enjoyable as possible. I wanted pictures, greeting cards, lights, stockings, and as much love in our store as I could provide. The store was my safe place, and I wanted my employees and customers to feel loved.

My heart danced as I picked up the box containing the black Christmas tree and placed it in the cart. Then, as I rounded the corner, I heard a loud thud and felt a large jolt as my cart crashed into a stand of Christmas lights.

"I didn't know you to be this clumsy," Teddy said, laughing.

"Oh my God, I don't know how I didn't see that!" I grinned. "I guess I was getting a little excited. What are you doing here?"

"I'm getting a tree for my store. What about you?"

"Same, actually. That's why I'm excited. My husband doesn't get into Christmas. It's kinda sad, but I love decorating, so here I am."

"Wow, you're getting them stockings and everything? Shoot, I wouldn't do all that."

"Why?"

"I wouldn't spend the money."

"I don't mind. I enjoy it."

"Of course, you do. You're a nice person. When can we have dinner? I'm off tomorrow."

"I think tomorrow is my early day. I can text you later and let you know something that works."

I almost forgot I was miserable as Christmas songs played their tunes in my head and glittering silver bulbs, diamond ornaments, and lights bounced in my shopping cart. Smiling, I tried to keep the rhythm of my cart's squeaking wheels in time with the beat that rang in my head. Humming to myself, I carried the items through the glass door of my store and headed to the back room. Meg's eyes lit up as I approached. She reminded me of a kid opening a new toy as she watched the promise of Christmas come to life.

Grabbing a new coffee pot from the packages, I quickly made hot cocoa and took it out to the girls. I loved the idea of setting it out on a table in the store for people to take while they waited for one of our team members to become available. It would be a great place to run credit applications. In less than an hour, I transformed our store from stiff to welcoming. And the excitement didn't slow down as I followed through on my promises and decided when we would set up the store's new look. Those few extra items made everyone smile. It was then that I made my first donations to local charity auctions and food drives.

As we prepared to close for the night, I remembered what was waiting at home. I knew that if I were smiling when I came home, Matt would interrogate me. He always wanted to know the reason behind every smile, always assuming it had something to do with another man, and it never did. Once again, I remembered my actual life and not the life I enjoyed while I was at work. I often felt like two different people: one happy, accomplished, and confident while the other was a crumpled rag on the bathroom floor.

"You look sad."

"I'm sorry, I didn't see you come in, Michael," I replied, jumping up from my seat. "What can I help you with?"

"My daughter is getting her nails done, so I thought I'd stop in again and say hi," Michael informed me. "I don't like staying over there. The smell can get bad."

My stomach was in knots as our eyes met. My toes curled in my boots, and I tried to regain my balance as Michael smiled. My hands instantly grabbed my hair and adjusted it from the mess I had tossed it into moments earlier. This time, Michael's green ball cap hid his hair as he glanced my way for an instant. But in that instant, I felt his essence radiate through me like a ray of sunlight, illuminating the shadows I hid inside. *I swear this man can see right through me.*

"Well, I'm glad you stopped by. How did your date with your daughter go?"

"Funny story, actually."

"Oh?"

"Yeah, so she gets ready, and I take two hours figuring out how to curl her hair and fix it for her. I get dressed up, and we head to the theater. I get up to the door, and it's locked. So, I look at the tickets, and guess what . . . I had the wrong date. The concert is actually next week. So, I dragged her out for nothing. I felt like such an idiot."

"Seriously?!"

"Yes. Oh my God, it was awful."

"That sounds like something *I* would do. I am so scatterbrained. Wait, did you say you curled her hair? I didn't know guys do that."

"Well, yeah, why not? She was having trouble, and I wanted to help. Here, let me show you a picture."

His daughter's hair was perfectly curled down her back, with only a few loose strands. Her smile seemed to reach her ears as she stared back at me. Her blue dress sparkled from the camera flash as she held her shoes in a brightly lit bathroom.

"She looks happy. You should be proud."

"I am, except I got the date wrong. So now, I'm going to have to do it all over again. How's it going with your husband?"

"I don't know . . . He says he loves me, but I don't know that I believe him. I've tried talking to him about doing more things together, but he seems to think that means I should play more video games."

"I'm not sure I believe in love. I don't think it's a real emotion."

"What do you mean you 'don't believe in love?'"

"Can you say that love is a real thing? Or is it something that corporations made up to sell chocolates, and flowers, and jewelry?"

"I think love is real. I can't imagine life without love. Isn't that why we're here? To love each other?" I suggested as much to myself as to Michael.

"I don't see how it's real because if it's real, then how can you explain how people treat each other? If it were real, relationships would be equal, but they never are. There's always one person putting in all the work."

"Maybe only one person loves."

"Or maybe they feel obligated, like it's something they have to do to feel normal? Seriously, how would you describe love, Sheila? What is love to you?"

"I don't know. I've never thought about it. But . . . maybe it's not one emotion, maybe it's many."

"How so? What emotions?"

"Ummm . . . maybe trust, respect, adoration, admiration . . ." I trailed off quietly.

"Maybe. But I will *never* get involved in another relationship again.

Never!"

"Why? That's sad. Won't you get lonely?"

"No! Why would I? Women are evil. Nothing good ever comes of a relationship. You get your hopes up, you say you fall in love, and then you give her everything you can. And women? They turn on you. They're like wild animals. Besides, I have enough drama with my daughter. She reminds me every day why I'm not in a relationship."

"Not all women are evil."

"I bet you're evil."

"Why would you say that?"

"Because you're a woman. You can't tell me that you've never done anything bad to a man, that you've never used them or manipulated them into doing what you want."

Just Lance . . . and all the guys I teased at the mall and hid from. That's not really bad, though, is it? "Maybe. I might have."

"*See?!* That's what I'm saying"

"I don't know, Michael. I think men are worse than women—at least, they have been to me. I'm not that bad. I'm human, I have my moments, but I don't think of myself as evil."

"Of course, you don't! That's because you're evil. Listen to me, though: not all men are like that. I think it's gotten that way because nobody cares about anyone but themselves. It's a big problem for me. I care too much."

"I know the feeling. It's sad."

"Yeah, it is. Can you imagine what this world would be like if people did things without getting any personal gain? No rewards, no strings . . . nothing."

Sitting down at my favorite spot behind the engagement rings, I looked up to see a closed-off shell of a man. In his eyes, I saw tenderness and pain, and I understood. In Michael's eyes, I saw a battlefield, and he was there hidden in the rubble, a wounded soldier after defeat. I wanted to hold him in my arms and be a light in his darkness. *What light do I have to give him? Michael doesn't deserve to be hurt anymore. What if I hurt him? What if I AM evil? Matt keeps telling me I'll never be happy with anyone. What if Matt's right?*

"Honestly, I feel weird saying this to you, Michael, but . . . I'm not sure I know how to love. Everyone has this fairy-tale idea stuck in their heads, and I don't think I'm capable of that kind of surrender. I'm doing good to love myself."

"Don't feel weird about it. I get what you're saying. I loved deeply, or that's what I thought it was. When I look back, I think it was obsession, and I know my ex didn't feel the same. I'm never going to go through that again."

"I feel you. I wish I could trust someone and feel that overwhelming sense of belonging. But I don't think it's ever going to happen. I think the best thing for me would just be to have someone around who I could walk through life with. Not someone in front of me and not behind me, but someone to walk beside me, to enjoy life with. We have these great expectations growing up, but really it should be that simple."

"That actually makes sense," Michael acknowledged. "Hard to find, though. Everyone has too much drama and wants to put labels on everything."

My conversation with Michael must have continued for an hour, sometimes serious, sometimes not. Still, I enjoyed Michael's company and hated to see him leave. It seemed like only minutes had passed before he had to return to his daughter, and I had to close the store. It took me a while to stop smiling, but once I got through the drive-through, I had buried the contentment of Christmas decorations and good conversation.

It was hard not to share my excitement for the day with Matt, but it was better not to. The only thing he wanted to know was my plans for seeing Teddy again. It seemed like he wanted to push me into dating when I would have loved the extra time to sit in the tub surrounded by bubbles and a glass of wine. *Heaven forbid I take time for myself or go shopping with Terra.*

* * *

Sitting on the bed before work the next day, I stared blankly at my closet. What do you wear on a date with your ex-boss when your husband is watching? Why am I in this situation?

"Matt, can you help me figure out what to wear?" I asked

"Sure, what are you thinking?"

"I don't want to be too fancy. But it's been a while since I've dressed casual. I'm not sure I remember how." *That sounds ridiculous.* With a sigh, I collapsed on the bed in my work clothes as Matt headed toward my underwear drawer. *Why is that? Where's he heading?*

Thumbing through my vast assortment of satin and lace, Matt pulled out a pink set and threw it at me. "I like this one," he told me.

"Well, I wasn't worried about my underwear. We're only going out for dinner."

"You can do more than that. Might as well."

"Why would I?"

"Why *wouldn't* you? You can do whatever you want, remember?"

"You don't mean that. And besides, maybe I don't want to do anything else."

"I don't care. Just make sure you check in with me."

"Yeah, okay. What should I *actually* wear?" I asked, holding up a couple of skirts.

"Whichever one is shorter," Matt answered while leaving the room.

Throwing a denim skirt in my bag, I slid on my boots and stood, staring at my reflection. I wish I would have been nervous, but I wasn't. It was my early day, and mostly, I looked forward to leaving the store while it was daylight. *This feels weird. I'm not sure I like this.* I leaned up against the wall for a moment, watching Matt smile at his phone, his legs spread out over the loveseat and his sweatpants hanging loosely over his feet. As he looked up, he stared directly at my tall black boots.

"You should go. You don't want to be late." He grimaced.

"Yeah, guess not."

"I love you."

"I love you, too." *That was weird.*

Reaching for the doorknob, I looked back at my husband as he texted another woman. *Please notice me. Tell me I look pretty and that you don't want me to go out tonight. Show me you care, and I will fix everything.* Matt was smiling at his phone as I walked out the door. I pretended not to notice the bulge growing in his pants as I left.

Looking back at the house I had purchased, I remembered the apartment. I'd been supporting us for years. Without Matt, it would be easier. I wouldn't be spending as much on video games. *Maybe he will find someone soon. If Matt doesn't notice me and keeps pushing me to see guys, maybe it's for the best. I need to make sure I have a plan for Terra.*

Work went by slowly that day, and as the clock wound down, I watched for Teddy. I didn't want to change until he arrived, just in case. I was aware—painfully aware—that plans change, and he had spent the day moving into a new apartment, away from his ex-wife. A bunch of guys from Teddy's church had volunteered to help, and then he planned to pick me up for our dinner date. I paced in front of the windows, confused as to what I wanted but excited for a night out that I didn't have to pay for.

"That's weird," Meg announced from the front of the store. "Teddy is out here. He parked beside your vehicle and is sitting there like he's waiting for something."

"Yeah, well, he's kind of here to pick me up."

"*What?!* I thought he was happily married?"

"Not anymore. They finalized the divorce, and he moved into a new apartment. Today, actually."

"And you guys are going out?"

"Yeah, but just as friends . . . I think. We went to lunch a while back. It was hard for us to get our schedules together after that."

Grabbing my bag, I headed for the restroom to change. As I glanced in the mirror, I took a second to try to forget Matt's lack of a reaction that morning. Hoping for the best, I took a second to freshen up my makeup and run my fingers through my hair.

Soon enough, Teddy and I were sitting at a booth sharing retail war stories about goals, deadlines, employees, applicants, and payroll demands. The evening was filled with laughter, and as the conversation turned more personal, I watched Teddy's expression change as his eyes began to wander.

"I never thought we would be going out." Teddy smiled.

"Me neither. But I guess I should have seen it coming." I winked.

"Why would you say that?"

"You treated me a little differently than everyone else."

"Well, if I knew it would have been a possibility, I think our evenings closing The Outlet would have gone a little differently."

"You know, I think you're right. But you were married."

"Aren't you *still* married?"

"Yes and no."

"Does he know you're here with me?"

"Yeah, he picked out my outfit, actually."

"Wow, that's crazy. Tell him I said he did a good job."

"Thanks, I'll let him know. Sooo, how was moving?"

"It went well. The new place looks nice. Do you want to see it?"

"Sure, that would be fun. I'd love to see how you put it together."

Teddy's eyes lit up, and his smile broadened as he scanned my body. A shiver trembled through my heart as he quickly stood. *What did I just agree to? CRAP!* Feeling a little nauseous, I followed him to his car and buckled in. Closing my legs together tightly, I glanced over at him and gripped my phone in my hand.

How's it going? Matt texted.

It's okay. We're running a little behind, but we're going to drive around for a while. He wants to show me his new apartment. He moved in today, so I doubt it's completely set up. He might want my advice.

Are you going to sleep with him?

I don't plan to.

Okay, well, keep your phone close so I know when you're on your way home. Try not to be too late.

I won't be. I have work tomorrow.

The drive to Teddy's place was longer than I expected, and by the time we got there, my stomach had found my throat. *I don't like the way he drives. Thank God I survived.* The stars twinkled brightly from Teddy's upstairs balcony, outside his apartment's front door, as I peered over the edge. The crisp night air eased my nausea as he unlocked the door and ushered me inside. The space was small and clean. A small table sat by the door, a leather loveseat sat in front of a small electric fireplace, and there were no chairs.

"That's cute," I said, gesturing toward the living room.

"Thanks, I don't have much yet. Some of the guys gave me a few things. I guess I don't need much, though."

"No, I think this is nice. Say . . . um . . . where's your restroom?"

As I finished calming my nerves in the restroom, I noticed Teddy's new shower curtain and the same towels I had purchased during my last trip to The Outlet. Feeling their thickness as I washed my hands, I tried to relax. *Teddy hasn't even kissed me yet or even tried to hold my hand. I'm sure everything will be fine. He's not like other guys.*

When I returned, Teddy was leaning back in the loveseat with his arm draped around the back. Soft music was drifting through the room as a candle flickered in the corner. His smile spread quickly across his face as I appeared, and I couldn't resist smiling back.

"Come sit beside me?" he invited.

Uh-oh, be careful.

Sitting on the edge of the loveseat as far from Teddy as I could, I looked over and tried to give him a smile. It didn't take him more than a couple of seconds to make his move. His arm reached down to me, pulling me closer as his lips swallowed mine. His hands gripped my thighs, and I struggled to breathe as he shoved my skirt up to my panties. Pushing them to the side, Teddy's fingers dove between my legs. *What did I get myself into? Why did I trust him? I'm alone, in the middle of nowhere, in his apartment with hardly any cell service. Oh my God, NOT TEDDY! His kisses, his hands . . .*

Cold rushed through my body as Teddy stripped my clothes off and led me to the bedroom. I barely had time to gather my senses before I was laying naked on his bed, with nothing but my boots to defend me. I tried to push away, to free myself from Teddy's powerful kisses, but he was too much for me. He didn't notice and didn't stop kissing me long enough for me to say no. Instead, I laid beneath him as he ravaged my body.

Teddy's strong hands gripped my breasts, and his mouth fiercely ravaged my nipple as he tugged at my body. His hands wrapped around my throat as I lay beneath him, my legs splitting around his waist as my fists dug into his blanket. *I might have wanted this with a little warning. But this man I trusted is just like every other man. If only he had given me more time, more respect, and let a relationship grow. I wasn't expecting this, not from HIM. If only I had known. I'm an idiot—a hopeless idiot.*

Thank God for autopilot.

By the time I made it back to work, I had forgotten how to speak. Staring out the window on the way, I lost myself in the stars. My legs had shivered as Teddy touched me. I had managed to escape his apartment quickly, lying that I needed to help Meg close the store, and he agreed to drive me there. As we pulled in front of my second home, I hopped out and slammed the door behind me. Swinging the glass door open, I headed toward the restroom to catch my breath.

"How did it go?!" Meg asked excitedly.

I stared at her face, then scanned the floor with my eyes. My hands were trembling as I pulled out a chair and sat down, knowing I wouldn't make it to the back of the store without explaining.

"I don't know, not what I expected."

"I thought you would come in all happy and stuff. You guys have a lot in common. I can't imagine it went badly."

"It didn't. I guess I just wasn't expecting him to be so . . . passionate."

"Oh, wow."

"Yeah, I didn't feel prepared—not at all."

"Well, I can tell by the look on his face that Teddy likes you. I'm sure he just surprised you."

"Yeah, he sure did. I'm not sure how I feel about all that."

Of course, I was sure. I knew *exactly* how I felt about it. I liked

Teddy as a friend, maybe more. And even though I was basically single, I hadn't wanted to sleep with him. But I had walked into it. I had been naïve, and that was my fault, not his. I should have told him that I wanted to build a relationship slowly, get to know him, and see what happened from there. I didn't want another lover, another man who only wanted to enjoy my body. I wanted something more, something real. I wanted to feel loved, and that's not what I had felt with Teddy. As I returned home to Matt, I felt the same thing I always did: the icy bitterness of men.

That night, Matt bent me over the bed and shoved my skirt to my waist. Tearing my panties, he ripped into my body. I clung to the mattress, knuckles deep in sheets as my body convulsed beneath him. I buried my face in the comforter, muffling lung-shattering screams. Closing my eyes against the pain, I hid my tears and planned my escape. *Two men in one night. If only I had known. I'm sure Teddy didn't mean to hurt me, but Matt will never stop hurting me.*

That's when I decided to make a trip to the bridge. I would place a letter in my journal and leave it where it would be found. Terra wouldn't miss me. She never saw me anyway. Every day, I told her things would get better, but they never did. Those lies reminded me of what our life had been: pancakes, dance parties, and pillow fights. But now, there was only silence.

I wasn't a mother anymore. Instead, I felt like a slave to my husband, who continuously robbed me. My body ached from the thrusting of men, and my mind was distant, barely functioning as I pretended to be confident and in control at work. I donated, I discounted, and I helped others accomplish the impossible. I spent my moments there, trying to save everyone else as I was drowning in the savagery of my own regret.

With Teddy, I wanted a friend who I could kiss. I wanted someone to make me feel safe, who I would know cared. I thought I saw tenderness in him and that he enjoyed our conversations, but I was wrong. He only saw me as a way to cure his frustrations, if only for a night. It was time to end it. I didn't want to be a rag doll anymore. This was not the life I wanted to live. So, I waited until the next evening, when the weather would be at its coldest, and I headed for the bridge.

The only other person I had anything in common with was Michael, and when my story was over, he would be my only regret—I would regret that I had known him sooner. But his fear of relationships suggested that I would never break through his walls. I wanted to know him, but it seemed too late.

* * *

The next morning, I carefully hid my favorite black satin nightgown in my purse, along with a plastic bag containing my journal. I let Matt know I might be a little late because I wanted to meet with my assistant after work. What I really needed was time to die. If Matt found me climbing the bridge in my nightgown, his fury would be harsher than the icy river. I wanted my last moments to be beautifully uninterrupted, like walking up a glittering runway to my death. I would be surrounded by the sparkle and lights that I had come to love, and diving within the treacherous depths that had captured so many before me would be a beautifully poetic death that only I would see.

As I sat at work that cold December day, I blankly placed new pricing tickets on diamond rings that I would never own, put information cards on necklaces I would never receive, and hung stockings that I would never fill. I knew that even if I stayed, there wouldn't be any gifts for me. There never were. I took comfort in knowing that my life insurance policy would go into a trust fund for Terra and that she would be safe with Tasha. As I stared out the window at snow falling heavily, my phone lit up with a text notification.

Hey, I wanted to check on you after last night, Teddy texted.

I'm okay. Why wouldn't I be? I lied.

I practically raped you. I didn't mean to. All I wanted was to kiss you. I don't know what happened. I'm sorry.

I appreciate the apology.

It's just that it's been a long time since I touched a woman.

Thanks, Teddy, but I'm okay.

Do you need anything? Can I bring you lunch?

No thanks, not this time. I have to go. I shouldn't be texting.

Can I see you again? I want to show you that I'm not all bad.

I never thought you were a bad person. I just wish you hadn't done that. You hurt me. I have bruises on my breasts. I had to hide them from Matt. He doesn't like it if I have marks on me.

Let me make it up to you. I'll text you when I have time.

Placing my phone face down on the diamond case, I again looked out at the falling snow. It was beautiful. The snowflakes were untouched, fresh, and innocent. They hadn't been stained from the touch of men that would trample them with muddy boots and salty tires—not yet. But like me, their beauty would quickly be destroyed by carelessness. *I wish someone would notice me the way I notice snowflakes. Each of them is beautiful, unique. I'm like that in a way—at least, I think I am. Maybe Teddy will make it up to me and prove that it was an accident.*

In my mind, I hoped Teddy could change. *No, if I allow him to use me now, it will only get worse.* As much as I cared about Teddy, I couldn't allow myself the luxury of doubt. Not even with his apology. I had no regrets. It was the perfect night to die.

Looking up at the green bridge, I shivered in the snow. From the bottom, I saw the sidewalk rise into the night. The bridge's lights cast their reflective glitter on the untouched path ahead. It was zero hour . . .

Chapter 17

A S I LOOKED OUT upon a desolate land, I watched what was left of the blue sky turn gray as streaks of red arose from the building in the distance. I saw cages against the walls as beastly men were captured. Their eyes were dark, and their faces contorted in voiceless screams as I watched.

Slowly, blue flames turned to ash as rocks arose from the trembling ground. The black ocean crashed its oil upon broken mirrors of the past, cresting gray against the shore as I hid in the tallest branch of the tree. The rhythm that once echoed through its branches grew silent as vines shrank into the ground, burying themselves in death. What once was wood turned to steel in my hands as the tree gave its final breath. All that was alive had withered, fading into The Gray, and even the screams within my mind turned to deafening silence.

As the smoke calmed, resting upon the ground, heat emerged violently in the silent desolation of The Gray. Sliding from my branch, I reached for the one below it as the tree's branches turned lifeless and scratched against my skin. Slowly, I descended into the ash below. The ocean beckoned me as shards tore my feet. Still, I walked, with my eyes upon the shore. I felt the waves gently beckoning me. The heat that surrounded me felt like a blanket pressing against me like a swaddled baby, and I sat on the edge of the shore.

The mirrors that surrounded me reminded me of the life I had been given. Each one taunted me with the past, with memories of shame and regret flashing before me until my eyes drifted away, locked upon the waves. As the black waves caressed my feet, I laid upon a bed of shattered mirrors and waited for death to finally take me. My body laid flat as the smoke rose around me and the waves reached farther up my body with each moment that passed. The black waters lifted me a little at a time, and I waited to be carried into the depths, to become one with the lost.

I remembered my journey up the icy bridge. The cars that passed threw their splinters of snow and ice on my legs as Christmas lights mocked me from apartments below. The smiles of happy couples flashed before me as I laid in the smothering heat of The Gray. My body rested on the splintered mirror shards as I awaited the fingers of black waves to drag me into the depths. *This is it; it's over. Now, The Gray will take me to my death.*

My tears evaporated quickly as I remembered every time Matt's fist had come close to me and the pain of every thrust that ripped into my flesh. Beneath me, the ground trembled. It quaked as light bolted through the darkness, flashing through my lifeless eyes and resting in the center of the waves. The light hung there, wavering as the black ocean rushed toward it. The light gathered waves like a stone crushing water. Around me, the sands cracked, and then only one mirrored shard remained, playing at my feet.

In the shard, I saw Terra smiling, with her radiant eyes glowing like a lantern in the darkness. Cradling a baby wrapped in pink, she bent down to kiss the plump cheeks of innocence. I smelled baby powder and formula as her tiny fingers wrapped around my pinky. My granddaughter's eyes sparkled as they looked into mine, and it reminded me of Autumn, when life embraced death and then vibrantly prepared for rebirth.

I saw myself laughing, a smile spreading across my face as an ivory veil floated against my lace wedding gown. I saw pink flowers covered in pearls and clear waves dancing with white sand against candlelight and a sunsetting sky. I saw Terra standing beside me, her red hair glowing in the sun as she walked with me toward my chapel in the sand. And in the darkness, I awakened.

As the ocean rushed toward the light, the silence was broken. The darkness vanished against the light that strobed like a newly born sun.

Slowly, the temperature changed around me, and the stench of sulfur faded. As the light bathed me in brilliance, I felt a surge of electricity echo through The Gray. Closing my eyes, I collapsed farther into the ashes as the light screamed, piercing through the darkness . . .

LIVE!

And my heart began to beat again.

* * *

I felt blank as sterile lights bathed me in emptiness. Rough blankets scratched my skin as my eyes drifted open and rested on the hospital curtains that separated me from the world. As my hand twitched around tubes that poked my skin, I felt the blood pressure cuff squeeze my arm. The sound of beeping machines and distant voices seemed like an evil circus against the sharp pain. And then, I felt a shadow behind me.

"What happened?" my voice managed to scratch out in a distorted whisper.

"I was on my way to the store," a muffled voice whispered from behind me. "And I saw the bag at the foot of the bridge. I stopped to see if I could return it to someone. I thought it had fallen out of a truck. I saw your name. Then, I looked up and saw you. If I had been a few minutes later, you would have been . . . gone."

"Where's my husband?"

"I overheard them call him. He sounded angry. He's not coming."

"Asshole."

"Sounded like it."

Turning my head, pain shot through me like a bullet, and my eyes collapsed as I strained to see the face of my rescuer. Then, as I struggled to move, I felt the shadow in front of me. A chair scratched against hard tile as my hand was covered in tender warmth. A thumb comforted my fingers. As my eyes slowly opened, I gasped in shock, and my heart skipped a beat as I saw his crisp button-up shirt, his fingers, and finally . . . his face. *It can't be! HE'S the one who found me?!*

"I'm cold," I scratched out. The only thing that felt alive on my body was the hand that rested in his gentle grip. Pulling the blanket tighter against my body, I looked down to see a plastic bag and the untouched gilded pages of my journal. Looking into his concerned eyes, my face warmed, and for the first time in my life, I knew I was safe. "Thank you . . . Michael."

As he released my hand from his, I reached for him and shuddered as the cold overtook me. *All I said was thank you, is he leaving? I know he's not into relationships, but he just saved me. Where's he going?* Hearing a heavy click behind me, I strained to turn my neck as the bed shook and my blanket tightened around me. Then, there was warmth as Michael's body pressed against mine like an extra blanket. As his arm wrapped around me, I grabbed it and held it close to me. His breath warmed my neck as he cuddled against me. His tenderness spread through my body.

"Does this help?"

"Yes . . . it helps."

I felt hidden tears emerging. They began as only a drop or two but quickly grew as my body shook in Michael's arms. Little tears grew to a sob, and within moments, a raging waterfall of emotions trapped within came crashing through my body like a tidal wave.

I remembered: cinnamon toast for dinner; the kids that tortured Terra; her tears when her bike was stolen; Trenton leaving me yet always coming back; Seth and his so-called friendship; Teddy and his trap; the perverse pastor; waking up to Matt's penis choking me; the way my neck snapped when he threw me on the bed and I wasn't allowed to say "no" or "stop"; the threesome; hearing my husband screw another woman; every moment that I felt trapped; every time Matt yelled at me; the hidden tears; the terror; Matt's fist hitting the wall, inches from my face; holes in doors; and being pushed against the countertop. And I heard Matt's voice screaming through my mind: *You don't matter, you're just here to please me; I want an open marriage; You will never be happy; No man will ever love you like I do; I didn't say that, so you must be crazy; It's your imagination;* and *I will NEVER leave!*

A volcano erupted within me as whimpers became screams. I clung to Michael's hand, my body convulsing as he held me tighter. His hand caressed my arm as I finally released the poison trapped within.

"It's okay, let it out," Michael whispered reassuringly. "I've got you. You're safe."

And I felt his *truth*.

Chapter 18

*Y*OU CAN *be brave. You can be strong. You can stand up for what you believe in. Remember what Michael said: "If you're not happy with your life, change it!" I can do this.*

"You need to find a job, Matt. And we're going to stop this open marriage thing. If you want to be with me and you say you love me, then we need to work on us. I tried to kill myself, and you didn't even visit me at the hospital. This is not the life I want to lead. If things don't get better soon, as in within the next three months, I will file for divorce," I stated firmly.

"What do you mean? I can't get a job. You know I can't! I have anxiety. I can't!" Matt answered, stomping over to where I sat on the sofa.

"You need to get a job. And I'm serious about the divorce. I want to give this a few months, and I'm going to try. We could get therapy, talk things out, and focus on us. If that doesn't work, it's over."

"I don't have anywhere to go! I can't go back to my mom's!"

"Maybe you should ask her. But if you had a job, you could get your own place."

"I love you! I don't want to lose you! Please, just stop!"

"Then let's work on us. If we both focus, we can see if this is worth saving. And if it's not, then that's it. I can't keep living like this. I keep telling you how I feel. I've told you thousands of times, but you act differently for about a week, and then . . . that's it."

"I'm not going to therapy. They will say everything is my fault. They never listen. Stop! None of what you're saying is true. I treat you well, so just stop! I don't want to argue."

"They're not going to say that. They have to be objective and help us figure out how to solve this."

"You can go, but I'm not going. I don't need it. There's nothing wrong with me."

"If I look at some books and articles, will you read them with me?"

"Yeah, but I'm not the crazy one here. You wouldn't be happy without me. You won't be happy with anyone because nothing is ever good enough. You need to stop."

"Then I will be alone. I want the option to be by myself, and you need the freedom to find someone who can love you the way you want to be loved. I may not be able to give you that."

"So, you're not even going to *try* to love me? Did you ever love me?"

"I don't love you the way I want to love you, and I don't think that's fair. I want to be happy with who I am, and if I have to be alone, then I'll be alone."

"I can't imagine you wanting to be alone."

"I want to work on us, Matt. I don't want to give up."

"Okay, fine. Are you done attacking me now? Are you going to stop?"

That night, Matt asked me how to get a job. Thankfully, he had a friend who helped him while I was at work. Within a month, Matt started his first job. He was working midnight shift stocking shelves, which meant I never saw him. We spent a few minutes together in the parking lot before he clocked in, which was the same time that I was leaving work. When I went home on the evenings that he worked, I took showers, ate real food, and spread out on the bed without him rolling over and hitting me with his elbow.

Sometimes, I would sit up all night writing. I made a playlist of songs that reminded me of my journey—songs that made me cry, songs that gave me hope—and I would type well into the night. I loved those moments, that time to express myself. I needed to tell my story, hoping it would help others along their way. Maybe if they saw my journey through The Gray, it would help others. And that's how my first novel began.

On Matt's days off, I cuddled up next to him and rubbed his feet. I watched movies with him and made sure I only answered text messages regarding work. I tried to smile and find the good in him, and for a few weeks, things were different. But my heart was as cold as it had always been. Still, I pushed forward.

I showed Matt articles about codependency, narcissism, and abuse. I talked to him about the different roles people play in relationships. I researched how to fall back in love with someone and how to save your marriage. But with all the discussions I tried to have, Matt always made me feel guilty for my demands. He blamed *me* for our problems, and I believed him.

I believed that I wasn't doing enough. So, I visited my doctor and was put on antidepressants. I convinced myself that I had been experiencing cycles of depression and mania or possibly a midlife crisis. They became the excuses for my indiscretions, and I clung to those ideas. I felt dirty and worthless. Even as I urged Matt to, he never went to therapy, never talked about the articles I sent, and never talked to a doctor about medication. The only difference was that he was happy to go to work, and I was happy to let him.

At first, it was hard not to entertain the guys that came around. Matt and I had both went through the tiring process of deleting our dating accounts and promised to focus on us for a while. There were plenty of men on my social media, and they contacted me when I least expected it. Unlike before, I didn't feel guilty when I said no. My writing routine quickly grew from an occasional distraction to a need. Sometimes, I worked on my first novel with Matt sitting only feet away. Still, I had to be cautious, and although I wanted to write my truth, I only wrote part of it. The rest was how I wished things would have been, and every day, I grew stronger as I left the mistakes from the past in the attic of my mind and on the pages I typed into my laptop.

Teddy contacted me from time to time. He seemed interested in being friends but more interested in my marriage. That's what he always asked about. I enjoyed the occasional lunches and snacks that he would bring by, and his kindness quickly led me to forgive and forget the pain he had caused. Visits from Michael were rare and always turned into deep discussions about relationships.

As the months drew on, I began to enjoy my independent evenings writing through the night. Now that Terra was older and Matt was working at night, I found the extra evening hours to be enough to remember who I had always wanted to be. I grew stronger as a manager, and our store grew. I took more showers and had time to teach Terra how to cook, do laundry, and take care of herself.

When several of my employees passed their diamontology exams, I threw them a party. Sneaking out of the store during lunch, I grabbed a cart and found the biggest chocolate cake in the store. Going through the different designs of paper plates and napkins, I landed on a diva princess theme with bright pink animal prints and crowns. I smiled as I added my party supplies to the cart. I had scheduled a meeting that evening, but my employees had no idea what I was up to.

It didn't take much to watch the minutes tick by as I slowly walked through the store. Then, I saw them: three glittering tiaras with clear rhinestones that sparkled under the lights. *What a beautifully fun surprise for the newly certified girls. They've worked so hard.* My smile turned to laughter as I imagined placing the tiaras on their heads. I made a habit of rewards and fun parties, so my employees were always excited to see what I would come up with. That night was one of the best.

The next year went by quickly, and soon, winter was calling. My baby store had grown into more, and it wasn't the store itself that I mothered and cared for but everyone within it. I had created the first Employee of the Month Award in the district and had named my first winners. Their eyes lit up knowing they were the first to ever receive that honor. Over time, our store became a family. Work wasn't work anymore; it was a safe place where I was respected and loved. Regardless, every evening I tended to drift away. The last few hours were always quiet, a perfect time to reflect. After a long day, I was exhausted, existing somewhere between life at home and a career I loved.

* * *

They danced. Within glass walls, I watched, mesmerized by their grace. I felt the snowflakes twirl in a silent symphony, watched from the nosebleed section of a giant opera house. I couldn't see their intricate details and stunning elegance, but I saw their journey. As water attached to pollen, the life the snowflakes carried was frozen in fractured crystals that dazzled the eyes like the diamonds sleeping in the bridal case. Each unique piece of delicate splendor danced to the concrete below, unaware of their folly. The ground grew silent as I watched from inside the store. The snowflakes' presence absorbed the sound of passing cars like crowds of spectators watching the symphony. They captured an unknowing world.

As the snowflakes continued to dance outside, I stood to greet my sister Tasha. I hadn't been able to see her unless she visited me at the jewelry store. As Christmas grew closer again, I had gone from fifty hours a week to a stunning seventy-two, but that was the life of a store manager. I often joked about putting a bed in the back room to save a little time. After all, what was the point of leaving?

"Hey girl," Tasha greeted me from the door, her usual smile fading as snowflakes followed her inside. "How have you been? You've been quiet lately."

"I don't know, busy, I guess. Trying to work things out with Matt and working, of course," I answered, gesturing to the engagement rings that sparkled like snowflakes on concrete.

"Oh, girl, I feel that." Tasha laughed nervously.

"What's up? You're not yourself."

Sitting down, she pulled out her phone. Sniffling, she looked up at me, her fingers shaking against the screen. Straightening her back, she cleared her throat. "I need you to see this. I couldn't keep it from you. Matt contacted me a few times. I thought it was innocent at first, but then . . . I swear, Sheila, I was trying to be a friend."

Slowly, I glanced at the words below, knowing what rested there. My heart slowed as I read through his flirtations in dated screenshots. Each message worse than the last, I continued until his intentions were not only clear but flashing like a neon sign. Checking the dates again, it was obvious that Matt didn't want to work on our marriage. Even if he hadn't cheated, he had tried.

Unfortunately, Tasha hadn't been the only visitor to inform me of Matt's indiscretions. In fact, she was the fourth in less than a month. After Matt and I had decided to stop our open marriage and focus on saving our relationship, I had received more calls and more proof than ever.

"I'm sorry you had to go through that, Tasha," I said.

"What do you mean *you're* sorry?"

"I don't want anyone to feel uncomfortable, and that's what he's good at."

"What are you going to do?"

"I gave him three months for us to focus on our marriage."

"It doesn't look like he's taking it seriously."

"Obviously not."

As Tasha stepped away, I watched the snowflakes in their folly. They were dancing quickly now, almost leaping to the concrete below. I knew their fate better than they did. Each beautifully unique individual would be lumped together, squashed, and scraped to the sides of the road. Like me, they would be abused. With their beauty only existing for a moment, they would be swept away, unappreciated. Their intricate elegance would be stripped away as the days wore on until they were frozen into chunks of ice. The life they carried with each particle of pollen, dressed like a radiant bride ready to conceive, would turn black to be swept away in sewage drains like abused wives unable to escape the mental torture of bad husbands.

"You always seem so distracted when I visit." Michael laughed, interrupting my thoughts. "Let me guess; I snuck in on you again?"

"Definitely. You have a habit of that." I smiled.

"Nah, you always seem to be deep in thought. I can't say I blame you. What are you thinking about this time? What has your attention?"

"Well, I was watching the snow falling outside, thinking about how something so unique and beautiful will be swept away, soaked with dirt, stomped on, and . . . abused."

"A lot of people are like that, too."

"Yes, they are. I feel that about myself a lot of the time."

"I know you do. I was the one who took you off the bridge only moments before you froze to death. Was that your plan?"

"I wanted to die at first. Then, I realized when I was somewhere else, in something like limbo, that I wanted to live—just not in the life I have been given. I'm tired, Michael."

"I know you are. And you know I'm here whenever you want to talk. Maybe I should always visit you in the evenings. I guess it's lucky that my daughter is looking at puppies tonight."

"*One* of you sure has good timing."

"I am your friend. I want to help. I am a psychology student, after all. Helping is what I do. I'm close to graduating, so think of me as your own personal therapist."

"I can't take advantage of you like that, and I want to do the right thing by my marriage. Although, I know for a fact that Matt doesn't feel the same way."

"You can't control his actions, only how *you* react."

That evening, Michael and I stepped into the snow as he awaited the return of his daughter, who was a few stores away. Together, we considered the snowflakes that fell, not on concrete but on soil. There, they would rest, almost sleeping, and they would never lose their beauty. Hundreds would appreciate their grace. Like a bride cherished, in the spring, the snowflakes' bodies would transform as they gave the precious gift of life. As I watched Michael's hair rescuing snowflakes from meeting the concrete, I smiled.

* * *

"I've discovered something," I stated as I stared at Matt over a cheeseburger that evening. "I've discovered what I wanted out of all of this—the men I've been with, the things that I've allowed."

"So, you're finally going to tell me what you want?" Matt answered, not looking up from his phone.

"Yeah, I guess so. You see, it's simple. I never felt like I was valued or cherished. When we heard weird noises outside or inside, you never went to check on your own. You always asked me to go so you didn't have to get out of bed. That seems like a small thing, but it's not. I wanted you to focus on our marriage, on us, to see if we could love each other the way we should. I've told you for years that I want you to touch me—"

"But I've been doing those things," Matt interrupted.

"No, you just think you have, and that's part of the problem. You can't seem to understand that I don't want to be groped, prodded, and screwed. I want to be touched in a way that makes me feel appreciated. I've looked everywhere for that—for a man who would see me as more than a piece of ass, who would touch me the same way you run your hand over the hood of your car. You wash it, polish it, buff it, and wax it. You touch it gently, examine it, and try to get rid of any flaw you discover. You cherish it like it's the most beautiful thing in the world. You look for ways to make it unique—you look at rims, lowering kits, or special headlights. When you drive it, you drive carefully, only revving the engine when you want to show it off."

"Of course, I love my car. I'm going to take care of it."

"Well, what if you touched me with the same care? What if you looked at me like I was something precious to be cared for? What if I felt important and beautiful? Instead, you ram your cock down my throat until I almost vomit, and you spread my legs open and screw me until I scream. You give me away to strangers. You record me and post it on porn sites without my permission. You even tried inviting over a group of strangers. What made you think I wanted any of that?"

"You always want sex. You always ask me to touch you."

"I want you to touch me like you care about me. Throwing me on the bed or grabbing my breasts for a minute before bending me over the bed or shoving my mouth on your cock is not the same thing as touching me. Pushing my mouth back down on you when I tell you my jaws hurt and you tell me I can't stop is not what I mean by touching me. I have come to realize that I don't care about sex. I need something else. Sex leaves me empty, and I'm tired of it."

"You're crazy. I touch you all the time."

"Only out of obligation. I can feel the difference."

185

"You don't know what you're talking about. How can you compare yourself to my car?"

"Most of all, I want to feel like you think I'm beautiful and that you love me, Matt. I've been asking for years. I've tried everything to teach you how I want to be touched. How am I supposed to feel when, after we agree that we are going to stop seeing other people and work on our marriage, woman after woman comes into my store telling me that you have been texting them."

"What?! Who said that? I haven't talked to anyone in a long time unless I was trying to be a friend."

"I saw the messages, Matt. You're a liar."

"Why would I lie to you? I haven't done anything like that in a long time. Did you check the dates? I'm sure they are trying to start drama."

"I know what you've been doing. There have been four or five women in just the last month. Why would you do that? You keep saying that you want to save our marriage, and then you never stop messaging other girls?"

"Here, let me show you how much I want you!" Grabbing my hand, Matt pulled me off the couch. Snatching my dress, he ripped it to the side, exposing my breasts. His mouth dropped to my exposed nipples as I struggled to breathe. "Can't you tell I want you?"

Pushing me to my knees, he grabbed the back of my head and blindly stabbed at my mouth until I gagged from the force of his cock. Pushing against his legs, I tried to block him. Pain shot through the back of my throat and traveled up to my head. My lungs felt like fire as I struggled to breathe.

"*No!*" I sobbed. "Please stop! I can't take this anymore."

"You like it when I take control."

"Please . . . *stop!*"

Grabbing my hair, Matt pulled me to my feet and bent me over, thrusting his penis into me as my arms braced against the window.

Thank God for autopilot.

As Matt finished with me, I sat on the couch, carefully trying to avoid the inevitable pain. Staring at my cold fries sitting on a paper plate and the ketchup now gathering gnats, I wanted to scream, but I only stared at the now inedible food. I glared at Matt as he casually went back to his phone, smiling at whoever was texting him.

"Who is she?"

"Not she. His name is Terry. He's a friend from work."

"A guy, huh?"

"Yeah, didn't I introduce you?"

"You had him run over to my vehicle once. He looked confused. You know, I was in there the other day after work and ran into a girl named Teri. Are you sure it's not her?"

"What does it matter? I'm allowed to have friends."

"I suppose it doesn't," I stated dryly.

"Don't you have that one guy who visits you in the store?"

"Yeah, I have a customer who comes in and talks to me for a few minutes occasionally."

"Why haven't you mentioned him? I saw him talking to you outside today. You were smiling. Why?"

"We were talking about snowflakes." I laughed. "His daughter was looking at puppies at a store nearby."

"I don't know about that."

"Whatever. I see you were spying on me again?"

"I have to, or you won't tell me anything. I know everything you do, Sheila. You can't hide anything from me. People tell me everything."

"Do you tell me about every person *you* talk to at work?"

"Listen, I'm not the one who cheated. Your doctor even put you on medication because you're not right. You need to accept that you need help. I think you're having a midlife crisis. That's why you keep talking about divorce. You don't mean any of it."

"I asked you to go to therapy with me, Matt. I thought it might help. Getting ideas on how to fix our marriage is a good thing. I don't know why you won't go."

"I tried that before, and they blamed everything on me. Besides,

I'm not the one with the problem. You're the one who keeps screwing up. You keep saying that I don't give you any attention. You're never going to be happy with anything."

"Do you wanna give up?"

"No, I don't have anywhere to go. I talked to Mom, and she said I couldn't stay there, and I don't make enough to get my own place. Besides, you don't want me to leave. You love me, and we're going to fix this."

"Not if you're texting other women."

"What do *you* know? You're always on your phone."

"Yeah, with work. I'm the manager. I have to."

"No, you don't. You're not going to let me be homeless. You're not that cruel."

"How much money do you think you will need to get a place?"

"I don't know, but you owe me a lot. I've been a stay-at-home dad for years, and that's like working a full-time job. You owe me all that money, and I want the house."

"Why would you want the house? Terra and I need a place to live. Besides, you couldn't pay the bills. And yes, you stayed home, but I paid for everything, bought you games, and even got you a car while I put off what *I* wanted."

"You better think of something because you can't make me leave. We're married, and I live here. You can't evict me."

Chapter 19

S TARING AT THE computer screen, my legs bounced like a rubber ball as I chewed on my freshly manicured nails, and I pressed print. Pushing back from my desk, I leaned my head against the chair, closing my eyes as paper hit the floor.

I remembered Matt telling me about his family members—his mother, grandmother, and uncle—and their mental illnesses. I realized why he had trouble understanding things, but as much as I hated what he had been through growing up, I was more concerned about what it was doing to Terra and me. I didn't want to give up on Matt, but I worried about what he was capable of.

I thought about things Matt had told me. *My uncle is crazy. He took a shovel and almost hit me in the head when I was little. He was inches away. He barely missed. My uncle says everyone is always trying to break his back. He sat in his trailer and starting shooting when the police knocked on his door. They had to drag him out. I'm surprised nobody died. My mom came home from school one day and found her mother covered in ketchup, screaming, saying she was dying.*

I remembered Matt talking about his previous divorce, the lawyers, and how his family had treated his ex-wife. When the lawyers accused him of neglect and abuse, his family had called Child Protective Services and tried to take his daughter from her. There was no limit to their cruelty, and I didn't want them as enemies.

Grabbing the papers from the floor, I figured out how much I could pay Matt. With a sigh, I filled in the sections for spousal support and other finances. I was going to give him a lump sum, and then monthly payments for a year. *Might as well, as long as I have my job. It's going to be a rough year, but it'll be worth it when it's over.*

"Sheila, you have a call on line two," Meg interrupted.

"I didn't hear it ring."

"They asked for you specifically. You've been out of it lately. Are you okay?"

"I'm going through a lot. I'm sorry."

"It's getting hard around here," Meg reassured me.

Turning my DIY divorce papers face down, I picked up the phone.

"This is the school nurse. I have Terra with me."

"Why, what's wrong?"

"Her teacher sent her down here. She was wearing a hoodie, and when she pulled up her sleeves, we saw cuts on her arms. She said she's been cutting herself. I think she needs to go to the hospital. We can't let her back in class. We tried to call your husband, but he didn't answer."

"Oh my God, did she say it was an accident?"

"No, that's what's bothering me. She said she hid a knife in her room."

"Can you send her home on the bus, and I will take her to the hospital tonight? I'm at work, and I don't think I can get there before school lets out."

"Yes, but make sure you take her. Let us know what happens, please. We've never known her to be like this. Is there anything going on at home?"

"Not that I know of, but I'll find out. I'll get this taken care of."

After closing the store, I rushed to take Terra to the hospital. The little girl I knew, who loved to watch princesses and dance to crazy music—my sassy little diva—was gone. In her place was a teenager with red curls that now hung in knots. Terra's pale skin only made the cuts more vivid as they swelled and scabbed, turning red from infection. There were many, starting at her wrist and ending at her shoulders. Everywhere she could reach had been cut. I felt my skin chill as she stared at the floor. *How did this happen? Where did my little girl go?*

"Terra," I whispered.

"What, Sheila?" Snatching her hand away from me, Terra's swollen eyes stared into mine. Her gaze was like a laser cutting through my mind.

Why didn't she call me Mom? "Why did you call me that?" I asked.

"You mean, by your name? I don't even know you anymore, Mom."

"I don't understand."

"Why is Matt in *our* house? I've tried to tell you that you need a divorce, but you don't listen. You never will."

"You act like it's simple."

"It *is* simple. Mom, I'm tired of having to stay in my room. He's angry all . . . the . . . time. I don't feel welcome in my own home, and he keeps crying about how I make *him* feel because I'm not interested in his stupid NASCAR game. He *literally* cries like I killed his puppy."

"Terra . . . I'm trying. I told him to get a job and that I want a divorce. He doesn't believe me."

"*MAKE HIM BELIEVE YOU!* I can't watch you being treated like this!"

"I will. I am," I answered. Pulling the neatly folded papers out of my purse, I handed them to Terra.

"What's this?" Terra asked.

"Divorce papers. I'm prepared to pay Matt to leave. I'm afraid of what he'll do, though. I don't want him to hurt you."

"I can take care of myself, Mom. You told me to learn how to do things, and I have. Defending myself is one of those things. A friend of mine is teaching me self-defense after school. You know, Matt hasn't even noticed I'm an hour late coming home every day."

"Are you ready for this? I don't know how he's going to react. I've been talking to him, but I don't know if he'll leave right away. He's going to suck us dry if he can. This is all I can offer him."

"I don't care what you give him. We'll find a way. We always have. We're a team. I don't mind you working all the time. I respect what you're doing, but Matt is hurting us, and we deserve better."

"I'm not worried about me. I'm worried about you."

"I can't stand to watch him hit walls and throw silverware, and I can . . . hear you sometimes. I'm old enough to know what he's doing to you. I feel like it's my fault. If it wasn't for me, you would have left Matt a long time ago."

"You can't blame yourself for what Matt does!"

"I don't, just for what I do. I know you want him to leave. You need to stop thinking about me. They should put me in a place where I can get help. My friends will never know. I'll tell them I got to go on a vacation with Aunt Tasha. Stop worrying about me and do what's right for *you*, Mom."

When Terra spoke with the doctor, she admitted she had been cutting and had planned on committing suicide. I shivered listening to her words, and when they loaded Terra into an ambulance, a part of me died. I watched until the taillights faded into the night.

Terra had always been by my side where I could protect her. Now, there was nothing I could do. Gripping the steering wheel, I pounded my head against the headrest. My organs twisted inside me, knowing I could've lost her. Screaming, I shook the steering wheel and cried for a while. Then, with divorce papers tucked neatly in my purse, I headed home. My eyes narrowed as I thought about what could've happened while I was away, and anger rose in me like a wildfire.

Throwing the door open, I found Matt stretched out on the couch with his pants around his ankles. Rolling my eyes, I stared through him as he struggled to hang up his phone.

"Just in time, come here. Why don't you take care of me?" Matt cooed.

"I'd rather not." I glared. "I was thinking about your requests last night. Will $100 a month be enough on top of what you make at your own job? And a $2,500 lump sum for the house? That's all I can afford. I'll have to hire a babysitter and someone to mow the lawn."

"You don't mean it. You won't do it. You can't make it without me!"

Sitting down beside him, I opened my purse and pulled out the paperwork. "Really? 'Cause I made two copies with those numbers. You sign, I file, and when it goes to the court, they put it on record and it's over."

"But . . . I love you, Sheila. I want to make this work," Matt pleaded.

"Maybe you should have thought about that before you started trying to sleep with half the county and before you raped me."

"I didn't do any of those things, and it's not rape if we're married. You never said no anyway."

"Being married isn't an automatic yes. Matt, I saw the messages, and that many women wouldn't be coming to me if it wasn't true. I could understand one or two but not four or five."

"You're never happy with anything, so what does it matter? You can be miserable alone. If that's what you want, then I'm going to need more money."

"How much?"

"Double it! I deserve to be paid for staying home with Terra all these years."

"You wouldn't get a job, remember? When you started working, it proved to me that you could have all those years when I cried missing my daughter, wishing I could take her to dance class. When we were barely making ends meet, you refused to get a job. But now that you don't have me to support you, suddenly you have one? And tonight, I came home without Terra, and you didn't ask why! You seriously had your pants down, on the phone, talking to God knows who while I had her at the hospital?! That says a lot about you. I have given you everything you have *ever* asked for, and you barely did the absolute minimum for me. I tried to love you, Matt, but then you betrayed me far more than I ever betrayed you. If you want double, then I will redo the papers tomorrow."

"Fine, but remember, double is merciful. I talked to Mom, and she said I am entitled to half of everything."

"Maybe *you* need to remember that I'm being nice by not having you arrested for everything you've done."

"Go ahead, tell the cops what I've done. They will just laugh at you, and that will give me the perfect opportunity to tell everyone how you cheated on me, how you slept with all those men. I will ruin you and make sure you lose your job. What *you* need to do is pay me and fuck me when I want, and you'll be just fine."

I didn't listen to him after that. I walked away and let him think he'd won. His words ripped through my mind like a razor blade, but I knew I had to push through. Even if I never spoke about the things that happened to me, at least Matt would be gone. That night, he stayed awake on the couch, on his phone, and for once . . . I slept. I missed Terra, but at least I knew she was safe. I made sure that by the end of the week, the dissolution was filed. We only had to wait for a court date.

Chapter 20

"**D**ID MY DAUGHTER'S RING come in from repairs yet?"

"Um, give me your name, and I'll check," I answered.

"This is Michael. You don't recognize my voice? You should be ashamed." He laughed.

"I'm sorry! I should have, but a lot of people ask for me by name. Yes, it's back in."

"Did you check it yourself? I want to make sure it's done right."

"I didn't, but Meg is picky, so I'm sure it's fine."

"I was hoping you could join me for lunch. I want Chinese, but I don't want to go alone."

"Sure, sounds good."

Fire shot through my body as I hung up the phone. My eyes grew wide as I leaned back in my chair. *Oh, wow . . . really? Wait, did he just ask me out? I'm sure he means as friends. He's not looking for a relationship. But what if he is? Oh my God, I shouldn't have answered so quickly. I can't go out with him. Matt is on a rampage. What will happen if he sees Michael? Would he bother him? Michael is too important. What if Matt runs him off and I don't get a chance to talk to him again? No. No. No. I can't, and besides, we're in the middle of a special event. Even if it's dead and nobody is coming in, the district manager keeps checking up on me. What am I going to do?*

In a panic, I looked through the wall of glass to the outside. The cold winter air drifted through the open glass door as I tried to silence my heart. *You never know what's going to happen.* The crisp air teased my senses as I drew farther from my desk. The sunlight teased me with its brilliance as I stepped outside. The breeze caressed my body as I closed my eyes and turned my face toward the sun. *Change is coming.*

I felt like I was standing on a beach as the sun washed my skin with light. Slowly, the wind increased as the sound of 80s rock tickled my senses. With each moment, it grew louder until it echoed against glass and concrete as Michael's two-seater convertible approached. His mirrored sunglasses reflected clouds as his arm rested on the door, tapping to the rhythm of drums and guitars.

"Are you ready to go?" Michael smiled.

"I don't think I can go. I'm sorry, I know I said I would, but it's a special event, and the district manager has been watching me."

"Oh, come on, the store will be okay. You're allowed to take a lunch, I'm sure."

"Yeah, but that doesn't mean I can leave the store. He isn't always the most reasonable. You can hang out here if you want, though."

"You do know I was asking you to lunch as friends, right?"

"Of course, yeah . . . I know," I replied as my heart wilted into the concrete. *Guys ask me out all the time, but the one I feel safe around just wants to be friends? Why am I doing this to myself?* "Maybe you can get takeout Mexican and hang out here?"

"I don't know. I might. Are you sure you can't go with me? It's literally just a few doors down."

"No, I can't leave. Maybe we can another time?"

"I don't know, maybe . . . if you're good." Michael laughed. "Can I at least get a hug?"

"Maybe."

As my face drew closer in the reflection of Michael's sunglasses, I closed my eyes and felt the warmth of his arms wrap around me. My arms gently tucked beneath his as my hands caressed his shoulders. I breathed in the warm scent of his cologne as it bathed me in his masculinity.

"You feel good," Michael whispered.

My hands stopped trembling, my breathing slowed, and my shoulders relaxed as his warmth overtook me. Suddenly, I was a little girl again, clutching my teddy bear when I was lost in the terrors surrounding me—when the screams echoed through my home, when the storms

196

raged in my family, and my world was covered in tears. I had only felt safe when I held my teddy bear, until Michael held me in his arms. I remembered the bridge and the warmth of his body against me in the hospital. Both times, his innocent embrace washed me in peace as my frantic mind grew still.

"You feel good, too."

"Hey, do you like music?" Michael asked.

"Of course, I do."

"I play around and write music sometimes."

"Do you have anything I can hear?"

"Yep, let me pull it up."

As music caressed the air, I stepped closer to him, straining to hear the gentle sounds that teased my ears. The notes danced around us, starting with the whisper of strings and twirling into the keys of a piano. The melody leaped like a veil of tulle around us, glimmering with the breeze that surrounded us with change. *You play around with music sometimes?* As a second song played, the low notes crawled through my spine as I imagined myself surrounded by candlelight. Each note felt like fingertips caressing my palms, drifting upward, teasing my flesh. And as the music grew, the notes captured my lips with warmth, kissing away the tears escaping my heart.

Where have you been hiding? Why? How? What? Wait a minute, could it be that my prince charming exists? And he didn't arrive on a noble steed but in a two-seater convertible blaring "Pour Some Sugar on Me?" It's not fair that this amazing man—talented, intelligent, compassionate, and tender—is HERE with me. And he HATES women. But when he looks in my eyes and when I feel his touch, I see something else. I see his heartbreak, but deep within, I see a glimmer. It's not possible, Sheila—just friends, remember? But maybe . . .

Business stayed quiet that evening. It didn't matter that there was a sale. Michael spent time with us at the store, and because I couldn't leave the store, he stayed beside me. It was four hours of discovery, and even now, I don't remember everything we talked about. When a guest visited our store, Michael quietly stepped back and allowed me to work. I remember his smiles as I taught people about diamonds, gemstones, and gold. At the end of the night, he waited patiently outside, leaving only to bring me coffee as I secured my store and readied it for the following day.

Standing beside Michael's car that evening, we drank coffee and talked alone under the stars. When he gave me his phone number, I smiled, knowing we had made a small step. He wasn't just another guest that loved to visit my store but a real friend.

* * *

"Where were you?" Matt demanded from the couch.

"I was hanging out with a friend after work. What does it matter? We already filed for divorce."

"We're *still married*! So, until everything is final, I want to work on us. You have to treat me like a husband and tell me where you are at all times."

"That's not right, Matt. I don't have to. I'm basically single. I can do whatever I want."

"You don't get to talk to me like that." He growled, climbing to his feet.

"I'm not going to talk to you while you're like this," I answered.

"What do you mean, 'like this?' You're my wife, and it's my job to take care of you. I just want to check on the van for you and make sure everything is good on it. You know I check the tires and fluids once a week. I actually need to do a rotation."

"Why do you need to rotate my tires?"

"Because I do, every six months or so."

"Well, I can take it somewhere and have it done. Don't worry about it."

"You're my wife. I'm going to worry about it."

"No, I'm not. We're legally separated. When are you moving out? I thought you would have by now."

"My mom said I could stay with her for a while, but I don't have to leave until the paperwork is final. Once we go to court, I'll leave. Until then, I have every right to stay here."

"Why would you *want* to be here?"

"Why *wouldn't* I?"

Without answering, I headed for the bedroom, locking the door behind me. I didn't know what to tell him. I hadn't been anywhere. I had decided to enjoy a little freedom after having coffee with Michael. I loved visiting the city park at night. It gave me time to think. The stars were always bright, and nobody was around. It was the perfect time to sit in my vehicle and think. It had been a while, but was it any of Matt's business?

Staring at the bedroom walls, all I could remember was nightmares with Matt. Our room wasn't the peaceful retreat I wanted it to be. His clothes were piled on top of a broken chest of drawers, and his side of the bed was cluttered with weird things he picked up. I hated the red curtains and peanut butter walls that surrounded me, only because he had wanted them. The black sheets and red comforter had seen better days. I wanted to make my own luxurious space that he'd never see.

Grabbing my phone, I went directly to my shopping app and started looking for bedding sets. I didn't know what I wanted until I saw it. It was a champagne gold with silver scrolls, trimmed with lace. It was elegant, classy, and shined like satin. It wasn't the frilly styles that my grandmother would buy. It was something that belonged on the bed of a celebrity—understated and refined. As I added it to my cart, I smiled, thankful for how far I'd come on my journey. I went from cinnamon toast for dinner to bologna, and now, I didn't have to worry about my budget. It didn't take long for me to find pillows and lamps and start considering paint colors. After I checked out, I thought of the rest of the house. I needed to erase Matt, even if he was sitting in my living room.

I fell asleep smiling, dreaming of paint colors. I knew that if I hired my mother and stepfather to paint, Matt would disappear for the day, and I wouldn't have to see him. It was the perfect plan.

"Hi, honey. I got up early and got your tires rotated for you," Matt informed me the next morning. "The ones on the back were pretty worn down, so I switched them with the front so they would last you longer. You should be okay for a while."

"Thanks," I answered groggily. "You didn't have to." *Why is he trying to be nice?*

"Of course, I did. You're my wife. Speaking of which, I want to sleep in bed with you tonight, and you can't tell me no."

"I like sleeping alone."

"Well, I work hard, and I don't want to sleep on the couch."

"But—"

"But what?"

"We're separated. Doesn't that mean anything to you?"

"No, not really."

"Then maybe I will sleep on the couch. We can rotate." *Should I feel guilty for not wanting to sleep beside him?*

"Fine. Are you going out with anyone? Which one is your boyfriend?" Matt demanded to know.

"I don't have a boyfriend."

"Of course, you do. That's why you want the divorce. He's pressuring you into it."

"There is no *he*. I want the divorce because I want to be alone. I don't plan on getting into a relationship for a long time."

"You don't have to lie to me."

"I'm not lying. I have no reason to." *There it is. Of course, he's accusing me of lying.*

"Well, I know you're dating someone. You can tell me."

"I'm not, Matt. Why is it so hard for you to believe that I want to be alone?" *Seriously, I'm making a friend, not dating. It will probably never be anything more. I really DO want some time alone. I need it.*

"Well, then, if you're still alone, you won't mind if I fuck you. After all, you have needs." He laughed.

"*What?* Are you *serious*? What makes you think I want that?" I answered, throwing myself out of bed. Gathering my things, I quickly got dressed and headed for work. Blaring my favorite songs, I escaped for a moment, letting the music invade my senses.

It was a few days later that I noticed a strange noise coming from my wheels. At first, I thought it was from a rough place in the road or something under the engine. So, I asked Matt to check it, but he found nothing.

After a few more days, I had my tires checked at a local shop. It was there that I discovered my lug nuts had been loosened enough that a tire could have come off at any moment. I could've been killed. When I asked Matt how that happened, he quickly passed the blame. His explanation was that another man was jealous because I had dumped them or wouldn't do what they wanted. Still, I knew nobody had access to my vehicle. When I was at work, it was under video surveillance, and nobody had approached it. There was only one explanation: Matt.

When it was time to pick up Terra, I listened carefully to every sound my vehicle made as I traveled toward the hospital. As I passed over the hills that embraced our town, the road flattened. The warm sunlight caressed my face as I headed north toward my little girl. With every rattle that quivered in my vehicle, my heart froze. *What if I hadn't caught what was wrong with the lug nuts? What if Terra had been in the vehicle? We could have died. How could Matt do that to us? He's a mechanic. He knew what he was doing.*

Approaching the glass doors of the hospital, I was greeted by a cocker spaniel in a vest. It reminded me of the dog we had when Terra was little, before we bought our home. I quickly learned that the dog was part of the therapy program, and as it climbed up beside me, I felt my body relax. I knew I wouldn't be around as much as I wanted after Matt left, and Terra would need someone to greet her when she got home from school. *Maybe a puppy would help.*

Staring at the conference room doors, I waited to meet Terra's doctors. The room was quiet, with only me and the dog warming the cold tile floors. When the meeting started, we went over the treatment plan, and I learned what had led Terra to suicidal ideation. It surprised me how much she knew about my arguments with Matt. Her main complaint was being unable to help me escape. She talked about watching Matt yell at me, the cries that came from behind my bedroom door, and the many times he had thrown me against the wall.

The hole in the bathroom door from Matt's fist flashed through my mind as they talked about Terra's treatment plan. With a sigh, I gathered my little girl in my arms. Her smile warmed my heart as her arms hugged me back, and she simply said, "Let's go, Mom." *At least she called me Mom. How am I going to handle things with Terra while I'm working fifty hours a week?*

Chapter 21

"**M**EG, RING ME UP for a bear, please," I requested, tossing a fundraising bear in the air.

"Sure thing! Are you going to take it home to Terra?"

"No, she's not into stuffed animals. This one is mine. I keep hugging different ones, and I want to designate one for my desk."

"Um, okay. That makes sense, I guess."

Grabbing a marker, I quickly scribbled on the tag of the soft gray bear: *Official therapy bear—store use only.* Then, I sat down, leaned back, and cried. Michael had failed a stress test. They found a blockage, and he had to go in for a heart catheterization. I heard from a lot of people that it was a lot like getting your teeth cleaned. It was routine. But it didn't feel routine, especially not when his daughter texted me that day, letting me know they found a huge blockage.

A vessel around Michael's heart had slowly closed up, and his blood had rerouted itself into smaller vessels. It had taken his endurance and his ability to function, and the smallest of blood clots could have taken his life. His doctors couldn't remove it. The blockage was like concrete. Michael was rushed to another hospital. He was medicated and strapped to the table when they transferred him in an ambulance from one cath lab to another.

Hearing the news, I felt barbed wire wrap around my heart, and I clung to Mr. Therapy Bear. I couldn't stop crying. My mind shook in terror as I waited, hoping they could fix Michael. My anxiety spiked, and I gasped for air as I held the soft bear, clutching it, hoping it would ease the pain in my heart. But it didn't help. I waited as I paced the floor, trying to control my insanity. *What's wrong with me? He's just a friend. It will be okay. It doesn't matter. Michael is another customer— just barely a friend, right? Oh my GOD! Why can't I stop crying?*

Terra had only been home for a week, and she and Matt were still fighting. Nothing had changed between the two, and with the divorce date approaching, she felt no need to be around him, and I couldn't blame her. Every day was stressful, and the only thing that gave me peace was my conversations with Michael.

As I sat in the manager's chair, I remembered the first time Michael and I had talked on the phone. What was meant to be a thirty-minute conversation quickly turned into eight hours. We talked about life, love, and all the mistakes from our past. Over the phone, I read him stories I had written and told him about pictures from my old photography business and paintings I had painted years before.

When it was Michael's turn to share during our first phone conversation, I listened quietly as he played guitar and told me about a band he had put together years before. I thought about my early talks with Trenton and how quickly they had flown by. But with Michael, hours felt like seconds instead of minutes. It was like Trenton was merely a preview for what was inevitably coming. He had given me only a glimpse of what I saw in Michael.

The only reason that first phone call ended was because I knew Matt would be home. When Michael and I hung up the phone, I pretended to be asleep as Matt rattled around in the bedroom. After he left the room, I locked the door behind him and curled up, thinking of all that Michael and I had shared. It was amazing to me how he hadn't tried to be sexual. He didn't ask for nude photographs, and I felt respected even after eight hours of talking.

Pacing in front of the glass walls at the front of the store, I held Mr. Therapy Bear in my arms, thankful for a quiet day. Just like my first phone call with Michael, our first date out as friends was unique. I hadn't known what to expect when he held his car door open for me, and when the wind swept through my hair, I marveled at how smoothly he drove a standard transmission.

Michael and I kept it simple that night with a last-minute pizza from a drive-through pizzeria that we ate under the stars at a table at the city park. We turned on the radio as the stars danced across the night sky, and Michael made me a plate and made sure to leave the last piece of pizza for me. That evening ended without a kiss. After all, we were just friends. I couldn't understand Michael's sincerity and respect. My other male "friends" always managed to cross the boundary of friendship, but Michael hadn't. He ended our first night out as friends respectfully.

When another employee arrived at the store, I headed to the back room. Staring at the walls, I traced the wires and pipes with my eyes. *I hope he's okay. Michael has so much he wants to give. He said as soon as he starts to figure things out, bad things always happen. I hope this isn't the end for him. That would be cruel.*

A few hours later, Michael's daughter finally texted again. She let me know that they had tried two more times but couldn't remove the blockage. Michael had three catheterizations in one day at two different hospitals, but he was stable and in recovery. I didn't know whether to be relieved he was alive or to panic because they couldn't fix him. I sat stunned, frozen. As I regained control of my breath, my phone rang.

"Sheila, my dad is awake. I thought he might need you."

"Really?"

"Yes, definitely. Here, hold on . . ."

For a moment, the phone went silent, and then Michael's voice rattled on the other end, groggy from medication. "Hey, Sheila. I'm . . . I'm . . . okay, I think. It hurts, though."

"I'm so glad you're okay, Michael. I've been worried."

"Well, I'm not okay, but I'm alive, so that's a plus."

"Hang in there. Do you have anyone to help you when you get home?"

"I don't know. My daughter is supposed to help, but I don't know other than that. Listen, I'm tired. I should go."

"I wish I could be there. I feel like you need me."

"I wish you were here, too," Michael whispered.

"Okay, take care of yourself." I sniffled. "Get some rest."

When Michael got home from the hospital, he wasn't able to lift anything. He needed help, but his daughter only stayed with him for a day before a friend picked her up. He was left alone as he tried to heal from the procedures. I was livid, knowing Michael wasn't eating well when he needed to rest and recover. I knew there wasn't much I could do for him with Matt's continued jealousy and my long hours at work. So, one night, I ordered a bucket of chicken with all the side dishes and headed to Michael's apartment, making sure to grab paper plates and napkins on the way.

Standing outside Michael's door, hands full of food, I tenderly knocked on the door, knowing he was waiting for me. As he yelled for me to come in, I opened the door slowly. The space meant for his living room was empty, mail from a week ago sat at the base of the staircase, and across the room, he sat at a small table. His normally well-groomed hair was tousled aimlessly as he greeted me in bare feet and gym shorts. Walking to him, I placed my bags on the table and sat in the empty chair across from him. *It's weird seeing him like this.*

"Thank you, Sheila. I'm sorry I couldn't help you carry everything in. I appreciate this, and it smells so good. Let me look and see if I have any clean plates."

"No, it's okay. I brought paper plates so you wouldn't have to clean up."

"You thought of everything, didn't you?"

"I tried."

"How did you sneak away from your husband?"

"I told him where I was going. No point in lying. Matt understood."

"That's good of him."

"I'm sure I'll pay for it."

"What do you mean?" Michael asked.

"Nothing, don't worry about it." I smiled.

Grabbing the paper plates, I quickly filled Michael's plate with food, and then my own. My stomach was growling after a long day. As Michael took his first bite, he leaned back in his chair and his eyes rolled back in his head in delight.

"How long has it been since you've had a meal?" I asked.

"Too long. Probably since I left the hospital."

"That's awful. Why hasn't anyone been here? They should be helping you—fixing you dinner, getting things you need."

"I know, but I'll be okay. They have their own lives to live."

"Yeah, but—"

"I'm a strong, independent man. I can take care of myself."

"I know you can." *Well, obviously, you can't.* "But it seems like the right thing to do."

"It is, but I'm not going to beg anyone to help me."

"I get that."

As our plates went from full to empty, Michael looked across the table at the remaining food. Picking up the paper plates, I began to gather trash and organize what was left to put it in the refrigerator, hoping it would last him a couple days. Then, as our eyes met from across the table, Michael's face changed. His casual gaze and the tenderness he hid behind walls of crystal blue were different. His gaze never left mine. Instead, his compassion was laid out in front of me like a flower freshly bloomed.

For a moment, the noise of passing cars stopped and the earth was silent. Fire ignited my toes and raced through my body, leaving butterflies in my stomach and a blush on my cheeks as Michael's eyes looked through mine, searching through the shadows and discovering what I had hidden within. My breath shook. *What was that?! What happened? Michael has never looked at me like THAT before.*

That moment was gone in an instant, leaving me wondering. The look Michael gave me shook me to my core as I remembered the way I felt when his gaze ventured into the shadows of my heart. *Maybe I imagined it. He's just a friend.*

Click . . . click . . . click. My heels echoed against the hard floor of the grocery store as I grabbed a few things on my way home. I saw the faces of men, one after the other. Their gaze tasted bitter as I looked ahead, feeling the caress of my skirt against my thighs, noticing the scent of strawberries as it wafted to my nose. Quickly, I chose my dinner and headed for the door. Looking back, I snatched the eyes of a businessman. I held his eyes until his mouth opened enough to speak so I could raise my eyebrows and turn my lips in an almost smile as I walked away, vanishing into the night.

I'd become quite adept at purposefully teasing the eyes of men. The game I played at the mall came naturally now, but the prizes weren't as rewarding. I refused phone calls and text messages now. It was my intent to get what *I* wanted—that momentary look of appreciative lust in the eyes of dangerous men before I vanished like a mist into the night. It was enough for me to know I was in control. I didn't have to bow to the fantasies of greedy men.

Matt's departure was looming, and I was ready for whatever lay ahead. I loved to hate the looks of men—the ones that frightened me and made my flesh shake. I felt their eyes on me, like ravaging hands stripping my body of its defenses. I was aware—aware of their desire to capture me. I let them frighten me, knowing their evils were nothing compared to the monster that awaited me at home.

Only that searching look from Michael had ever shaken me, though. My guard was up, and I was determined to enjoy those moments when other men stared at me. In my enjoyment, I felt hatred for the knowledge of what was at the base of every man's mind: sex. I just wanted to be desired for who I was and not what I could give. Those reminders made me feel sexy but also made me feel that no man was worth the pain. *How can I find a man who doesn't see me as an object?*

My phone never stopped after the news of Matt and me separating. The men of Gallia County were like vultures, and I hated them. Every day, I rolled my eyes a little more and took fewer messages. During the day, I was strong—independent and powerful—but at night, I felt like I was in prison, waiting for the divorce and Matt's departure. I loved when he was working because I could work on my novel and call Michael. When Matt was home, I watched him text other women as he demanded that I watch him play video games and watch movies that I wasn't interested in.

On those nights, I felt the seconds pass like a bass drum pounding through my soul. I was empty, missing the intense conversations of the only man I wanted to speak to. I barely slept at night without Michael's voice whispering goodnight through the phone. He was my real-life therapy bear, after all. My mind ached for him on those nights as I waited for midnight. I counted the minutes like a prisoner, waiting so I could text Michael goodnight, knowing any conversation would be questioned by Matt. I was tired of being accused of lying.

Over the months, Matt grew accustomed to my goodnight texts as being simply that, and he stopped questioning the way my eyes lit up when Michael responded. After a while, Matt ignored my longing gaze as I saw Michael's convertible across the street when he visited his daughter. It no longer mattered whether Matt knew I was innocent. *I* knew, and that's all that mattered.

When I was alone, Michael and I continued our conversations well into the night, every night. As I grew closer to him, he resisted me. Each time I saw his emotions, he pushed me away. Still, I wanted to prove that not all women are evil and out to destroy him. As I laid alone only hours before it was time to return to the store for another twelve-hour day, Michael's words would echo through my thoughts: *I don't want the responsibility of a woman in my life. I can barely take care of myself. I can't expect you to wait for me. I might not ever get there. Women can't be trusted.*

Eventually, I began pushing away from Michael. I wanted to be alone but not alone. I wanted to have someone beside me who cared, who wanted me. Of course, I couldn't stop my conversations with Michael—I craved them like a pancake breakfast on Sunday mornings. They were a part of me. But Michael's visits to the store became less frequent as his classes dominated his time. I think Michael was oblivious to how much I enjoyed his presence, but he told me not to wait . . . continuously.

When I was ready, the men around me had a sixth sense and started showing up without an ad or invitation. They knew I was ready to entertain them. One by one, I rejected them until . . . I didn't.

"Sheila, do you want to go out for pizza again?" Teddy whispered from across my counter on one of those days I barely remember.

"Um, sure, why not?" I answered as I examined diamonds under the gem scope.

"You remember last time, don't you? Pizza has a bit of an effect on us."

"It sure does." I tried to laugh. "Matt works at 10. Do you want me to meet you around then?"

"That sounds great. That'll give me time to go to the bank after I close my store."

"Okay, Teddy. I will see you then."

When I walked inside the pizza place that night, Teddy was waiting with his favorite pizza. I smiled when he remembered my drink— probably because it was the same as his. Teddy's eyes were bright as I sat across from him. He leaned forward in his chair like he wanted to grab my hand but didn't.

"I'm glad you're here. I've missed you." Teddy winked. "It seems like you're the only person I can be myself around."

"That can't be true. I thought you had a lot of friends at church?"

"Yes and no. I have to be careful with what I say around them."

"I guess I can see that. I assumed you guys talked about everything in those men's groups."

"Not really. We do but don't," he answered with a smile. "Anyway, how was work? Are you and Meg getting along?"

"Seem to be. But I've been going through a lot with the divorce, and she's upset with me because I'm distracted."

"She applied for a job at my store. She even called. I'm not sure I want to do that, though."

"Oh, wow! When? I don't want to lose her."

"I'll talk to her but will tell her I don't have an opening."

"Thanks, Teddy. I appreciate it. That makes me feel bad, but I can't talk to her about it. We're not supposed to talk like this about applicants."

"No, but she's a mutual friend, so I think we're okay."

"True."

We talked mostly about business that evening, and Teddy smiled a lot. It wasn't long before we went to his new home, but this time I had my vehicle with me. When I stepped inside his place, I was shocked. Instead of one small loveseat, there was almost too much furniture. Black sofas lined the walls in front of a large TV and coffee table. I smiled when Teddy asked me what kind of music I wanted to hear. That simple act turned into an hour-long debate as our laughter filled the room.

Somehow, Teddy had become like an old friend. This time, when he sat beside me and his lips covered mine, I wasn't afraid. I felt empowered. I welcomed his aggressive hands as they pulled me close to him and pushed my bra to the side. He was quick to find my breasts, and his lips quickly covered my nipples a little too roughly, leaving me with the discolorations of passion. As he reached between my legs, I stopped him. So instead, Teddy wrapped his arm around me, and we talked.

I remember staring at Teddy's pictures. My favorite was a casual portrait of him with his kids. They were standing in front of a cross, holding their bibles. It seemed like a different man than I knew. Their joyful smiles seemed innocent as they stared at the photographer. It reminded me of my childhood dreams, and a part of me wanted—wished—I was standing beside them with Terra. I wanted to be part of a real family. *Remember what happened before? Do we have anything to talk about other than business?*

As midnight approached, I drove the twisting road that would lead me home. I waited for a cell signal to return to my phone. I held it in my hand, waiting to press send as I struggled to see the road. The rain fell in cold tears, pounding against my windshield as the roads mirrored my headlights and slowed my progress.

"What are you doing up?" Michael asked when I was finally able to call him.

"I . . . um . . . went out with someone tonight," I stuttered.

"That's good. How did it go?"

"I think it went okay. He's a nice guy. I've known him for a while."

"You need to be careful. You're not divorced yet."

"I know, but legally we're separated, and I thought I would give it a try. We've been out before."

"Well, you need to do what makes you happy," Michael quietly answered.

"But . . . I don't want it to take time away from you."

"I don't want to stand in the way if you have a chance at happiness. I couldn't do that to you."

My heart dropped as our conversation continued. A part of me wanted Michael to admit there was more to us than our conversations, but he never did. Instead, after a few minutes, we talked about the weather, work, and whatever else came to mind as we always had. *At least I will always have Michael, even if he's only ever just a friend.*

* * *

Pulling my hair into a ponytail, I stared at my reflection and the walls around me. Smiling, I headed for the door to greet my mom and stepfather. Today, we were finally getting started painting, but not my bedroom because Matt had too much in the way. I had simply placed the boxes that arrived from Amazon on my end table, waiting for him to leave. Instead, I was starting with painting the kitchen and the accent walls in my living room.

Wearing an old shirt and shorts, I welcomed my mom and stepfather into my home with two gallons of paint and a smile. I'd never looked forward to manual labor as much as I did that day. The only problem was that they brought a friend—one they had mentioned at least a dozen times in half as many conversations. Jackson went to church with them and was an usher with a self-proclaimed beautiful vocal range. I was always a sucker for music, so my curiosity was heightened.

Jackson was a gentleman. I was shocked to learn that he was only a couple years older than me, and he, too, was recently divorced. He painted, bought everyone drinks, and pressure-washed my porch. By the end of the day, we had exchanged phone numbers.

Sitting by the river with Jackson was an awkward déjà vu. I had spent plenty of time in cars with Matt, and I knew that even seemingly innocent situations could turn dark. Taking over my radio, Jackson was quick to find a southern gospel station and start singing and talking about God. While that all seemed very positive, I wanted to get to know him as a person and not just his religion. I knew enough about Christianity and didn't need someone trying to save my soul. From listening to him talk, I knew more than he did anyway.

Even with all of Jackson's righteousness, he quickly reminded me

212

that he was still a man when he climbed over my center console and started trying to swallow my face with his lips. His hands were rough as they grabbed my breasts like a pit bull clinging to a fresh steak. My nipples were sore as he squeezed and pulled. It didn't take me long to end the almost date and return home to my newly painted kitchen. I'd had more than enough from stupid boys that thought they were men. Sure, I let Teddy touch me, but I considered him a friend. Jackson hadn't earned that privilege. *It would be nice if men would just talk to me. It just proves that none of them are good.*

"How was your date?" Matt asked as I walked through the door that night.

"It was . . . whatever. I was just trying to get to know this guy Mom goes to church with," I answered. "I wasn't impressed."

"I figured he would be a good choice for you."

"No, I'm not really interested in him. I thought I might be. It seemed like a good idea but no."

"Did he kiss you?"

"I don't see why that matters."

"I just wanted to know."

That night, I hustled to the bedroom so I could be alone. My thoughts were deep as I considered what it would be like to be alone. I couldn't understand how easy it was to find dates as a plus-sized woman. I fell asleep wondering if everything I thought I knew had been wrong.

Pain shot through my neck as I strained to move my head the next morning. Struggling for air, my eyes shot open only to be filled with the sight of Matt's hairy thighs. His knees were on my hair, and my scalp burnt as he inched his knee closer to my head. As my mouth opened, gasping for air, he forced his cock into it as I pushed against his legs, forcing my head back, trying to escape. *I can't even open my mouth to say no! I can barely breathe!*

I felt my hair ripping from my head as Matt grabbed my neck, thrusting his erection to the back of my throat until my throat convulsed and acid filled my mouth. I coughed and gasped for air as his knees pinned me to the bed. My body shook as I collapsed, and tears escaped my body to pool on my pillow as I drifted away. *So, this is what I get for trying to go on a date? This should have stopped by now. How much does he think he can put me through? I'm never going to forget this. I'm never going to forgive him. This hurts so bad. I can't breathe.*

Thank God for autopilot.

When I finally escaped from Matt and settled in my vehicle, I headed to the park as I frantically searched for a crisis line. Finding one in the next county, I quickly dialed, hoping for advice or a way to get Matt out of my home legally.

"You're married? Just filed for divorce," the lady on the other end of the line suggested after hearing my story.

"Yes, I want him out. I want to feel safe in my home. Or maybe there's somewhere that I can go?"

"I'm looking now, and I don't see anything close to you that has openings. I'm sorry, I wish I had better news."

"What if I call the police?"

"You could call them and make a statement, and they would decide if you have a case. I know they usually want you to go to the emergency room and have a rape kit done, though. Did he leave any bruises or marks on your body?"

"No, I don't think so. I'm probably missing some hair, though. He's been doing stuff like this for years. He doesn't give me a chance to say no. He talks me into things, and I felt like if I didn't initiate sex, he would take it anyway. So, I tried to make the most of it. I made myself have a huge sex drive for him. It was constant. But now, I know better. Sex won't save me. We're legally separated, and this morning, I couldn't breathe or move. It was scary. I was crying. There has to be something I can do!"

"Unfortunately, when it's your husband and you don't have any marks on you, it's going to be hard to prove anything," the lady informed me. "The police might be able to remove him, but there's nothing stopping him from legally coming back. You might not even be able to get a restraining order. They can argue that you are just an upset wife and claim you're just trying to hurt him. I know that's not what you want to hear, but I've seen a lot of cases, and that's what usually happens. I hate that. We need a better system. I hear stories like this all the time, but with no shelter openings right now, there's not much I can do to help. If you ever want to talk, I'm here for you. I'm sorry I don't have better news. I feel bad for you. I really do."

Even the lady on the crisis line says there's nothing I can do. I hate my life.

My eyes were hypnotized by the darkness beyond the store's glass walls that night as the closing printers rattled through the nightly paperwork. *I can't believe there's nothing I can do. But Matt will eventually leave. Once we appear in court, he won't be able to stay legally. It won't be long, and then I'll finally feel safe. I will redo my bedroom, redo my house, and erase him from our lives. It won't be long . . . It won't be long . . .*

The cold air pressed through the glass and crawled through my mind like a spider. Snapshots of previous weeks ripped through my body as warm tears found my lips. I remembered pizza with Teddy and music with Jackson—two Christian men who encompassed everything I had desired as a child. Their presence reminded me of watching couples sitting together in church, praising God together, listening to the pastor preach as they cuddled in pews. Then, I remembered Pastor Ram and our conversations, and his voice echoed through my body in a hypnotic whisper: *I want to fuck you on the pulpit and bend you over the Sunday school table. My wife will never know.* Memories of our forbidden kiss at the mall, the way he looked at me, and the way he wanted me sent shivers through my mind.

Then, I remembered Trenton and his work with church youth groups, years of empty promises, and my desperation for him. I had wanted him, but looking back, I felt like a fool. *Why did I tolerate Trenton's insanity? I never felt safe with him and never believed him. I hoped blindly in a fantasy. How could I believe that a liar could ever be my personal prince charming? He was never the man I wanted him to be. He never gave me peace, only pain. That's all any of them have ever given me. Lies—they all lie. I'm better off alone. I deserve to feel safe, and with men like them, I never will.*

Michael's face flashed through my mind. I remembered when he rescued me from the bridge and his arms wrapped around me, holding me to keep me warm. Michael had never lied to me or pretended to be something he wasn't. When I was upset, he calmed my fears. I had only frozen from fear in the arms of other men, but in his, I had melted against him and the world was silenced. Michael was my peace—my safe place—and he *couldn't* be just a friend.

I'm going to risk it. I can't stay silent forever. I can't take this. I can't believe I will never have someone I want. Even if Michael and I are never more than friends, he is enough. I don't need anyone but myself. I can sleep alone and live alone, but if I were to have anyone that I could enjoy life with, it would be him. If there is a possibility for more, I will try. I've only felt peace in the arms of a man once, and I'm not going to let that go. Grabbing my phone, I didn't think. I just dialed.

"You're calling early tonight," Michael said when he answered. "Is everything okay?"

"Yeah . . . um . . . I have something I need to say. And I really, *really* need you to listen and think about what I'm saying, okay?"

"Of course. I always listen."

Listening to Michael's voice, it felt like claws digging into my heart. My sobs wouldn't stop, knowing—fearing—I might lose him. My voice froze like I had swallowed a gallon of ice as I tried to speak. Bending over the granite counter, I clutched Mr. Therapy Bear against my chest. "Michael . . . wake up," I whispered. "Wake up," I said again, gasping into the phone as a hammer beat against my chest.

"What do you mean?"

"Think about it. I'm dating all these guys. I get calls and messages all the time, and I . . . I need you to wake up. Please, wake up."

"Do you mean I need to wake up before I lose the best thing that's ever happened to me?"

"Yes. I mean, maybe . . . I don't know. Ugh. Is that what you want? Do you want me to slip away?"

"No, Sheila. I—"

"Please, wake up," I gasped again. "I'm . . . sorry . . . I, um, needed to say that. I have to go. I . . . I . . . have to finish closing the store."

"But can I talk? You can't keep me hanging."

"I have to go. I will call you back in a few minutes. I have to close the gate, lock the doors, and go to the bank," I informed him.

Hanging up the phone, I watched Meg scurrying to close the store without me. She rushed to the safe with pads of diamonds and gold as I stood trying to stuff store receipts into an envelope. My heart shook as hard as my hands while I fumbled through our procedures, hoping Michael would answer when I called back. Clutching Therapy Bear, I collapsed in my chair, clicking computer keys through a veil of tears. *Get it together, Sheila. You have to call him back. It's going to be okay.* As I locked up and ran to my vehicle, I swallowed my heart and called him back before I had time to change my mind.

"That was a lot to think about," Michael said.

"I know, I'm sorry. Before you say anything, I need you to know that I care about our friendship. I mean . . . you mean a lot to me, and I . . . I . . . don't want to lose that."

"I don't either. But I also don't want to complicate it. I care about you deeply. But you're married. You're going through a lot. You might not be ready for a long time. You need to be honest with yourself."

"I know. I know I'm messed up from everything. And I don't want to lose you or lose your friendship—whatever this is going to be."

"You're not going to lose me, Sheila. I'm always going to be here."

"How can you say that to me, Michael?"

"Because I mean it. I don't want you to get ahead of yourself. If you do with me or anyone, you could set yourself up for failure, and I don't want that."

"What if one day you're ready, and then I'm not? Is there something more than us being friends, or—"

"I care a lot about you. More than I do other friends. I think there's something there, even if I don't want there to be."

"I know what you mean. I keep fighting it off. Some days I can feel it strongly. It creeps up on me, this feeling, and I do everything I can to push it away because I know you don't want a relationship. But the feeling keeps coming back. At first, it was a passing thought, and it would go away for a few weeks. But now, it's almost relentless. It won't go away."

"Same here, Sheila. I keep trying to hide from it, push it away, and pretend it's not there, but I can't stop thinking about you. There's something there, and it scares me. I don't want to go through this again. I know you're not ready. You don't want to bring everything from the past into this. I've been alone for years, and Matt's still in your house. You have to get him to leave. You want to do this right. It matters. You don't want him coming back on you, calling you a cheater. You don't need that."

"Yes, it's not easy. I'm afraid of what he'll do, and I'm trying to do the right thing, find him a place to go."

"I know, but how are we supposed to try to be in a relationship if he's there?"

"I know, I know . . . you're right. I know I need to be fully ready. I want this to be right. You mean too much to me, and I'm so afraid of hurting you. But being around you . . . our conversations. I can't lose that. I barely sleep on those nights when we can't talk."

"I want you to be happy, and I'm not sure I'm ready either. I don't want to promise you something I can't give. My ex screwed me up. It was like a part of me died. I'm not sure I'll ever be the way I used to be. But I always look forward to talking to you."

"Maybe that's not all bad, ya know. What if . . . would you *try* with me?"

"I can't predict what will happen. But if I would ever try to be with anyone again, it would be you. You're like a precious gem. You're rare and unlike any other woman. You deserve better than this, better than me. But . . . you have to be ready. I know you can't stop how you feel, and neither can I. You have to realize that it's going to take you a long time to be ready, to get through what you're going through. You need time to heal—you and Terra both. This isn't just happening to you. It's happening to her too."

"What if it takes me years to be ready, to get through this?"

"Then it takes you years. I'll be here."

"Will you wait for me?"

"Yes, I will wait for you, Sheila."

Chapter 22

OVER THE NEXT few months, I worked on myself relentlessly. Who knew it took so long to get a divorce? I stopped taking calls from other men. I stopped texting. I stopped everything. I wrote in my journal and found a program through work where I could speak to or text a therapist at any time. So, I did, constantly. I searched my mind and my heart, wanting to find the roots of my pain and dig them out one by one.

It didn't help that when I went home, I was faced with Matt and his relentless demands. He was already asking for spousal support, and I quickly obliged. I didn't want to argue with him anymore, especially not when I was trying to understand my own emotions. I wanted to heal, and there's nothing quite like the month of February to bring a woman's emotions into the spotlight.

As Valentine's Day approached, every day was torture. I hated every man that walked through the doors of my store. I hadn't had a Valentine's Day gift since high school, and every purchase made reminded me of that. Watching them pick out gifts for their girlfriends and wives—sometimes both—felt like torture as I prepared for my divorce and spent time with Michael, knowing we were only friends. As the day came closer, I wanted to do something for Michael that wouldn't be noticed by anyone else, that would tell him how special he was to me.

Armed with the knowledge of Michael's love for old-fashioned things, I went online. I searched diligently for stationary paper. I wanted something you couldn't find at a local department store. Finally, I found the perfect package. It had beautiful old-fashioned tan pages with pink roses in the corners. Both of us loved vintage, and while it was a small detail, when I saw them, it made me smile.

I would write Michael a letter on stationary—a classic idea for someone who appreciated things full of character. Grabbing my pink pen, I sat down and wrote the first love letter I had written in over thirty years. The last letter I remember writing was when I was a kid, but *this* was different, and I knew it was something Michael could appreciate.

Michael,

I remember the day I met you like it was yesterday. I could never have imagined that one simple meeting would grow. You were more than the average guest. You were more than the average guy. You were always more. Now, I can't imagine a day without talking to you. Yes, I search my emotions daily. I don't want to care about you for the wrong reasons.

Then, I remember the journey I have taken over the past couple of years. I remember the men who cared or tried to care. I remember the ones that didn't. Maybe it's hard to believe, but this is different. This is a unique feeling that I can't completely explain, but it's quite possibly the realest thing I have ever felt. That is a little scary at times, but I do know that even though you have never touched me and never kissed me, you have touched me in a deeper way.

You said you would wait for me, and I hope that you do. I hope that you will always be there. I don't want to be generic in any way, but you have broken down more walls than I even knew existed, and I was helpless to stop it. I adore you even though I tried not to. You have captured a part of me that has never been touched.

I adore you because I enjoy our time together. You're silly and tend to say the things I only think to myself. You always make me smile even when I'm crying. I want us to learn how to spoil each other and experience life together. Even in the simple things, I enjoy spending time with you. I hope I have captured you—at least a little part—like you have captured me.

Happy Valentine's Day to the only man who has ever even come close to deserving me. One of these days, I just might kiss you.

Always,

Sheila

There was no coffee to greet me the morning of the divorce, just the rustling sound of Matt's clothes being deposited into bags. Lying there, I didn't bother opening my eyes. I just listened, knowing it would be the last time I heard his morning slithers. When the door closed behind him, I pushed the blankets away from my layers of pj's and locked the door behind him. Grabbing my best dress, I covered myself in confident armor. As my eyes narrowed and my breath stilled, I headed to the courthouse with Matt in the driver's seat because he had refused to drive alone.

When the judge questioned my agreement to the amount of money, I stiffly affirmed that it was correct as Matt smiled. I knew I was being screwed and that he didn't deserve it, but it was the price of peace and a quick settlement. When we returned home, Matt quickly gathered his things into the car that I had given him a year earlier—the thing he loved more than anything. But he didn't leave immediately. Squatting beside it, he replaced his rims and rotated his tires like it was just another day.

I cried softly behind the locked door of my bedroom with its freshly painted burgundy walls. Matt was free from emotion or obligation, but in my driveway, he sat loving, caressing, and dressing his precious car to impress. All the times he claimed to love me but ignored me came rushing back. Fiery cold tears plummeted from my gaze as I counted the years I'd lost in the ceiling tiles above me.

Obviously, Matt never loved me, and I am alone. Didn't he say, just yesterday, that he would never give up on me? Didn't he say that nothing was more important than me? What did I expect, though? Matt has always been heartless, frigid. While I fought to save us, he stared at video games and the car I gave him. Why couldn't he love me? What did I do to deserve the years of mind games? I always made sure to pleasure him, but Matt wanted more than I could give. I was just one woman. I was never enough for him because I couldn't be controlled with a controller and didn't have four wheels. It never mattered how much I gave him. What if Matt is right, though, and I'll never be able to love and never be happy with anyone?

Wrapping a blanket around my shoulders, my swollen eyes stared through the windows at the man who had taken my life from me and had tried to destroy me, and my heart quaked with loss. I must have stared, frozen, for hours as I waited for him to leave. *He should care that it's over. I've wasted too many years on something I didn't want, just because I thought it was the right thing to do and because I was afraid for me and for the life of my child. I won't be afraid anymore. Matt won't be telling me how crazy I am or crying that he doesn't want to cook. This proves that I can make it on my own. I made it this far, and I can live. We won't just survive; we will thrive without Matt holding us back.*

When gravel spun as Matt drove away, my heart began to beat again as I turned to my newly painted walls and the boxes that awaited me. Longing for transformation, I swung into action. I moved furniture, stuffed pillows, and dressed my bed in luxury. I traveled through the house and trashed everything that reminded me of Matt. Pictures left the walls to hide in dusty corners, replaced by inspirational quotes in blue. By evening, my tears had quieted, and for the first time in years, I could breathe again.

Chapter 23

THE UNSEASONABLY WARM March air whipped through my hair and the sun kissed my face as Michael put his convertible top down. Leaning back, I stared at the clouds that painted the sky like cotton angels. Warmth blew through the vents as I clutched my coat like a blanket.

"This is crazy. It's barely March!" I giggled.

"I know!" Michael agreed. "I thought you might enjoy it for a few minutes. A little crazy never hurt anyone."

"I'm so glad to get out for a while. It gets so tiring, the same thing every day."

"That's what I thought. You need to be reminded that you're alive occasionally, that there's more out there than Gallipolis."

"You're probably right."

"Of course. I'm always right."

"No, you're not." I laughed, slapping the side of his arm. "*I'm* always right, though."

"Ouch. Don't hurt me just because you're only right when I agree with you!" Michael laughed.

"You know better!"

"Yeah, maybe."

As we walked through the mall doors, Michael's legs carried him quickly while mine were still half asleep. The stores went by in a blur as we scurried toward the watch kiosk.

"Slow down." I laughed. "I can't keep up."

Michael's footsteps slowed as he looked back at me. Smiling, I ran up to him and slid my arm into his. I felt the warmth of his flesh through his button-up shirt, and my body froze as I looked into his eyes. *Oh no, what did I just do? We're just friends. This is something a girlfriend would do. I didn't mean to. It just happened.* My eyes grew wide as Michael stared into mine, and then he smiled. Quickly, I let go of him, and then he slid his hand into mine. He squeezed gently as he laced his fingers through mine, and with a wink, we walked together toward our destination.

My face must have been red as we casually looked at watchbands like nothing had happened, and each time Michael took his hand away from mine, he quickly returned to my side and laced them together again. That simple touch felt like a flush of sunlight traveling from my fingertips and tingling through every inch of my body. *I can't believe we're holding hands. I'm so happy. It feels nice. It's so weird that something so small seems so special—beyond special. Only couples hold hands. Is that what this means?*

"Oh, you know what we should do?" I asked.

"What?"

"Do you see that jewelry store over there? Let's go play a little game. We'll pretend to be a couple and give them a little hell."

"Who's pretending?" Michael winked. "You want to give 'em hell? Let's do it if it will make you happy."

As we played in the jewelry store, we asked for everything and wanted nothing. Every time that I looked at a diamond ring, Michael stated that it wasn't good enough. And, of course, the watches we looked at for him weren't quite what we were looking for. I acted ignorant about diamonds, and for the day, Michael was the expert as he discussed their quality and asked to look at them under magnification. We were never rude, and while it was fun, it felt playfully serious. After all, we had spent many days examining the same merchandise. We both loved jewelry, and when the sales associate made a mistake, we politely educated them. By the end of our little game, we weren't the only ones laughing, as they joined in on the same pleasure that jewelry brought to us.

My mind had been heavy from changes happening rapidly. My life had been completely transformed. As we drove back to our humble town, I was thinking almost too much. Spring was fast approaching, as evidenced by the warm day in the midst of snowstorms. Like the world around us, my heart was being reborn, and with that comes much reflection.

When we are young, barely old enough to understand, we await our first kiss—that magical moment where we discover passion and intimacy in what's meant to be its purest form. We talk about it in movies, songs, and books. It's a cherished moment and a rite of passage that we all enjoy, but it's only the beginning. Our *last* first kiss—with the person who will be with us and endure our shortcomings, who makes us want to be better people, and who helps us along the way—we tend to forget when it's the one we should remember the most. It's something that sneaks up on us like the last ray of light in a sunset or the last warm day of summer. It's gone before we realize it.

As headlights sheltered Michael and me against the darkness of night, words I had scribbled down ran through my head. *I've been kissed a thousand times and had moments take my breath away. I've been in love, felt my heart quicken, and felt my body shake with anticipation. Each time is a little different yet still the same—another lover, another man to take my time away. But one of these days, when I least expect it but know it's right in my heart, I'll find my last first kiss—a moment that will burn within my mind and last a lifetime. I don't want part-time lovers or temporary affairs. I want to give someone my last first kiss, my last true love. In him, I will find my last first date, my last story of you and me, and my last time to say I love you as I look into your eyes, trying to understand why.*

As the streetlights bathed us in light that evening, Michael opened the passenger-side door for me. Holding his hand out to mine, he politely helped me out of his car. Taking a deep breath, I looked into his eyes and waited for him to say goodnight.

"So, I remember that letter you gave me a few weeks ago, and I just have a question," Michael started.

"Oh . . ." I answer curiously. "That's a little scary."

"Why would it be scary? I enjoyed your letter."

"You did? We never actually talked about it."

"Of course, I did."

"So, what is the question?"

"Why would you want to kiss me?" Michael asked with a devilish smile. With streetlights glowing behind him, he stepped closer to me as the sun burst its heat within me.

The night air caressed my cheek as I tried to speak, my breath catching somewhere between my lungs and my throat. *Uh-oh, I'm in trouble now.* "Why wouldn't I?" I smiled, looking down at his feet.

"No, seriously. Give me a good reason why. I mean, I know why *I* want to kiss *you.*"

"Oh yeah? Why?" *Oh my God, he wants to kiss me? Oh shit!*

"You have to tell me first. You started this, after all. Didn't you say that someday you just might kiss me?"

Why did I say that again? Oh yeah, 'cause I stare at his lips all the time, and I desperately want to see how he kisses. Will he kiss me tenderly, passionately, or like he's trying to swallow my face? That will tell me his true character—the true character I already know that's warm and compassionate and has only ever been completely gentle. Oh, this is going to be good . . . I hope. Crap! Even my thoughts are rambling. This is really going to happen, isn't it? My . . . last . . . first . . . kiss . . .

"I want to kiss you, Michael, because you are tender, handsome, and you have shown me what it feels like to be respected," I answered. "You have shown me what it feels like for someone to care. And I want to feel what it's like to be kissed by a man who values me."

"I definitely value you. I'm glad. Believe it or not, that's the same reason I want to kiss you. You have shown me a lot, and I never thought someone like you existed. Are you sure you want this?"

"Yes, I'm sure." *What? That's a question? Of course, I want this! Why would you even ask? Damn!*

Stepping closer to me, Michael's eyes met mine again, and he reached his hand up to my face and caressed my cheek with his thumb. Leaning down toward me, his hand reached to the back of my neck as his fingers wrapped themselves around my hair. *This is it. This is my last first kiss. It's really happening.* Looking around me for one last moment, I took in the scent of the night, the feel of the air, and the warmth of Michael's hand on my neck as he pulled my head back. Watching his lips come closer to mine, I closed my eyes just as his lips met mine for the first time.

Our kiss started as a whisper—a firm tenderness that swept through my body with a wave of sunlight, caressing my body in warmth. As the kiss deepened, I wrapped my arms around Michael's neck while he pulled me closer, our lips talking only to each other as the stars twinkled against a dark velvet sky. Pulling away for a moment, his eyes smiled at mine as he dove in to taste me once again. My breath escaped into his lungs, and my body melted into his embrace. *He's so tender and his lips so sweet. I want to kiss him forever.*

That night, I curled up in a cocoon of blankets and soft pillows as I talked to Michael about our kiss and how it felt for our hands to finally be together. We talked about how we were finally free to be together and how important it was for us to have waited until after the divorce was final. We could step forward into a relationship that we didn't have to feel guilty about, knowing we did the right thing. Balancing my phone on my cheek, I pulled the blanket closer to me as the sound of Michael's voice soothed me like a lullaby, and I imagined falling asleep in his arms.

* * *

"**Y**ou owe me money! It's time to pay up!" Matt yelled as he burst through my bedroom door early the next morning.

My body still slept as Matt pulled my silky blanket off me. As my eyes cracked open, I froze in place. *Thank God I was too tired to take off yesterday's clothes. Why is HE here?*

"What the hell?! How did you manage all this?" Matt asked, looking around at the newly decorated room. "Why didn't you do this when we were together?!" he screamed.

"What do you mean? I tried, and you just piled it full of junk, and you never liked any of my ideas."

"Whatever, I'm here for my money."

"I'm not even awake yet. You know I have to get cash. What makes you think you can just bust in here? I want my keys back, *now*!"

"No! I have stuff here, and you owe me money. You're not getting them back until I have everything I want."

"Excuse me?! You have no right to be here, and you need to leave! *Now!*"

Shrinking against my blanket, I pulled it against my body, shielding myself from the eyes that stripped my flesh. My jaws clenched as I stared up at Matt, now an invader in my home. "I said *GET OUT*!" I yelled. "I told you I would let you know when I have cash. What is wrong with you? You *knew* I would be asleep."

"If I wait, I know you won't give it to me!"

"I will get it to you later today, maybe after work. You know how this works."

"Fine. I'm going to grab some things from downstairs. The whole house looks like you're moving. You should have told me."

"We're not moving, just making some changes."

Matt was relentless that day. I felt like I was being chased by the mob for $200. After entering my home without permission, he continued to text me, and when I wouldn't answer him at work, he started calling. After four or five attempts on my cell phone, he called the store phone, and I put it on speaker. I wanted witnesses. It was already harassment. Matt hadn't allowed ten minutes to go by without texting or calling, refusing to take no for an answer. He didn't care that I was at work. He wanted money, and he refused to wait for me to get off work.

When Matt realized he was on speakerphone, he told my employees I hated them and was working with my district manager to fire them. Their eyes were wide as my blood froze in my veins. Still, throughout the day, he persisted, until the store was closed and the cash was in his hands.

When I collapsed on my sofa that night, the house was quiet. Staring at the doorknob, I thought of Matt's endless begging. *I can change the locks. How hard could it be?* Leaning back, I rested my neck and allowed the tension to drift away with every breath I took.

"Mom, I think I need to go back to the hospital," Terra stated from the hallway.

"What? Why?"

"I'm scared. I've been cutting again, and I'm still thinking about suicide, and I . . . I know Matt was here. It freaks me out that he just came into the house."

"How do you know about that?"

"The neighbors told me. Besides, I could just tell. Can we go back to the Emergency Room and see if they can send me to a different place?"

"You seem okay, Terra. Are you sure you need that?"

"Yes, I wouldn't ask if I wasn't sure. I need to go."

That evening, Terra was sent to a hospital closer to us. This time, it was in Huntington, which was only an hour away. On the way, we picked up Michael, who spent most of the evening talking to her. They sat together in a meeting room while I filled out paperwork. I was relieved to have him with us. His presence took some of my tension away as I watched my little girl talk about suicide and show him the cuts on her arms.

Will our lives ever be okay? I hope they can help her, but I thought she was already doing better. Maybe she's just freaking out because Matt got into the house. Watching Terra and Michael together, I struggled to understand her. This wasn't like the first time she went to the hospital. This time, she seemed normal, if only a little sad. I could tell from her smile that she wasn't in danger of hurting herself. She just needed a little extra time.

At first, Michael and I sat in silence as the moon peeked at us from behind the clouds on the way back to Gallipolis. I had handed him my keys just so I could stare out the window and chew my fingernails without worrying about crashing into oncoming traffic. My eyes were distracted, torn between missing Terra and wanting to stare at Michael as the dash lights bathed his skin with light.

"What's wrong, Sheila?" Michael asked. "And don't tell me the obvious. I can tell there's something else."

"I don't know. There's a lot going through my head."

"Like what?"

"I was thinking about how much I adore you, and I was wondering how strongly you feel about me and about us. I'm not used to waiting for things to happen."

"I care a lot about you. I thought that was obvious."

"It is. My mind is just messing with me."

"How so? What are you thinking?"

"I'm just worried that I care about you more than you do about me. I used to tell myself that I would never have someone who I actually wanted. I've always had to settle, and that scares me. You're so good to me, and I want to keep that."

"I get it, but you don't have anything to worry about. I care a lot about you—more than you know. You're just waiting for me to say the L-word, aren't you?"

"I don't know, maybe." I blushed.

"Here's the thing: I don't want to get in a hurry to say that because, once we do, there's no turning back. It means something. I don't want to say it until the time is right. Once that happens, it starts the ball rolling, and there's no way to stop it. If and when I do, it means a lot more than just words. I thought I had my future planned out, and then you showed up, and everything changed. That left me with a lot to figure out."

"I know I wasn't exactly in the plan."

"I'm glad you are now, though. I'm glad I took a chance with you. You make me happy, and that's what I want for you: to be happy. You deserve it, Sheila. I just don't want to say it too soon. But please know that I care *a lot* about you."

"You mean a lot to me, too. I completely adore you, Michael. I feel like I'm ready for more, and that scares me because I know you've been through a lot too, and I don't want to push you. It makes me feel like I'm crazy because I'm afraid to tell you how I feel sometimes."

"Don't be afraid of what you feel. Your feelings are valid, and they're important to me. Having emotions and asking questions doesn't make you crazy."

Reaching for my hand, Michael raised it to his lips and kissed the back of it like I had seen on the bridge months before, and I smiled as my body filled with sunlight and my heart swelled with joy. *So, that's what that feels like!*

"Do you think Terra will be okay?" I asked after a few moments of silence.

"Yeah, I think she's okay. She's not as bad as she's letting on. I'm sure she'll be home soon. You don't need to worry about her. It just takes time, and I will help in any way I can."

"Hopefully, she'll talk to you. I know Matt hurt her too. I don't think he did anything to her. I've asked plenty of times. But she saw him change too, and neither of us felt safe. There were times when I honestly feared for our lives. He had a gun, and I was afraid he would use it on us if he got too angry."

"I'm glad he's gone. Nobody should be afraid to go home."

"*I* was. Matt never actually hit me, but he did everything else, and it was getting bad. Every time I tried to say something, he would turn it around on me. I saw his anger increasing, getting worse every day. I tried to get him help, but he refused. He said he didn't need it."

"Not to downplay physical abuse, but mental torture is worse than being hit in a lot of ways. When they mess with your mind—the yelling, screaming, manipulation, and all the things you've told me about—that is abuse. The things he did to you in the bedroom, all of that is rape. Rape has many forms: manipulation, coercion, not giving you a chance to consent. Even if you're married, it's still rape. That's why I haven't made love to you."

"Wait . . . *why* haven't we had sex?"

"Because I have a feeling that you haven't ever been made love to. You've just been screwed, and honestly, I want to give us time for our relationship to build, for us to really connect. If we do it too soon, it could really mess things up, and I want to do this right. I want it to mean something. I'm a little afraid, too. My heart is still messed up. That blockage is still there, and I can tell. I have trouble carrying in the groceries and doing little things around the apartment. I don't think it's safe for me to make love to you. I want it to be special and to do it right, and I can't right now. So, there's that, too."

"I've been thinking about that a lot lately. It worries me. Has your doctor made a plan yet?"

"Yeah, I have an appointment with him in a few weeks. I'm going to try to talk him into attempting to remove the blockage again. He keeps saying I'm okay and that the blockage won't kill me, but I know that if I have even a tiny blood clot, it could get stuck in one of those rerouted veins and kill me. I don't have any energy, and I want to be able to give you the best of me. I want to be healthy for you and know that I'm okay rather than make you promises that I can't keep."

"I get that, but you don't have to worry about that with me. I will help you through this."

"I know you will. You did last time, and we were just friends then. But I'm afraid he won't be able to fix it, and then all of this will be for nothing. Life is cruel sometimes."

After weeks of waiting, discussing, and fearing, the cardiologist agreed to another heart catheterization. Sitting in the waiting room, I stared at the clock. Every second felt like a pounding drum, beating on my heart. My chest was raw and sore from the heavy beats. I tried to distract myself, but my gaze never faltered. *These normally take around thirty minutes if everything is okay. This shouldn't take longer than that unless they can't fix it. The doctor said they might not be able to, and then he would require open-heart surgery. I know people who died in the cath lab. Michael will be okay, you'll see, Sheila. It's all going to be okay.*

It didn't matter how hard I tried to convince myself, my chest still pounded in rhythm to the second hand, only twice as fast. I flipped through social media, texted friends, and chatted with anyone willing to listen, but still, I watched the clock and the door . . . waiting. *Michael deserves a better life. He wants to feel like he can conquer the world. And I want him to be in my arms for a long, long time.*

Sitting there, I thought back to the night before, cuddled up with Michael in his apartment, fully aware of our early morning and the procedure that loomed ahead. Michael's eyes were tender, his touch gentle. After a while, he had laid his head against my chest as I ran my fingers through his hair, caressing the worries away. We had only been a couple for a few months, but we had been friends for over a year. *I can't imagine my world without him—or any world without him. Michael has so much to give. He has a purpose, a reason to live. Don't let this procedure take his life. Don't let it happen to him. Don't let him fade away.*

Seeing Michael's hair and a glimpse of his hospital bed through the waiting room window, I ran into the hallway. Grabbing the wall, I gasped as he was wheeled into his room. Then, as employees left the room, I rushed to his side. He was mostly covered with the hospital blanket, and his eyes quietly smiled as I stepped into the room. Brushing Michael's hair from his eyes, I gently kissed his forehead as he grabbed my hand, squeezing it tightly.

"Everything went okay," the doctor stated from the doorway. "He handled the procedure well."

Went okay? What does that mean? Were you able to fix it, or are we going to have to open him up? You said that was a possibility, so we were freaking out that it was a possibility. You said it would take a miracle. Did we get a miracle today? Please . . .

"Were you able to remove the blockage?" Michael asked.

"Well, sir, I did a lot of thinking, and I believe the reason it was a problem was because it wasn't a clot. Your vessels had collapsed. It happened slowly, but with a little creativity, I was able to put in four stints. Now, everything is open, and you should start feeling better."

Yes! Finally, good news! I can't believe it. Carefully, I climbed into the hospital bed beside Michael and rested my head on his chest. His arm wrapped around me as his lips gently brushed my forehead. *Thank you, God. Thank you for letting me keep Michael. I love him, and he's not ready to tell me, but I know he loves me. He says it in so many ways, just not with his words. This world wouldn't be the same without him.*

Peace encompassed Michael and me as together, we closed our eyes, waiting out the six hours required before he could walk and change from his paper-thin hospital gown. With Michael's arm draped around me, I laid my head on his chest. My fingers traced his cheek as we squeezed together on the narrow bed and fell asleep. When it was time, and the medicine had worn off, he got sick, nearly passing out in the hallway. Once again, we waited, hoping for better results so I could take him home. When Michael got up the second time, we walked together through the halls. I stayed by his side as he waddled from the painful incision in his groin.

Stepping back into the darkened hospital room, the door closed softly behind us. The room was quiet, and the machines were quiet. The hospital floor had been silenced as the other patients had found their way home. Holding his arms out to me, I cuddled up against Michael, and as I looked into his eyes, a smile spread across his face. Caressing my lips with his, I felt his tears drop onto my cheek.

"I love you," Michael whispered.

Reaching my arms around his neck, I gasped, my eyes closing against the sunburst invading my senses. *He said if he told me that, it would be because he meant it and it would mean much more than three simple words and would start the ball rolling toward the future and couldn't be stopped.*

"Did you really just say that?" I whimpered in Michael's ear. Pulling me tighter against him, I felt his breath against my cheek. His arms were warm with tender strength. I was afraid to look at his face—afraid that . . . I had heard wrong.

"Yes, sweetie, you heard me right. I love you," Michael whispered again.

"I love you, too."

It felt like Michael's life was given to him that day, like the procedure had healed his heart in more ways than one. I watched over him closely that night until his daughter came home. I made arrangements with her, to make sure he was taken care of. Thankfully, this time, there wasn't anyone to hold me back from nightly visits.

* * *

*W*hy did you change the locks? You have no right to do that!

That was Matt's first text message the day after I was bold enough to make some changes. Glancing at my phone, I turned it over, ignoring him. *He's interfered enough with my store. Meg and Tilly hate me, and my district manager is angry because he keeps getting calls about a man driving by revving his engine.*

I thought it was pretty obvious, I replied after Matt texted a few more times.

You can't do that! I have stuff there.

I told you to get everything out. The court papers say that you should have everything you own in your possession. You don't live in my house anymore. We're not married, and you entered my home without permission. It is my right to protect my home, and that includes changing the locks. I asked you to give me the keys, and you refused, so I had to change the locks.

I told you I would give you my keys when I got everything out. You better give me a copy of the key.

Why would I do that? You can arrange a time to come and get everything you want. I won't stop you from getting things out of the basement, but I won't allow you to enter my home anytime you want. And you need to stop contacting me at work. You drove by and saw my vehicle. You know I'm working! Don't bother me. I have told you hundreds of times to STOP!

I'm just going to work. I didn't do anything wrong.

There are about five other ways for you to get to work that don't include driving by my store as slowly as possible, putting your turbo car in neutral, and revving the engine. You are coming in from the opposite direction, and you park on the other end of the parking lot. There is literally no reason for you to keep doing that.

I don't do that. I drive by normally. It's your imagination.

Is it the imagination of everyone in the plaza? Because you're do-

ing it constantly.

I don't do it constantly, just when I'm on my way to work.

Listen, Matt, I texted. *I'm not playing your mind games anymore. You need to stop driving by, stop contacting my employees, and stop harassing me at work.*

I can contact anyone I want, Matt replied. *Besides, I thought we were going to try to be friends for Terra? I care about you.*

If you cared, you would respect that I'm trying to work. You can't keep contacting me here. You can stop spying on me, too. I wanted to be friends. I wanted this to be peaceful, but you're not letting that happen. I'm not afraid of you anymore. You have abused me for years and accused me of cheating when you were the one actually cheating. You used me and drained nearly every last cent I had earned, spending it on fast food, video games, and your car! You can't control me, push me up against walls, or rape me anymore! I'm done. You need to stop, or I'm getting a restraining order. I'm not kidding! I already talked to a lawyer.

You can't get a restraining order from me driving by your store.

Yes, I can. You're going to get a letter in the mail, and if you don't comply, they will set a court date.

You wouldn't.

I would. What do you want anyway? Just pissed that I changed the locks?

I know you just paid me, but can you go ahead and pay me for next month? I ran into a little problem, and I need the money.

You have GOT to be kidding me! No, I don't have money to give you whenever you ask for it!

When do you think you can pay me again?

I don't know. I will let you know. Probably when it's due. Don't contact me anymore.

Can you try to get it to me sooner? Then we can hurry up and get this over with, and you won't have to worry about it anymore.

I will think about it, I guess. I seriously doubt it. I told you I will let you know.

My text messages meant nothing. Every day, several times a day, Matt continued to drive by. Each time a car drove by, I stopped moving, stopped talking, and waited for it to pass. I waited for his text messages, asking me where my vehicle was, when I would see Michael again, and other ridiculous questions. Were Michael and I sleeping together? When did I get off work? When could I pay him? It never stopped. Nothing mattered.

I asked Matt for his address so I could drop his money off there instead. I asked to meet somewhere else. I talked to a lawyer, and a non-communication letter was sent, but Matt ignored everything until I paid him again. I didn't have time to wait for the restraining order to be processed, and there was no guarantee I would get one because I hadn't filed a police report, which I couldn't file because he hadn't left any marks on my body.

As Matt pulled away, the engine of the car I bought for him echoed against concrete and glass. I looked inside the store I called home, at the place I had fought for and at the people I loved like my own family, and I felt my heart shatter. When I looked inside, I still saw the birth of our beautiful store, with the fresh drywall and the ladders scattered across the floor before the wallpaper was hung. I saw the boxes blocking the aisles as we made the first displays in the new store. I remembered my interview with Meg and the first time I had sat in the manager's chair. Like a loving mother flipping through an old scrapbook, I thought of all the milestones I had witnessed. Looking at the thank you notes from organizations and people I had helped, I was sad as I knew I . . . had to leave.

My family—the employees I had trained—were turning on me. They hated Matt's interference, and it didn't matter how many times I told him not to drive by the store or block the entrance because he wanted money, he wouldn't meet me anywhere else. He had called my employees and told them I hated them and planned to fire them. He had wrapped his coils around everything I loved. Not only my daughter but the store I had built and the people I had nurtured.

Matt is going to destroy everything if I'm not careful. I can lie and tell my employees I want to take writing classes, that I need a change. They will never know that I actually had to leave to protect them. I can't stay and let Matt poison the thing I built, the one thing I love almost as much as my daughter. It might just be a store, but it has always been my baby. I was always meant to make it something beautiful. I've done that, and they don't need me anymore, not like they used to.

I have to leave, and maybe one day, they will understand. I love them too much to let Matt hurt them anymore, to let what he's doing to me affect them. This is my home, too. I will lie to myself as much as I will lie to them. I will lie to everyone to protect all of us, and eventually, life will go on, and maybe someday everything will be okay.

And soon enough, I had a new job—selling mattresses—and I enrolled at Marshall University. As I prepared to leave my store, I hoped for a reason to stay, but my employees never gave me one. They never said goodbye. There wasn't a farewell party. Because of all Matt had done to poison my staff, there was nothing, and I simply walked away.

As the apartment door closed behind us, I collapsed into Michael's arms. Hidden tears teased my cheek as he cradled me in his arms. His lips were tender as they caressed my forehead, and soon, my body settled in a purgatory between relief and sorrow.

"You need to relax, Sheila. This is a big step. You're standing up for what you believe in. There's no shame in that," Michael whispered. As he took my bag upstairs, I followed quietly, letting my mind rest as the finality of my position coursed through my body like an eternal shiver. Sitting beside me, Michael's hand squeezed mine as his face nestled gently against mine.

"I was going to get in the shower, but do you want to go first?" Michael offered. "Maybe the warm water will make you feel better?" he suggested, kissing the back of my hand.

"Maybe. It's worth a try."

Pulling me to my feet, Michael led me to the bathroom and turned on the water as I stared vacantly into the mirror at an empty shell hidden by my eyes. Taking my hands in his, he placed them on his shoulders as his hand gently unzipped my dress. As it fell to the floor, he removed each hook that held my bra in place, and as my breasts were released, his hands were waiting. Tossing my bra to the side, he caressed the side of my face with his hand before his lips found mine. Pulling my body against his, Michael's lips caressed my throat while his hands lovingly caressed the small of my back. His kisses trailed down my body as he kneeled in front of me. Sliding his hands beneath my panties, he gently tugged them away.

Leaning forward, I pressed Michael's head against my breasts, holding him close to my heart as my fingers ran through the back of his hair. His breath was warm against my nipples as his tongue danced across them. His hands caressed my buttocks as my breath escaped in moans from deep within my throat.

Pulling Michael's face to mine, I fell against him, my lips dancing against his throat as he held me. Gently, he cupped his hand beneath my chin and leaned my face up to his as his lips whispered against mine. Taking my hand, he gestured toward the running water that covered the small room in steam, and he guided me within its massaging streams. Leaning my head back, I let the water release the soft curls that framed my face until it covered my back in wet satin. Turning to face the water, I washed away the tears staining my cheeks and rested my eyes in the massaging tendrils.

When the shower curtain opened again, I felt Michael's arms wrap around my belly as his head nestled against my neck. Together, we rested as the water washed away my pain. Then, as his hands traveled up my body, he guided my neck back as he grabbed the shampoo from the ledge beside us. He caressed the shampoo through my hair, washing each tendril with his fingers. Shielding my eyes, Michael guided the water through my tresses as my sadness was evicted, escaping with the water that trailed down my body.

Filling his hands with body wash, Michael pressed his thumbs on either side of my spine. As he massaged my body with his hands, the tension in my shoulders relaxed, and I leaned my flesh against his. Pulling me closer, he cupped my breasts in his hands as he teased my nipples with his fingers, twisting them and pulling them until they hardened against his touch.

Turning to face him, I pushed Michael against the shower wall and grabbed the back of his neck, pulling his face to mine. Gasping against his lips, I teased them until his mouth devoured mine and his tongue danced against my upper lip with tiny flicks. Wrapping my arms around his neck, I pulled his lips closer to mine. Breathing in the kisses that engulfed me, I tugged at his body, pulling him closer.

When the water ran cold, Michael wrapped me in a towel and twisted the water from my hair. He held me in his bed all night that night, only pulling away to refill our coffee or start a playlist on his computer. His arms were warm and tender as they caressed and loved my pain away. His skin warmed mine as we embraced beneath the sheets, our bodies remaining separate with only kisses uniting us.

* * *

My mood was dark again when I went to retrieve Terra from the hospital. She smiled when she saw me, and this time, there wasn't a long conference and there was no treatment plan. Our instructions were to follow the previous plan set by the other doctors. I was disappointed because they had nothing new to say. It seemed like more of a vacation for her than anything else.

"Mom?" Terra called me, turning down the radio.

"Yeah?"

"Why did Matt have to be such an ass?"

"Don't say ass, baby girl." I glared. "I don't know why. I tried talking to Matt, asking him to get help and suggesting therapy. But he wouldn't do anything. He believed he was in the right."

"How could he think that? Why did he think it was okay to treat you that way, especially if you talked to him about it?"

"I don't know, and nothing I said mattered. He always found a way to turn the conversation, trying to make me believe I was the one who was in the wrong. He always made me feel guilty."

"That's crap."

"Don't say crap. But I agree. That's the way it is, I guess. I did everything I could."

"Mom, for what it's worth, I think you did more than enough. I don't want another dad, not anymore. Men can't be trusted. They have only ever hurt you. You know, kids at school talk, and they told me that Matt has talked to their moms. I swear there's someone new every day telling me that my dad has been trying to get their mom, dad, sister, aunt, or even cousin to sleep with him. I thought he was dating a girl from work. Why is he still talking to all the other moms?"

"Yeah, he's with Teri. Remember, I introduced you to her? He used to lie to me, saying he was spending time with a guy named Terry. He really used that to his advantage so he could keep accusing me of cheating. But of all the women who contacted me, she seems nice. It's not her fault that he lied to me. Nothing has changed, though. Matt's already cheating on her. I feel sorry for her. She has no idea. I tried talking to her once, and I told her that the rumors about him were true, because she asked. But she believes in giving people a second chance. I admire that, but with Matt . . . it's a mistake. I'm sorry people are talking to you about it at school. You shouldn't have to deal with his drama."

"It's okay. It doesn't bother me too much. I get mad sometimes, but not at my friends, just at him! I hope you don't get involved too soon."

"What do you mean?"

"Like I said, I don't want a new dad. What have you been doing anyway? I know that you have been going out sometimes, but please don't get serious."

"Well, you know I really like Michael. How do you feel about him? You two were getting along when we dropped you off at the hospital."

"I do like him. He seems like a nice guy—almost too nice. It's suspicious. I don't want to see you get hurt again."

"Well, we have gotten really close, and I love him."

"I know you do, but I don't want a new dad. I don't want it to be like Matt again."

"I know you're not a little girl anymore, and whatever relationship you have with Michael will be on your terms. It's up to you. Maybe you could be friends? Would that be okay?"

"I guess. But it's going to take some time."

* * *

At my new job, I was quickly labeled "The Jewelry Queen of Gallipolis." Each time my co-workers said it, I found a reason to smile. When I started classes at Marshall University, I quickly gained respect, and my classmates even started calling me the "cool kid in class." I thought that was hilarious because I was considerably older than them, although most of the time, it didn't feel like it.

The sun was bright and the leaves were golden as I stepped outside on what I remember as one of my favorite days at Marshall University. As the breeze tousled my hair, I strutted to my vehicle, my arms full of binders holding my latest creations. Michael was always waiting for me after class, but that day, I looked over to find him with the window rolled down, his head leaned back with a guitar in his hands. The low music teased my ears as I approached him with fast runs and gentle strums that sang in random notes as he tested his newest acquisition.

Surrounded by people running for class, Michael hopped out of the vehicle and headed toward me, leaving his new guitar propped up in the driver's seat. Wrapping his arms around me, Michael's lips met mine passionately. The world around us stopped as our mouths collided in the open air. His arms drifted up my back, and my fingers ran through his hair as we were cocooned in the protective haze of love.

"Let's get out of here!" Michael suggested.

"But I have another class," I whispered between kisses.

"You mean the one you keep complaining about? The one that zaps the creativity from you and leaves you emotionally numb for hours?"

"Yeah, that's the one."

"My point exactly."

Opening the door for me, Michael held out his hand as I sat inside the vehicle. With a gentle kiss before he closed the door, I awaited him. That day, we traveled around Huntington, tormented the mall jewelry store, and drove home with the wind in our hair. We talked about class and the story of our love. I enjoyed asking questions about when we met. I'm sure I had asked enough times to be annoying, but Michael always answered. Those answers always made me smile. We had been together nine months—long enough to realize that neither of us was going anywhere.

Running to his computer when we returned to his apartment, Michael started flipping through playlists as I leaned against his bed. Sitting beside me, he tenderly brushed my hair away from my forehead before leaning down to caress my lips with his. Stretching out beside me, his fingers traced my cheek like a whisper. My breath caught in my throat as I bent my knees, allowing my skirt to raise to my hips. Slowly, Michael's kisses grew stronger as his hands caressed my body, removing each piece of clothing separating our flesh. Kneeling beside me, his kisses greeted my forehead and traveled down my nose to my lips. Arching my neck, I pushed his head further down as my breath escaped in gasps against his touch. Obediently, his lips trailed down my neck as his fingers caressed and teased my nipples.

Is this going to happen, or is it just another make-out session that leaves me wanting more? We've been together for a long time, am I ready for this? Oh GOD, please don't let my mind drift away! I don't want to go on AUTOPILOT again! I want to be here for this moment. I want to feel every emotion. I want to open myself to him—Michael, so handsome, so sweet, and so tender. Please let him show me what this is supposed to be like, how I'm supposed to feel.

Taking my hands in his, Michael pulled them above my head. Overwhelmed with hopeful fear, I closed my eyes and embraced the rhythm that echoed through the room. My lips quivering, I arched my back and pressed my body against him. Reaching for me, Michael's hands released mine, and I wrapped my arms around his shoulders, pulling him closer to me. Gently spreading my legs, he climbed on top of me.

Michael's kisses grew stronger as they drifted down my body, and he opened my body with his until his fiery breath rested against my belly. He laid there . . . waiting. Looking into my eyes, he smiled as he lowered himself between my legs. One hand cupped my buttocks as the fingers of his other hand spread open the gentle folds of my most delicate place and his tongue flicked against the tip of my clitoris. Burying his chin against my vagina, Michael squeezed my body as my legs opened in a gasp of pleasure. My back arched as his tongue worshipped me. His hands lifted me like a golden chalice to his adoring lips. Burning, my body moaned against his flesh as he explored and moaned against my lips with delicious sounds of passion.

OH GOD, don't let him stop! Don't let this be the only thing that happens tonight! I want to feel him inside me!

With my hands buried in Michael's hair, I caressed him and guided him against my clitoris until the fire inside me had erupted into a fierce volcano. As his lips caressed mine again, he took his hand behind my neck and propped me up against his arm. With a longing glance into my eyes, I felt his essence whisper to mine in the darkness. Pulling me tightly against him, Michael's hips moved against mine, and his penis finally entered me. Softly, tenderly, his hips raised and lowered against mine as I gasped, my mouth opening as fire erupted between us.

Thank GOD! I'm still here. I can feel everything, see everything!

Our bodies worshipping, colliding, caressing, stretching, and turning against each other, my mind exploded with passion. My lips moaned against Michael's body as my hands clung to him, constantly tugging, reaching for his kiss. Caressing my thighs with his hands, Michael looked down at me for a moment, his eyes full of love. He arched his back, and his lips parted in pleasure.

"You look so beautiful, lying there. Your kisses are so sincere, so passionate. You feel even better than I could have ever imagined," Michael said as he gasped.

"You feel amazing." I whimpered beneath him.

Lowering himself against my body, Michael brushed the hair from my eyes and caressed my forehead with his lips. My body quaked beneath him as I wrapped myself around him, arching to meet his every thrust. My arms clung to him, and my lips explored his neck, tasting the small beads of sweat that arose on his skin until he collapsed above me, resting his head between my breasts.

"I love you so much," Michael whispered.

"I love *you* so, so much, baby," I replied. Kissing Michael's forehead, I wrapped my fingers in his hair, caressing his face and shoulders with my hands. My body relaxed, relishing the moment. *Finally, I have given someone not just my body but my mind as well. I stayed in the moment and didn't drift away.*

Throughout the night, our bodies danced. Our lips never grew weary, and my arms never grew tired of embracing Michael. Only out of duty did we fall asleep, cuddled into each other's arms just as daylight broke the horizon.

* * *

The months flew by as I traveled while selling mattresses at different stores, went to classes, and enjoyed my time with Michael. Still, Matt didn't go away. The money I had enjoyed before had vanished, and I was left with barely enough to scrape by after traveling expenses. But it didn't matter because I loved where my life was heading. Terra and I didn't need as much as what we had grown accustomed to. Now, I had life. I was true to myself. Matt's harassment continued, but now, it didn't matter. He couldn't keep track of my schedule or watch my vehicle. Occasionally, he asked where I was, but I never told him.

Women still came to me after the divorce, confessing that they had received messages from Matt while we were together. And some confessed to newer messages while he was with his new girlfriend. There was nothing I could do because I was the "crazy ex-wife." He would contact me complaining about living with his mother, and then moments later, he would show off new games and car parts he didn't need before asking for money.

Matt tried accusing me of starting rumors, which I hadn't. There had been more than enough women to gossip about him for me. He seemed to enjoy tormenting me whenever he got bored, and I continued to stand up to him. Eventually, he ran out of manipulation tactics, and things grew quiet. It just took eighteen months to do so, and when the money was finally paid in full, I changed my phone number and blocked Matt from social media.

Chapter 24

LEANING BACK INTO Michael's arms, I watched Terra escape the house with her friends. It was the end of her sixteenth birthday party, and I was exhausted from the constant noise of teen laughter. Tilting my head up, I pulled Michael's face to mine, kissing him gently. *It's time. I don't think I can wait any longer. It will only take a second to go get it.*

Pulling away, I headed toward the bedroom, searching for the gift I had prepared for him. My heart raced as I dug it out of my drawer and looked at it one last time. *I can't believe I'm doing this.* My cheeks grew warm as I stood before Michael, my breath rattling as I tried to find the words to explain, yet hide, what I was dying to say.

"Michael, I wanted to do something for you to let you know how much I appreciate you, so I wrote down what I was feeling. I know Valentine's Day is getting close, and last Valentine's Day, I gave you a letter. I wanted to do something similar this year, but I wanted it to grow like we have. I want to explain something to you first, though. You see, I thought about giving you a real rose with the letter. But real roses die, and our love will never die. Then, I thought about getting you a silk rose. But they're fake, and our love isn't fake. So, I went to a specialty store, and I found these beautiful real roses dipped in twenty-four karat gold. Not only is it real, but it will last forever, and it is more precious and unique than any other rose." I smiled.

Reaching into the gold box, I pulled out a rose. It was white with pink faded petals trimmed in gold. It felt delicate yet strong in my hand. Michael's eyes grew soft as I walked toward him, placing the rose in his hand.

"You didn't have to do anything for me," Michael stated, smiling.

"I know. And that's why I love doing things for you. You appreciate it. Here, let me read the card to you . . ." I pulled the card away from the rose and read. "Sometimes, when we're not looking, something unexpected happens that changes our life forever, and we finally understand that the simplest things are often the most important. Finding someone to enjoy life with—the good times, the bad times—and who will stand beside you and help you achieve your biggest dreams is one of those somethings. You inspire me every day to be better than I was. I love you more than you could ever know."

A smile spread across Michael's face again as he reached for me. Pulling me into his arms, his lips caressed mine, and he wrapped his warmth around me. Turning the rose in his hand, he traced each petal with the tip of his finger, memorizing the curves and the lines of his new masterpiece.

"Do you like it?" I asked. "It's hard to buy for a guy. I didn't want to buy you any more jewelry."

"I think you did wonderful, but I'm not prepared to give you anything yet."

"This wasn't your Valentine's Day gift. It's just something I wanted to do."

"I guess our anniversary is coming up, too, isn't it?"

"Yes, it is." I giggled.

"You're going to make it hard on me. This is going to be difficult to beat."

"Baby, I wouldn't try." *This is only the beginning.*

* * *

The pancakes smelled heavenly when they arrived at our table. Terra and I had always loved trying different syrups and combinations when we went out for breakfast. The servers always seemed confused when we asked for extra plates, especially when she was little. Now, we just hung out like old friends.

That day was no different. Terra had shut herself in her room a lot, so I was thankful to be able to drag her out of the house. Most of the time, I didn't see her, and it just reminded me of the promises I had made her—that I would be home soon, that it would get better, and that I wouldn't be working as much. I always felt like I was lying to her. Our freedom from Matt had taken its toll on me, and sometimes, it seemed to take away my most important relationship, the one with Terra. But she was almost grown, almost gone, and I only wanted her to be a baby again so I could have another chance to raise her. Looking back at a life full of regrets seemed like poking needles in my eyes, and I felt that pain often.

"You know I miss you, right?" I asked from across the table.

"I know, and I miss you, too."

"Am I a horrible Mom?"

"No, of course not. You've sacrificed everything for me. I can see that. Sometimes, you're a bit of a snob, but I know you do things because you care. I'm just not like you, that's all. We are very different, and sometimes, you're more of a friend than a mother. But I think it's more fun that way. I know that if I need something, you're going to be there. I get it. I think that makes you a great mom because you can be both a friend and a mother."

"Thank you, Terra. That's sweet," I answered, trying to hold back the tears that dared to escape my heart. "I feel guilty for all the things I've done, for not telling you about them sooner, and for not being there for you. I missed everything."

"Not everything. And you shouldn't feel guilty. I don't blame you for the things you've done. I'm glad you told me and didn't lie. I like that you're a real person. I've learned a lot from you."

"Are you sure all of this didn't happen because I wasn't there all the time?"

"I'm sure."

"Terra, I need to tell you . . . Michael and me, we're getting . . . really close. He's important to me, and I want to keep him around . . . forever."

"*Forever*, forever?"

"Um . . . yeah."

"Has Michael asked you to marry him? Please tell me he hasn't. I don't want another man in our home yet. I like that it's just us."

"He hasn't asked me that, not yet. I don't know if he ever will, but he might someday."

"I don't really care, Mom. I told you, I don't want another dad."

"I know. It won't be like that, though. You know, Michael and I have been together almost a year now."

"So. That doesn't change how I feel."

I guess that's enough of that conversation. "We have to go. I need to pick something up. I um . . . decided to buy something, and it's time to meet up with the seller," I informed Terra with a smile.

The ride out of town was filled with questions I refused to answer. Terra asked if it was something for her, and I just smiled silently, letting her nag me. But she never guessed. Thankfully, it was a short trip, and when we pulled into a rest area, I saw it. At the edge of the parking lot, a woman stood with a purple leash and a red and white spotted puppy standing alertly. Its docked tail shook as its nose sniffed the air. The curls on its ears blew in the breeze. Terra's eyes widened as she caught sight of the little furball, and the tears I had been holding in trickled down my cheek.

"Mom! Seriously?! Mom! Oh my God, Mom. Is that . . .?" Terra pleaded.

Looking over at her, I couldn't speak through my laughter as I pulled beside the woman and climbed out of the vehicle to greet her. As the lady handed me the leash, I shook her hand and handed the puppy to Terra.

"Mom! I love you! What gave you this idea?"

"I'm not always home, and I remembered the dog at the first hospital and how it helped all the patients. You've done so well. I never have to worry about what you're doing while I'm at work, and you deserve for there to be someone waiting for you when you get home from school. I think this little girl will help you. Honestly, we both deserve a little extra love at home."

"Thank you! Do you really think I'm doing good? I saw pictures of her online, and I never thought it was possible. She's the same type as Lady in *Lady and the Tramp*. She's so beautiful! Can we stop and get her toys, and a brush, and I don't know . . . *everything?*" Terra laughed through her tears. "Oh, Mom, thank you! And thank you for understanding. This is probably the best thing you have ever done for me."

"Happy late birthday, baby girl. This was your real birthday present, and yes, I wouldn't do this if I didn't think you could take care of her. You're old enough to have a little responsibility, a little extra purpose. So, tell me, what are you going to name her?"

Holding the puppy to her chest like a baby, Terra closed her eyes and sighed. Her face lit up as the baby cocker spaniel licked tears from her cheeks and snuggled against her neck. "I think her name is Hazelnut Angelica Dot." Terra laughed. "She's just like the one we had when I was little: Dot. That's why I want to keep that in there. But let's call her Hazy for short." Terra smiled, holding Hazy to her chest again. "Thank you. I love her."

I finally got something right.

Hazy seemed to bring out the best in Terra, and suddenly, my stubborn teenage daughter was smiling again. Her eyes lit up, and I knew that it wasn't only the right decision but the best decision I could have made for my daughter. It was going to be nice having Hazy around to make our home a little warmer. Her spots and curly ears were irresistibly adorable—a ray of sunshine in a world once full of darkness.

* * *

Staring at the glowing lights of the mattress store sign, I shut off my vehicle and headed inside, wishing I was at home with Terra and Hazy. That day, I knew I would be working with one of the managers. I guess he was technically my boss, but it didn't feel like it. He'd been flirtatious the day before when he called to confirm that I was coming to work at his location.

Like most men, the manager tended to go after what he wanted. That was the problem with selling mattresses; there was too much opportunity. Almost everyone that worked for the company was male, and the atmosphere was hostile to women. Every time I worked with one of the guys, they either let me know what they were thinking, or I would catch them looking down my shirt.

With a glance down at my red dress, I sighed. *I miss working in jewelry.* When I asked my new boss about the dress code, he kept telling me to dress comfortably, but I had grown comfortable in dresses and heels. They made me feel classy, which was something I desperately wanted to hold onto. I had gone as far as to discuss it with one of my co-workers at another store, and he told me I needed to be myself.

We rarely saw other employees except in passing. The days were lonely now. Sometimes, I didn't see anyone or make a sale for weeks. I simply drove to whatever store they wanted me at, stayed there all day surfing the internet, and then did homework before driving home.

"Don't take this the wrong way, but you look nice," John stuttered as I walked inside.

"Why would I take that wrong? There's nothing wrong with a complim—"

"No, I mean you look *really* nice. I see you took my advice about being more comfortable at work."

"Thanks. It's a lot easier to make a sale when I feel confident. Red is my power color."

"I can see why. I love the lipstick and heels," John whispered.

"Well, this is how I used to dress for work, but I was afraid it would make customers here uncomfortable. That's why I've been wearing leggings. It's hard to lay on mattresses when you're wearing a dress, though. Hey, show me what you did with the back showroom. You told me you were making some changes and moving the low coil counts yesterday."

"Of course! You know, I think it would make people more likely to buy a mattress with you looking like that. You should let me see what you look like laying on one. I bet you look tempting. I, um . . ." He sighed, shaking his head. "I put some of the clearance mattresses in the shadows so people are less likely to see them. I would rather them buy the newer ones. We get more commission that way. God knows they don't pay us anything."

"No, it's pretty sad," I agreed, looking down at a small pile of men's clothes stuck in the corner. "It looks like you might have been a little more comfortable yourself earlier. Big plans tonight?"

"No, of course not. I haven't been able to have any big plans for a long time. My wife doesn't exactly care about what I want if you know what I mean. It makes me understand why a man would do crazy things for a little attention."

"What do you mean?" I asked.

"You know *exactly* what I mean," John replied, running his hand up my arm.

It felt like a bucket of ice crashing over my head as John touched me. His eyes were chilling probes, tearing away my clothes as he stared at my breasts. Shaking my head, I stepped back. I felt his desire, his loneliness. Taking another step back, I stumbled, falling back against a mattress. My body tensed as I quickly sat up, my hands gripping the sides of my dress. My eyes darted to the door, searching for the closest security cameras but finding none. *If I say anything, I can't prove it. There's no evidence. He's friends with the district manager. No one would ever believe me. I would be labeled a troublemaker.*

"Well . . . it looks . . . like you . . . put a couple of the memory foams back here, too," I stuttered. "And not just the clearance ones."

"You never know when you might catch a little time to enjoy a mattress, right?" John winked.

"Pretty sure we're not supposed to sleep on the job," I answered as I stood, quickly pulling my dress down.

"I didn't exactly mean sleep."

Of course, you didn't! "You know, just because I talk to you a little bit about work, that doesn't mean—"

"Are you sure? 'Cause, just say the word, and I'll lock the door. No one will ever know."

"I don't think that's a good idea."

"Is there no way I can sell you on this?" John pleaded as he sat down on the largest mattress.

"*No!* You can't sell me on this. I love who I'm with. There's no way I'm risking that."

"Why? He would never know."

"*I* would know, and I told you, I'm not going to betray him. It doesn't matter how tempting you think the offer is. I'm not desperate. I have been used by enough men to know how this ends."

"What do you mean . . . 'this?' There is no *this*. It's just two adults having fun."

"I know how I'd feel if he ever did something like that to me, so why would I do it to him?"

"You're not doing anything to him. You're doing it to me. Or, well, I could do it to *you* if that would make you feel any better." He laughed.

"No, not really. It's not worth it."

"Okay, okay. I will go then. Just text me if you change your mind." John winked.

Watching him walk away, I plopped down in the chair and threw my head back. My heart was racing, and my eyes grew warm with tears. Logging into the computer, I stared at Michael's picture. Learning to say no hadn't been easy, not after years of surrender. Those desperate moments had given me false value for most of my life. Now, I knew better. I knew I was worth more, and so was my love for Michael. As I went through photos of Michael and me, my sadness turned to pride. I had resisted. I had said no. *I SAID NO!* Without hesitation, I had done the right thing, and that was something I couldn't have done before knowing what it felt like to be loved.

Chapter 25

GRABBING THE GOLD BOX holding the second rose, I placed it beside Michael's coffeemaker before heading upstairs. Opening the box, I pulled out the second part of the letter. I made a small, folded card and placed it on its side, knowing he would see it either that night or first thing in the morning. Opening it, I read the words in my head again as I thought of my journey with Michael.

I don't have it all figured out, but what I know is this. I wanted someone who could challenge me, who I could be proud of, and who would understand my heart and my mind even at its craziest. I never thought I would feel anything again, and then somehow, without ever meaning to, I fell in love with you. Now, I know I can't picture my life with anyone else.

Walking upstairs, I headed for the sound of running water and quickly accepted Michael's invitation to join him in the shower. It had become one of our favorite things to do together. In his arms, it was okay for me to be vulnerable, to let go of my worries, and to forget the men that flirted and propositioned me. I had abandoned teasing men in grocery stores, wanting only the attention of Michael because with him, I felt loved. Even when there was nothing separating our flesh, his hands were gentle and his kisses loving.

Now, when other men looked at me, it reminded me of past regrets. I felt vulnerable and afraid, knowing what men were capable of. So, I stayed close to the safety of Michael's arms. When we were together, he watched over me. The gentle touch of his hand on my lower back let me know I was safe. When I was farther away, it only took one look for him to see my fear and return to my side.

I'll never forget Michael's face lighting up when he found the second rose as we prepared to leave for class. It was somewhere between confusion and joy as he smiled. Michael held me in his arms after he read the card and discovered the beautiful turquoise and white rose trimmed in twenty-four karat gold.

* * *

"**W**ow, you look nice today. What's the occasion?" my store manager for that day asked when I walked in.

"This is just how I dress."

"You might give me problems if you dress like that all the time." He winked. "John already called, wanting to talk to you. You seem to have really hit a nerve with him."

"Not exactly." I glared back at him.

"Well, it's not like your man has put a ring on it, so you might as well have friends, right?"

Why is it that you men keep thinking the MAN has to propose? I am more than capable of asking for what I want, when I want it, if I decide to want it. I can be in charge of my own destiny. "I'm very loyal," I answered, sitting behind the desk. "Did I get any other calls today?"

"Nope, that's the only time the phone rang. So, what are you doing today?"

"I finished writing my book, and I'm going to do some editing. What about you?"

"I brought a book to read. But I'm still curious since you changed the subject awful fast. Is Michael ever going to ask you to marry him?"

"I don't think we're in a hurry. Besides, he wants to finish his master's degree."

"Then what's the problem? You should call John back."

"I'd rather not."

"Well, we talked about moving you there permanently, but I told John no because I like it when you're here. I'll tell you what, if I was

Michael, I wouldn't let you out of the bedroom."

Seriously? I left the jewelry store for THIS? I hate men.

"Well, unlike you, Michael respects me. It's nice."

"Respect, huh? I respect you, darlin'."

"If you say so."

I have to keep this job for a little while longer. I don't want to be here. I mean, damn . . . they lied about how much money I would make, said I'd have control over promotions and advertising, and then took it all away. But what am I going to do? I guess I can make it without a job. I've done it once; I can do it again. I've worked hard for a long time, and I'm tired of being around all these rude ass men. Come on, just fire me already, please!

With a sigh, I pushed away from the computer I was using and began walking around the showroom. I wanted to get away from the uncomfortable stares of my manager. As I walked, I thought about cinnamon toast for dinner, bologna sandwiches, and finally, shopping sprees. Ideas for my photography business popped into my head as I made my second lap, and after that, I just started to dream. I wanted to be home.

"Your phone keeps going off," my manager pointed out. "Maybe you should check it. I'm going to go next door and get some snacks. Do you want anything?"

Shaking my head no, I headed back to the desk. Glancing at my phone, I was greeted with messages from John. *What does he want now?* As I investigated further, I realized it wasn't only him messaging but several guys who had managed to add me on their Snapchat and a few customers who had come into the store as well. Sighing, I placed my phone face down and leaned back in my chair. *I changed my profile picture to one of Michael and me. Can't they take a hint? Why do men think that if I accept their friend request that I'm interested in dick pics and sex? These guys have a serious problem. Hell, I'm just trying to sell mattresses and make a living.*

As my phone continued to alert me of new messages, I reached down and quickly deleted Snapchat and started blocking some of my admirers on social media. *I just can't talk to men at all, apparently.*

This is getting old, fast. As my manager reentered the store, I pulled up a picture of Michael and me, and I started looking through hotels in Florida, hoping my manager would leave me alone. Of course, he didn't, so I excused myself early and headed to the park to think before finding my way to Michael's little apartment.

Taking the third golden box from its hiding place, I placed it on the passenger seat, knowing I would be driving to class the next morning. Opening it up, I smiled at the white and purple rose, the edges of its petals and the stem and thorns all covered in gold. Opening the card, I read the third part of the letter and placed it on top of the box so it was ready for Michael to discover.

A long time ago, I decided you were more than enough. I knew who you were, and even now, I can see the worst and the best of you, and I am not afraid. Whether you succeed or fail, I want to be by your side. I love and respect you more than I thought possible. You are different, and you are the only one who has ever seen me and loved me as I am. I don't want to lose myself in you because I am always going to be me. I don't want OUR life to be based on YOUR successes but on OURS. Sometimes, two people are better together than they are alone because together, they can push the other to achieve the impossible. We are both impossible . . . as was our LOVE.

When Michael opened the car door the next morning, he froze for a moment. His smile broadened as he read the card, his eyes resting more on me than the rose. *"Three* of them? What are you up to, Sheila?"

"I'm not up to anything. I just want to do something special for you to remind you of how much I love and appreciate you."

"I love you, sweetie," Michael gently whispered.

Leaning over to me, his lips captured mine, and I nestled my face against his neck, enjoying his fresh cologne and the warmth of his breath in my hair. *It's almost time for the fourth and final rose.*

* * *

259

Hey, how are you? Teddy texted as I finished my breakfast.

After driving an hour to sit all day in a mattress store with no customers, I was happy to answer. It had been a while since I'd seen a customer, and sometimes, those stores were too quiet. Sometimes, I waited to get ready for work until I was *at* work. After leaving my jewelry store, it was hard to be as committed to work, especially when my new employer made promises and didn't deliver on them. I had stopped talking to employees because the men were flirtatious when they saw me. Now, my new work uniform was solidly in the sweater and leggings family.

I'm doing okay, I replied to Teddy. *Just staying busy-ish. What's up with you?*

Well, I might be taking a job in Cincinnati and moving, Teddy informed me. *I miss talking to you.*

I miss it, too, sometimes. But Michael keeps me busy. It seems I'm busier now than when I was a store manager.

Of course. You never slow down, do you?

Not if I can help it. Although, when I'm at work, it's really slow.

I'm glad you and Michael are doing well. You deserve it. I haven't found anyone. Women don't seem to understand me. I can't relax and be myself.

I always saw you as you are, Teddy. I think you should give them a chance.

What do I do?

Just talk to them. I mean, to her. Are you talking to the same girl who wanted to get married?

Sometimes. Why do girls always want to get married?

Commitment is important. She must really like you. Do you like her?

Yes and no. I just don't think I'm ready for any of that.

I understand. Michael wasn't either, but it's been beautiful. It surprises me sometimes.

After discussing our relationships and his new job, Teddy asked if he could stop by and meet me at work sometime for lunch. With new cameras being installed in the Gallipolis store, I obliged and was looking forward to seeing him before he left for Cincinnati.

When the doors swung open and Teddy entered the Gallipolis store the next week, his smile brightened the room instantly. Walking up to me, his arms wrapped around me. I had left my shoes behind the counter, and he towered above me as he pushed me against his chest. Gasping for air, I pulled away, laughing.

"You look good, girl!" Teddy smiled.

"Thanks. So, what are you up to? When are you leaving?"

"A couple days. I wanted to see you before I'm gone because I don't know how long I'll be gone or whether I'll be coming back."

"If it were me, that would make me nervous."

"A little bit. So, I do need a new mattress. What do you recommend? My back has been hurting a lot."

Taking the professional approach, I asked a few questions and led Teddy to the most popular mattress for back pain, sitting down beside him as was customary. His large fingers gently caressed my cheek as his warm eyes caressed mine and he smiled.

"I really do miss you," Teddy whispered.

"I miss you, too, but . . . I'm happy with Michael. It's not like before."

"I'm glad you're happy. I wish *I* was." Running his fingers through my hair, Teddy cleared his throat and pulled me into his arms again. I felt him sigh as I pushed him away.

Stepping away from Teddy's arms and the hands that reached for me, I headed for the sales desk. "Teddy, I mean it. I'm happy."

261

"Yes, I know. I don't want to come between you and him. It's good to see you smile again. You're glowing. He must treat you well. I just wish I could kiss you one more time before I leave."

"How about a hug? You know I care about you, Teddy. I think if you're careful, everything will be okay. I'll always be your friend, but I'm not going to kiss you . . . or anything else. It's too late."

"I understand, and I promise to be happy for you."

"Thank you, Teddy. If you come back, let me know, but remember . . . just friends."

Wrapping his arms around me, I felt Teddy's breath in my hair, and I sighed. I remembered our moments alone, when he was too forceful and I couldn't say no. I remembered his apology afterward and our pizza nights discussing employee gossip. I remembered when he cleaned off my vehicle in a snowstorm and watched over me at The Outlet, and I smiled. It felt like I had passed a test—one that I had often failed years before. I had learned to stand up for myself and demand respect. I didn't just feel safe in Michael's care anymore. Now, I felt safe in my own decisions.

As I pulled away, I looked once more into Teddy's brown eyes and saw the love he had trapped within himself. Grabbing his phone, he pulled me into his arms one last time.

Goodbye, Teddy.

Chapter 26

STRUGGLING TO GET ON the sofa, Hazy whined until Terra picked her up and cradled her in her arms. Terra put her hand up, and the little cocker spaniel smacked it with a well-trained high five before snuggling against her.

"Is tonight the night?" Terra asked.

"Yeah. I was going to wait until our one-year anniversary tomorrow, but I forgot it's a leap year, and there's this tradition . . ."

"Really? So, have you given him all the roses yet?"

"Just the first three. I have everything ready, though . . . I think. I'm really nervous."

"You shouldn't be. He loves you, Mom. I think it's a good decision."

"You think so? I thought you hated the idea of me getting serious?"

"I did, but I've been paying attention, and I've never seen you this happy. You're at peace, you smile a lot, and you're more patient. Besides, Matt has been gone for a year now, and you've known Michael a long time."

"I still don't expect you to call him Dad. You know that, right?"

"I do, and I appreciate that. He's been respectful and been good to me. He's becoming a friend. I'm always going to be nervous about it after everything Matt did, but if you want this, I'll support you."

As Hazy sat up against Terra, the little dog leaned her head back, looking into Terra's eyes as she scratched her belly. Laughter erupted through the house as we finished our freshly baked chocolate chip cookies and the newest live-action princess movie began. Since Matt had left, Terra and I had both become addicted to them as more and more old animated films were modernized and transformed from old cartoons to beautifully modern love stories. It was our guilty pleasure, and it was one that we indulged in with a bag of popcorn and freshly baked cookies.

When our movie was over, I took a deep breath as Terra smiled knowingly. I had prepared my usual overnight bag but with a few additions to make the night special. I was going to catch Michael off guard. I'd made up an excuse so I could take him out for dinner a day earlier than planned. With a final hug from Terra, we both smiled as I left for the evening, my bag extra heavy. I just needed a moment to myself before my plans went into action.

The cold was bitter as it crept through the window of my vehicle. Looking at the steps where I used to imagine standing with Trenton, I smiled. *Sometimes we don't get what we want because there's something better waiting for us. I wish I would have known that. I wish I would have known my value. I could have saved myself a lot of pain. I've been through so much, and now, my life is a miracle.* I remembered sitting at the park talking to the crisis prevention line, meeting Matt and Jackson there, and every other memory that the park held for me. *I'm glad I changed. If I hadn't gone through everything, then I wouldn't have made it to this moment.*

As the shrill sound of my cell phone ringing echoed through my vehicle, I jumped, my heart skipping a beat as I was jerked back to reality. I didn't recognize the number, so I braced myself, hoping for a telemarketer who I could chat up. But that wasn't the case.

"This is Doug from Mattress Fantasies. I have human resources on the line with us, and this call is being recorded."

Oh please, oh please, oh please . . . FIRE ME! I dare you! "Um, sure, that's fine," I replied.

"Sheila, we are closing a couple of our lowest-performing stores, and that means we won't need as many people in sales. Because you are one of our newest associates, we're going to have to let you go. But we won't fight your unemployment. You should be able to get it easily."

"Okay. Thank you for letting me know. I appreciated the opportunity to work with your company."

YES!!! My heart leaped for joy knowing I wasn't required to return to the uncomfortable boys' club that was Mattress Fantasies. *Whoo-hoo! No more sexual harassment at work that I can't do anything about because of their shield of testosterone.*

Then, my heart dropped as I realized . . . I just got fired. But the fear only lasted for a moment as I considered the alternatives. *I will be okay for a while. I can work on writing and painting. I can spend time with Terra and finally be able to rest. I've spent the last several years in chaos, and now, I can be safe at home.* As I glanced around the park one last time, I smiled. *The past is gone, the last chapter is closed, and it's time.*

As the moon rose on the horizon and the world turned from light to dark, warmth shot through my body like a quick glass of wine as the wind changed and the world continued to turn. Michael and I shared food from his favorite Chinese buffet and laughed over the past, but my thoughts quivered in anticipation, waiting for the moment with thoughts of my bag lying at the bottom of his apartment staircase.

"Since you don't want to leave the apartment tonight, not even for a few minutes, you have to sit over at the table, eyes closed until I message you, okay?" I instructed Michael.

"Are you sure? This seems a little crazy. I don't need to keep my eyes closed. I won't be able to see anything."

"Fine." I laughed. "But that's kinda the point!" As Michael took his seat, I walked over to the door, looked down at my bag, and quickly opened it. *Speed is of the essence. I only have an hour before midnight and leap day will be over.* "Can you see me, Michael?"

"No, and I'll look at my phone the entire time. I don't want to ruin the surprise for myself."

"You're sure?" I confirmed. "No peeking!"

"I promise."

As the sound of Michael's favorite TV show echoed through the room, I watched him as tears filled my eyes. *This is going to be amazing. And maybe a little crazy, but hey, crazy is who I am, and he loves that. So, here goes nothing, or rather . . . everything.*

Pulling the silk rose petals from their container, I removed my shoes and quietly tip-toed up and down the stairs, leaving a trail of their beauty on either side. As the petals graced the stairs, I found and turned on twenty-four flameless candles, placing them with the petals. On each step, I left enough room for our feet so Michael could pass by easily. The flameless candles flickered against the shadowy staircase, enveloping it with warmth as they danced against the beauty of soft pink rose petals. Finding notes I prepared, I folded them in half so they could stand on their own.

Between the candles on the first step, I placed the first rose and the first note. The note read:

Our journey wasn't just one step. Many steps were taken before we were ready to admit how important we are to each other.

Taking a few more steps, I considered the early days, when Michael hated the idea of love, and all the fears we both overcame. Closing my eyes, I placed the second rose and the second note. The note read:

The past tried to hold us back, but things happened naturally, and our journey couldn't be stopped.

As tears filled my eyes, I looked back and smiled, my heart quickening with every step. My hand was shaking as I placed the third rose and the third note on the stairs. The note read:

Each step was an unexpected moment that rippled through our hearts, and we realized what the past has taught us.

When I reached the top of the steps, I glanced down at the beautiful candlelight that graced the staircase. Rushing into Michael's bedroom, I pulled out twelve real candles and lit each of them. Quickly, I found and laid out the previous three roses and opened the fourth and held it to my heart. Closing my tear-filled eyes, I took a moment and thought about all the moments that had led me to Michael, my own personal prince charming. Finally, I placed the last note on the top of the stairs, knowing it had the most meaning. The note read:

Sometimes, you have to go through artificial beauty and false pas-sion to appreciate what's real.

Closing the door behind me, I sat in the middle of the burning candles and cradled the final rose in my arm. I gasped, my heart quickened as tears flooded my eyes, and I texted Michael, letting him know I was ready. As I waited a few moments, I closed my eyes and took a deep breath, counting and shaking. My palms sweating and my heart pounding, I let the rhythm of our song echo through the apartment. As I waited for Michael, I thought of the notes spread out on the staircase, the rose petals, and the candles flickering with their beautiful imitation flames. I waited, with my body trembling, for the door to open.

Michael's eyes were wide when he saw me kneeling amid the soft candlelight, holding the fourth and final rose. Blinking away my tears, I grabbed the letter that I had broken into four pieces, one with each rose. Slowly, through the tears, I began to read the words I had written months before.

Handing Michael the first rose, I read the first letter to him. "Sometimes, when we're not looking, something unexpected happens that changes our life forever, and we finally understand that the simplest things are often the most important. Finding someone to enjoy life with—the good times, the bad times—and who will stand beside you and help you achieve your biggest dreams is one of those somethings. You inspire me every day to be better than I was. I love you more than you could ever know."

Smiling, Michael sat on the other side of the candles as I wiped the tears from my eyes. I handed him the second rose, and again, I read. "I don't have it all figured out, but what I know is this. I wanted someone who could challenge me, who I could be proud of, and who would understand my heart and my mind even at its craziest. I never thought I would feel anything again, and then somehow, without ever meaning to, I fell in love with you. Now, I know that I can't picture my life with anyone else."

Quietly—silently—Michael watched as I shifted on the pillow and handed him the third rose as I quietly continued. "A long time ago, I decided you were more than enough. I knew who you were, and even now, I can see the worst and the best of you, and I am not afraid. Whether you succeed or fail, I want to be by your side. I love and respect you more than I thought possible. You are different, and you are the only one who has ever seen me and loved me as I am. I don't want to lose myself in you because I am always going to be me. I don't want *our* life to be based on *your* successes but on *ours*. Sometimes, two people are better together than they are alone because together, they can push the other to achieve the impossible. We are both impossible . . . as was our *love*."

Pausing for a moment, I took a breath. Michael had heard my words up to that point, and now, there was no turning back. *This is the moment I've been waiting for, that I've longed for. Now, my personal prince charming kneels beside me, with only candlelight between us.* With a deep breath, I closed my eyes, and as my body quaked, I handed Michael the fourth and final rose and read the accompanying letter.

"Every day, our love evolves into something deeper and more magical than what most ever experience. I've never heard of anyone quite like us. There are many things that make up the many layers of our *love*. The journey over the past year has been beautiful and has allowed me to see love for what it can be. And because we took a risk a year ago, I want to ask you to take another. As I give you the fourth and final rose, I want to ask you, will you give me the honor of being my *final* husband and allow me to be a bride one *final* time so that *finally*, we can get it right? Michael . . . will you marry me?"

My body gasped in anticipation as tears trailed down Michael's cheek. Michael looked past my eyes to a heart that trembled, took my hand in his, and quietly whispered, "Yes, I'd be honored to be your husband."

Author's Note

*S*HEILA'S MEN is a memoir based on my personal journey through the most difficult decade of my life. While nearly every scenario is completely accurate, some are metaphorical and emotional truths that show my mental state and the devastation that I was experiencing.

In the writing of this book, I have changed names, places, and descriptions to hide the identity of many characters for my safety and the safety of others. I also made the character of Terra into a composite character as she represents the thoughts and actions of all three of my children. The events surrounding her are all true and show the effects that this journey had on them. It is always important to realize that these situations affect more than just the victim/survivor.

I hope that this book can start much-needed conversations about the struggles many face. Their stories are hidden, but now, mine is not. I hope that my survival will encourage others to realize that they are not alone. I encourage all who have suffered sexual assault, coercive sexual assault, or domestic violence to find help through local crisis centers, advocacy centers, counseling services, or suicide and crisis hotlines. Don't be afraid to ask for help because no one should have to travel the journey alone. Happiness is possible on the other side of despair.

From the Publisher

Thank You from the Publisher

Van Rye Publishing, LLC ("VRP") sincerely thanks you for your interest in and purchase of this book.

VRP hopes you will please consider taking a moment to help other readers like you by leaving a rating or review of this book at your favorite online book retailer. Depending on the retailer, you can do so by flipping past the last page of your e-book (to the rating and review page) or by visiting the book's product page (and locating the button for leaving a rating or review).

Thank you!

Resources from the Publisher

Van Rye Publishing, LLC ("VRP") offers the following resources to readers and to writers.

For *readers* who enjoyed this book or found it useful, please consider receiving updates from VRP about new and discounted books like this one. You can do so by following VRP on Facebook (at www.facebook.com/vanryepub/) or Twitter (at www.twitter.com/vanryepub).

For *writers* who enjoyed this book or found it useful, please consider having VRP edit, format, or fully publish your own book manuscript.

You can find out more and submit your manuscript at VRP's website (at www.vanryepublishing.com).

Thank you again!

About the Author

JENNA ASHLYN is a volunteer for Southern Ohio's Survivor Advocacy Outreach Program, providing support and services to victims of emotional, physical, and sexual abuse. She studied creative writing at both the University of Rio Grande and Marshall University, where she worked for the campus literary magazine *Et Cetera*. Jenna's writing has appeared in numerous literary magazines, including *Night Roses*, *The Atwood Review*, and *Poet's Choice*.

In 2015, Jenna won the overall writing award in the StarJewel Nationals and Talent Showcase arts contest, and in 2019, she was nominated for a Maier Award, which celebrates the best writing by Marshall University students. In 2020, she released her debut novel, *Within the Gray*. Jenna currently resides in Ohio with her three children, her fiancé, and an assortment of pets, including two cocker spaniels and a guinea pig.

For more about Jenna, including updates on her upcoming projects and appearances, please be sure to follow her on Facebook (www.facebook.com/AuthorJennaAshlyn), Instagram (www.instagram.com/JennaAshl), or Twitter (www.twitter.com/JennaAshlyn1).

www.ingramcontent.com/pod-product-compliance
Lightning Source LLC
Chambersburg PA
CBHW070321260626
47160CB00003B/906

* 9 7 9 8 9 8 5 1 0 9 9 0 0 *